FINAL CUT

FINAL CUT

A NOVEL

SJ WATSON

HARPER

NEW YORK ⋅ LONDON ⋅ TORONTO ⋅ SYDNEY

HARPER

A hardcover edition of this book was published in 2020 by HarperCollins Publishers.

An original trade paperback edition of this book was published in Canada in 2020 by HarperCollins Publishers Ltd

HarperCollins books may be purchased for educational, business, or sales promotional use. For information, please email the Special Markets Department in the U.S. at SPsales@harpercollins.com or in Canada at HCOrder@harpercollins.com.

FIRST HARPER PAPERBACKS EDITION PUBLISHED 2021.

Library of Congress Cataloging-in-Publication Data has been applied for.

Library and Archives Canada Cataloguing in Publication information is available upon request.

ISBN 978-0-06-238216-0 (pbk.)
ISBN 978-1-4434-4406-4 (Canada)

21 22 23 24 25 LSC 10 9 8 7 6 5 4 3 2 1

FOR ANNA, ARCHIE, NEIL, AND OLIVIA

AND

IN MEMORY OF ANZEL BRITZ (1979–2020)

My life closed twice before its close—
It yet remains to see
If Immortality unveil
A third event to me

—Emily Dickinson

THEN

She runs across the moor, as hard and as fast as she can. The sliver of an old moon hangs above her and, somewhere far behind, the village lights shine anemic yellow. But she keeps her eyes fixed forward. She sees nothing but the road ahead and hears only the wheeze of her dry breath and the cawing of the gulls as they swoop and dive. There are no sounds of pursuit, no shouting, no howling of dogs. She is safe, she thinks. She can calm down, stop running and walk. It's over.

But still she runs. She pushes herself harder, her limbs wheel, momentum carries her until she is on the edge of tumbling like a marionette, wires snipped, head over heels. A car flashes past on the horizon, and then it happens. Her body goes numb, as if she's fallen into cotton wool. Her arms and legs circle in front of her but they look alien, they're moving independently, she has no control. It's like looking through the wrong end of a telescope.

She tries to draw breath, to blink herself back to reality, but it's too late. Her body has rebelled. When she tries to stop running she finds she can't.

Her foot hits something then. It registers only as an abstract pain, dull, like the dentist's drill after the needle, but still she trips in slow motion as if falling through sludge. Her hands fly forward and she hits the cold ground, squeezing the breath from her lungs like air from a paper bag.

She lies still. She could rest, she thinks; forever, if need be. She sees herself as if from a distance, as if she's in a documentary. She's lying there in the dark, her eyes open, her lips blue. They'll find her in the morning, frozen. It wouldn't be so bad.

But no. She won't die here, not like this. Energy rushes in, a shot of adrenaline, and she gets clumsily to her feet. She walks, putting one foot carefully in front of the other, over and over, until finally she reaches the junction. Her eyes dart. She shakes, though she doesn't feel fear. She doesn't feel anything. She puts her rucksack at her feet then holds out her hand, thumb up.

It's early morning and the road isn't busy. Cars pass infrequently, but eventually one stops. The driver winds down the window. It's a man, of course, but beggars can't be choosers.

"Where to, love?" he says, but she doesn't know how to answer him, she hasn't thought that far ahead. She imagines Bluff House; it's as if it's right in front of her, silhouetted against the pale sky, huge and looming with a solitary light shining in an upstairs room. She can never go back.

"Love?"

She shakes her head; she knows where she wants to end up, but not how to get there, and she has to choose somewhere before he drives off.

"Anywhere," she says, before opening the door and climbing in. "Anywhere. Just . . . away."

Evening Standard, 14 March 2011

NEWS IN BRIEF

MYSTERY GIRL FOUND ON DEAL BEACH

Oliver Johnson | No comments

Authorities are baffled by a mystery girl who was taken to the hospital last week after being found unconscious on the beach in Deal, Kent, by a passerby.

The teenager, who carried no identification but is believed to be around 15–18 years of age, was soaking wet and was admitted to Queen Elizabeth the Queen Mother Hospital in Margate, where she was found to be suffering from hypothermia. On regaining consciousness, she was unable to tell doctors her name, where she lives, or where she was born, and claims to have no knowledge of how she came to be in the seaside town.

She was described as extremely anxious, terrified of any new face, and reluctant to talk. Doctors have found no sign of injury and the police report notes that there is nothing to suggest foul play.

She remains in the hospital while doctors decide whether she requires any further treatment. The police are thought to be considering a public appeal for information if her condition does not improve.

She is described as 5 feet 7 inches tall and overweight, with shoulder-length brown hair. She was wearing a black jacket, a white vest, and blue jeans when found.

NOW

I mustn't fall asleep. I know that, it's obvious. You hear the stories. People get trapped and eventually stop trying to escape. They succumb to exhaustion and close their eyes. The body shuts down. They die.

But what do I do to stay awake? That's the question that spins in my head and won't go away.

I'd just crested the hill when it happened. The dead thing lay in the road, leached of color and completely still, and even as I registered its presence I knew I had no chance of avoiding it. It was too late to do anything but slam my foot on the brake and hope for the best.

The car began to skid. I saw myself as an observer might, someone filming the incident for posterity. I wondered if I'd get out of this alive. I imagined the vehicle turning slowly in a balletic curve before plowing into a low stone wall with a sickening crunch. I saw the bonnet concertina, then a moment of perfect stillness and utter quiet before a fireball lights the scene from within.

I start to burn. My red flesh is eaten up by the inferno before a cool, sweet blackness washes over me. I know that when they find my body it'll be twisted, unrecognizable. They'll have to work out who I am from some clue—dental records perhaps, the chassis number of the car—but even then they'll wonder who to tell. There's no one, not really. A flatmate I barely know. An ex-boyfriend who I doubt would really care.

And Dan, I suppose, though his interest will be purely professional. If the papers pick up the story, he'll tell them it's such a shame. A real tragedy. A promising career, wonderful to work with, her next film was shaping up to be really something, taken from us too young. Blah, blah, blah.

Something like that, anyway. They'll write it down and stick it on page seven, as long as nothing more interesting comes along. No better than I deserve.

But it didn't happen like that, of course. The car turned through a quarter circle and lurched violently into a shallow ditch bordering the road. The seatbelt bit into my shoulder and the dashboard jerked toward me, then my teeth crunched painfully together as my head struck the steering wheel. Everything outside went black and for a second or two I heard a curious, high-pitched tinnitus. When I opened my eyes I saw double. Shit, I thought, the last thing I need is a concussion.

But a moment later everything cleared and I pulled myself together. The lights were dead, and though the engine started after a while, it was with an odd, grinding noise, accompanied by the caustic stench of burning rubber. The wheels spun.

I gave up and let the motor die. Silence rushed in; the moor swallowed me whole. The car's interior was cramped and airless and I had to force myself to breathe.

Why here? The nearest town is miles back; the next, the one I'm heading for, miles ahead. I've seen no other traffic for half an hour at least and one thing I do know is there'll be no phone signal.

I tried to look on the bright side. I was uninjured. Winded, but alive. My knuckles bled to white as I gripped the wheel; my skin burned with cold. I had to do something. I couldn't walk all the way, but neither could I sit there forever. And whatever it was that had sent me spinning off the road was still out there.

My camera was on the passenger seat and I reached for it instinctively; I'm here to make a film, after all. I braced myself, then opened the door. The air outside was rotten, heavy with decay. My stomach roiled but I swallowed it down. I've smelled worse, after all, or at least as bad. Back when I made my first film, for example. *Black Winter*. Out there on the street I slept in garbage, lived amid the stink of rancid food, of open wounds and festering abscesses, of clothes that'd been worn so long they were fused with the putrefying flesh they were supposed to protect. Next to that this was nothing, just a dead animal bleeding into the pale snow.

Still, I wasted no time. I set the camera recording and began to film. It calmed me instantly. I had a purpose now. A curious detachment set in, one I'm used to, one that I first noticed when I lived with the girls on the street, shooting them for *Black Winter*. I become passive and invisible. I can zoom in and out, reframe as necessary, but my decisions are artistic, creative. I'm only recording, not part of the story. I'm not even there.

It was a sheep, its fleece matted and filthy. Something dark and gelatinous—blood, it must be, though in the dismal light it looked like oil—stained its upper quarter. I crouched down to frame it with the thin blade of the horizon in the background, the stars above. From this angle I could see its neck was twisted, the face blackened. Its torn lips spilled a bloody pink onto the ice; the eyes were glossy marbles. I began to shiver as I panned down the creature's lower body to the source of the fuliginous stench: a gash in its side, from which its innards oozed, dark and steaming. It must have been dead when I hit it, but dimly I wondered whether it was me who split it open, me who visited upon it this final, horrific indignity.

I carried on filming, but my defenses were cracking. I was back in the middle of it all. My car was wrecked, the road iced over, and I knew soon the route might become impassable. My hands were numbed, my ears too, and I was standing over a body, a dead thing, bleeding, disgusting. Alone. I switched off my camera. I needed help, I thought, but who could I turn to?

I didn't think. I left my luggage in the car. It was much tougher going than it looked. The snow wasn't deep, but beneath the new fall it'd already frozen hard, and by the time I'd gone just a few yards I'd almost fallen twice.

"Shit," I muttered under my breath, then a second later my ankle twisted beneath me, liquid pain shot up my leg, and I stumbled once more, this time landing in the wet snow. I knew straightaway that nothing was broken, but I also knew that I was defeated. I was going to have to wait it out. I hobbled back to the car.

That was an hour ago, maybe two. It's hard to tell. The temperature has dropped farther; my breath mists the air then disappears. The car seems to be shrinking, hemming me in, but it's too cold to open the window. I look up at the stars. I search for Betelgeuse, the belt of Orion, fiery Venus. I make promises. Let me get out of here and I'll turn around and go straight back to London. Screw the channel, screw Dan, screw the film.

But I've no idea with whom I'm bargaining. Not God. Even if he exists, he gave up on me years ago. And in any case, there's no reply, just the empty, spectral howl of the wind over the moor. The snow falls silently, no longer even melting on the windshield. My teeth begin to chatter. A car appears in the rearview mirror, but it doesn't stop; I probably imagined it. I wonder how I'll look when they find me. My lips frozen, ice in my hair, my face covered with frozen snot, but still hugging my camera like it's the only thing that matters. She died for her art, they'll say. Ha ha ha. My head tips forward as I begin the slide into the dark, into the soft, black nothing.

I catch myself in time. No, I tell myself. I didn't make it through what I made it through, didn't achieve what I've achieved, to die here. And in any case, this isn't a war zone, or even the wilds of Alaska, where it's forty below. This is the north of England. Not far from here, there'll be teenagers queuing outside nightclubs, the girls wearing not much more than their makeup, a short skirt, heels, and a crop-top. The boys will be luckier, in T-shirts and jeans, but not much. I can see them, might have even been with them once, shivering not with the cold but with the anticipation of the night ahead. Eager for a drink and to dance, for the laughter and the lights, for the sickly sweet smell of dry ice and warm flesh pressed in tight. Cigarettes, vodka. Pills and powder.

No. I'm not going to freeze to death. I just have to stay awake, that's all. I dig my nails into my palms, so hard I think I might draw blood, and then, in the rearview mirror, I see the light.

At first I think it's my imagination again, but when I twist round to look over my shoulder I see I was right. There are headlights shining over the hill. Salvation. For a second I wonder if my bargaining worked, but as the vehicle itself appears I tell myself to drop the crap. It's coincidence, nothing more.

The car approaches cautiously on the treacherous road and doesn't slow. Almost too late I realize my own vehicle is in darkness, half off the road and easily missed. I have to move. I have to get out. It would be ironic if whoever's driving were to have an accident, too, end up skidding along the same path, winding up in the same ditch. I need to flag it down.

I pick up my phone from the dash and get the door open. The cold brings with it a surge of energy and I manage not to stumble. I wave the phone's lit screen as I shout, and this time I'm in luck. The car slows to a halt, then a tall figure steps out. I think instantly of the women I'd filmed on the streets, the strange vehicles pulling up in the gloom, mysterious figures inside who may or may not want to hurt you.

Well, I think as he approaches, let him try. "You okay there?"

His voice is muffled by the wind, but friendly. Though I can't yet make out his face, my shoulders sag with relief.

"I just . . . not exactly." My teeth chatter and I nod toward my stricken car. "Can you give me a hand?"

He steps forward and into the beam from his own headlights. "Broken down?"

He's about thirty, I guess, and tall—very tall, definitely six foot plus—and rangy. He wears square, thick-framed glasses and his face is long, his features angular. Though warm, his smile seems some-how wary. He has the same build as Aidan—my friend from back then, from before—but also the same awkwardness. I remember how Aidan made me laugh and begin to relax. He seems innocent enough, though I know as much as anyone how deceptive looks can be. Those first few months in London taught me that, if nothing else.

"I came off the road," I say. "There's a sheep . . ."

He glances past me to where the creature lies in the middle of the road, a black shape on the ice just visible in the gloom.

"You hit it?"

I look back. The head lies angled toward us. Staring. Accusing. *You did this*, it says.

"No. It was already dead. I didn't see it."

Does he believe me? I can't tell, but either way he holds out his hand.

"You want me to help?" he says. "I'm Gavin."

3

It takes me a moment to place the name. Gavin. My assistant, Jess, had been looking for someone local to put up flyers for a meeting at the village hall to get the project up and running, and he ran the film club there and offered to help. We have a shared interest, at least.

"Alex."

No sign of recognition; perhaps Jess didn't mention my name.

"I suppose I'd better take a look. At the . . ."

He motions toward the dead sheep, seemingly reluctant to name it.

"Thanks."

We approach together and, torch in hand, he crouches at the pitiful creature.

"Something hit it hard," he says, his face twitching with discomfort. "It'd have been quick."

I look down at the beast. A pool of blood spreads blackly from its hindquarters, staining the snow.

"We can't leave it here."

His head falls. "Suppose not." He sighs. We kneel side by side and each grab two legs, then, together, we begin to pull. The thing is heavy but slides relatively easily over the ice. The viscera smudge the snow and a cloud of stink erupts. I hold my breath and glance at a grim-faced Gavin, who's doing the same, but after a moment it's done. We heave the body into the ditch.

"Right," he says, standing up. "How's your car?"

I step back over the creature's smeared remains. I wonder what he thinks of me. That I'm helpless, just waiting to be rescued, clueless about the car to which I've entrusted my safety? I watch his face but can read none of that there. Only a willingness to help.

"Screwed, I think. I just need to ring the breakdown service. As soon as I get a signal. I'll be fine."

He shakes his head. "Look, I know a guy who'll help."

"He can fix it?"

"Or tow it. He's got a Range Rover."

A Range Rover? I think of the vehicle I thought I saw earlier. I could see nothing in the glare of the headlights: the driver was invisible and I couldn't even tell what make of car it was. Something big, some kind of four-wheeler.

"He wasn't here?" I say. "Your friend? About half an hour ago?"

Gavin laughs. "No. I just left him. Why?"

"There was another car," I say. "It looked as though it was going to pull up, but then it drove off."

"You're sure?"

"Yes. But it doesn't matter."

For a second I think he'll ask more, but he seems to change his mind.

"Where you headed?"

"Blackwood Bay."

He smiles. "Hop in. I'll give you a lift."

He drives in almost complete silence, cautious in the snow. I wonder what he's like and look for clues. The car is spotless and completely devoid of the kind of junk that litters my own; the only evidence it's not brand new is the packet of licorice sticks in the cup-holder between our seats. My stomach growls.

"It's lucky you came along," I say, more to puncture the quiet than anything else.

He smiles. I look out, toward Blackwood Bay, the constellations clear above. There's a flash in the distance, the lighthouse on Crag Head strobing the low cloud. I was nearer than I thought. Again it occurs to me that I was a fool to come in winter. Not that I had any choice. After a minute or two he accelerates a little. The headlights pick out something, a brightness pricking the blackness, the glimpse of an eye, but it disappears as we pass. Another sheep? A rabbit? A deer? It's impossible to tell its size; the perspective is unknowable. Gavin cranks up the heating.

"You still cold?"

I tell him I'm fine and ask where he's from. "Not Blackwood Bay?"

He looks puzzled. "What makes you so sure?"

"The accent. Or lack of."

"Oh, yes," he says sheepishly. "My folks are from Merseyside. But we moved down south. London."

"And now you're here."

"Yes. I felt like a change. I was working in the city and I'd just had enough. The commuting . . . pressure . . . you know how it is."

I, I think. Not *We*. I say nothing. I've already clocked that there's no ring on his finger, though I'm not sure why I looked. Habit, perhaps.

"How long have you been here?"

"Oh, wow. About a year now."

He whistles under his breath as he says it, as if he's surprised it's been so long, as if he came intending to stay a fortnight and then got stuck.

"You like it?"

He tells me it's okay. He keeps busy.

"How about you? Where're you from?" he asks.

I keep my answer vague. "London. You're not married?"

He laughs. "No!"

He slows to take a blind bend. "You're not from London originally, though?"

So he's picked up on my accent, too. No surprise. It's mostly gone, but some things will never change. A temptation to use "were" instead of "was." The way I pronounce "glass" to rhyme with "ass" not "arse"; ditto "castle," "bath," "class." Not that I've used any of those words, as far as I can recall, so I guess he must've spotted other, more subtle, clues.

"Near Leeds," I tell him.

"Oh, right. Come for a visit?"

Now I'm faced with the question, I'm not sure how to respond. I'd wanted to stay under the radar. After all, it was never my plan to come here. But this isn't an ideal world, and I can't stay hidden forever.

"Sort of," I say. "I'm here to work on a film."

He laughs. "Thought you might have something to do with that! So how do you fit in?"

"Oh, I just help out. You know?"

He drives on. A minute later he coughs.

"So what's it about, anyway?" He pauses. "Zoe?"

My breath catches in my throat at the mention of the vanished girl, but he doesn't notice.

"Not exactly," I say.

"You know about her, though? And Daisy? Yes?"

I tell him I do. I think of the research I've been doing, the conversations I've been having with Dan. I know too much, if anything.

"But really the film's about village life," I say breezily.

"So why here, if it's not about the girls?"

"No particular reason," I say. "You'd have to ask the producer, I suppose. He makes all the decisions; I just do the work."

He laughs, but there's an undercurrent of disappointment. I remember Jess telling me about him. Lovely guy, she said; asks lots of questions, though.

I think back to how the project started. I'd met Dan at the festival in Amsterdam, and he'd told me he loved *Black Winter* but thought my second film—*Adam, Alive*—was "worthy, but not what I should be doing." I admired him for that; he was probably the only person who'd been honest. He asked me if I had anything in the pipeline.

"A few things," I told him, although this wasn't true. He gave me his card and a few months later I invited myself to his office. It was all white furniture and glass partitions, ergonomic chairs and chai lattes. His awards glowered down at me from the wall behind his chair and my mind went to the night I won mine. I'd bought myself a new outfit—a trouser suit with a white jacket—and felt good. Even so, by the time they came to the Audience Award the last thing I was expecting was my name to be called out. The announcement came as if through a fog and I felt everyone's eyes boring into me. I stood up, feeling suddenly drunk and regretting the heels I'd bought on a whim. I stepped carefully to the front of the room and at the podium made a dry-mouthed speech before threading my way back through the smiles and claps. As I did, I thought of all the girls I'd filmed and put into my documentary. They were just a few miles away, those who'd survived. Shivering on the same streets, their world and mine now so far apart the distance was incalculable. I felt the champagne begin to rise and strode past my table, only just making it outside before vomiting onto the pavement. No one saw, but that didn't make me feel any better, and as I crouched, staring at my own disgust, I thought that at the very least I had the decency to feel guilty. I vowed to go back, to find the girls I'd filmed, to give them the money I'd just won.

"Alex?"

I looked up. Dan was waiting for me to begin. "Well, what I thought is . . . let's do a film about ordinary life. About community. Mortality. Change. I mean, nowadays, what does 'community' even mean? People are more likely to find it online than they are next door, or that's the popular myth anyway. But is that really true, once you get out of the city? I thought we could look at life in a small village in Britain. One with a dwindling population, or whatever. See what life's really like."

He nodded. He was about to speak, but then his eyes went to my arm. My sleeve had ridden up, my scar was visible. I froze, holding his gaze, resisting the urge to tell him the story, and folded my hands neatly under the table. He shifted in his seat.

"It's very different from *Black Winter*. And I can't see what would make it unique."

"Well," I said. "It could be mostly observational, self-shot by its subjects on their phones, digital cameras, iPads, or whatever. That way we'll get people's own perspective—everyone can contribute."

"So, sort of *Three Salons* meets *Life in a Day*, then?"

"Exactly."

He smiled, and I wondered whether he'd been testing me. Though a classic, *Three Salons at the Seaside* came out in ninety-four, or something like that. Long before my time, and—with its focus on northern women getting their shampoo and set—is, on the surface, the last thing anyone would think I'd be interested in.

Unless they knew me. And he did. He knew I'd done my GCSEs late, had gone on to get a diploma in Filmmaking and Photography. He knew I'd come to this with the passion of someone who has finally found their direction after a long time drifting, someone who found the guts to pitch her first film—uninvited, and despite her northern accent and shitty clothes—to one of the guest lecturers.

"The important thing," I continued, "would be that the film finds its own stories. Then all I'd need to do is amplify them. I thought I'd set up a website, people could upload their contributions, anonymously—"

"You'll get dick pics."

I stared at him. If only he knew the things I've seen. If only he had the barest idea of just how many tiny, shriveled pricks I've witnessed in my life, of how little a few more will bother me. "You think I'm worried about that? Anyway," I went on, "I'd have administrator access. That way I can go through the submissions and delete any that are clearly no good. And any that I'm not sure about but might want to use I can mark *Private*, keep them out of the general pool. The rest would be public. People would need to sign up, but once that's done they could watch what other people are uploading."

"Could be interesting. Have you thought about consent?"

"Yes. There are a few options. We could bury it in the Ts and Cs, for a start. When people log on for the first time, you know?"

"When they'll click on anything . . ."

"Exactly."

He shrugged in agreement. These were all details we could work out, along with the ease with which people could upload their contributions. I knew it'd have to be as simple as clicking a button.

"How about a location?"

"Not sure, yet. I could do some research . . . scout around."

That was my mistake. I should've done my research first, found a location, presented it to him on a silk cushion tied up with a bow. Then I wouldn't have ended up in Blackwood Bay.

I didn't know that then, though.

"I think I could really do something here, Dan. Something fresh and interesting."

"You know I love your work," he said, after a pause.

"Yes?"

"It's just . . . I think it needs more."

"More?"

"Yes. I think you should find somewhere with a story. Not something major, just a focus, something that people can talk about."

I hesitated. I was broke, living in a shared flat, working behind bars whenever I got the chance, waiting tables, looking for admin work, trying my hand at a bit of journalism, though that paid next to nothing now. I had no parental funds to draw down, nobody I could go to, cap in hand.

"Okay," I said, and he smiled and said he'd make some calls.

It was a couple of weeks before he invited me back into his office. "So I heard from Anna at Channel Four," he said as I sat down. Hope rose like a bruise.

"And?"

He grinned. "Congratulations."

"They're going for it?"

"Well, they're offering three grand. They just want a taster. A few minutes. Ten, tops."

A taster, just to give an idea of what I wanted to do. Then they could decide whether to expand it into a series, a one-off, or drop it completely.

But three grand? It wasn't much.

"They want it by the end of the year, and Anna wants to know about location asap." He paused. "Drink? To celebrate?"

For a second, I was tempted, but who knew where it might end up? And I'd promised my boyfriend I'd be back early; I couldn't let him down. Not again.

"I'm sorry, but I need to get on," I said, gathering my things.

Was he disappointed? I couldn't tell. He walked me to the door.

"You'll have to make it amazing, Alex. But I know you can do that. You did it once, you can do it again. And don't forget," he added, "you need a story."

"I'll find one," I said. I had to. My second film had failed. This was my last chance.

4

My last chance. The car rounds a bend and I catch sight of the sea, a cluster of lights in the distance, nestled at the water's edge.

Blackwood Bay. Tiny, tucked into its cleft in the hills; beyond it, cliffs and the endless coastline, shrouded in the gloom. The moonlight shines white on the rooftop snow. It looks beautiful but treacherous; it's not hard to imagine the smuggling that used to go on here, clandestine activities in the filthy night. My body tenses in the seat, as if preparing to open the door and leap out, to take my chances in the wilds.

It was never the plan to come here. At no stage did the list of possible locations for my film feature Blackwood Bay. I knew exactly the kind of place I was looking for. One that had that indefinable something; like the feeling you get viewing a new flat when it already feels like home. Or the feeling of meeting someone in a bar, eyes across the room, nothing really, but as soon as you speak you know there's something more, that you're going to fuck. I looked at various places, but nothing grabbed me. Then a card arrived at Dan's office and everything changed.

I was at home when he called me, researching some place in Oxfordshire with little to recommend it. He launched straight in.

"I've never heard of it, but if you're sure, then I'm sure."

By now I knew this was typical Dan, to begin as if we were already mid-conversation. No doubt he had his phone on handsfree and was typing an email as he spoke, an intern hovering at the door with an urgent message from another hungry director.

"Sorry?"

"The postcard."

"What postcard, Dan?"

"Blackwood Bay."

At first I thought I'd misheard him.

"What?"

He repeated himself, his voice reverberating thickly down the line, and this time I knew what I'd heard.

"Blackwood Bay? What about it?"

My own voice echoed.

"The card," he said. "It's not from you? Weird." The word sounded like a shrug, and pointedly didn't answer my question. "Anyway, you know it?"

"What the hell are you talking about?" I said, failing to hide my tetchiness.

"I've had this card," he said, ignoring me. "Picture of a harbor on one side. Blackwood Bay. The message is *How about here?* I just thought it must be from you."

My hands shook as I took a swig of coffee. It was too hot, and my throat began to burn.

"Nope."

"Anyway, it doesn't matter."

But it does, I thought. It does matter. I could feel myself begin to panic and forced myself to count my breaths. "No one else knows about the project, do they?"

"Well, Channel Four does, obviously."

"They're not likely to send postcards, though."

"True, but maybe it's someone they've asked to sniff round. Anyway, this Blackwood Bay. You've been there?"

I considered lying, telling him I'd never heard of it.

"Yeah," I said. "Spent some time there as a child. I wasn't impressed, to be honest."

"But it's a possibility?"

"No. I don't think so."

"Why? That bad?"

"It's just . . . I mean, it's a long way. If one of us does end up having to go up there."

"The channel are keen for the location to be in the north. So—"

"You didn't tell me that."

"Pretty sure I did. Too much southern bias, apparently."

"It's small. Maybe *too* small. I don't know how many people we'll get submitting films in a place that size. It's just . . . it's not the right place. Okay?"

I thought I heard him sigh. For a second I thought he'd suggest we pull the plug, try something else or give the money back to Channel Four, along with our apologies and the tattered remains of my career.

"Have you still got the card?" I said.

"Why?"

"Keep it," I said, my laptop already open, Google up. I typed in *Blackwood Bay*. If Dan was going to argue, I'd need to have a pretty solid reason not to film there. I wanted to see the same pages Dan would look at. I wanted to be prepared.

My eyes danced over the articles as I clicked through. I was relieved at first: it was mostly banal, ordinary stuff. Restaurants that'd closed their doors forever, prettiest village in Yorkshire for the third year in a row, although that article was years out of date, a campaign to prevent the closure of the local lifeboat service that looked about to fail. I began to feel hopeful, but then I saw it. A missing teenager—a girl called Daisy—her suicide now confirmed beyond any real doubt.

There's no way Dan would miss that. No way he wouldn't seize on it as my story.

"We need to talk," I said. "I'm coming in."

I arrived later that afternoon. The postcard was on his desk, a photograph of Blackwood Bay taken from the cliffs. It was faded, as if it'd been out in the sun. I held it but felt nothing.

I turned it over. Those three words in black ink. *How about here?* The postmark was smudged and illegible.

He handed me a coffee. "Weird, huh?"

"You're sure it's not from someone in the office?"

He tipped his head. "Well, I've asked. No one's owned up to it. But . . ." I knew what he was going to say. "Why are you so bothered?"

I couldn't answer that. In any case, it was obvious he couldn't care less.

"You're certain this wouldn't be the right place?" he said. "I looked it up. Population's low, but it's not tiny, and it's going down. Seems to be what you were looking for. Small enough to have a community, but I don't think it's so small you have to worry that only a handful of people would do any filming." He turned his monitor toward me and began to scroll through a Google Image search. "Pretty, too. Look."

I glanced at the screen. A photo of the main street. Slate Road. A bright day, the middle of summer. The shadows were keen, the steep street looked vertiginous, the houses, cafés, and gift shops cute. Quaint. I leaned in and pretended interest. A view of the whole village from the cliffs above, the lighthouse in the distance, a photo taken from the shingle beach, the slipway looming in the foreground.

"It'd look good on camera. But then you know that. If you've been there."

"We're filming in winter, though. It might be difficult."

"It's not like you're doing the filming, though, is it? I thought that was the point. And any bad weather might add atmosphere."

He pulled up another picture. A cobbled street, too narrow for traffic. Hanging baskets, leaded windows.

"There aren't many vehicles, apparently. Road's too steep. And, most important thing, it's got a story."

I stood up. I didn't want him to carry on. "I'll consider it," I said. He tilted his head. I'd snapped. His gaze drilled into me.

"You know a girl went missing there?"

I hesitated, but there was no point in pretending. I thought of Daisy. "Years ago. And it was suicide. What's—?"

"No. This is more recent. And there's no mention of suicide." He pulled up another browser. "Look."

The story was from the website of the *Malby Messenger*. "CCTV clue in desperate search for missing teen Zoe Pearson," it read, above a blurred photograph taken from video footage. It showed a girl in a black jacket, her dark hair tied back, her pixelated features indistinct. The caption said she'd been spotted at a bus station in Meadowhall. I looked away, trying to focus on something else, but my vision felt distorted.

He scrolled down to a better picture, the same girl, now facing the camera, hair loose, almost smiling, but not quite.

"She disappeared from near Blackwood Bay. About three and a half years ago."

I shook my head. *No*, I wanted to say. *That's not possible. I'd have known.*

But is that true? I've been avoiding the place for so long now anything might've happened.

Dan looked up. "What's that you mentioned? A suicide?"

Fuck. I couldn't back out now.

"A girl called Daisy," I said. "She killed herself."

He flicked to a different screen, entered a search term. "Daisy Willis. Ten years ago." He sat back. "First her, and then Zoe Pearson."

He grinned, as if he'd won a jackpot. Part of me despised him.

"Don't you think it's strange?" he said. "Two girls disappearing?"

I heard myself speak.

"Daisy was suicide. It was confirmed."

He was skimming the article.

"There was no body, though. I mean—"

"It was suicide."

"Whatever," he said, looking once more at the screen. "She jumped from the cliff. Disappeared. And seven years later this Zoe whatever goes missing as well. There's your story right there." He stared straight at me, and for a second he looked exactly like the smug, self-satisfied prick I'd once thought he was.

"I have every confidence in you, Alex. But, well, not everyone else might."

"Meaning?" I tried to keep my voice from breaking. I failed.

He shook his head, like I was a child, like he was disappointed in me. And then the sucker punch.

"I told them you'd find a place with a story, something unresolved, some tension. They wouldn't have given you the money if I hadn't."

I couldn't afford to have the project pulled and, anyway, the image of Zoe must've had tiny hooks: it snagged me, got under my skin. When I closed my eyes I saw Daisy, too, the dead girl. She was reaching out, telling me I was the only one who could help. And yes, I admit it, when I thought about it there was a tiny rush of pride, like hot metal. Maybe I could be the one to help her find peace. I rang Dan the next morning.

"I've decided," I said. "Blackwood Bay it is."

He was delighted, and we spent the next couple of weeks making the arrangements and getting the website up and running. Jess found someone local—Gavin, who ran the film club there—to help and went up in early October. They organized a meeting in the village hall, just before a showing. She explained the project, said it was a portrait of life in a small town, all very lighthearted. No one was out to get anyone.

The clips began to arrive. Slowly at first, just a trickle, but then, when people saw that their friends and neighbors had been filming, more came in. Mostly they were of everyday life—kids playing, people cooking, a party in a back garden. There were lots of pets, views of the cliffs. A few dick pics, yes, but I deleted those. Scenes in the pub, a shortish guy pushing a boat out onto the water. All good background. Nothing of Daisy or Zoe, no mention at all, and while I wavered between relief and disappointment, Dan came down squarely on the latter, as did Anna, who, he reminded me, held the checkbook.

"There's only one thing for it," he told me. "You'll have to go up there yourself. See what you can dig up, okay?"

So here I am, sitting in a car on the way to Blackwood Bay; a place I never wanted to go, to explore a story I never wanted to look at. Yet somehow I don't mind. Maybe it will make for a better film, after all.

Gavin is still talking. I tune back in.

"Where you staying?"

"A cottage," I say. "Hope Lane?"

"Oh, Monica's place?" he says. "Lovely. I can't take you down there, though. Road's too steep."

"I know," I say, too quickly, before I remember I'm not supposed to be familiar with the area. "Monica's already warned me. If you drop me at the top, I can walk down."

"Okay," he says, and we drive on. The air gets heavier the closer we get, suffocating. I fight it, glancing at Gavin as I do, but he's oblivious; he looks perfectly happy. He pulls into the car park and shuts off the engine.

I stare out into the night. A penumbra of light shines around the lamps and the streets are empty: no sign of life at all, not even a dog or a fox rooting at the litter bins. As I get out of the car and gather my things I feel as if I'm about to descend into the past. I can see the smugglers, oilskins damp and glistening, heaving barrels of rum or tobacco, heading for the lost tunnels that are rumored to connect the cellars in a vast, arterial network. Legend has it that it was once possible to smuggle contraband from sea level all the way up to the clifftop without it ever seeing the light of day and, looking now, I find myself believing it.

"You okay?"

"Fine," I say, my eyes adjusting to the gloom. A few lights are on in the houses below, but not many.

"I'll give you a hand with your bags."

For a moment, I think he's going to invite me for a drink later, or to dinner, and it occurs to me that maybe I'd like him to. He seems a nice guy and it'd be good to have a friend here.

"Okay."

We get out. I look north, toward the grassy peninsula that extends out into the water, rising as it does to a shallow cliff. Not much is visible in the dark, but there's a light on in the distant house at its very edge.

"What's that light?" I say.

"Oh, that's The Rocks." He pauses. "Bluff House."

The words echo. It's been so long, I'd forgotten there was even a house there. It's as if my mind has erased it from the narrative.

"Bluff House?"

He looks at me, as if about to say something else, but then just smiles self-consciously. "We'd better get going."

I collect my things and we begin our descent. We fall into silence as we go: the quiet is enveloping, inhibiting; even the sound of our footsteps is deadened by the snow, shrunk to a soft crunch. Nothing is quite as I remember it; it's as if I'm seeing it through a filter, a distorting prism. The road seems to narrow farther with each step, and as it becomes increasingly steep I notice a rusted handrail by the side of the road. I grip it as I go down. I know the sea is out there, ahead and below us; there's that familiar smell, of oil and seaweed, salty and sulfurous. We pass darkened cottages and empty cafés, lonely shops shuttered for the night. Here and there, footpaths and alleyways begin to appear, springing off from the main lane at improbable angles, but they're unlit and disappear into inky pockets of darkness. I wonder who might be lurking, and I'm glad I'm not alone.

I'm spooked, that's all. Being here, miles from home. Stuck without a car, without friends. Thinking about Daisy and Zoe; one dead, the other missing. I watch Gavin and wonder who sent Dan the postcard. Could it have been him? But how could he have known we were looking for a location? How could anyone?

Suddenly, Gavin stops.

"Well, this is me." He points toward an alleyway a little farther down Slate Road. "You know where you're going?"

"Yes, thanks. I looked on the map."

He passes me the bag he's been carrying.

"I'll let you know. About your car, I mean."

"Thanks."

He pauses, just for a moment.

"Well, nice to meet you," he says. "See you around."

I tell him I hope so, but he doesn't move. He stands there, ill at ease. He has something else to say.

"Bye, then."

I'm turning to walk away when he calls me back.

"Daisy . . ." he says, and I freeze.

"What?"

"It's just . . ." He lowers his voice. "You ought to know. There are people here who think it wasn't suicide. Zoe's disappearance, too. Some people think they're linked."

"Who?"

"I can't say. Just . . . people."

"But—"

"That's all I know." He glances over his shoulder. "I have to go."

He turns away then, quickly and decisively, and disappears into the dark. I draw breath. I wish even more that I'd never come here, but there's no going back now. I have a film to make, a deadline to hit; progress is necessary. I look up toward The Rocks, toward Bluff

House and the tall cliffs, then lower my gaze and walk, head down. I go on toward the upturned rowing boats and rusted lobster pots. I go on, toward the pub—The Ship Aground—and down, toward the slipway, thinking of the missing girls as I descend, going deeper and deeper into Blackwood Bay.

THEN

5

CASE REPORT

Name: Unknown
Hospital number: 87498565K
Date of birth: Unknown
Address: Unknown
Date of Report: 28 March 2011

The case is of a young female of unknown age but thought
to be around fifteen to eighteen years old who was
referred to the memory disorders clinic in March 2011.
She first presented at the emergency department of Queen
Elizabeth the Queen Mother Hospital (QEH) in Margate,
Kent, with hypothermia and a suspected head injury,
having been found unconscious in Deal. At the time of
presentation she had no identification, and in fact no
possessions other than a mobile phone. It is reported
that on regaining consciousness she exhibited confusion,
claiming to have no recollection of any autobiographical
details, including her name, date of birth, address, etc.
Following subsequent treatment at the QEH, the patient
demonstrated extreme confusion when questioned about her
life prior to being found. She was subsequently referred
for inpatient assessment and further treatment.

On arrival the patient was extremely fearful,
confused, and reticent, though alert and not entirely
uncooperative. Reports from the local hospital suggested
that her head injury was minor, and certainly not
consistent with brain damage severe enough to account
for her symptoms. She maintained that though she could

recall some fragmentary details of events in the year or so leading up to her hospitalization, she had not regained knowledge of her name or any other significant autobiographical details, other than an impression that she had lived in the north of England, which was consistent with her accent, and that she thought in the days or weeks prior to hospitalization she had been living rough in London. No other details of her previous life were forthcoming. She could not recall how she had made the journey to Deal, what forms of transport she had used, or how she had funded it. She denied hitching a lift, claiming that she "wouldn't do that sort of thing." She admitted to having low mood and a poor appetite. She slept badly, with early morning wakefulness. She reported no suicidal ideation.

ON EXAMINATION

Examination revealed a young woman who was clean, somewhat overweight, though with evidence of recent poor nutrition, with poor eye contact. Judgment and insight were unimpaired. The patient was distressed during examination, and oriented in time and place but not in person. Her mood was depressed. There were symptoms suggestive of both derealization and depersonalization disorders, though no thought disorders were evident. Immediate recall and short-term memory were intact. Her memory was largely intact for the period since hospitalization and very significantly impaired for the period prior to hospitalization.

Though necessarily incomplete at present, due to the patient's incomplete recall, examination revealed no symptoms suggestive of seizure, bipolar disorder, a manic episode, schizophrenia, anxiety, or other

organic disorder. Though she denied abusing psychoactive
substances, physical evidence suggested the possibility
of recent intravenous drug use.

Medical, psychiatric, family, and personal histories
were all incomplete, due to the nature of the patient's
presentation.

Physical examination was unremarkable. Laboratory
testing revealed no abnormalities. Neurological
assessment was unremarkable. An EEG suggested no seizure
activity and there was no evidence for epilepsy.

The Dissociative Experiences Scale was administered,
though, due to the lack of long-term memory and the
patient's distress, the results should be interpreted
with caution. They certainly do not rule out a
dissociative disorder, however.

CONCLUSIONS AND TREATMENT PLAN

The working diagnosis is currently dissociative fugue
with dissociative amnesia. The patient will be engaged
in psychotherapy as an inpatient and has been reassured
that in this condition symptoms will often resolve
spontaneously. Though discharge is not imminent, a
current concern is her housing situation, and the
patient has consented to appropriate referrals to social
services and other agencies. She cannot remember the
four-digit pass code on her mobile phone (and, rather
frustratingly, has not yet agreed to allow us to ask the
police to investigate), but she seems certain (and I am
optimistic) that she will do so eventually.

Report prepared but not signed by,
Dr. Laure Olsen BSc PhD MRCPCH

NOW

6

*H*ope Cottage, along with three or four almost identical stone-faced buildings, is off a quaint, cobbled square at the bottom of Slate Road, accessible only through a narrow L-shaped alley and so close to the sea I can taste it. It's perfect, sparse but comfortable, with everything I need. A cloistered bolt-hole to which I can retreat.

Downstairs comprises the kitchen and a living room in which a deep sofa and matching armchair complement a carpet of seagrass. A television stands in one corner, a circular mirror on the wall to the left, and in the opposite one, by the door, hangs a barometer, the needle hovering seemingly permanently between *Rain* and *Stormy*. Upstairs there's one bedroom, plus a bathroom. Everything is tasteful: all biscuits and grays with throw cushions in contrasting colors, extra blankets on the bed, framed photos on the wall featuring picture-postcard scenes in arty black and white. More photos decorate the stairs, though here a couple seem to be family pictures. A woman—Monica herself, I'm guessing—features in several. In one she sits in front of a photographic backdrop, half turned to the camera, smiling, and in another she stands near the slipway with a group of kids, two girls standing slightly off to one side. Best friends.

I pour some coffee and drink it black. It's bitter, but as soon as I've finished it I have another. I've been here for two days now and I'm not sleeping well. The village is almost exactly as I remember it, yet somehow also different, as if it's a familiar person wearing different clothes. But there are more people around than I'd thought there might be. I see them, popping in and out of the shops, climbing the hill, relaxing on the benches down near the water. It's hardly bustling, a long way from busy, but it doesn't seem as forlorn and empty as I'd feared. More are submitting clips than I'd dared hope, too, and

I've even spotted a few people filming. Everything's going to be all right. It has to be.

I think back to yesterday's submissions: a guy waking up, his wife handing him a card and wishing him a happy birthday. A girl running along the beach, as fast as she can, until she trips and falls. An old woman in a nursing home. Girls eating fish and chips by the water. One was particularly interesting, if almost certainly unusable. A teenager standing at the slipway beside The Ship Aground in the weak afternoon light, staring out at the waves. She grips the railing then slowly begins to climb over. She clings to the metal, then, with a dramatic, campy flourish, lets herself fall. It's as if she's throwing herself into the water, and instantly I think of Daisy. I can almost believe it's her, though Daisy can't have jumped from the same place, as it's only a few feet drop to the beach. But what is the girl doing? As I watched, she reappeared, running up the slipway, giggling. The camera zooms in and she grins, as if to say, *Did you get it? Did I do well?* and I realize she was taking the piss.

My mind goes to Daisy, and Zoe. Apart from Gavin, no one has mentioned them, but I've done online research of my own. I searched Daisy's name, delving deeper this time. It was almost Christmas when it happened; she jumped in the early hours, nearly ten years ago. At home, in the trailer in which she lived, her clothes were untouched and her belongings as she'd left them. A few days later, one of her trainers washed up on the beach a few miles down the coast, followed shortly after by the remains of her jacket. The fact that her body was never found means she's still classed as a missing person, but there can be no doubt she killed herself. No one suspects a third party was involved.

Zoe Pearson's story is different. She went in late spring, over three and a half years ago. She was there one day, gone the next. Her bed empty, her parents thought she'd snuck out to meet a boyfriend, but she never returned. A runaway, that's all; no one has talked about suicide, no one thinks she was abducted. So why, according to Gavin at least, do "some people" think they're linked?

I finish my coffee and find my coat and camera. I won't find out sitting here.

I squeeze through the narrow gap and out onto Slate Road. The village is more or less deserted. A lone man sits down by the slipway, and a little farther on a group of girls has taken over one of the benches near the pub. Smoking, I suppose, though I'm too far away to tell. There's no one else. I record the scene for a moment, then head down. On the slipway I film the gulls wheeling and diving over the lobster pots, the weed-tangled ropes slapping in the wind. I film The Ship Aground—or The Ship, as I know it's called locally—the gift shops, a bookshop I find up one of the alleys. I film the light-house and make a mental note to return at night. Beyond the pub the coastline curves sharply toward the promontory that juts out into the water—The Rocks, Gavin called it—and on it, the black house sits. Bluff House. I film that, too, then decide to climb the steep path up toward the car park.

I avoid the black ice, using the steps where I can and stopping every now and again to get my breath back and film the view. I scan the horizon, recording the distant trees as they bend in the wind. The air seems thinner up here, easier to breathe. I turn left, past the car park and the village hall. There's a grocery store on the right, plus a post office with a voluntary community shop attached. Both sell postcards, an almost identical selection, and I check to see whether either stocks the one sent to Dan. I'm certain now that it came from Blackwood Bay, and though I have visions of sleuthing my way to an answer, this time I'm not in luck. The photos are views of the village and the surrounding area, pictures of the pub from centuries ago, but none matches. I'll have to keep looking.

The park is across the road and I push through the sprung gate and go in. It's tiny, just a playground really, a few swings and a see-saw, a tiny bandstand in the center, but from here there's a great view over the village and down into the bay itself. In the distance sits Bluff

House, silent and still. I feel drawn to it somehow, connected, even from here. The pull is hypnotic, a black hole at the edge of the water, sucking everything toward it, even light. I feel suddenly certain it's the place where Daisy jumped.

I tear myself away and look beyond it. Way in the distance, just visible across the water, is the next town along. Malby. A metropolis by comparison. There're estates there, new homes with neat lawns and expensive cars parked in the driveways. The schools are there, the supermarkets, the fast-food restaurants, plus a tiny cinema and solitary nightclub. But it might as well be a million miles away.

I decide to get a hot drink before returning to Hope Cottage. There's a café halfway down Slate Road and I head there. The door clatters as I enter. An unreconstructed greasy spoon: plastic table-cloths, bowls of wrapped sugar cubes, egg and chips, tea served in a chipped mug. There are plenty of free tables. A tiny Christmas tree pulses on the counter at the back, the end of each branch lit with tacky fiber optics, and I order coffee from the woman who stands behind the counter in a spotless apron and smudged glasses. She's in her early forties, I'd guess, and has cut her prematurely gray hair short, in a stylish pixie cut.

I've just sat down with my drink when the door jangles open and a man enters, wearing a waterproof jacket. He's short—only a little taller than me—and solid. Unshaven; his hair is long and looks art-fully disarranged. He orders a bacon roll and we almost make eye contact as he turns to choose a table, but then he skims past me to say hello to a guy sitting in the corner instead. He takes a seat and opens a magazine before settling in to wait for his food. He looks famil-iar, though only distantly, and I can't place him. In one of the films, perhaps? In any case, there's something about him that's magnetic; though not particularly attractive, he has an aura, a glow that draws the eye. I go back to my drink, but too late. He's spotted me staring.

"Nice day," he says, and I look back up. He's grinning, but his eyes are strange; one is darker than the other and has a curious, beady pulse. He lowers his magazine. "You visiting?"

I tell him I am. "Seems pretty quiet?"

He laughs.

"It's always bloody quiet nowadays."

"Really?"

"Yep. You staying here?"

I glance out of the window to where a group of girls are walking past, cackling as they go. I'm not sure why I'm pretending nonchalance; it just seems like the right thing to do.

"I am, yeah. Down in the village."

He pauses. "Anything to do with that film?"

Before I can answer a shadow passes and I look once more out at the street. A lone guy is walking past and for a second I think he's following the giggling girls I saw a moment ago, but then I tell myself I'm being paranoid, just projecting my own experience from when I was first down in London.

"Only, I saw the camera, like."

I'd put it on the table in front of me, next to the bowl of sugar. I smile.

"You caught me out."

"I'm a real Sherlock Holmes, me," he says, grinning. "I think I'm sorting out your car?"

"Is that right? You're a friend of Gavin's?"

"Yep." He reaches across and holds out his hand for me to shake. "Bryan. It'll be done in a few days. Damaged suspension." He gestures toward the chair opposite mine. "Mind if I join you?"

"Not at all. I'm Alex."

He comes over and settles himself. This close, I catch his aftershave, sweetly spicy, though with something else, too. A hint of leather, perhaps. Something dark and dirty. He puts his magazine on the table—*Sea Angler*—and I remember where I've seen him. One of the news stories I'd skimmed had covered the campaign—ultimately doomed—to save the lifeboat service, and he'd been in one of the photos, wearing a yellow jacket, handing out leaflets.

"How's it going?"

"Sorry?"

He laughs. "The film?"

"Oh, okay," I say. "Early days."

"So what're folk filming?"

"All kinds of things." I think back to the clips from yesterday. The girl faking a suicide. Teenagers eating a takeaway on one of the benches by the pub. "They're all online. Take a look."

"Maybe I will. It's good, you know? It'll be nice to see the place on the map at last." He glances toward the woman at the counter, though she seems determinedly engrossed in wiping the surface while she waits for her customer's food to cook. He lowers his voice. "It's tough, you know? Bein' this quiet. Your program might be a nice little boost for folk." He sits back. "That's what we're all hoping for, anyway."

"Well, I'll see what I can do," I say. I hesitate. Dan's words echo. *See what you can dig up, okay?* "I suppose you want to see the place in the news for the right reasons?"

His eyes narrow, just slightly. "What's that?"

I pick up a sugar cube from the bowl. "I'm just saying. That girl who died. Daisy, was it?"

"That's right."

"It must've been a bad time. Small village like this . . . You were around back then?"

"Aye. But I don't live in the village. My place is over near Malby."

"You didn't know her, then?"

"Not well. But a little."

"It's a small place."

He sips his drink. I wonder how far I can go.

"They said it was suicide . . ."

"Well, if that's what they said, I guess it was."

"But why?"

"Who knows? She were a teenager. Boyfriend trouble?"

"That hardly explains why someone would kill themselves."

He smiles ruefully and I find myself wondering if he has children. There's something about him that makes me think not, though I can't pinpoint what. There's a sadness about him, an emptiness, despite the charm. He looks like, if he's freighted with anything, it's the weight of lost opportunities and wrong choices.

"That's what a few people were saying back then," he says carefully. "But truth is, I don't think her family life helped. Her mother was on her own. Drink. Drugs. You know they lived in a trailer?"

I nod. The woman behind the counter is fiddling with the radio, pretending not to be listening. I lean forward and lower my voice.

"There was another girl, too? Zoe? Zoe Pearson?"

He hesitates. I wonder if I've pushed too far. After all, why should he trust me?

"Yeah," he says slowly, "but that were different. She ran away. That's all I know." He puts his cup down. "Is this what your film's really about?"

He sounds disappointed, wary, and I shake my head. "No. It's just . . . I'm interested, I suppose. Two girls from the same village—"

"Not the same, though," he insists. "One ran away. The other jumped off the cliffs."

I can see him deciding whether or not to talk to me, but I'm doing something right, because he goes on: "And there was her friend, of course. Went missing around the same time, about ten years ago now." The room goes cold. "Some folk reckon there was something going on there. Some falling-out or something. But who knows?"

A silence falls. The sugar cube I've been fiddling with bursts, and I sweep the table with my hand then look out at the darkening sky.

"Is Daisy's mother still around?"

He shakes his head. "It were the last straw for her, from what I heard. She were half dead with the drink anyway, and the shock of it all pretty much finished her off."

"So is there anyone who knew them?" I say. "Daisy and this friend of hers? Anyone who might know what happened between them?"

He thinks for a moment. "Monica, maybe?"

"Monica? My landlady?"

"You're in Hope Cottage, then?"

I nod. His lunch arrives, wrapped in greaseproof paper, along with a coffee. He thanks the waitress.

"Try her, if you want to go delving into all that, but like I say, I reckon it were just one of those things. You can't live your life like she did and not pay the price."

"Like she did?"

He smiles ruefully. "She could be wild. Anyway, I'd better go." He gathers his things with a cheerful wink. "See you around, I hope."

7

sit at my computer. I've persuaded Monica to meet me later this morning, but there's still time to work. A film of an older guy petting his dog has come in; another of a woman baking while, next to her, a baby gurgles happily in a highchair. I crank up the ancient machine and there's a short-lived grinding noise from deep within. I used this computer to make my first film and, though I know it's sentimental and ridiculous, abandoning it now would feel like Samson cutting off his own hair.

I wait for it to recover, then press *Play*. The next film opens with a black screen and noise, shouting that sounds wordless, and then the camera steadies, showing first a yellowed wall and then a woman appearing in front of it. She's overweight, dressed in a cardigan, her hair tied back in a tight ponytail. She yells at whoever is holding the camera.

"No!" she's saying. "You can forget it!"

The reply comes from close by. Just behind the camera.

"That's not fair!"

"Fair?! I'll give you fair, you little . . . and what the fuck're you doing with that?"

"What?"

"Your phone, Ellie!"

"Nothing."

"Put it away!"

There's no answer. The woman looks to her right, where a man in a shirt and jeans leans against a doorframe, watching the argument but apparently reluctant to join in.

"Are you gonna tell her?" she says. "Or just stand there?"

He shrugs pathetically.

"Chris! For fuck's sake!"

Now he turns to whoever has the camera. "Ellie," he says. "Listen to your mother."

"But it's not fair!"

"You were told," he says. "No more dance class unless you start improving at school."

"But—!"

He holds up his hands. "Enough. Go to your room. And turn that bloody thing off."

The frame lurches as the girl holding it—Ellie—swings to the left. There's a mirror on the wall next to her father and, in it, and only for a frame or two, I glimpse her reflection. I press *Rewind* and freeze it. She looks young. Thirteen or fourteen, with pale skin and beautiful ginger hair framing an innocent, freckled face.

I hesitate. Should I make this public? It's been filmed in anger, and no doubt uploaded in a fit of rage, a kicking out against the impotence of being a teenager. But she might regret it later. She might realize she never wanted it to be seen by anyone else, let alone the rest of the village. She might wake up tomorrow and worry about being in even more trouble with her parents when they find out what she's done.

I move the clip to the section marked *Private* then go upstairs. I need to get ready and think about how I can get Monica on my side.

We've arranged to meet at the end of the lane, and she greets me with a cheery "Morning!" when she sees me emerge from beneath the archway. She holds out her hand; plastic bangles crackle on her wrist. "Nice to finally meet you!"

"You, too!" I say. She looks younger than in her picture, early thirties perhaps. Only a few years older than me. She's heavier, though. Her hair is longer now and today it's tied back with a pale-yellow bandanna. She's wearing faded blue jeans and a purple waterproof jacket. At her neck I glimpse a knitted sweater in a garish yellow and she's wearing a plastic necklace of blue beads the size of marbles. Her eyes spark and she has a strange, twitchy nervousness; she looks like some kind of earth-mother, like someone who'd make her own muesli and buy everything organic and Fair Trade. Or perhaps a schoolteacher, friendly but slightly lost.

"Settled in? Everything okay?"

I tell her I'm fine.

"I left all the details. They're in the folder."

She means the one on the coffee table in the lounge. I skimmed through it the first night. It's stuffed with information leaflets, things to do, places to go. Most are out of date.

"And I'm just next door."

"Right," I say. "I didn't know that." She glances at me, her eyes curious. Has she sensed the discomfort in my voice? "Must be handy."

"It is," she says. "But don't worry. I won't disturb you." She pats my arm. "Shall we go for a brew? I'll take you to Liz's."

I tell her that'd be good and we begin to climb the hill. Once we reach the café—the same one in which I met Bryan yesterday—we sit in the window and Monica picks up a laminated menu.

"Tea, then?"

The woman from yesterday comes over—Monica introduces her as Liz—and today she smiles thinly as she takes our order, without quite meeting my eye. While it's not exactly hostile, it occurs to me she's found out who I am and doesn't like it. Well, I think, let her disapprove. Not everyone has to be onboard for the project to work; the odd sour-faced old cynic won't matter.

"Anything else?"

I say no and she retreats. Monica leans forward.

"So, was there something you wanted to talk to me about?"

I hesitate but think of the documentary. I have to get the channel to bite. I got the girls in *Black Winter* to open up, so I must have it in me.

"Daisy," I say.

She recoils, just slightly, but then seems to recover her composure. "Daisy Willis? Is that why you're here?"

"It's just background for the film. I'm interested in the effect it had on the community. You knew her?"

She's about to answer when the door opens and a group of girls comes in. They're teenagers, fifteen or sixteen I'd guess, still in uniform. They're gossiping, giggling; they transform the place with their frenetic energy. One is taller than the others, clearly in charge; she's leading the conversation, her eye rolls exaggerated as they talk about someone who evidently isn't there.

"What makes you think that?"

I glance over at the girls. I think of Daisy. I wonder if she'd have been like that.

"Oh, just something Bryan said."

She seems to relax a little.

"Oh, you've been talking to Bryan. Well, I guess I did a little. Everyone knows everyone here, see?"

"Is it okay if I ask you a few questions?"

There's a curve to her lips, not entirely encouraging.

"I thought the film was supposed to be lighthearted. Wasn't that what your friend said? *No one's out to get anyone?*"

My friend. She means my assistant, of course. She must've been at the meeting.

"Yes," I say, as warmly as I can. "And believe me. No one is."

Before she can answer, Liz arrives with the tea. She puts down a cracked teapot and gives each of us a mismatched cup and saucer, then, once she's exchanged a few words with Monica, withdraws. I remember Gavin saying that not everyone thinks Daisy's death was suicide.

I go on: "I'm just trying to understand what happened."

She takes her time to answer. Discomfort flits across her face.

After a second she glances over to where Liz sits watching us, then to the girls who followed us in. She lowers her voice. "Come outside for a smoke?"

We step out into the cold. She lights a cigarette with jaundiced fingers before offering the pack to me. I'm tempted, but resist. There's no way I'm going back to that, not after all this time. She blows the bluish smoke out through her nose.

"What've you heard?"

"Just that some people aren't so sure she killed herself."

"That so?" She takes a deep breath and lowers her voice. "Look," she says, "all I can tell you is she were a lost soul. From what I heard, she were having boyfriend problems. The usual, you know."

A lost soul? Boyfriend problems? My ex floats into view. I see him telling me he'd had enough. It was my work. I was cold. It was over. I was upset, yes. Much more than I let show. He was the first man I'd trusted. I cried. I swore I'd never fall in love again. I stopped short of watching a shitty movie with my flatmate, just. But I didn't reach for the bottle. I didn't jump off a cliff.

"Monica. People don't do that just because someone dumped them!"

"Some do." She hesitates. "Look, I don't know. Maybe it was more than that."

"Like?"

"Who knows?" She stubs out her half-smoked cigarette on the wall. "Look, it were tough, back then. With no body and that. Folks don't want it raked up. It's history. They want to forget. That's all. An' I reckon you'd be better off forgetting it, too. I mean, it's not like knowing why she jumped is going to bring her back, is it?"

"Of course not. But—"

"So what's the point?"

The truth, I want to say. That's the point. The truth. And it's what I do, my stock-in-trade. But then I think of *Black Winter*. Did the truth help any of those girls?

"Look," says Monica, her voice softening. "Whatever you make of us, we're just ordinary folk, y'know? Minding our business like anyone else. I mean, you may not realize it, but my livelihood relies on visitors here, now. Most folks' does. We can't have this film putting anyone off coming. Understand?"

For a moment it sounds like a threat, but she's smiling.

"Of course," I say. "But I'm not making an advert for the village, you know. *Come to Blackwood Bay and have all your dreams come true.*"

She grinds the stubbed cigarette into the ground with her boot. "I've been watching the films."

I hesitate. I don't need her approval. Yet I can't stop myself.

"Yes?"

"We all have. We just . . . we want the village to be known for something other than that."

"I get that."

She smiles sadly. "Daisy was lonely. That's what I think."

"I was told she had a friend? What happened to her?"

"She ran away. Don't recall where."

The wind blasts up the hill and, even though I feel it only in the most abstract, distanced way, I shiver.

"Who was she?"

My words sound wrong, mangled, like someone else is controlling my tongue, but she doesn't notice.

"Girl from out near Malby way. They went to school together but, like I say, she ran away. There were rumors she turned up in London, but I don't know anything about it."

No, I want to say. *No. It wasn't that. They barely knew each other.* Maybe Monica is confused. Maybe she has the wrong person. Maybe another girl went missing back then.

But no. I'd know about that. Surely?

"So three girls went missing?" I say, aware of how stupid I must sound. "Daisy, Zoe, and this friend?"

"Daisy didn't go missing. She killed herself. And her friend turned up, they say. But yes."

"This friend," I say, and it's like my throat is stoppered. I have to force the words out through thick sludge. "When did she run away?"

"I don't remember exactly. Around the same time Daisy died. Why?"

I feel like I'm clinging to a cliff face, about to fall.

"What was her name?"

"Sadie," she says, and though I suppose I should've been prepared for it, should've braced myself, the name thunders through me. It echoes like a scream in a darkened room and threatens to tip me off balance. "She were called Sadie."

THEN

8

So many of those days in the London hospital blur into one, but I do remember the day I found out who I was, the day I was born again. The day I became Alex.

I woke early to a pale light streaming in through thin blue curtains and tried to work out where I was. The room smelled of cheap air freshener and had few clues, just a chest of drawers with a television on it next to a vase of flowers, a mirror on the wall opposite, a bedside table with a lamp and an empty glass. For a second I thought I was in a hotel, that any minute I'd hear the toilet flush and some guy would reappear and tell me to get lost, but then I remembered. I was in the hospital, where I'd been since I was brought here from Kent.

I saw Dr. Olsen after breakfast. She met me in the day room; it was more comfortable in there, she said, as if we were just going to have a chat, a catch-up like old friends. I knew the real reason was I hated her office: it was too small, it felt cramped and stuffy and whenever I was in there I began to sweat. We sat on the stained chairs, and she shuffled hers nearer to mine. That day she was wearing a dress and smart leather boots, even though the weather was warming up.

"How're you doing?" she said, her accent barely perceptible.

I shrugged, then remembered to speak too. I like Dr. Olsen; she's done nothing to hurt me. "Fine."

She smiled.

"Fine?"

"Yes."

"Want to elaborate on that?"

"Not really."

She waited. The silence grew until, eventually, I felt compelled to fill it.

"There's nothing much to say."

"Still no luck?"

I shook my head. Dr. Olsen thinks muscle memory might one day kick in and, without thinking, I'll start to remember, maybe remember the code to get into my phone, but so far she's been wrong.

"And nothing has come back to you?"

A little, I thought. I remember a coach. Next to me, a huge man ate cheese-and-onion crisps and swigged a bottle of Coke before burping his rotten breath all over me. A cute kid with a mass of corkscrewed curls was told off by her mum.

But those memories are mine, I thought, they're all I have. And was that the journey I must've taken to Deal, or some other journey, from before?

"No."

"You're sure?"

I nodded emphatically.

"Yes."

She looked disappointed but tried to hide it. I felt sorry for letting her down, but there was nothing else I could do. After ten more minutes she told me she'd have to go.

"Oh, by the way," she said, standing up. "I wanted to ask you something." She took out her phone. It was a new iPhone, the latest model. "You know more about these than I do, I expect. I want to film my grandson, only I can't figure it out. There's a video, apparently, but . . ."

She shrugged helplessly. I held out my hand and she gave me the phone; without thinking, I tried to unlock it.

"What's the code?" I said, but she was looking at me strangely, watching my hands.

"You just tried thirteen seventeen," she said. "I want you to try that on your own phone. Okay?"

I stared at the phone in my hand, then gave it back to her. She'd tricked me, and I felt a hot, stabbing resentment. But, on the other hand, maybe it'd worked.

"I will," I said.

• • •

I lay on the bed staring at the ceiling, my open phone heavy in my hand. I'd found only one number in the memory. It seemed simple. If I wanted to find out who I was, all I had to do was dial it. So why couldn't I do it?

It was ridiculous. I sat up and tapped the number. I waited for it to connect, and when it did the silence seemed to stretch forever.

"Hello?" I said, finally. There was a pause, then a slick voice, velvety and with a hint of an accent that I couldn't quite place.

"Hello? he said, sounding concerned. "Sadie?"

The name was like a pin puncturing a balloon and I recognized it instantly as my own. There was no doubt; it felt like a lifeline thrown across the abyss, a secret code that might lead me out of the damp, musty cellar in which I was trapped. Memories flooded back in an almost overwhelming rush. I remembered Blackwood Bay, I remembered hitching as far as Sheffield, spending a few nights there before continuing to London. I remembered, too, that I was in danger, that I mustn't tell anyone anything, not even my name. I just couldn't remember why.

"Sadie?" the voice said again.

Maybe this person knew why. His was the only number in my phone, after all.

"Who's this?" I said.

"What?"

I repeated the question quickly. "Who am I speaking to? I don't—"

The line went dead. "Shit," I muttered, before calling back straight away, hopeful that it was just a dropped call. This time it didn't ring out, and neither did it the second time I tried, or the third. In the end, I gave up. There was nothing else I could do.

Dr. Olsen tapped on my door a little while later.

"Any luck?"

"It was the right number," I told her. She smiled, but she could see from my face that it wasn't good news.

"And?"

I remembered the conviction I'd felt that I mustn't tell anyone.

"There was only one number." I sighed. "Whoever it was hung up."

She sat on the bed next to me. I could tell she wanted to put her arm round me, but she didn't. Perhaps she wasn't allowed to.

"Did they say anything?" she asked instead, and as I looked up at her expectant, hopeful face I realized this was it, the breakthrough she'd been waiting for during our work together. All that time spent asking me whether I ever did anything and then couldn't remember it ("Doesn't everyone?" I said), or if I'd ever found anything at home that I couldn't recall buying ("What home?"), or if I ever felt my body didn't belong to me or was being operated by someone else. When it was all done she told me she thought I'd experienced something called dissociative fugue, and that it could be caused by lots of things, and it was obvious my life hadn't been easy recently, and that it usually just got better by itself.

And this was the breakthrough she'd been hoping for? Again, I felt I had to give her something, or else she'd never stop asking.

"Just my name," I said.

"Well, that's good!"

"My first name."

"Right," she said, a little more hesitant, a little more disappointed. "And?"

I had to think quickly. I couldn't give her my real name; she'd already talked about a TV appeal, or more contact with the national press. A name floated up from nowhere.

"Alex," I said. "My name is Alex."

"Alex?"

I nodded.

"Well, it's something," she said. "A big thing! Your name . . . We can ring them back. You want me to? I can explain—"

"No," I said. "I'll do it. Later."

She hesitated.

"Promise me you will," she said doubtfully. I told her I would, and

I did. Every day for a week, and every day she asked me and I told her the truth. The number was never answered again, and on the eighth day stopped even ringing out. She gave the number to the police at that point but they said it was unlisted, probably a pay-as-you-go mobile. Dr. Olsen told me not to worry, that more would come now I had my name.

"There's something else, though," she said. "I don't want you to worry, but we do need to think about discharging you to Outpatients soon. You can't stay here forever. You have somewhere to go?"

She knew I didn't. She'd already referred me to someone who'd said she'd help with that, not that I had any faith they could.

I shook my head. She put her arm on my shoulder and, for once, I didn't flinch.

"Don't worry, Alex, dear. I won't abandon you. It'll all be all right. I promise."

NOW

9

Monica and I finish our tea, then I return to Hope Cottage. I know I look nothing like I did back then, but still I'm shaken. I've lost the excess weight I was carrying, which was considerable. I dye my hair black—along with my too-bushy eyebrows, which I now pluck assiduously—and wear it short. Laser surgery has removed the need for the glasses without which I never left the house. The gap between my teeth closed up naturally, but I've had them straightened and whitened, plus I used some of the money I made from *Black Winter* to have my ears pinned back, my too-large nose trimmed down, and my slightly protruding jaw recontoured with fillers.

But there are other differences, too, more significant. Everything changed when I became Alex, when I got myself off the streets and into employment, when I started taking my filmmaking seriously. Everything. The clothes I wear, the way I hold myself, the way I walk and talk, my confidence. Even my own mother would struggle to recognize me, though that's not something I'd relish putting to the test. But people who knew me back then? A passing resemblance, they might say, as if Sadie and I could be sisters perhaps. But no more than that, I'm certain of it, or else I'd never have come this near Malby. I'd never have let Dan bully me into coming back to Blackwood Bay. I'd never have talked to Monica.

I reach for my glass of water. My laptop sits in front of me, a browser already open. Google is fired up and ready to go. I think back to what Monica said. That maybe me running away was the last straw for Daisy. But she's wrong. She's misremembered, or made a mistake. Daisy and I weren't friends; I barely knew her. I'm not even sure I'd recognize her if she were standing in front of me now. Not that she can, of course. So it can't be my fault she decided to jump. Can it?

And what did she mean about the rumor I'd turned up? Can it be true? I type my name and press *Search*. The machine hangs for a moment, but then the list of results fills the screen. I don't appear on the first page, nor the second. I try again, this time adding *Blackwood Bay*.

And there I am, right at the top. *Local Teenager Missing*. My hand hovers over the trackpad. I could click the link, go in deeper, find out what they said about me, whether they linked my disappearance to Daisy's death, or I could close the window and focus on what I want the documentary to be. I hesitate for a moment longer. Who knows what I might find out, where it might take me? And I've gone this long without looking. I should concentrate on my film, not on myself.

But what if the two things are linked? I click.

The article is from the local news. It tells me nothing I didn't know. I just disappeared, it says. I left home one day—from our house near Malby; I was on my way to visit a friend, according to my mother—and never returned.

I click another couple of links, hoping for more articles, but though there are a handful, the story seems to have died quickly. When I skim what there is, it becomes apparent that they all report the same thing, with few new details. I was seen trying to hitch a lift, carrying a bag. Details are sketchy, and of course, how can they know I ended up first in Sheffield, then London, and then, after who-knows-what happened to me down there, how I wound up unconscious on a beach in Deal? But still, I was expecting more than this.

I select the next link. In this article there's a brief interview with my mother; it's completely out of character, she says, her little girl would never run away. She appeals for me to get in touch. Whatever's wrong, we'll sort it out together. Yes, I think. Like you sorted everything else out: by siding with your new boyfriend and telling me to like it or lump it, to shape up or ship out.

There's only one picture of me, though it's used in most of the articles. It's in black and white, taken at school but cropped at the neck. I'm glad. I glance at it only briefly—it almost doesn't look like me. The girl I used to be had one of those generic, unremarkable faces that can map onto almost anyone. Only the gap between my front teeth is remarkable. My hair is a light brown, the color of milky coffee, tucked neatly behind my ears, and though my eyes are bright, my skin is blotchy and pocked with acne, my face puffy, my chin indistinct. Plump, they called me, when they were being kind. Which wasn't often.

I close the window, suddenly ashamed. What did I do? Why do some people think I'm linked to Daisy's death? The truth is, I can't remember; I know something terrible must've happened, something that made me run all the way to London and vow never to go back, never to use my real name, but, however hard I try, I can't remember what it was.

I open Google once more, and this time search *Daisy Willis*. There are more news reports, though by now the story is old, details even more scarce, the whole affair shrouded in uncertainty. A suicide note is mentioned, which I hadn't picked up on before, but nothing else. Nothing about me, so nothing to suggest she and I had been close, or that me running had anything to do with her death.

And yet there's something here, I'm sure of it. A memory bobs like jetsam, beneath the surface but unreachable, catching the light before sinking once more. I dig deeper, try an image search, but then it comes to me. Daisy and I standing on the slipway with a group of kids. Someone taking a photo.

I find the picture halfway up the stairs. I'd noticed it the first night I got here but hadn't recognized its significance. Monica with the kids, two girls standing off to one side, pretty much ignoring the camera. They look conspiratorial; they're up to something. I reach out and touch the cool glass, leaving a greasy mark. I lean in close, though I hardly need to. Now I look again it's obvious who they are, and I whisper their names under my breath.

Daisy. Sadie. Daisy. Me.

It's true, then. We were closer than I thought. I turn away from the photo and go back downstairs. I remember Gavin telling me that some people think Zoe's disappearance is linked to Daisy's. She's part of the puzzle, too, even if she did disappear years later. I'm sure of it.

I pick up my phone. He answers after the third ring.

"Gavin?"

It takes me a moment to realize he hasn't recognized my voice. My head drops, but so what? What did I expect?

"It's Alex," I say. "We met the other—"

"Oh, hi!" he says. "How're you? Everything okay?"

I ignore his question. "Listen," I say. "About Daisy's suicide, and Zoe Pearson?"

"Yes?"

"Well, I just wondered if there was anything else you could tell me."

"You're going to look into it!"

"Just as background to the film. I've been thinking about what you said, and I just wondered . . . Is there anyone I can talk to? Do you know whether Zoe had any friends that might still be here?"

"Well," he says eventually, "I heard she had a boyfriend, but that ended. And I think someone said she used to hang out with Sophie Steadman. I suppose you could try her."

I jot the name in my notebook.

"And where will I find her?"

"She works at the tattoo shop," he says. "Ink and Steel." He hesitates. "Want me to come?"

I almost consider it for a moment, but things will be simpler if I go alone.

"No," I tell him. "I'll be fine."

10

The words *Ink and Steel* snap to sharpness as the camera finds its focus, fancy gold lettering on black woodwork that's beginning to peel. I pan down slowly; screens in the window shield the rest of the shop and in front of them someone has arranged candles, a gold skull, an open book of tattoo designs. A sign next to the entrance offers piercings, plus more. *Enquire within*, it says.

I continue filming for a minute longer then go inside. The front of the shop has been set up as a waiting room, and there's a woman in here already, sitting in one of the wicker chairs arranged around a low table. She looks up when I enter but we make eye contact only briefly before she goes back to her phone. There are hushed voices from behind the screen.

The place is decorated with hundreds of tattoo designs. There are flowers, creeping vines, thorns dripping blood. One section of wall is taken up with butterflies and angels and on another there are snakes, birds, a revolver, skulls. Above the door is a photograph of a man's back, and on it a dragon breathes fire. It's stunning, rendered in blues and reds and yellows, its talons and teeth sharp, the scales on its skin intricate. I wonder how it looks in reality, glistening with sweat, shifting with the muscles under the skin.

I went for a tattoo, once. Perhaps here. Though vague, it's one of the memories that came back to me. I went with a friend but at the last minute I chickened out, scared of the pain perhaps, or my mother's anger. This was when we were still getting on.

My hand goes to my arm as I feel the bite of an imaginary needle. What would I have now, were I to try again? Something personal, perhaps. Something the relevance of which is known only to me. A line from a poem or a song? Or maybe it would be better to go for something beautiful, decorative but meaningless.

Not that I could, not there. Not with the scars that have turned my forearm into a battlefield since I was burned badly, years ago. I was in the hostel, pouring out tomato soup, of all things, but the pan was heavier than I'd expected and I caught it on the lip of the stove, spilling its contents over me. The pain was indescribable; the flesh seared and bubbled, it was like being flayed. Sometimes the skin is still sensitive there, still raw like it happened only yesterday, but most of the time it's the opposite. When I press it I feel nothing; the only pain is in my memory, but still I couldn't drag a needle across it, injecting myself with ink. Not now.

I look enviously at the woman opposite, at her unblemished skin. She's young, eighteen I'd guess, if that. She wears a T-shirt under a jacket, blue jeans, a beanie hat. She looks familiar, from one of the films I suppose. I lean forward and clear my throat.

"Sorry, can I ask? Are you getting a tattoo?"

She looks up at me. She's puzzled, as if I'm speaking gibberish.

"What're you having?"

She returns to her phone with a shrug but says nothing.

"It's just . . . I'm here to help with the film."

"I'm not—" she says, flinching at the sound of her own voice. "I can't—"

I force myself to laugh. "Don't worry! I'm not forcing you!"

She relaxes, just a little, but the wariness remains. Her eyes glisten, fixed on the patterns pinned to the wall behind me.

"I'm sorry if I—"

"Just leave me alone, will yer?"

I'm about to apologize when the door behind me opens. There's a dark-haired woman there. Sophie, I imagine. She's younger than I'd expected; not much older than her customer. Behind her I glimpse a sink, a leather chair, shelves stacked with plastic bottles.

"Kat?" she says. "Ready?"

The girl stands up. For the briefest fraction of a second her eyes melt.

"Excuse me," I say to Sophie. "Can I have a quick word when you're done?"

She looks me up and down. "I guess," she says, then she turns to Kat. "Come on."

The girl emerges after half an hour. She glances at me only once she's left, as she crosses the street. I'm surprised at the emptiness in her face. Surely she must feel something, even if only relief? If any-thing, she looks as though she resents it, has had it done for someone else. She removes a phone from her pocket—a different one from the iPhone she'd been staring at earlier—and presses it to her ear. She lis-tens intently, then nods in silent acquiescence before replacing it and disappearing down the street.

Sophie appears a moment later.

"You're still here," she says. "Come through. I have to tidy up."

I follow her into the back. I take in the machines, the sheathed needles, the jars stuffed with cotton balls, the trays of disposable ra-zors. I'm anxious; my chest is tight.

"Is this about Zoe?"

I'm not prepared for her to be so direct. It feels like going into battle.

"Partly," I say. "What makes you say that?"

"Why else would you be here? I'm guessing that's what your film's really about."

Her tone is sneering, condescending. I don't react.

"Is Kat okay?"

She glances away. She turns to one of the machines and begins dismantling it. "Fine. So?"

"Zoe was your friend?"

She stares at me, unblinking. I hold her gaze. Neither of us speaks. There are voices outside, someone walking down the street. I know exactly what she's thinking. Me, with my posh voice and nice clothes. What do I care about Blackwood Bay? About Daisy and Zoe? If only she knew.

"The film's about her, then? Or Daisy?"

I shake my head. I wonder if she knew her, too, but then realize she's probably too young.

"No. It's not *about* anything."

"Right."

I try again.

"Zoe was your friend?"

She goes back to the equipment. Her movements are methodical and precise. "Yes. She was. Okay?"

The air between us crackles.

"What d'you think happened to her?"

"Dunno. You'd have to ask her."

"I can't, though."

She says nothing. I remember the story of her being seen, the grainy CCTV footage from Meadowhall.

"You think she's alive?"

"How do I know?"

She's too defensive. Something's wrong.

"Was she happy here?"

Her laugh is brittle. "Would you be?"

"It doesn't seem that bad."

"No?"

I ignore the sarcasm.

"Look. I'm just trying to find out what happened. Maybe I can help. Did she tell you anything, before she went?"

She sighs, then turns to face me. "Zoe didn't fit in. She was pretty. Clever, too. Work it out."

"So she was bullied?"

Despite herself, she wants to talk. "It was nothing at first. Just having a go, you know? But then they started sending everyone photos on Snapchat."

"What kind of photos?"

"Zoe in the showers, and . . . well . . ."

I can imagine it. The word FAT, used as a weapon. The word BITCH. Worse.

"Didn't she tell anyone? Her parents?"

"They weren't really talking by then. She was staying out late. Drinking. They said it was affecting her schoolwork."

"Was it?"

"Like I said, she was clever. Her parents wanted her to go to university."

"And what about her?"

"Don't think she knew what she wanted." She puts her gum in the bin. Her T-shirt rides up as she does so, and I notice her arm. There, half hidden by a tattooed rose, there's a purple, thumb-shaped bruise. I force myself not to ask what caused it.

"Did she do drugs?"

She laughs. "What d'you think? You've seen the film. Everyone does. There's not much else to do."

"What film?"

She sighs theatrically. "Kat and Ellie. Eating chips. Are you blind?"

I resist the urge to rise to her bait, to tell her I've seen a thing or two and she needs to be careful before pissing me off. Instead, I smile thinly. I remember the clip she's talking about. I'll look at it later. "Did she have a boyfriend?"

"What's that got to do with anything?"

"I heard she did. It ended."

"Maybe, but she was really weird about it. She wouldn't even tell me there was anyone, for ages. Kept saying she was busy whenever I asked her to go anywhere."

She sounds hurt. I wonder if she feels guilty. Her friend ran and she has no idea why. Maybe she and I aren't so dissimilar.

"Any idea who it was?"

She glances past me, toward The Rocks. "Someone told me they'd seen her up there."

"What? That big old house?"

She nods.

"Who lives there?"

The room falls quiet. It feels like Sophie and I are at the bottom of a well. I can see the sky above us, but the walls are smooth and greased with sludge.

"David."

David? The word is cold, it's like plunging into freezing water, but when I try to remember why, nothing comes.

"Alone?"

She laughs, as if the question is ridiculous.

"Yeah. He lives alone."

"Why's that funny?"

"Go and see him. You'll see."

I just might, I think.

"What's he like?"

She shifts awkwardly. "Old."

"How old?"

"Older than Zoe, put it like that. And he's weird."

"How?"

"You never see him. And when you do he's always got binoculars. Goes and stands on the beach at night. Always by himself." She pauses. "And Daisy 'jumped' from right outside his house."

The air fizzes with her sarcasm. I can hear the quotes around the word.

"What d'you mean?"

"Look," she says. "I don't know anything. But they say Daisy weren't the type to kill herself. But she did. And I know Zoe weren't the type to run away. But she did."

Before I even know what I'm doing I'm asking the question.

"And the other girl? Sadie?"

"Sadie?" she says. She stares right at me, and for a second it's as if she's seeing straight through me, past the reshaped teeth and the lasered eyes, past the plastic surgery and the lost weight and the dyed hair, and seeing me for who I am. Poor, awkward Sadie. "No one ever really talks about her. They say they found her but she wouldn't come back. And I suppose with Daisy dying she kind of got overshadowed."

"But—" I begin, but a door at the back of the shop clatters open and someone enters with an urgent "Sophie?"

"I need to go," she says, her voice low. "But, like I say, some people think Daisy killed herself. But some people don't. They think she was pushed. Stick that in your little film, if you like. Only don't say it were me that told you."

11

I find the clip. The bench at the bottom of Slate Road between the slipway and The Ship, overlooking the water. Two girls are sitting, each with a packet of chips. The cliffs are visible just over the taller one's shoulder. The other looks younger; she has ginger hair and a dirty pink rucksack sits at her feet. The camera zooms in with that peculiar wobbliness of a handheld device. We're close now. The younger girl devours her chips anxiously, barely tasting them, while the other is more measured, taking a mouthful between drags of her cigarette.

I lean forward, closer to the screen. As well as Kat, I recognize the shorter of the two girls; she'd recorded an earlier film, the one in which she's arguing with her parents. Ellie. Now I watch the film again, I realize they're unaware of the camera. The person filming must be standing somewhere out of sight—in the alley that runs between the visitors' center and the pub, perhaps—watching them.

And listening, too. We can hear them speaking, though the sound quality is poor, and there's not enough context to snatch any meaning. We hear *It's okay . . . others . . .* We see the older girl blow out her smoke before handing the cigarette to her friend. She shakes her head, we hear *No*, and *I don't want to*, and *Just because, okay?* The older girl is unmoved. *Try it*, she says. *You have to*, and then, though it's too far away to see clearly, I realize it's not a cigarette but a joint. The younger girl resists, her eyes hollow, her thin face fearful, but her friend is relentless. *You might as well*, she says, and eventually the redhead takes the joint, puts it to her lips and inhales. *Hold it in*, says her friend, and though she tries, she coughs before handing the joint back.

The film ends. I almost want to smile. Weed? Is that all? It was so much worse in my day. I think back to what Sophie told me about Zoe and her boyfriend. Perhaps it was worse in Zoe's day, too. Perhaps she got mixed up in something she couldn't cope with.

My fingers hover over the mouse. Should I make it private? I remember what I learned at college—you can't afford too many scruples if you want to make a decent film—and decide against it. It's too late now, anyway. It's already been seen, nothing to do with me anymore, and anyway, I have things to do. Sophie told me Daisy jumped from The Rocks, from outside Bluff House. It's time I took a look, shot some footage I can post for the documentary. Maybe it will stir up someone's memories of back then, prompt them to talk about what happened, bring her story into the foreground.

The icy air blasts, sharp as glass. The only sound is that of the waves as they pummel the rocks below, the gulls' banshee shriek. It's dark; the bloody sky is jeweled with stars. It's impossible to imagine anything here but emptiness.

Head down, I force myself to carry on, but it's like wading through oil. My ears burn. Behind me, Blackwood Bay appears murky; even The Ship's cozy glow is curiously subdued. Ahead of me, the ground rises toward the glowering shadow of Bluff House, beyond which there's nothing but the sea and the black, precipitous cliffs.

Suddenly, I don't want to be here. I don't want to be doing this. But I take out my phone and film for a minute, recording the vast, unknowable water, studded as it is with pinpricks of light from dozens of minute ships. I think of the villagers watching the clip, imagine them wondering who's taken it, and why. I press the button to upload it before I can change my mind. Let them wonder.

Daisy must have stood right here, nearly ten years ago, gazing out at the same black water. But what compelled her to turn around, to face the edge and walk forward? What made her want to choose oblivion? Is it possible she didn't jump at all, that instead she was pushed, flung into the water like an armful of rags?

Or perhaps there's another explanation: it was no one's fault; she was running, being chased. She might've lost her footing on the wet grass, slipped and gone over the edge. It was an accident. Sort of.

I try to imagine where she is now, what might be left of her after all this time. The currents here are unpredictable; they can sweep you out in an instant. Swimming from the beach is discouraged. Her jacket washed up on a beach halfway to Malby, but no sign of her. Almost as if she were weighed down, or dead already.

I position my camera on its tripod and look up at Bluff House, silhouetted against the night. It's sadder, up close. Two forlorn stories with a pitched shingle roof. There's a light on in an upstairs room, but otherwise the place is in wretched, resolute darkness.

Who would choose to live here, in this godforsaken place? Despite its size—it must have three or four bedrooms at least—it's hard to imagine it containing any life at all.

I frame the scene, the house at one edge, and set the camera to record. The wind whispers through the long grass. *Sadie*, it says, *Sadie*. It sounds like a warning. I take a deep breath and stride purposefully into shot. I walk up to the front of the house, the side that faces the cliff. There's a gate here, a path that leads across the lawn, terracotta pots, their contents long dead, just visible in the dank moonlight. The door is closed; there's stained glass in its window, reflecting and distorting the light within, orange and green and red.

Now, up close, there's the tingle of familiarity, as if I've stood in this spot before, though I have no recollection of when. What memories I have are blurred; recalling them is like standing too close to the TV. The pixels are there, but not the image they form.

I stare up at the windows. There's a light on deep inside, and the whole place shudders. I knock on the door and the dull thud echoes through the house.

There's no answer. "David?" I say, peering through the stained glass. "Are you there?"

Nothing. I wait, then try again. I knock at the door so loudly this time that it judders against the frame, rattling the letterbox.

Now there's a noise. It sounds odd, like it's coming from deep in the house, or beyond it somehow. A light flicks on in the hall, then through the pus-colored pane of glass I see a figure approach, head down, blurry and wraith-like. Only when he's right in front of me, when all that's separating us is the door itself, does he look up. His features are indistinct, distorted by the window. He slides a bolt and the door opens a fraction, held back by a chain.

"Yes?" His voice is thin and reedy.

"Is that David?"

"What d'you want?"

I can't see him well. The hall light is behind him; the porch is in darkness. He's tall, though, and thin, his body angular and his movements awkward. I try to keep my voice even.

"Hi," I say. "I hope you don't mind me interrupting you."

I hold out my hand, but he makes no move to take it and I'm relieved. I don't want him to touch me. His attention seems focused on a spot a little way beyond me.

"I'm Alex. I'm just—"

"I know who you are."

He leans forward. His thin face catches the moonlight. His complexion is waxy; he looks bleached, overexposed. He gives me the creeps and I fight the urge to run, as hard and as fast as I can, until I'm miles away.

"Why've you come here?"

To find out about Daisy, I think. *About Zoe.*

I drop my hand and he flinches; his eyes dart with a feverish intensity, though he avoids looking at me directly. He scans my neck, my cheek, the side of my head; anywhere but my eyes. He doesn't blink. Even in the dim light I notice a patch of stubble on his neck where the razor missed, a tiny scar above his lip. He seems desperate to escape, even though he's standing in his own home and I'm the one trespassing. "I just wanted to ask you about—"

"Why have you come to Blackwood Bay?"

I open my mouth, but the words catch in my throat. Nothing will come.

"You need to get out."

His voice quivers. He sounds odd. Scared. Drunk, perhaps.

"What?"

"It's not safe for you here. You shouldn't have come."

His tone is menacingly low. I lean in, just a little, though my body is pulling against me. "I just . . . I want to talk to you."

"Leave. You should never—"

"Wait!" I say. He's closing the door. I'm desperate; my chance to speak to him is disappearing. "You knew Zoe Pearson."

"No," he says. "No. I'd never . . . not after what happened."

"What happened?"

He says nothing.

"Talk to me." I glance toward the edge of the cliff. "Daisy jumped from here, didn't she?"

He shakes his head. He looks haunted.

"David!" I say. "Please! Will you help me?"

"I can't!" he says. "I can't! Leave me alone."

He lets the door go and it snaps shut. The house shivers. I peer in through the glass, but all I can see is his silhouette, the back of his head.

I lean in close. I know my words won't be picked up by the camera, but I'm not sure that matters now. My focus has shifted. I need to know what happened, to Daisy, my friend, and to Zoe.

"Tell me what happened to the girls, David."

He speaks then. "You should know," he says. "You should know more than anyone."

I don't react. I can't. What does he mean? In any case, the light goes off and the house falls silent once more.

I walk away, back to my camera. It's not possible. He can't have recognized me, surely. Not in the half-light, not if I didn't recognize him. He can't be the one person in Blackwood Bay who knows I'm Sadie Davies.

But then it comes to me. What if he's not? What if I'm kidding myself that no one knows who I am? I look back toward the house and see something there, a figure half hidden in the dark. It's David, I think, and again I want to run. But then I realize I'm wrong. It's not David at all, but a girl. She's just standing, watching me. I take a step toward her, but my feet are suddenly heavy, mired in the sludge. I don't know what makes me, but I almost say it. *Daisy?* But the words catch in my throat, and when I look again there's no one, nothing at all. The place is deserted, but there at the back of the house, glinting in the moonlight like cold steel, I see it.

A trailer.

THEN

12

From: Alexandra Young
Sent: 22 June 2011 17.06
Re: No subject
To: Dr. Laure Olsen <olsen.laure@gstt.nhs.uk>

Hi Dr. Olsen,

I know you asked me to write to you when I got settled,
but I haven't been able to until now. There's only one
computer in this place and we all have to share it, and
anyway, the internet is down half the time.

I'm still in the hostel. St Leonard's. It's okay. Noisy,
though. There's a girl three doors away who has a baby
that won't stop crying, but it's not too bad. He's cute,
so that makes it okay. We're not really friends, but she
lets me hold him sometimes and one time asked me to
look after him.

I have made a friend, though. His name is Aidan. He's
about five rooms down on the same corridor as me, but on
the other side. He came here about three weeks ago, when
I'd already been here a couple. He makes me laugh, I
like him a lot. He says the only thing he wants in life
is to meet a nice man and settle down! It's a shame that
he's gay. His dad threw him out because he found him
writing about it in a diary (I know you said I ought to
think about starting a diary, but I haven't yet, sorry!
I have started filming things on my phone, though, just
so I don't forget them) and he had to come to London.
He slept in a sauna for a few days until he met someone

who took him home. He won't tell me what happened, but
he ended up here. He's nice to me. We share cigarettes
and stuff. We've promised each other we're going to be
friends forever, no matter what. He said he thought I
was gay, too, at first, because according to him I go
really quiet around men, like I wish I was invisible.

He's trying to help me remember what happened before
I ended up in the hospital, but not much has come back.
I think I slept on the night bus sometimes, and on
benches. Aidan said he once stole someone's handbag just
so he'd be arrested and be able to sleep in the cell,
but I don't think I've ever done that and, anyway, it
didn't work. I think I had a friend down here, before I
ran to Deal, but it's just a feeling, I can't remember
anything about her. I wish I could. Maybe I told her
about who I was, before I lost my memory in Deal. If I
could remember who she was and talk to her, that might
help, don't you think?

And I'm trying to remember back before then, too,
but it's like I just get vague feelings, nothing that's
specific, and sometimes I can't work out whether it's
a dream or not. Sometimes it's scary, like I'm not in
control of my body, like it's not even mine or something.
I remember that I liked school, and I think I did okay. I
remembered my mum, and that we used to get on pretty well,
until she met someone. I don't really know what changed.
I just remember not being as happy once he arrived. I
suppose that must be not long before I ran away, but I
have this weird feeling that something really bad happened
right before I left home. I can't remember what.

Anyway, I should go now. There's a massive queue to
use the machine! I hope you're well too.

Alex

NOW

13

A girl, she's lying face down on a couch, her shoulder exposed. A gloved hand appears and begins to smooth the skin. It takes me a moment to realize where we are, what I'm watching. It's Kat. She must've propped her phone on the counter, or maybe Sophie filmed it for her. The needle appears.

"It'll feel like a scratch," Sophie says. "Try to be as still as you can."

Kat says she will. Her face is pinched, her brow knotted. The machine buzzes.

"You're sure this is what you want?"

She doesn't answer. She's biting her lip. Sophie works slowly, wiping with a cloth every few seconds. The ink flows, pulsing under the skin. Blood rises to the surface and Sophie wipes it away. Still more comes.

When it's done, Sophie moves back. There, on Kat's upper arm, in black ink, is a perfect circle. It resembles an "O," or a wedding ring.

"Done," says Sophie, and Kat sits up. She's mostly out of shot, which is unfortunate. Her body twists.

"Stop filming now," she says. A moment later, the screen goes black.

I feel lightheaded. I've not eaten much, and my sleep was fitful. In the kitchen I cut and eat a slice of cheese, following it with another. I think of the trailer in David's garden and wonder whether it might be there by chance, unrelated to Daisy; I wonder whether he was lying when he said he didn't know Zoe. I'm angry. A weird, diffuse fury courses through me, as if searching for a focus. I can't work out what's upset me. Is it the documentary? I'm running out of time and it's shifting away from what I wanted it to be. Maybe it's Dan, taking it over and insisting on a story. I didn't want to make a film about Daisy's suicide, I didn't want to get involved in Zoe's disappearance. And I didn't want to end up worrying about Kat and Ellie.

At least when I was making *Black Winter* I was on home turf; I could go home if it got too tricky, sleep in my own bed. But here? I'm trapped; there's no crew, no camera operator or sound guy. I don't even have my car. But I can't give up. I'd be kissing my career good-bye; I'd have nothing left.

I return to my computer and select the film I shot last night. The footage is blurred but, slowly, it resolves. The trailer at the back of the house on The Rocks, barely visible in the gloom, but definite, defiantly solid.

It's a coincidence, I tell myself again. Daisy lived in a trailer; David has one in his garden. It doesn't mean they're linked.

But who am I trying to kid? I open Google once more and pull up the news stories. I don't know what I'm expecting—an address, perhaps, confirmation that Daisy's trailer was still parked on the site up the coast when she jumped—but I search them again. This time my eyes snag on a photograph of Daisy's mother, taken several months after Daisy's death. She's sitting at a kitchen table, holding a framed photograph of her daughter. She looks devastated, and ill.

I've seen her before, I know I have. But where? I go through the films, one by one, until I find it. A carpeted floor, a coarse dark brown, the color of chocolate. Flower pictures on the walls, a cage with two budgerigars, a wipe-board with the words *Resident of the Day! John R, Happy Birthday!*

The camera pans, a jagged left. An empty corner lounge behind glass windows. In the distance there are trees.

We follow the corridor and reach a brightly lit room. Two arm-chairs have been pushed close together. In one sits a woman; she's tiny, her hair is white, swept back, her scalp visible through it. She's looking at the person in the other chair. A man, he's in his forties, perhaps late thirties. Her son? Grandson?

The woman is smiling; her expression is one of almost childlike excitement. The man is speaking to her, though we can't hear what he's saying. His lips barely move. It's sad, but weirdly beautiful. Behind her, another resident sits in a gray tracksuit, staring at the camera, her eyes blank and empty, and I know I'm right without even having to check.

It's Daisy's mother.

14

According to Google, there's only one care home in the area, Holbrooke House. I take a taxi. The open road is like coming up for air and I realize I've been feeling like I'm in a sealed room, holding my breath, anxious for my next gulp of oxygen. I shiver as we drive past the spot where my car ended up in the ditch, remembering the vacant, unseeing stare of the dead sheep. I half expect to see it still there, but there's no sign anything happened. The view is desolate, just miles and miles of emptiness in the dank afternoon light.

We drive through a village even tinier than Blackwood Bay—just three or four houses and a pub that looks closed—and a little way after it pass a narrow track leading down toward a church. The road winds until we turn off and into a lit drive that curves toward a large red-brick building. It's more modern than I was expecting and seems to consist of two wings. Above the main door a sign reads *Holbrooke House, Residential Care Home*. We pull into the car park and I unbuckle, suddenly nervous, and get out of the car.

The doors slide open with a sigh. I introduce myself to the woman at reception. She looks me up and down—I'm glad I've put my camera in my bag—and asks if she can help.

"Yes," I say, smiling. She has a pink streak in her hair, a ring through her nose. "I'm here to visit Geraldine Willis."

"Oh, right," she says. "And how do you know Geraldine?"

I look her in the eye. "She's my aunt."

Her head tilts with evident suspicion, but I hold her gaze. "I've been away."

She dithers for a moment then pushes a book toward me and asks me to sign.

"How is she today?"

"The usual."

It tells me nothing, but I smile sadly. "You must know her well. She's been here . . . how many years now?"

She shrugs without interest. "At least six. That's when I started, and she were here then."

I thank her and she points me up the stairs.

I pause on the landing. The air is thick, invasive like smoke and far too hot, and I begin to sweat. A little way along the long corridor there's a brightly lit nursing station at which sits a woman in a pale green tunic, and at the end I can see a glass-walled room, a few armchairs, the flicker of a television.

"I'm looking for Geraldine?" I say to the nurse.

"Halfway along. If not, try the day room."

I head toward the light. An old woman shuffles toward me using a frame, her skin parched and liver-spotted, her hair glowing like orange floss. A little farther on I find Geraldine's room. Her name is on the door, alongside a laminated photograph. I hesitate outside; I want to prepare myself.

I think back to what Bryan told me about the drink and drugs. I know what they can do; I saw it on the streets. People whose addictions had left them with memory difficulties, motor problems, as good as killing them in some cases. People who barely even knew who they were, people who'd never be independent again.

I steel myself to enter. Geraldine is sitting hunched in an armchair, dressed in a tracksuit several sizes too big, staring at the TV that's bolted to the wall. She seems almost unreal, but recognition shudders through me. Only now do I wonder why I'd assumed Bryan meant she was dead.

"Geraldine?"

She doesn't look away from the screen and I call her name once more. This time, she moves her head, her movements slow and unco-ordinated. There's a slight tremor, a doll-like wobble, as if some joint is working loose, as if she's in danger of falling apart completely.

"Is that you?" she says. I take another step toward her. It's doubt-ful she, of all people, would recognize me, but I can't be sure. "Ger-aldine?"

The remote sits on the arm of her chair and her hands shake as she reaches for it. Up close, she looks much older than her years; her features are sunken, her hair loose and untidy. She seems hollowed out, eaten away from the inside. Her eyes are dull, a gray-green color, but when she turns her gaze on me they flash for a moment, as if something has sparked, some internal connection made.

"What is it, love?" she says. Her eyes have dulled once more and she's looking past me now, over my shoulder. "Is it time?"

There's a jug of water on the table. I pour myself a cup and, with trembling hands, pass one to Geraldine, too. I shouldn't have come here, I shouldn't be disturbing her. I need to retreat. I need to find my safe place.

I take out my camera. At first, I think she hasn't noticed, but then her eyes swivel toward it. "What's that? Are you taking my picture?"

"D'you mind?"

She answers only with an ambiguous shrug, so I press *Record* and put the camera on the dresser.

"My name's Alex."

Her cup wobbles as she brings it to her lips, but when I go to help she shoos me away. She spills only a little, then hands it back.

"I saw you, y'know?" She waves vaguely toward the window. "I were watching you. That yer fella?"

Does she mean the taxi driver? He's down there, in the car park. I wonder how much Geraldine sees, what connections she makes. How she fills the gaps that are left.

I think of my own gaps. I managed to piece most of my story to-gether, but so many of my memories seem borrowed, and so many are absent completely. In some ways, that's merciful. Maybe some gaps are protective.

"You deserve someone nice."

She's waiting for a comment. "He's all right," I say, feeling guilty as I do. It seems unfair to lie, to string her along, but I'm just trying to build a bridge. It's what I do.

"Good."

"Geraldine?" I say gently. Again, that flash of lucidity, quickly extinguished.

"Aye?"

"Can I ask you something?" I lower my voice. I need to find out whether the trailer parked in David's garden has anything to do with her. "Something about Daisy?"

She blinks, but there's no other reaction. I was worried it might upset her, she might close down, but instead it's as if she doesn't even recall her daughter.

"Do you remember the place you lived before you came here?"

She looks up.

"Aye! Over in the bay. A trailer. Up near Malby. I cleaned there."

I smile—I almost want to laugh—but then she says, "On'y they got rid of me. We had to move."

The relief vanishes.

"Move where? David's?"

She says nothing. I take her hand. It's cold, hollow-boned; there's a crackle of static as we touch. I can almost feel the blood as it pulses through her veins. Down the corridor there are voices, laughter from the nursing station, but it seems a thousand miles away.

"You'd moved the trailer to David's by the time Daisy went?"

Geraldine hesitates. She seems confused, almost as if she's forgotten her daughter is dead. But then another connection forms, another synapse fires. She smiles warmly.

"How is he?"

"Why did you live with him?"

"He were our friend. How is he?"

"Your friend? Or Daisy's?"

She stares straight at me, as if the question is ridiculous.

"Did you trust him?"

"'Course I did."

"With Daisy? Didn't you worry something might be going on?"

She gazes into the distance, toward the mirror bolted to the wall over the dresser. For a second I think I've lost her, but then our eyes meet and she smiles.

"Nowt were going on. He were decent. He were decent to us both." Her eyes shine, determined. "You'd do well to remember that. It weren't him that hurt them."

"Someone hurt Daisy?"

"Aye."

"You said *them*. Who else?"

She doesn't seem to hear me. There are footsteps in the corridor outside, as if somebody's approaching, and I become aware of the camera on the dresser, recording us.

I lean in. "Someone hurt her, so she . . . killed herself?"

Her head bobs.

"She'd never do that. She were too strong."

She's faded out.

"There was a note? Do you have it?"

She doesn't answer. I say it again, and this time she laughs bitterly. "A note . . ."

"It wasn't real?"

Her response is mumbled, incoherent, almost as if she's talking to herself, arguing with voices in her head.

"Geraldine?"

"They reckon someone saw it, too." She laughs, as if it's the most absurd thing.

"Saw her jump?" I say. "Who?"

"But it's all lies."

"Who? Where's the note now?"

"They took it. But it weren't true," she mumbles sadly into her chest. "I knew it. I felt it."

The room falls silent. Outside, a door opens, then closes. There are voices. Whoever's approaching must've stopped en route. I want to stand up, to walk away, to never look back, yet I also want to stay with her. Or take her with me, look after her, try to give her back her daughter.

But how can I do that? I sit on the bed next to her chair. For a moment, it feels like a normal visit, like I've come here with flowers and her favorite cake, just here to hold her hand and gossip or take her for a trip out in the car.

But it's not. How could it be?

Suddenly, she raises her head. "Poor Sadie . . ."

The word reverberates. The walls shake.

"Sadie?" I whisper. "What about her?"

Nothing. It's like I'm not here, as if I haven't spoken. She's drifting in and out of lucidity, bobbing to the surface before being sucked under once more. She glances away, toward the floor. Her head falls but when she looks up her eyes dart like minnows.

"Poor girl. All that to live for. They said she wrote a note an' all. Did you know that?"

"What?" There was no note. I'd remember.

"Her mum told me."

"Sadie's mum?" I say, trying not to sound as exasperated, as desperate, as I feel. She's confused, misremembering. She must be. It makes me wonder whether there's anything she's said that I can believe. I'm about to give up, to turn around and switch off the camera, when something takes hold of me. I can't. I have to find out, this one thing at least.

"Where is she?" I say. "What happened to Sadie's mum? After she went?"

Nothing. I put my hand back on her arm and she looks down at it, resting there.

"Thick as thieves."

"Who? Daisy and Sadie?"

"What happened to your arm?"

She's staring at my scar.

I don't answer. I don't want to tell her about the accident, but then she grabs it, her movements surprisingly quick, surprisingly strong.

"You should get it seen to."

I pull my arm back. "Tell me about Sadie. You said she wrote a note, too?"

"They killed her."

"Daisy? They killed her?"

She folds her hands in front of her and stares out of the window. There's nothing there, just a blank gray square in the wall, flakes of snow drifting beyond it, catching what's left of the afternoon light like burnt paper.

"Geraldine?"

More voices. This time there's a knock on the door.

"Geraldine?" comes a voice, echoing mine. "Everything okay?"

I look back over my shoulder, but before I can answer Geraldine grabs my arm again, her face crumpled with pain. I feel terrible for what I'm doing, for the places I've taken her.

"She's here. My Daisy." Her gaze rests at a point over my shoulder.

"Here?" I say. I look round. There's a woman there, dark hair, a pale green tunic. I wonder if she looks like Daisy, or like Daisy might now.

"Geraldine?" The newcomer looks from Geraldine to me. She notices the camera, clearly angled toward us both. "Miss?"

Suddenly, there's another hand on my arm. The grip is strong, firm.

"Miss, I think you're upsetting her."

I shrug off the woman's hand, but it's no use, too late. I've lost Geraldine completely. She's returned to the television, apparently unaware that it's no longer switched on.

"I was just leaving," I say. I'm about to hold out my still-shaking hand when I'm gripped with the desire to do more, to embrace her, with the conviction I won't see her again and that that will be a terrible shame. So I do, I hug her, and though at first I think she's going to recoil, she doesn't. She's still for a moment, then she leans into my embrace, her hands go around my back, she holds me tight. We melt into each other. She whispers in my ear, her voice tiny and desperate.

"Please . . ."

"What?"

"Has it stopped?"

"What?"

"The girls. You have to help them."

"Who?" I say. "Which girls?"

"Help them. Please."

My mind goes to Kat. And to her friend. Ellie.

"Who? What's wrong?"

She looks at me, her expression impenetrable. "Miss!" says the voice from behind, stern now. I stare into Geraldine's eyes, but something has dimmed. I hold her instead. It's all I can do.

"I have to go. I'm sorry."

"Come back for me, then."

"I will," I say, standing up. I feel terrible, even as I lie, but what else can I say? Her eyes close in relief.

"Daisy . . ." she says, but it's half murmured; she's drifted off once more, hovering somewhere between the past and the present, between pure fiction and misremembering.

"Don't leave me here," she says, and for a moment I wish more than anything that I could tell her I won't.

The doors hiss open, but my taxi has gone. The driveway is empty save for a solitary car over by the entrance. Inside, I can make out a silhouetted figure, and I get the feeling they've been watching the exit, waiting for me to come out. When I turn to look for the car park, the road is lit by the mysterious car's headlights. It reverses and turns, the driver's profile flashing momentarily into view. I'm filled with the sudden conviction that it's David, though as it recedes doubt creeps in. No one is watching me, I tell myself. It's a coincidence, that's all, another visitor leaving in a hurry. I'm being paranoid.

Back inside, I call Gavin; he arrives after twenty minutes.

"You're a lifesaver," I say as I get in, and he laughs.

"Well, I couldn't leave you stranded here, could I?" He leans toward me, just slightly. "You're not cold?" he says. "Did you wait inside?"

I ignore his questions. "Shall we?"

We pull out of the car park. At the bottom of the drive he turns left, back toward Blackwood Bay. I can tell he's itching to ask what I was doing there and, sure enough, after a minute he coughs delicately.

"You went to see Daisy's mother?"

"Yes. I wanted to find out what she thought."

"And?"

"Well." I sigh. "She's really confused. But she insisted Daisy didn't kill herself."

"She's not the only one. Like I said."

"Who else?"

"A few people. The woman who ran the guest house I stayed in when I first arrived, she said there'd been loads of talk when Daisy was first presumed dead but then it kind of fizzled out." He hesitates. "But if her own mother said she didn't do it . . ."

"I know. But she's pretty muddled."

"So, you believe her? What does she think happened?"

"Who knows?" I say. "She just said, 'They killed her.'"

"They?"

"She didn't remember anything else. She seemed doubtful about the note, too. And she told me someone saw Daisy jump but she doesn't believe it and didn't say who." I stare out the window.

"It'd still be good to know who said they saw her," he says. "Want me to do some digging? See what I can find out?"

"Why would you do that?"

He shrugs. "Dunno. I'd like to make myself useful."

I smile. My instinct is to say no, but maybe I could do with some help. He's got to know the people here, he knows who to ask.

"Okay, then." I pause. "She says David up at Bluff House had nothing to do with it."

"What made you think he did?"

"Just something Sophie from the tattoo shop said. She thought Zoe might've known David. Would her parents talk to me, d'you think?"

"Zoe's?" He shakes his head. "I doubt it. To be honest, I'd steer clear. From what I've heard, they don't like people reminding them about what happened."

"As if they could forget."

"You know what I mean." He hesitates. "Did you know about Sadie Davies?"

My breath catches, just for a moment. I don't think he notices.

"Daisy's friend?"

"Yes. She disappeared just before Daisy killed herself."

No, I think. *He's got the chronology wrong.* I can remember it. Daisy went first. I can see myself back then, though it's like a dream. I'm sitting on the floor in a strange room; there's a mattress on the floor with no sheets and a weird smell. I have my legs crossed, my arms folded over them. I'm crying, because Daisy's gone and I couldn't help her.

He coughs. "Did Sadie know David, too?"

I stare down at my hands. They're turning over and over, each stroking the other as if they have a will of their own. I force them to be still.

"No," I say. That's one thing I'm sure of.

I gaze up at the cloudless, star-studded sky as it turns from dark blue to black. A pinprick of light flies over, too fast to be an airplane. A meteor, I suppose, a shooting star. I remember London. I used to lie there at night, in a doorway, near a vent if I could find one, and look up at the sky. Looking for the stars. Usually, it was cloudy down there, there was too much pollution, too much light, but even knowing it was there made me feel better. It made me feel less hungry somehow, less hopeless. Less alone.

"Maybe Zoe's got nothing to do with the other two," he says. "She wasn't the kind of girl to run away, it seems. Whereas both Sadie and Daisy—"

"What? Were?"

"There were rumors that Daisy, in particular, was a, well . . ." He shifts uncomfortably then takes a deep breath, like someone about to plunge in the knife. "She was promiscuous."

"What?" I can't help but laugh, though I'm grateful he at least found it difficult to say. "She was fifteen, for fuck's sake!"

He seems to shrink. "Don't judge me. I'm just telling you what people have said."

"Who? Who said that?"

"Oh, you know." He shifts again in his seat. "People."

I say nothing. I let it go. I have to. I remember one of the women I filmed for *Black Winter* saying that social services had told her she was a slut, that she'd asked for it. She was thirteen.

But I don't want that argument now. Not with my new friend.

My mind trips on the word. Is that what he is?

"Have you been watching the clips?"

"Some of them, yeah."

"You see the one of the two girls eating chips?"

"Kat and Ellie. Yes."

"And? It was a joint, wasn't it? Sophie says all the kids do it."

He laughs. "That's why I do the film club."

I hesitate. He seems honest, at least about that, but I'm still not sure how much to trust him, whether I can let him in. I don't want to sound like a crazy person, a conspiracy theorist desperate to inject interest into their film, but still I go on.

"Geraldine said something else," I tell him. "Whatever happened, she doesn't think it's over."

THEN

15

ALEX'S DIARY, 29 JUNE 2011

I'm on my own. I can't trust anyone, I know that after what happened today.

I feel sick just thinking about it now, but I'll try to write it down like it happened. So, we were supposed to go up to Deal—maybe it would trigger my memory and I'd know what I was doing up there. Aidan suggested it, and Dr. Olsen said it was up to me but that I should definitely take a friend and tell her when I was going to go. I didn't, though. I mean, what was she going to do? Come with me?

We cobbled together what money we had and got the bus to the coach station. On the way, Aidan was telling me about how he just wants to meet someone and be looked after, and he asked me what I wanted to do. It seems crazy now, after today, but I realized I haven't really thought about the future because I've been so obsessed with the past, trying to work out what happened to me, back in Blackwood Bay, and here in London, what made me run. Anyway, I said I thought I'd wanted to be a vet once, or a doctor, and he said I should look into doing GCSEs, or a BTEC or something. I could talk to Dr. Olsen about it.

When we reached Victoria I seemed to know the way and when we got on to the main road it felt like I'd been there before, too. At the station the stink of exhaust fumes and fast food hit me like a train, and when I saw the sign for the toilets—they're down some stairs—I knew exactly what they'd look like. It came back to me in a rush: I used to buy drugs down there, that was where I used to hang out.

Aidan came over with the tickets, but I couldn't go to Deal now, I was getting too close to who I was here. He followed me through an exit at the back. Outside, it was all posh cars, Bentleys and stuff, on one side of the road, and on the other it looked like public housing. Then we were in front of an Italian restaurant, next door to a place that did dog-grooming. Between them was a metal gate that led up to some flats, three or four floors of them. There was a panel with all the door buzzers and without even thinking I pressed the one for thirty-two. My heart was beating so hard, but when it opened I went up, and Aidan came too, even though he kept asking if it was a good idea. When we reached flat thirty-two the door was ajar and I could hear music. It stank of cigarettes and dope, but we went in anyway. It was disgusting; the walls were yellow and peeling and there was rubbish everywhere. There was a bedroom with a tatty mattress on the floor, then a disgusting kitchen, and in the room at the end of the corridor I could see a folding table and on it there were drugs and plastic bottles, bags of powder and some scales.

There were two men sitting on a sofa, and a girl between them who looked like she was nodding off. As soon as he saw me, the one on the right stood up and said, "You!"

Who? I wanted to say. Who am I? But he looked like he wanted to kill me, it was dangerous, he'd have a knife or something, and when Aidan came in he got even angrier.

I kept looking at the girl on the sofa, and I knew that'd been me once. And the mattress on the floor next door. I'd slept on it, I'd fucked on it—or been fucked, I don't remember it being something I wanted.

I was frozen to the spot, even though I knew I had to get out, but Aidan pulled on my arm. "Come on!" he said, and then he said my name, Alex, and the guys started laughing. "Alex?" said the other one. "So that's your name now, little Sadie?"

We ran, then. Back down the stairs. I didn't know whether they were chasing us or not, I just knew we had to get away. But at the bottom I saw someone on the other side of the street. She was looking straight at me, and somehow I knew she was the one who'd been my friend, the one who might know who I was and why I ran away.

"Wait!" I shouted, but she ran away. I tried to catch up with her, but it *was no good, she disappeared down a side street. Aidan shouted after me to stop. He asked who it was I was chasing and I told him the truth.*

"I don't know."

I knew he'd ask, then, and I was right. "And who the hell *is Sadie?"*

He sounded almost angry. But I didn't tell him. I'm never telling anyone, not even—no, especially—*Dr. Olsen. Like I say, I'm on my own.*

NOW

16

I remember that day, the day a memory came from one place and led me to another and I walked straight into the shooting gallery I hadn't previously known existed. So I know it's worked before, and that means surely it can work again. It's like picking up a track at the edge of the forest, following it, going deeper in. Even though I want to know, I'm nervous about what I might find in Daisy's home. Lightless, Bluff House seems even more desolate; it glowers resentfully in the dark. I go around to the far side, where there's a garden, separated from the land by a low wall and some hedging. A clothesline is strung diagonally across it from a pole in one corner, and in the other, battered and decrepit, is the trailer.

I switch on my camera and attach the light unit, then film for a moment. But when I put it down, something's wrong. The van appears almost pixelated, as if I'm still looking at it through the camera's lens. I blink and shake my head, but it's no better, and when I step toward the gate that separates me from Daisy's van it's like I haven't moved at all. It's as if I'm floating, an inch outside my body, above and to the left, watching myself as I unlatch the gate, invisible.

This is wrong. It's like déjà vu, except more intense, like something terrible is about to happen. I glance round but there's no one there; Bluff House remains in stoic darkness.

I breathe deep. Nothing will happen, I tell myself. It's a short-circuit in the brain, that's all, and it'll pass. Dissociation. Dr. Olsen warned me this might happen occasionally, way back then. But it's not until I lift the camera to my eye and begin to film again that things go back to how they really are, as if they're in front of me and I'm in control of my body once more.

The van sits at a strange angle, half off its support, sinking into the mud. What's left of the paint is streaked with blood-red rust and there's a crack across the front window; the wheels are so corroded they look almost moth-eaten, flimsy as gauze. The door hangs off its hinges; the steps that would once have led up to it have long since disappeared. There's a brand name inscribed above the window: *Pegasus*.

I peer inside. The stale, sulfurous smell hits me first, an ammoniac undercurrent of stale pee, possibly worse. I shine the flash into the dank interior, still filming. Meaningless slogans cover the walls: names and dates, a weird, cartoonish figure, the odd tag in garish spray-paint. Beer cans and bottles litter the floor; there are pieces of wood, pizza boxes, magazines. Teenagers, I suppose, using it until it became too unsafe, or too disgusting. I wonder if David let them; perhaps he didn't even try to stop it. I picture him, holed up in his house while the kids outside partied, played music, took drugs, screwed. Perhaps he hid himself away, retreated to the depths, or maybe he peered out of the window and watched them. I wonder what he thought. Whether he envied them.

There's a rusted cooker right in front of me, plus a filthy sink. A concertina doorway at the back leads, I presume, to the only bedroom, with another that I'm guessing is the bathroom. I try to imagine a different time. Daisy living here.

Is that where she would have slept? There'd have been posters taped to the walls—Katy Perry, perhaps, Lady Gaga? The Twilight films?—a soft duvet cover in a bright purple, something like that. I doubt she'd have an iPod—a tinny stereo, maybe? I see her mother, waiting until her daughter went to bed, then releasing a catch to fold down the tiny dining-room table and arranging the cushions from the living area to double as a mattress. The two women on top of each other. Fine for a fortnight's holiday, I suppose, but every night? Who would want to live like this, amid this dinginess? It must've been suffocating; it reminds me of the hostels in London. What teenager would want to have her life pressed so tightly against her mother's, every day?

I check myself. Any, perhaps, if the alternative is . . . well, whatever did happen that day she went over the edge. Could it really have been something to do with me, the thing that caused her to jump? I close my eyes and try to see us. In the café, perhaps, just like the girls the other day. Pushing and shoving, bitching about our friends, but it's playful, we don't mean anything by it. Or maybe we're down on the beach, she's telling me about a boy, she's met him again, and this time he kissed her. She can't believe her luck, her first kiss, and someone she really likes. He's older, she says, nearly a man, and she could taste cigarettes on his breath, only she didn't mind because they were his cigarettes that he'd smoked, and it was his breath she could taste them on.

I'm jolted out of my reverie. It doesn't make sense. Mooning over a boy? What was it Gavin had told me? People say she was a slut, or words to that effect.

Anger bubbles up. *People* know nothing. *People* can take their judgmental bullshit and shove it. *People* can fuck off.

And yet . . . we're supposed to believe she took her own life? Flung herself to her death just a few feet from here? My eyes flick open as I remember where I am. Perhaps it wasn't like that at all. Perhaps her first kiss was right here, in this stinking van. I see that, too. Hands on her, despite her wanting them gone. Her own mouth stoppered with that of another. Or maybe it was in the park, in the bandstand, at the amusement arcade. Or over there, inside the black house, with a man as old as her father.

But where did I fit in, at the end? What did I do? I use both hands to lever myself up into the van. I carry on filming as I explore, still not sure what I expect to find. Anything she or her mother might've left would be long gone by now. I wait, but the smoke isn't clearing. I steel myself against the weight of the stink. The van creaks as I go in deeper, treading carefully. There may be anything buried here, discarded needles hidden among the wrappers. At least I'm wearing my boots. I shiver in the cold and scan the defaced walls with my camera, then try to push my way into the bedroom area. The door that separates it from the rest resists as something bunches behind it. I push harder—it's a thin mattress, it turns out—and eventually get in. The smell in here is worse, the air staler. I want to escape but, over by the remains of the bed, low down and half hidden by a bundle of rags, something catches my eye. A mark, scratched on the wall.

It's a message, I think, but even as I draw closer I'm telling myself not to be stupid. And I'm right to be skeptical. It's just a series of dots, joined together in two lines that converge at one end to form a horizontal V. Meaningless, I think at first, it's a surprise I even noticed it, but then I feel a peculiar jolt of recognition and realize it could be Andromeda. Seven major stars, part of the Perseus group. Named for the beautiful princess who was sacrificed, chained naked to a rock to be eaten by a sea monster. A constellation visible only in winter.

But why would Daisy have that scratched on her wall? Just as I'm about to stand, to get a better angle with my camera, I notice something else next to it, two words. They're both unclear, but one is almost certainly *Daisy*.

As I crouch down to the other the déjà vu returns, stronger this time. It's like I know what the word is. I make out an *S*, a *d*. *Sad*, it looks like. My heart thrums as I rub away at the debris and dust, and there it is. *Sadie*.

I stand up. It's true, then. We were close. Best friends, just like I thought when I first saw the photo in the cottage. I must've been here. So why don't I remember?

I lift my camera to frame the shot, but then I hear a sound, some movement outside. An animal, something big, unless I'm imagining it. It comes again, heavier this time, more distinct, and with it there's something else, a shuddering bang that shakes the whole van, and I realize it's the trailer door, slamming shut.

I drop my camera and tear open the door to the living area. The door to the van is closed but there's a movement outside, I'm sure. The door handle rattles uselessly and I slap the fiberglass with the heel of my hand. "Let me out!" I shout. I try the handle again, then I'm turning around, sliding to the floor, and after a moment of blackness everything bursts into life.

I'm not here, it's like the channel has changed; a burst of static on the screen, then I'm in an empty room, yellow walls, a stained mattress on the floor. There's the stink of cigarettes on him, stale sweat, clothes that have gone a touch too long without a wash. His hand is between my legs. I feel nothing. This isn't happening. Or not to me, at least.

Leave me alone! I say, but his hand is over my mouth. I kick out but I can't connect, and then he's trying to kiss me. His breath is the worst, and even in the middle of it all I find myself thinking that at least the fucker could've sucked on a mint or brushed his teeth. He takes off his belt and my mouth fills with a metallic taste.

I've bitten his tongue. He spits. Right in my face. And I want to spit back but I can't feel anything and, anyway, I don't have any choice. I never did. I need what he's got and he'll only give it to me if I do this, so I do, I lie there, and I deserve it, I deserve it, I deserve it, and it doesn't matter because I'm not here anyway.

My eyes open. The trailer's interior shimmers in front of me, like I'm looking at it through fire. My heart hammers in my chest; my mouth dries. *No,* I think. No. *That wasn't here. That was in London, in the flat by Victoria. That came later.*

Didn't it?

17

I keep my head down as I walk off the rocks. I'm shaking. I don't look back. My camera hangs off my neck like a noose.

When I tried the door a second time it flew open, so easily the lock might as well have been greased. I stumbled out, almost falling to the ground, anxious to get out of the van's toxic interior, and gulped the air thirstily, desperately, as if I'd been drowning. Bluff House still loomed over me, silent and cold. Is someone trying to warn me off? Am I in danger here?

All I wanted was to get away, but not to Hope Cottage. Not yet. I need something to calm me down and there's nothing in the house. I wait outside The Ship for a moment, breathing deep, but still I'm skittish as I go in. A trickle of sweat runs down my lower back, despite the cold. But maybe coming here will help me remember. Maybe I came here with Daisy.

The place is as I recall, pretty much. Shinier, if anything; in color, as opposed to the black and white of my recollection. I look around as I shake off my coat at the door. A log fire burns in the grate; the dense air is muggy but comforting. Brass plates hang on the walls, along with framed maps and prints, the usual pub decoration, though unlike back home in London, at least here the scraps have accumulated over years, rather than been picked up as a job lot from some warehouse.

I imagine the teenagers in here. Sophie and her friends. Lock-ins after hours, lights out, candles lit, no need to even draw the blinds way out here at the edge of the world. Too many rum and blacks, drunken fumbling as barriers are dissolved, hands where they shouldn't be. Hot, wet lips. The acidic sting of regret the next day, swallowed down with warm water and a couple of aspirin. I can picture it—me and Daisy here, in the middle of it all—but is it a memory or just a forced imagining?

No one acknowledges me as I approach the bar. Not even a dipped chin.

"What'll it be?"

The interruption startles me. I look round and see it's Bryan.

"Let me buy you a drink," he says.

His words slur, just slightly, and the glass in his hand is almost empty. He's been here a while, I can tell, but some company might be nice. I ask for a gin and tonic.

"A double," he says to the woman serving. She's tall and solidly built, her hair blond but cropped close, an inch or so all over. I notice she's missing the ring finger of her right hand. It's absent from the second knuckle, severed neatly, leaving only a stump.

"How're you?" she says to Bryan as she pours the drinks and hands them over. Her voice has the gruffness of a heavy smoker. I find myself wondering how she lost the finger. An accident? Somehow, a fight seems just as likely.

"You 'eard about David?"

"No," he says. "What?"

"Apparently he's had a visitor. The other night."

Shit. She means me. My stomach balls itself into a fist and Bryan glances at me for a moment. Almost like he knows. "Really? Who?"

"No idea. This were according to our Matt. Says him and a group of lads were down on the beach and they saw someone up there."

No, I want to say. *There was no one there, no one on the beach.* No one saw me. I'm sure of it.

But am I?

"Looked like a girl."

Bryan shrugs. "I wouldn't worry about it."

"Aye," she says. "I guess you're right. Seems whoever it was filmed it an' all." She glances at me, then winks. "Not that it's much to look at." She means the shots I took, the black sea, the ships in the distance. "Anyway. I'll leave you to it."

We take our drinks to the table nearest the fire. I sit as close as I dare, edging nearer until the heat scours my legs. I look over at the landlady as she serves the next customer. Her wink had been friendly. She's watching the films, then. Maybe they all are. I scan the room. A couple of people look away as I do. It's obvious they know who I am.

"How long has she run this place?" I say, once we're settled.

"Beverly?" He looks back to the bar. "About nine years now. Maybe ten."

"Right," I say. I find myself doing the math; I can't help it, it's automatic. She must've taken over not long after I left.

"She's from here then?"

"Born 'n' bred," he says. "Just like me."

I go cold, despite the fire. But there are no signs either of them has recognized me. I look at Bryan and try to imagine him ten years ago. I can't.

"You okay?" he says.

I look away and tell him I'm fine.

"Shit!" he says. "I nearly forgot! Your car. It's done." He fishes clumsily in a pocket and hands me the keys. "I parked it up top."

I grin with relief. I can escape now. I don't have to rely on taxi drivers who take off on a whim and leave me stranded.

"Great! Thanks. How much—"

He waves me away. "Let's sort it out next time, eh?"

He thinks there'll be another time, then. It won't be so bad; he seems nice enough. I'm about to tell him how grateful I am when he fixes me with a stare.

"I wanted to ask you something."

Suddenly, I feel pierced, right through to my core.

"Those films . . . The one with Button and Kat—"

"Button?"

"Sorry. Ellie. It's a nickname." He hesitates. "They're eating chips."

I sip my drink.

"What about it?"

"Well . . . You must know what I mean?"

I smile. "The joint? Not that unusual, I guess—"

He laughs. "No! Not that! We're more bothered about someone sneaking around filming teenage girls."

"We?"

"Me and a couple of the fellas. Y'know? Any idea who it is?"

I shake my head. "We said that the films should be sent anonymously." I hesitate. I wonder if this is why he was keen to buy me a drink. "You think something's going on?"

"What makes you say that?"

I lower my voice. "I saw Kat getting a tattoo. She looked . . . I dunno. Scared. And she had two phones."

"So?"

"Like a burner."

"A what?"

"A burner phone," I tell him. "You know. Cheap. Pay-as-you-go. Easily replaced."

"Why would she have that?"

I shrug. "Usually it's to do with drugs."

"Not Kat," he says.

"Or, you know . . . if there's a boyfriend that needs to get hold of her, even if her parents confiscate her mobile."

He laughs. "Not Kat either. How come you know so much?"

I think of the girls in *Black Winter*. I think of their burner phones, and of my own.

"I've been around," I say. "Tell me about David."

He puts down his drink. "Listen," he says. "I'd love to help, but, well . . . we don't want all that raked up again. Not after last time."

"What d'you mean? All what?"

"All that stuff about Daisy and whatnot."

"What's that got to do with David?"

He lowers his head.

"Nothing."

"No," I say. "Come on. I mentioned David and you started talking about Daisy. What is it?"

"David . . . well, he . . . he kind of had a breakdown. Just after Daisy killed herself. He'd been okay before then—I mean, odd, but friendly enough. Then he just kind of disappeared. When we did see him in town, he was acting weird. He'd come in 'ere and not speak. Just sit on his own, watching people. Muttering to himself. It was freaky. He even got into a fight. He just started on this guy. I don't remember who, now. But it was over nothing. He lost of course, got smacked in the face then ran off. Then, when Zoe went, he got worse. Smashed his car up. Drove into a tree. There were rumors it was deliberate."

"He tried to kill himself?"

"That's what people said."

But he told me he didn't know Zoe, I think. I almost say it out loud. Again, I wonder whether it's time to approach Zoe's parents, despite Gavin's warning. It's easier now I have my own car. I needn't tell anyone.

"Do you think he was involved?"

"David?" He picks up his glass and takes a swig. "I mean, he's always been odd. But I like him."

"But how well d'you know him?"

"Well enough to have a key to his place," he says. "I look after it when he's away, stuff like that. It's just . . . well, some folk were being pretty nasty to him. After first Daisy, then Zoe, I suppose they put two and two together. No smoke without fire, an' all that. Painted stuff on his car, smashed his windows." He sits back in the seat. "Anyway . . ."

"Why're you telling me? If you don't think I should be putting any of this in my film?"

"I dunno." He puts his glass down clumsily. "You seem like a good sort. And it's obvious you care. About the girls." He sighs heavily. "Maybe I'm secretly hoping someone can find out what went on. Just . . . don't make us look bad, y'know? In your film." He gestures to the half-empty pub. "Things are hard enough for folk as it is."

"I'll do my best," I say.

"I'd like to help, if I can?"

"Help?"

"You know I've got a boat?"

I nod, though I'm not sure why he's telling me.

"There was a clip of you with it, I think."

"Aye. I do some fishing. I were thinking, I could take you out on it, if you fancy it?" He nods toward the camera on the table between us. "To get some footage, I mean. Lovely views of the place from out there. Just if it'd help, like."

"Oh," I say. "Right."

Never, I think. I can't. I hate the water, can't stand boats, never learned to swim. Even now, imagining it, all I can see is blackness, above and below, the icy cold invading me, plugging my breath, pressing in until I'm nothing, merged with the void.

But I can't tell him that. It sounds ridiculous.

"Maybe. Sounds like it'd be good."

He grins, then takes out his wallet and a pen.

"Here's my number."

He jots it down on the back of a receipt and, even though there's no chance in hell I'll go on his boat, I take it.

"By the way," he says, lowering his voice. "About Gavin . . ."

"Gavin?"

"Watch him."

It's a surprise. I thought they were friends. It was Gavin who suggested Bryan sort out my car.

"Why do you say that?"

"Nothing. I'm just saying he was asking lots of questions. Digging around, especially when he first arrived. Bit like you."

"Really? He seems to me like he's just someone trying to fit in."

"You think? Trying a bit too hard, if you ask me. Almost like he has something to prove. And there's something else."

"What?"

He leans forward, even though the bar is noisy and no one is paying us any attention.

"This is probably nothing. But the night you arrived? He asked me to tell you he was on his way from seeing me, when he bumped into you."

Despite the fire, I go suddenly cold.

"And?"

He shakes his head. "He wasn't. I hadn't seen him that day. Not at all."

18

Zoe's parents live on the outskirts of Malby, in the same house from which their daughter disappeared. I leave after breakfast, telling no one where I'm going, happy to be driving once more, though anxious about where I'm headed. The morning sun shines weakly through thin cloud and I'm startled by a memory; a morning, it must've been not long before Daisy died. We were sitting on a bench on the cliffs, not far from Bluff House. It was pre-dawn, we'd been up all night, messing around, talking and smoking and staring out to sea. And then the sun appeared, a glow at first, then a sliver of golden light over the horizon. A new day, but back then it'd felt as important as a new year, a new millennium. A new beginning, but what had we done with it? Look where we'd ended up.

I push the thought away then drive on toward Malby. As I reach the town the road curves round to cross the river. Behind me, way in the distance, sits the ruined abbey, blackly illuminated in the morning light. A minute or two later the GPS tells me I've reached my destination.

The house is small, 1930s I'd guess, with a pebble-dash front and a tiny overgrown garden sloping up toward the door. There's a light on in the hall, and as I watch one comes on in the front room, too. A woman opens the curtains, glancing out with curiosity to where I've parked. Zoe's mother, I suppose. I get out of the car, walk to the door, and ring the bell.

The house is quiet, but after a moment the door is opened. A man stands there, dressed in jeans and a gray hoodie. He's balding, his hair is cropped short, his skull craggy and pitted. I hold out my hand.

"Hi."

He makes no move to return the gesture.

"We're fine, thanks."

"I'm not selling anything—"

He goes to shut the door. Maybe he thinks I'm with a religious group, a Jehovah's Witness, or perhaps some politician canvassing for votes.

From somewhere in the house I hear his wife. "Who is it, love?"

"Mrs. Pearson?" I say, before he can shut the door in my face.

His wife appears. "How do you know my name?" she asks. She's younger than her husband, dressed in a baggy sweatshirt and tight jeans. She resembles her daughter. "What is it you want?"

"My name's Alex," I say quickly. "I'm staying in Blackwood Bay."

"That right? And what's that got to do wi' us?"

"I'm wondering if I can talk to you about Zoe."

A wave of pain rolls over her face, but she extinguishes it before it can take hold.

"That so?" she says, regarding me now with undisguised hostility. "Well, you can fuck off."

"I'm not a journalist," I say. "I don't want to cause any trouble. If you could just give me ten minutes." She begins to react, but I interrupt her. "Please? I'm worried that something's going on with the girls—"

"What?"

"Give me ten minutes and I'll explain."

She hesitates. "You can have five."

I thank her. "Can I come inside?"

"No. Here's fine."

Zoe's father breathes deeply. "Love," he says. "It's freezing. Let's let the lass in."

Again she stares at me, but then relents. I follow them through and into the living room.

"Sit down."

She indicates a chair. The room is comfortable; there's an old-fashioned TV, a sideboard, china figurines. The two of them sit on the sofa. I feel like I'm being interviewed. Or judged.

"Say what you've got to say, then."

I open my mouth to begin but am interrupted.

"I'm Sean," says Zoe's father. "This is Jody."

I nod in acknowledgment, but Zoe's mother makes no sign she even heard what her husband said.

"You must be sick of people asking questions," I say.

"That we are," says Jody.

I look over at Sean. He's chewing his lip. I realize what I'd thought was defiance might just as well be fear. But of whom? It can't be me, surely?

He turns to his wife. "Let her speak, love."

Not her either, then. She fixes me with a glare.

"I came up here to make a film," I begin. "But it's not about Zoe. I promise you."

"So what is it about?"

I explain it to them briefly, aware of the five minutes I've been granted.

"An' what's any of that got to do wi' us?" says Jody when I've finished.

"Well," I reply, "I keep hearing about Daisy's suicide, and then Zoe running away—"

"Ha!" She laughs, a mordant, hollow laugh, then quotes me, her voice rich with sarcasm. "'Suicide' . . ."

Sean shoots her a look of admonishment. "Love."

She falls silent.

"What?" I say. "You don't think Daisy took her own life?"

She pushes the hair from her face. "Who knows? Plenty of people had doubts. Until Zoe *ran away*."

Again, the sarcasm.

"You don't think that's what happened?"

Jody pins me with her gaze but says nothing. She looks like a still photograph; I can almost see her in black and white, half in shadow, half in the bright light from the window, a harsh chiaroscuro. She seems desperately sad, yet defiant, too.

"Tell me what you're thinking."

Sean takes her hand. "We talked about this," he says softly. "Remember?" He turns to me. "Of course she ran away. What else?"

Jody snatches her hand away. "Or was driven."

"What?"

Sean jumps in before she can answer. "That's enough!" he says, but she won't be deterred.

"No," she says. "Why would she run? Away from us? Away from me?"

Sean looks at me. "I'm sorry," he says, but I ignore him.

"There was that other girl, too," I say. "What was her name?"

"Sadie."

"Yes. She ran."

"So they say. They reckon she turned up, too. But I'm not the only one who has their doubts."

"No? Who else have you spoken to about it?"

Another warning glance from Sean, but again she ignores it.

"Liz, for one. In the café?"

I remember her. She'd seemed unfriendly, suspicious. Of me. I wonder how I could get her to talk.

Something to worry about later, perhaps.

"Okay," I say. "Well, as I said, I'm concerned, too." I hesitate. "And whatever drove Sadie to run away and Daisy to . . . do what she did . . . and then Zoe . . . well, I'm worried it's still going on."

Neither of them looks surprised.

"Jody," I say. "What d'you think happened?"

Sean shifts uncomfortably in his seat, but she doesn't look at him. She sighs heavily.

"I don't know," she begins. "But for starters, back then there were folk who said Daisy wouldn't have jumped like that. Reckoned something else was going on. And as for our Zoe? She changed. She weren't our girl anymore."

Sean cuts in. "It were just typical teenage stuff," he says. "Started staying out, booze and cigarettes, y'know?"

Jody turns on him, venomous. "Just tell the fucking truth."

"What?"

"It was worse than that. She were such a good girl, 'til she met him."

"Who?"

"Some boyfriend. She wouldn't tell us. But she was skipping school. Staying out 'til all hours. Hanging around Blackwood Bay. Coming home drunk. Stinking."

"Stinking?"

"Cigarettes. Weed. She even got a tattoo."

"So she was taking drugs. Where was she getting them?"

"Him, of course. He was older than she was."

I think of David.

"How much older?"

"No idea. We never saw him. She'd sneak off to meet him. We just know he wasn't from school. One of the neighbors said she saw 'er with an older boy, but—"

"Boy? Not man?"

"That's what she said. On'y I'm not sure I believe her."

"Why?"

"Because I don't know what to believe, anymore."

She's almost whispering now. I want to reach out, to take her hand, though I stop myself. Sean does instead, and she lets him, though without any obvious signs of reciprocation. All the defiance I saw earlier has vanished, leaving behind a shell, a vessel holding nothing but pain.

I did this to my mother, I think. This exact same thing. But then I remember her boyfriend. I see his relief that I'm no longer around, and for a moment I'm sure that, secretly, my mother was glad when I went, too.

Still, guilt knots my stomach, a hard lump. Jody lowers her gaze. "She were fourteen. Fourteen."

I hesitate. "Was she having sex?"

Jody laughs, but again Sean tries to silence her.

"Enough—" he says.

"I'd say so. She were pregnant."

The room falls silent.

"Pregnant?"

My voice sounds hollow. At first, I'm not even sure I've spoken out loud, but then Jody speaks.

"She didn't want to tell us. But it were obvious."

"Did she tell you who the father was?"

"That were obvious, too."

"Him."

"Who else?"

I hesitate. "Was she . . . promiscuous, d'you think?"

"Promiscuous? You sound like the police." She leans forward. "She were *fourteen*, love. It were rape, whichever way you cut it."

I grip the edge of my chair.

"I'm sorry."

"We told 'er we'd look after 'er. There were no need to run," says Sean.

"And she were just a girl," says Jody. "A child. It were his fault. Whoever he is. And now we'll never know."

"Did she ever mention a guy called David?"

She considers for a moment, then says, "I don't think so. Why?"

"I don't know," I say. "But . . . well, he's an older man. Lives in Blackwood Bay. There're rumors . . ."

"Rumors?"

"You haven't heard of him?"

"I've heard *of* him," she says, "but . . ."

"We don't go there," says Sean. "Not now."

"No," says Jody. "We're stuck here."

Her husband lowers his voice. "We're not stuck. We could move."

She laughs but doesn't answer, and I know what she's thinking. *What if she comes back? What if she comes home and we've gone?*

"Can I look in her room? Maybe there's something there that might be a clue as to who got her pregnant, or why she ran away."

"I'm sorry—"

But Jody stands up. "Come on." She faces her husband. "I like this one. It can't do any harm."

This one. I should be flattered, I suppose. We climb the stairs together, her in front. Sadness follows her in a cloud; I can almost smell it, the lingering grief.

"We kept everything the same," she says. She opens the door at the top of the stairs. There's a stale smell, like old perfume. The room is small, the walls painted mauve, a pinboard over the desk. Just a single bed with a bedside table, a chest of drawers next to it, a wardrobe in the far corner, all mismatched. Clothes spill out of the drawers and are strewn on the bed, an explosion of pink and white and purple and black. An acoustic guitar rests against the foot of the bed. It's as if Zoe left this morning, as if she's at school right now, will be home any second demanding a snack and to be left alone in her room.

"I haven't tidied," says Jody, as if apologizing. "Well, not much. There were bottles. Cigarette packets . . . I cleared those out."

"It's okay. You mind if I film?"

She says that she doesn't, and I go in. I look at the bedside table first. There's a phone charger plugged in behind it, a lamp with a broken base, a glass, a box of tissues, makeup remover. The drawer is open but empty. I take my camera and film it all.

"Was there anything in here?"

Jody shakes her head, but I can tell she's lying. I wonder what she found. Love letters? Condoms? I wonder what else, what might be too shameful for her to tell me. Wraps of coke? Lubricant?

Part of me wants to tell her there's nothing left that would shock me. I've seen it all, things that she can't even imagine. I go over to the desk. It's littered with detritus. Scissors and tape, some old headphones, pens and books and scraps of paper.

"She had a computer?"

"She used the ones at school. And her phone, I think."

I examine the pinboard. Her school timetable, and postcards, mostly. Among the photos there are pages cut from magazines and a few pictures of Zoe with her friends. Carefully posed selfies, the odd candid picture of her laughing with a mate. She seems happy, carefree, just like Daisy was at that age, I suppose, just like I was. If only she'd been aware of what was in store. If only she'd known how to avoid it.

"There's nothing there," says Jody sadly. "I went through it. The police, too."

I lean closer and study the pictures. In one she's standing in the sun, dressed in a vest-top, looking much older than her years. The edge of her tattoo is just visible on her shoulder, under the strap of her bra. It looks like a circle, a tiny "O." I film it, then lift a couple more of the photos, looking at what's underneath. As I do, I see a familiar pattern. A series of dots, joined together with lines, sketched in felt-tip on a piece of card. I unpin it.

"What's that?" says Jody.

"It's Orion," I say. "A constellation. The hunter. Was she into astronomy?"

"No," says Jody. "Not that I know of."

I replace the card and search through the rest.

"What about this?"

I show the photograph to Jody. It's of Zoe; she's dressed in her school uniform and has her back to the camera. She's leaning forward, looking into a short, fat telescope. Jody tells me doesn't recognize it.

Suddenly I don't want to tell her what I know. That her daughter isn't the only one with a perfect circle tattooed on her flesh. That Daisy had scratched her own constellation on the wall behind her bed. That she and Zoe and myself are linked, we all have this one thing in common: astronomy, staring at the stars.

"You're sure?"

"Let me ask Sean."

She takes it from me and goes to the top of the stairs and calls. A minute later Sean joins us, and she shows him the photograph.

"No idea," he says. "I never saw that before. Maybe when she was out on one of her trips."

"With her boyfriend, you mean?" I try to swallow but my throat is dry.

Jody glances back at me. "No. He means her uncle. My brother. She used to see him sometimes, after school and whatnot. They were close."

"Where is he now? You don't think he might've had something to do with what happened? With her running away?"

She shakes her head. "Maybe once. Not now. The police talked to him, any road." She examines the photo in my hand. "He were never interested in telescopes, though. Whoever got her into that, I don't think it were him."

THEN

19

CHAPMAN SEXUAL HEALTH CLINIC, MALBY

Chapman Sexual Health Clinic, Malby

Notes

Date: Tuesday, 10 April 2017 (6.15 p.m.)

Zoe in again today (still won't give me her surname).
Arrived at about 4.20, again with the older girl (Hannah?
Laura? The same girl has been in with others, and I've
heard her called both. Again refuses to tell me her
name. Quite aggressive. I'm certain it's the same girl,
as she has a distinctive circular tattoo on her upper
arm). Zoe asked for condoms and, after some persuading
from the older girl, also asked about STI testing. I
asked her about her partner and she refused to answer;
the other girl said she had a boyfriend and asked why
I wanted to know. Zoe seemed very quiet and withdrawn.
I wondered whether she'd taken something and asked her.
She refused to answer, instead telling me it was "none
of my business" and she just wanted to "get sorted
and then get out as she had to be somewhere." When I
asked her where, she ~~didn't want~~ refused to tell me. I
told her I was concerned and asked whether there was
anything Zoe wanted to tell me. She said no, but again
I got the distinct impression that she was scared of
the other girl, even that Hannah/Laura was there to keep
her quiet in some way. I asked directly whether all the
sex she was having was consensual, and she nodded, but
said nothing. I gave her the condoms she'd requested and
suggested Zoe come with me into one of the consulting

rooms in order to discuss her concerns over STIs. She
agreed, but when I suggested that Hannah/Laura stay
in the waiting room the older girl once again became
aggressive and said she wanted to look after her friend.
I felt it best not to push the issue as I don't want to
scare the girls away completely, but I am concerned that
something is going on with Zoe that she is ~~reluctant~~
scared to talk about.

I went into the consulting room to get the leaflets,
however, and when I returned to the waiting area the
girls had left.

Plan: When (if?) Zoe returns, attempt to get her to
divulge her surname, and if possible talk to her alone
about drugs and/or the possibility of sexual abuse.
She needs to be handled with care, though. Consider
a referral to social services and/or the police if
appropriate.

Shreya Divekar, Sexual Health Nurse Specialist

NOW

20

I wake, wet and shivering. My mouth is dry, I can't breathe, and for a moment it's like I'm drowning, my lungs full. But then I remember. I'm here in Hope Cottage. I'm Alex, I'm making a documentary. Everything is going to be okay.

I throw back the duvet. Soaked with sweat, but also too cold. My breath plumes in the moonlight. I reach out and check the radiator. It's not even lukewarm.

I want to crawl back under the covers, to pull them over my head and cling to what's left of their warmth. But I'm awake now and won't sleep again. I'm certain, now. Daisy, Zoe, Kat. The girls are linked, all of them. Me, too, though I don't know how. And every time I close my eyes I see Daisy in the dark, standing on the edge of the cliff. Is there someone behind her? Was she physically pushed, not goaded by circumstances alone? I have to think back; I have to remember.

David? Did he have anything to do with it? Geraldine was sure he didn't. It'd been a moment of lucidity amid the confusion; her memories had seemed real. But what does that mean, really? Of all people, I should know how unreliable memory can be. My phone buzzes on the table with a call from Dan. I watch it skitter across the hard surface but can't bring myself to answer. Whatever he wants, it can wait. Even though he pushed me toward Blackwood Bay and the story, I feel close to the girls now, the missing ones in the past and the ones here now, and I want to make the documentary my way.

I pull on a chunky sweater, my jeans, and the same pair of thick socks I was wearing yesterday, then pad downstairs. There's a smell here, burnt toast and coffee, the crappy air freshener plugged into the socket in the lounge that stinks of apple. Not unpleasant, but it reminds me of St. Leonard's. In the kitchen I fill the kettle and take a plate from the drainer. There's a mark on it; it looks like ash, like a cigarette's been stubbed out on the edge. I think of what Bryan told me about Gavin; and I think about the dead sheep, too, conveniently placed where it would send me spinning off the road, needing to be rescued. I need to find out more about my new friend. But that can wait.

I can't stop thinking of Ellie and Kat. Kat's tattoo, identical to Zoe's; the fact that they were filmed unknowingly, smoking a joint. In my mind, the two girls have merged with Daisy and me, though I'm not sure which is which. Sometimes, Daisy is Kat and I'm Ellie; at others, the other way around. But it's always the same fate I see. They go the same way as we do: one dead, one disappeared. And even though I know it won't help, not really, I can't help believing that if I were to find out what's happening to them, I'd also know what happened to us.

The snow has cleared. A thaw overnight, but the sky is overcast, more like late afternoon than almost lunchtime. As I reach the end of Hope Lane I see a tall, gangly figure lurking in the gloom on the other side of the road. It's Gavin, I think, though I'm not sure. What does he want from me? Should I be more wary of him? He's lied, and if he set out to ambush me . . . I cross the street, but when I look back he's disappeared, vanished up one of the alleys, presumably. I climb to Liz's café.

The lights inside are glaring, unflattering fluorescents, and I feel exposed. But my hunch was right: the girls are here. A group of them sits at one of the Formica tables in the corner, the lit Christmas tree flashing above them. I choose a nearby table and take out my phone so that I can pretend to be engrossed, but my spirits sink as I realize Kat and Ellie aren't among them. I decide to wait anyway. I order tea from Liz, who's friendlier today, but not by much. By the time it's arrived, though, the door has opened again, and this time I'm in luck. Kat and Ellie walk in, along with an older boy. I watch them as they head toward the table next to the others, Kat shouting a greeting as she goes while Ellie and the boy are both silent.

Kat is tall, coltish. She's wearing a bottle-green school uniform and a puffer jacket. Ellie is dressed almost identically, carrying a pink rucksack that clashes with her red hair. The boy is older, at least eighteen, I'd say. Old enough to be shaving, not old enough to have grown out of the acne that must make it difficult. Pretty, though, in a kind of cocky, boy-band way. After a minute they stand up together, then order at the counter before returning to their table, each with a can in front of them. Kat and Ellie put their jackets and blazers on the vacant chair. There's a tiny rip on the elbow of Ellie's sweater; Kat's wearing a short-sleeved shirt, despite the cold. She fiddles absent-mindedly with one of the wrapped sugar cubes from the bowl in front of her. She reminds me of myself.

They settle and become absorbed in one another. I can only hear the odd word. It's Kat talking, mostly. Something about another girl, it sounds like. Teenage gossip. She talks quickly, her leg bouncing under the table as if there's a surplus of energy within her, too much to contain, while the boy is the opposite; he seems bored. At one point he mumbles something to Ellie, then laughs. She doesn't join in but sinks further into herself.

I pick up my tea; it's cold, but it was pretty awful anyway. When I glance up the boy has taken a half-bottle of vodka out of the pocket of his parka. He glances round, and we lock eyes. I look down at the bottle, then smile, just slightly, just enough to let him know I've seen but won't be saying anything. I go back to my phone. Some things don't change.

I wonder if I'll get a chance to speak to them later. Alone. I don't like the boy, he has an arrogance; he's slouching on his chair, arm over the back, legs spread. A hand rests lightly on Kat's shoulder, though it looks more like ownership than affection. I take a photo with my phone but they don't notice. I'm invisible, so much so that I consider filming.

Suddenly, there's a commotion at the other end of the room, raised voices. It's the girls; a scornful cackling that reminds me of the gulls out on the cliff.

"Get lost!"

"I saw it! We all did!"

One of the girls is shaking her head. Laughing, but it's obvious she wishes the spotlight would move on to one of the others. A second is swiping at her phone, while a third seems to be filming the whole thing.

"Look!"

A phone is passed round.

"That ain't me."

"It so is! Amy! That's so you!"

More laughter. A hooting, cawing; they do sound like the gulls, dive-bombing kamikaze-like over the rooftops.

"What you even talking about?"

"Look! You're wasted!"

"Am not!" she says, almost shouting. One of the girls holds the phone straight up and I glimpse the film they're playing. It's an early one, one of the first, if I remember. A girl, falling on the beach as she runs toward the water. They're in hysterics; it's the funniest thing they've ever seen. Then the girl stands. She's red-faced; now, it isn't a joke. I watch to see what else she'll do. Fight back. Defend herself. She won't get far like that. But instead she slaps herself, bangs her own cheek, as if she deserves punishment. As she does, I notice Ellie sliding farther down into her seat, as if terrified that at any moment the spotlight will move on to her.

She's spared, though, for now at least. "Leave me alone!" sobs the girl who's the current target, but she's ignored; there's a chorus of snickers. She snaps, grabbing her phone off the table, sending her chair scraping back over the laminate floor, then picks up her coat and leaves. Part of me wants to go and comfort her, part to confront the girls who've attacked her, part to stay with Kat and Ellie. The last choice wins; what comfort could I be, anyway? It's my fault; the film of her falling wouldn't have been public if I hadn't made it so. It's me who handed them the ammunition.

Still, part of me is glad. At least they're watching the films. Joining in.

I look back over at Ellie. She's staring at her hands. Kat's still grinning, laughing at the other girl's exit. Either she hasn't noticed Ellie's distress or doesn't care. The boy isn't ignoring her, though. He's
watching her, a creepy half-smile twisted on his lips.

I'm shoved from behind as one of the girls barges past me. Tea slops
out of my cup and on to the saucer. "Fuck," she says, though it's not by
way of an apology, more an exclamation of annoyance that something
was in her way. A moment later there's the screech of chairs and the
babble of excited voices as the rest of the girls prepare to leave, too.

And then we're alone. Just me and the teenagers at the next table,
plus Liz in the back. The whole place seems too silent, too still. The
moment stretches, then the boy looks at Kat. "Stay here," he says, and
then he leaves, too.

I seize my chance. Without thinking, I switch my phone to *Record*
and slip into the chair he's just vacated. Ellie flinches; Kat's pupils are
wide.

"What—?"

"Don't worry," I say, interrupting her. "I just want to talk."

She glances toward the door, no doubt hoping her boyfriend will
return to rescue her. I hold my phone casually in my hand, hoping it
won't look like I'm filming her.

"To talk?"

"Yes."

"About what?"

"I just wondered . . . are you all right?"

"All right?" She laughs, but it's empty and humorless. Her face is
pale and bloodless, the color of porridge. She holds my gaze for one
second, then two. In that moment she seems much older than her years
and I begin to suspect the reason she can't seem to keep still.

"Are you on something?"

She laughs once more. "Fuck off."

"Ellie?"

The younger girl glances at her phone on the table between us, as if she wants to call for help, then looks up.

"What?"

Her voice is high-pitched, tiny. It seems to belong to a much younger girl than her face would suggest. It's as if both girls have seen things they shouldn't have seen, been to places they shouldn't have gone.

But Ellie? She seems so timid. Button, Bryan told me they called her. Yet someone this timid wouldn't have filmed her parents as they grounded her. Something must have happened since.

"Are you okay?"

She shrugs. The other girl answers.

"Why?"

"I'm asking her, not you. Ellie?"

"Of course she's okay. Aren't you?"

The younger girl glances up at her friend. Something passes between them. It looks like it might be love, though if so, a desperate sort. A plea for rescue, perhaps, or maybe forgiveness. I reach out my hand, but she shies away.

"I'm not here to hurt you."

"Then why don't you just get lost, then?"

I stare at Kat. I can't work her out. She's definitely on something or coming down from it. Speed, maybe? There's clearly no point in asking her again, or asking her who's selling it. Again, I look at Ellie. She must be a year or so younger than Kat and looks it, until she makes eye contact and tries to smile, at least. Is it possible she's taking something, too? I'm about to ask when Kat reaches forward to pick up another sugar cube. The sleeve of her shirt rides up and I see her tattoo. That perfect circle, inked in black.

"Your tattoo?" I say. "What does it mean?"

She sneers, but it's false. She's rattled. She tugs down her sleeve.

"Get lost."

"I'm trying to help, you know?"

"Who says we need it?"

"You know David?"

"David?"

Her response is quick—too quick, if anything—and urgent. But her eyes tense, momentarily. She's scared.

"Yes. David. Up at Bluff House."

She shakes her head. "No, I don't know David"—but she's too late. I've seen her fear. I know she's lying.

"You're sure?"

"Yeah," she says, her voice laced with mock disgust. I realize now there's no point in telling her I'm on her side; she'd never believe me. "I'm sure."

"Ellie? Do you? Does he give you drugs?"

The other girl shakes her head, but I catch her looking at Kat, as if for confirmation.

"What is it, then?"

"Nothing."

"Ellie!"

I turn to Kat. "Just let her speak. Ellie?"

"Please," she whispers. "Don't hurt him."

"I won't," I say. "I promise. I'll just talk to him."

Her face clouds; I think she might erupt into tears.

"No! No, don't tell him we've spoken to you!"

Kat grabs the younger girl's arm. "Ellie, that's enough!"

I lean forward. "I can protect you. Both of you."

Kat laughs. "How?"

Before I can answer, she grabs Ellie's jacket and shoves her friend toward the door. "Come on," she says. "We're leaving."

Ellie glances back as she goes, her expression identical to that of her friend as she left Ink and Steel, her new tattoo still wrapped in plastic.

There's no point in giving chase. They're lying, I can see it. Lying, and scared. Both of them. If I'm going to help them, I need to speak to David.

21

I find him by Smuggler's Way, the alley just past The Ship. It's like I knew he'd be there. He's standing in the near-dark, motionless, head cocked, as if waiting.

I watch from a distance but, abruptly, he moves off. I follow as he squeezes up through a narrow alley to a row of cottages, beyond which steep steps lead up and on to the southern cliffs. I take them carefully—they're slippery and the light is failing—and at the top see that David is a little way ahead of me on the overgrown path.

I keep him in my sight. After a minute he leaves the track to disappear down another, tiny path that drops sharply toward the edge of the cliff. I follow it, pushing through the undergrowth, and after a few paces it opens up.

He's standing with his back to me in the half-light. Beyond him the sea wall, built to stop the cliffs from eroding, I suppose, drops precipitously to the water. He's looking over it at the waves beyond.

I freeze. For a second it seems like he's going to throw himself over, down and onto the beach. But he doesn't. He raises something to his eyes and I remember what Sophie told me. They're binoculars.

I crouch in the shadows and film him for a minute or two, but then I can wait no longer. I stand up and stride out.

"David."

The word clings to my throat. He recoils. The binoculars fall around his neck. "Who—?"

He sounds scared, and I'm glad. It gives me the power.

"I need to speak to you."

He peers through the dim light as I move closer.

"It's Alex."

His breath catches. "You!"

I'm a couple of yards from him now. He's even paler in the gloaming. His ashen skin is translucent and I almost imagine I can see the veins beneath squirm and pulse.

"Leave me alone," he says. "Please."

I shake my head. "I can't. You know Kat." He doesn't react. "And Ellie."

Now there's a twitch, I think. But, really, it's too dark to tell.

"Admit it."

"I never . . ." he begins, but then his sentence seems to swerve, to take a different route. "No. I don't know them."

"If you've hurt them—"

"No!" he says. He sounds desperate. "You know that. I'd never . . ."

"They're taking drugs. You know that, right?"

He says nothing.

"Where are they getting them? You?"

"Me?"

He sounds genuinely shocked, as if it's the last thing he expected me to say, the very idea is preposterous.

"No. Not me. You might want to talk to your friend."

My friend? Who does he mean?

"Gavin?"

He says nothing. It can't be; when would he have seen us together? But who else?

"Why him?" I say. He doesn't react. "Who are you?"

He ignores me.

"What's happening here?"

"You know what's happening. Better than anyone."

He steps forward and I think he's going to reach out, but then he says, "Look."

"What?"

He motions toward the sky. "Look."

I can't help it. I follow his gaze. Something streaks overhead, too fast to be a plane. A meteor.

"Is that—" I begin, but he interrupts.

"The Geminids."

I look at him. He's scouring the sky. "Another! Look!"

I look up and just catch another flash. It's debris, burning in the atmosphere. A shower. I think of the photo of Zoe with the telescope and see David scouring the sky with his binoculars and something happens. I'm losing control of my body. My limbs have become gelatinous, like I've smoked too much dope.

"Amazing. Isn't it?"

"You hurt Zoe," I say, my voice barely a whisper. I step forward and grip the sea wall, but David mistakes it for awe. He rubs his hand through his hair.

"No. I didn't."

He says it softly, but determinedly. I can't work out whether to believe him. I can't understand why I seem to want to so badly. He tips his head again and I seem to recall the gesture, but from a very long time ago.

"She ran away. You know that. I never hurt her. I never hurt anyone. Why don't you believe me?"

Life returns to my limbs, but still my breathing is loud in my ears. I try to focus, to stay present. I look down at the hugeness of the sea, at its quiet, unstoppable power. Spray hits my face and I'm on an unmapped road; I want to turn away, to go back, keep walking and never stop. But I don't. I can't. I watch my exhaled breath swirl and disappear, blown out like hope, and look up once more. Another meteor flies over and now I'm imagining Daisy, on the other side of the world, perhaps, lying on a beach in India, backpacking in Mexico, visiting Cambodia. She'd be doing the same thing, following the same stars, the same pieces of rock as they burn themselves up in the ether. Maybe there's a man with her, a husband, a lover. She's considering settling down. Children, perhaps. I wonder if she ever thinks of me.

Except she's not. I know that. She's dead. One way or the other—whether she jumped, or fell, or was pushed—she's dead.

I turn around. David is still staring at the sky.

"Who are you?"

He looks straight at me. His face is unreadable, shot through with pain, and hope, and defiance.

"You know who I am," he says.

22

*B*ryan kneels at the top of the slipway, next to a motorboat that rests on a rusted metal platform. It's his own, I suppose, though it appears to be smaller than the one in the film, just a few yards long and with a tiny cabin at the front. When he hears me approach he looks up.

"Alex!" he says. He sounds pleased to see me. He glances back at his boat, his eyes glowing proudly. It's sweet, a boy with his toys, but I hope he's not getting it ready for me. Seeing it now, I'm even less keen to take him up on his offer; it seems minute, far too insubstantial to cope with the brutal water.

"Always good to keep on top of repairs in the winter . . ." He wipes his hands on an oily rag but in doing so seems to transfer more filth onto his skin than off it. "How's it going?"

I pause. "I wanted to talk to you about something."

"The car? Everything all right?"

"Fine," I say. "It's David."

"David?" He tosses the rag into the boat. "What about him?"

"You said he was your friend. You trust him? With the girls?"

"Aye," he says. "Why?"

"You know where they might be? Kat and Ellie?"

He glances at his watch. "Now? The arcade, maybe?"

"Thanks."

"Want me to come with you?" He looks hopeful. "We could get a drink?"

I hesitate. The girls may be more forthcoming if I arrive with a friendly face.

"Okay," I say. "Come on."

. . .

The place is garish and bright; a huge glitter ball hangs from the middle of the room, the pinball machines strobe and flash and, undercutting it all, there's the sinister bass thrum of a rap song. It all seems to belong in another town, a different era altogether, and at the back of the room a guy sits in a change booth, looking down. He's reading, I suppose, or staring at a screen, apparently unaware that anyone's come in. There's no sign of the girls.

"We can wait," says Bryan. "I just need to have a word with Pete."

I watch as he moves off and have the same frisson of recognition I had the other day, the same I had with David, and for a moment wish there was some way I could ask whether he remembers me, whether we knew each other before.

But I can't, of course. I turn away, and a moment later there's a voice at my side.

"Alex!"

It's Monica. She's holding a bagful of twenty-pence coins. I greet her, forcing as much cheer into my voice as I can muster, and she asks how I am.

"Listen," she says, glancing toward Bryan. "I'm glad I caught you. I hear you've been talking to Kat and Ellie."

"From who?"

"They told me."

"You know them?"

"Oh, aye," she says. "I just wanted to let you know there's nothing to worry about. They're fine. Kat was annoyed they'd been caught smoking and you'd made it public, but—"

"Smoking a joint?"

"Kat said it weren't a joint."

"You believe her?"

She lowers her voice. "Not really. But it's not like it's that bad, is it? And anyway, the point is, they say there's nothing to worry about." She looks up as Bryan returns. "I'll leave you to it."

Leave us to what? I think, but before I can ask she moves off toward one of the fruit machines, greeting Bryan as she goes. A minute later a group of five or six girls arrives and joins her. I scan them anxiously and, sure enough, one is Kat, though at first glance she seems totally different. She's dressed in ankle boots, tight jeans, a black leather jacket. She's wearing lipstick, plus blush. Her eyes are dark. She looks much older and, next to her, wearing less makeup but still some, stands Ellie. Neither has noticed me, and I watch as Monica gives each of the girls a handful of coins, then puts her hand on Kat's shoulder. The gesture is maternal, protective; it's clear she has their trust, and I feel the urge to take out my phone to film them. To counteract the bad things I've seen, I tell myself.

"How about that drink?" says Bryan, and I turn away. In the corner four plastic chairs are arranged around a Formica table and we sit opposite each other. Between us there's a saucer, a few wrapped chocolates. He takes out a hip flask.

"Want some?"

I nod and he pours what I presume is whiskey into plastic cups. I watch Kat and Ellie. They're both on their phones now, flicking through who knows what. Easy in each other's company, they're so relaxed it almost borders on indifference. Ellie holds her phone up to Kat, who examines it conspiratorially, but then each goes back to her own browsing as Monica leans against the machines like a mother hen.

"They're okay, you think?"

He glances over. "They look fine to me."

I sip my drink. "I've been thinking about what you told me. About Gavin, on the night I arrived. Any idea why he'd lie?"

He shakes his head. "None."

"David told me Gavin's the one who's been selling drugs to the girls."

He cocks his head.

"He said that?"

"Yes."

"Gavin? You're sure?"

"Well, no. Not by name, He said "my friend," but who else could he have meant?"

He hesitates, then downs his drink before pouring another measure. He swallows hard.

"He didn't mean Gavin. I think he was talking about me."

The words sound wrong.

"What?"

"I used to do that," he says.

"What? Sell drugs?"

"A little bit, yeah. It was just a bit of weed, and I stopped years ago, though David might not know it. But mostly I used to take stuff. Heavy stuff, you know? But it was when I was a kid. Not anymore. Not much else to do, back then. You know what it's like, surely?"

He's said it pointedly. As if he knows.

"I fell in with a bad crowd," he continues. "Took me a while to see it. And that lady there"—he gestures toward Monica—"is the person who saved me."

"Saved you? You were together?"

"I wouldn't say that, but she persuaded me I was on a route to prison. Or worse."

"It was that bad?"

He laughs. "Oh, yes. I was a wreck. Stealing things, you know. The works."

What? Selling your body, too? Breathing in the fat burps of drunk strangers so you could get your next hit? I don't think so, though I suppose it's possible.

"That's why I help out when I can. You know?"

"What d'you mean?"

"I rebuilt the village hall. Give the kids something to do. And Monica helps out, too, makes sure there's a few things for the youngsters to do up there, keep 'em on the right track. It's all about building a community," he continues. He nods toward where Kat and Ellie stand with Monica, laughing with their friends. "They look fine to me."

I smile. He's right. The sight of them takes me back for a moment to the reason I wanted to make this documentary.

"Maybe I worry too much."

"Maybe."

But then I remember Zoe's pregnancy, the rumors that Daisy didn't kill herself, Bryan saying that she and Sadie had fallen out.

"Do you think Daisy's death was related to Sadie running away? You said they argued."

"I don't know." He sighs, then leans forward. "Maybe. There were rumors that things got nasty between them. One of them threatened the other."

"Who?"

"Daisy. Daisy threatened Sadie, I think. She said she'd kill her. That's what I heard, anyway. Don't know how much truth there is in it. It was a long time ago."

"Almost ten years," I say without thinking. "To the day."

"A long time, anyway." He looks right at me. He wants to change the subject, I can tell. I glance at Kat and Ellie, and again I see the two of us. Me and Daisy.

You're not wearing that, are you? It makes you look like a slag.

Well, isn't that the idea?

"You okay?"

I blink the image clear. Bryan puts his hand on my arm.

"I'm fine," I say. "It's just . . . a couple of people have told me they don't think Daisy killed herself."

"Who?"

"Zoe's parents, for one."

"Well, what happened to Zoe hit them hard. I wouldn't take that much notice." He smiles sadly. "Of course she killed herself. People just . . . they feel guilty, I suppose. She was so young . . ."

For a second it seems almost as if he's about to cry. I sense someone watching and look up to see Monica's gaze fixed on us, her expression unreadable. She looks away when we both notice. He retracts his hand, but something's happened over there. Ellie's shoulders have fallen and she appears suddenly, desperately unhappy. As I watch, she glances up at me, almost as if she'd felt my gaze burning into the side of her face. Her eyes are wide and beseeching, her mouth set in a hard line, and I feel the urge to go over to her, to ask her what's wrong, what's happened. But I can't; Kat would step in, as she had in the café, she'd begin answering my questions for her friend and I'd get nowhere. I'm going to have to be cleverer than that.

I look back at Bryan. He's noticed nothing.

"Can I have some more?"

He unscrews his flask and begins topping up my drink.

"Say when."

I watch him tip the flask, watch as the amber liquid flows into the cup, but it's as if I'm not there, or rather that I'm disconnected from it, as if I'm somehow watching it both from a great distance and in extreme close-up. And when I see that he's added as much of the alcohol as I'd like, I can't work out how to say stop, how to send the signal from my brain along the nerves and into the muscles of my jaw. Instead I watch mutely as he continues to pour, until after what seems like minutes I manage to force myself to shake my head.

"Enough."

He looks up. He's grinning. I hear myself thank him, then stand up.

"I just . . . I won't be a second."

I head toward the toilets at the back of the room. On the way I manage to catch Ellie's eye and, though she looks away instantly, I hope she's seen where I'm going and got the message.

I go in. The light in here is even brighter; there's a sink, a broken paper-towel dispenser, a cracked bar of pink soap. The noise of the arcade drops to a muted thud as the door closes behind me, but still it's too loud. I drink some water—stale and lukewarm—then go into the cubicle and lock the door behind me. I listen out but hear only the distant music, the muffled voices and the stomping of my chest. I breathe in as deeply as I can. I try to calm down but can't.

The door opens and someone comes in. I step out.

It's Ellie. She's standing in the doorway; she looks tiny.

"Ellie," I say. "Are you okay?"

She doesn't move. She stares straight at me, utterly still. I get the sense that if I were to move toward her, she'd run, like a startled animal.

"Talk to me," I say, as softly as I can, but she shakes her head.

"I can't."

"You can," I say, nodding. "You can trust me. I promise."

"He was listening," she says quietly.

"Who? What?"

"The other day. He was listening."

"The boy?" I say. "Kat's boyfriend?"

She shakes her head.

"Who, then?"

She doesn't answer. I remember the phone I saw on the table, remember Kat's burner phone.

"What's wrong, Ellie? What's going on?"

Still nothing.

"Is it David?"

She looks up at the mention of his name but says nothing. She's terrified.

"Tell me. What's he done?"

The door opens once more and Kat comes in. This close, I see her eyes are blackened with kohl and she's wearing lipstick the color of a ripe plum. She looks from me to Ellie, and then back. Her face is like a bruise.

"Oh, you're here."

Her arms are bare and I see the circular tattoo on her upper arm, brand new. She stares at Ellie. "We have to go."

"Ellie, don't—"

Kat steps forward. She grabs the other girl's arm. "I said, come on!"

Ellie looks at me, but she's already being dragged toward the door.

"I'd better go," she says, and I know then I need to find some way of speaking to her alone.

23

I return to Bryan, only to tell him I need to leave. He bites his lip.

"Everything all right?"

"Yes," I say, vaguely. "It's just . . . getting late."

He laughs briefly at the excuse, and I glance over to where Monica was standing with the girls. She's drifted off a little now, and both Kat and Ellie stand with the others, looking happy enough.

I smile as winningly as I can. "It's just . . . work, you know. I have to try and get an edit done soon. I'm on a deadline." I add: "For my producer." He nods slowly, his disappointment evident. "I'll see you soon."

I avoid Ellie and Kat as I leave but walk right past Monica. I smile at her, and she reciprocates, but half-heartedly. If she's so keen to help out the girls, I wonder why she told me that Ellie is fine, when it's clear she's not. I wonder what she really believes.

I turn left. The air is cold and damp, and a few steps up the street there's a recessed doorway from where I can keep watch on the arcade. I will Ellie to come out by herself, but after fifteen minutes or so I'm disappointed; Kat appears with her friend in tow, Monica straight after them, with others trailing her. She and the girls huddle in a group, then she glances at her watch. "Come on, girls," she says. "We don't want to be late."

The girls trill with confident excitement. One peels off, saying she can't make it but will come next time, while the remaining five or six accompany Monica toward The Ship. I wait until they've almost reached the corner before following and keep them in sight all the way up Slate Road. They chat, they look animated, happy to be going wherever Monica is leading them. Even Ellie is joining in, though she seems much younger than the others, looks almost like she's trying to copy them, taking her cue from Kat.

At the top of Slate Road Monica waits for the stragglers, then they enter the car park, a clutch of chicks scampering after their hen. Monica approaches a battered Volvo estate and gets in the driver's seat, Kat next to her, while Ellie is helped into the boot by one of the others. Once they're loaded, Monica begins to reverse and I head toward my car, intrigued.

I set off unnoticed, aware suddenly of the whiskey coursing through my blood. Monica drives out of the village and turns left, not toward Malby, as I'd expected, but toward Crag Head. We go past the turning for the lighthouse, then she takes a side road that heads inland, then another lane, even narrower. I watch Monica drive up it but don't follow, parking instead a little farther on before continuing on foot.

She's left her car next to a metal gate. I climb the trail as it rises gently, my view blocked both left and right by tall bushes between which the path meanders. I hear voices in the stillness, Monica and the girls chatting happily, a distant crow's plaintive caw, but little else. I jog a few steps, fearful of losing them, but as I round a bend I see they're directly ahead, standing in a huddle just past another gate, at which Monica fiddles with a padlock. I film them for a moment then step back, still unseen, and wait until they've moved on before following them through that gate, too, and into the fields.

I hold my camera in front of me, still recording. The group is ahead, striding purposefully toward what looks like a large shed that sits in the near corner of the field with a yard in front of it. I skirt the edge, staying as close to the undergrowth as I can, and get as near as I dare. I spot two horses over in the middle of the field—one gray, the color of the sky, the other chestnut brown; both wearing rugs—and it all makes sense.

I creep closer. Monica is unlocking the smallest of the three doors on the stable, chatting as she does. "Kat?" she's saying. "Give us a hand, would you, love?"

The others wait while Kat and she disappear inside what I'm guessing is the tack room. They reemerge a few minutes later with blankets and halters, then Monica takes the girls into the field itself.

She's too far away for me to hear what she says, but she gets one of the girls to whistle; it's surprisingly loud. Both horses look up from their grazing and, to the girls' evident delight, begin to trot over. Monica makes a fuss of the gray one while the girls crowd around the other, then she shows them how to attach the head collar and a rope. When that's done they lead the snorting horses gently back to the yard and tie them up, then Monica demonstrates removing the rug and lets the girls do it, before they scratch the withers. Monica rubs a hand over each horse, explaining something as she does, and the girls coo enthusiastically. They look like they're enjoying a rare treat; even Ellie looks in her element, a long way from the anxious girl who'd left the arcade. Kat and a couple of the others erupt into laughter; I consider trying to get nearer, to hear what's being said, but it's too risky, I don't want to be seen; I have no earthly reason to be here.

Still, I decide to try. I wait until Monica and the girls are engrossed. She's kneeling at the horse's foot, picking at it with some kind of metal tool while the girls watch, fascinated. I step forward, as slowly as I can, still filming. "Then we use a brush," she's saying, and Kat passes her something. "Like this."

"It doesn't hurt?" says Ellie, and Monica shakes her head.

"No, love. You can't hurt her. Look, have a go?"

"Can I?"

Monica hands the pick to a thrilled Ellie. The others watch as she attends to the hoof, though a couple seem to be getting restless, giggling among themselves.

"Girls?" says Monica, looking up. "Can you get the feed? Kat?"

Kat leads them into the stable, emerging with two brightly colored tubs, one yellow, one green. They finish picking both horses' hooves and Monica puts a different rug on the gray horse before letting the girls do the same with the brown. They pet both horses, stroking their muzzles, then Monica asks the girls to lead them into the stable and watches fondly as they begin to untie them. Ellie in particular seems to enjoy the connection with the neighing creature.

I move a little to the left to get a better shot, but my foot lands on a soft clod and my ankle goes over. A sharp shock, over in a moment, but still I gasp. Monica cocks her head slightly.

"Kat?" she says. "Come here a minute, would you?"

Kat does as she's been asked. Monica murmurs something to the girl but, luckily, both are looking the other way, into the field, rather than toward where I'm hiding. I creep, as carefully as I can, backward and to the right, keeping the horses between me and Monica as the girls lead them into the stable. Now, I'm right behind the building, out of sight. I crouch while Monica puts the day bars across the stable door and leads the girls into the tack room, then take my opportunity to escape, retracing my steps to the car, then driving back to Blackwood Bay.

I pull into the car park and sit for a moment. It's afternoon; soon, it'll be getting dark. I pick up my camera and watch the footage I've just recorded. It's sweet. It'll work really well in the edit, showing the girls in a positive light and a community spirit. But how to get Monica to agree to me using it? I could be honest, I suppose, tell her I followed her. Or perhaps I should deny all knowledge, tell her it was submitted by someone anonymously. Either way, there's no reason she shouldn't let me use it, not once she's seen it.

A shadow falls across the windshield. Almost before I've reacted, the door right next to me is open and a figure is standing there, wearing a waterproof jacket, hood up, and though I want to react, to lash out, something stops me.

"Move!" comes a familiar voice. It's a woman. "Get in the passenger seat."

I find my voice.

"No. What the—"

She takes down her hood, just for a second, and I see who it is.

"Move over," she says, more softly, though no more kindly. "We haven't got long."

Liz drives erratically, as if she's being pursued. Her hand shakes when she takes it off the steering wheel to change gear; the car whines as she releases the clutch. Is she as scared as I am?

"What is it?" I say, my voice weak and tremulous. "Where are we going?"

She remains silent. She's agitated, at her limit. I wonder whether she's acting against her will, she's been forced to pick me up, she's delivering me somewhere.

Or to someone. My flesh sings, sweat runs down my back despite the cold, and I panic. I reach for the door handle, but my hands are numb, they won't close around it, and what am I going to do, anyway? Hurl myself onto the roadside? Hope for a soft landing in the heather?

I think of the dead sheep. Burst and bleeding.

"Liz?" I can't keep the fear from my voice.

The car swerves. Not much, but the road is narrow, barely more than a car's width, and with a ditch on each side. What does she mean to do? Will someone be waiting for me? Again, the dead sheep appears in front of me.

"Just . . . shut up. Okay?"

She glances in the rearview mirror. There are headlights behind us, a car in the distance, and she speeds up. She barely slows for the crossroads and goes straight over. There's nothing this way for miles, nothing but the empty, desolate moor.

We cross a low stone bridge and, once more, my hand goes to the door handle. My knuckles are white.

"Don't—" The threat, if that's what it is, hangs in the air.

She pulls off the main road and onto an even narrower track, then into what serves as a lay-by. She cuts the engine.

"Come on."

The undulating moor is ghostly in the afternoon light, but there's no one else in sight. She strides out and, instinctively, I take my phone from my jeans pocket. It's already filming, though I don't remember starting it. I'm safe, for the moment.

She reaches a stone wall on the moor and follows it, then scrambles over a stile and heads off, climbing toward a distant tree. I can see it only dimly, in silhouette. It's a yew, I think. When Liz reaches it, she turns and beckons.

I'm torn, but my instinct to find out, to document, wins out and I jog toward her. There's a bunch of flowers under the gnarled tree, in plastic wrapping, secured with an elastic band. They're white, bedraggled. Dead. The edge of each petal is turning to brown, as if stained with nicotine.

"What the fuck is this?"

"A grave." Her face shifts; it softens in the half-light, the shadow of the tree. "The girl's," she whispers. "The one who disappeared."

"Daisy?"

She seems to recoil at the name, and I flinch, too. My spine tenses and contracts, as if I'm trying to shrink myself to nothing.

"No," she says. "Sadie."

"But she ran away. They found her."

"No," she says, and I shiver. Wind blasts up the hill, driving out thought.

"What happened to her, then?"

She hesitates, and when her answer comes it's a lament.

"She's here."

The ground tilts, even though it can't be true. This must be what they mean, someone walking over your grave. She shakes her head sadly, her eyes cast down.

She can't be, I want to say, but I can't risk giving myself away.

She's brought me here to tell me something, and now she seems unable to do so.

"What are you saying, Liz?"

She begins to speak, but the words escape as a sigh, a breeze of defeat, and her whole body seems to deflate with them, as if she's crumpling, collapsing in on herself.

"I didn't know. I swear."

"Didn't know what?"

She ignores my question. She's whispering now.

"He said he never meant to hurt her."

"Who? Who said? Hurt who?"

She gazes back toward the car. Anywhere but at me. "My father," she whispers.

Her father? I force myself back, into the past. I don't remember him any more than I remember her. How old would he have been back then? Forties? Fifties? I can imagine him, though, understand what she's saying. God knows I've seen plenty of people like that in my life, with their pudgy jelly-mold skin, their rotten popcorn breath, their slobbering eagerness as they unthreaded their belts and unzipped their trousers.

But all that was later, after I'd run. There was none of that here, I'm certain of it. Or at least not for me.

"You're saying your father killed Daisy?"

I haven't said the wrong name deliberately, but I notice that she doesn't correct me. She shakes her head.

"He said he didn't kill her, but . . ."

"But he was involved?"

She nods once.

"What did the police say?"

"He never told them what he knew."

She says it bluntly. Her voice is cold.

"He told me a couple of years ago. Just before he died. He had cancer. He knew he didn't have long." She hesitates. "And there was that other girl. Zoe. He said it just felt so . . . similar, I guess. Like history was repeating itself. Everyone said she weren't the type to run away."

I think back to my friend, Alice, to meeting her in London. Is that what they said about us? We weren't the type? Maybe no one is the type to run away, to get out of a bad situation, until one day they find they are, and they do.

"It was then he told me that Sadie didn't run. She was dead."

Daisy, I think. *He meant Daisy.* Maybe he was confused; he must have been on medication for his illness.

"He said they killed her."

"Who?"

"He died before he could tell me."

The words catch in her throat. I can almost see the grief inside her, battling it out with the resentment, the disappointment, the shame.

"He drowned." The word echoes. Liz blurs, shifts out of focus. I have to concentrate to bring her back. "They found him halfway to Malby."

"Suicide?"

She answers quickly and with contempt.

"That's what they said. All I know is, he was scared."

"Of those involved in Daisy's death?"

"Sadie's," she says, this time correcting my slip. "Maybe. Who knows?"

"Look," I say. "Are you sure he didn't mean Daisy?"

"I don't know. He were on drugs, for the pain . . ."

Exactly, I think, but I say nothing.

"I suppose it'd make more sense," she goes on, "what with them saying they found her."

"What?"

"Sadie. They found her, they said. My father said they must've faked it . . ."

They couldn't have found her. It's impossible. The only people who knew my name were Alice and Dev. And Aidan, I suppose, though I think he only heard it once. I was never found. Unless . . .

"When did they find her?"

"I can't remember. I just know the police got in touch with her mother. She'd been frantic."

Frantic? I almost laugh. How did she pull that one off? The truth would have been closer to the opposite. I see her calm shrugging of the shoulders: *She'll be back, or not, I don't much care.* I see the new boyfriend telling her not to worry, all the time secretly—or not so secretly—hoping I'll never return and that I'm off his back forever; good riddance. Frantic? My arse.

"Where?"

"Sheffield, I think it was."

No. It's not true. It never happened.

"Not London?"

"No. Why?"

I ignore her question. "But they'd have brought her back, surely?"

"They told her mother she didn't want to come back, said she'd told them she wasn't safe at home, that her mother's boyfriend had raped her."

I freeze. *No*, I think. *No.* I remember the boyfriend. Eddie. He worked on the rigs. For a month I'd have my mother to myself, then he'd return and I was forgotten. She was out every night, drinking too much, not bothering to tell me where she was going to be or when she'd be back. It was like living with two different people, and when, after a few months, she moved him in, it got even worse. His sole purpose seemed to be to get rid of me. But he never touched me. That much I was sure of. He used to tell me he'd rather chop it off than stick it anywhere near me.

"Raped her?"

"They said they'd rehome her, just until she was old enough. They wouldn't tell her mum where she was. Said she didn't want to be found. Her mum never believed it, said the police were lying. Said Sadie never got on with her boyfriend, but there was no way he'd . . . do that. And Sadie wouldn't make something up. She was a good girl, underneath it all. She'd never run away."

I fight the urge to laugh. A good girl? My mother always was fond of rewriting the past. So skillful she'd end up believing it herself. Suddenly, I want to see her, to find out the truth. But I can't. A bit of plastic surgery isn't going to fool my own mother.

Some instinct kicks in. I can't get lost in my own memories, my own story, not now. I count—one, two, three—but it doesn't work. I name what I see. Car. Wall. Road. Yew tree. Liz.

It's enough to snap me back. *Daisy*. What happened to her? I steel myself to ask.

"And Daisy? Do you think she took her own life?"

"Maybe," she says. "Plenty don't. Or didn't. There was a story about some boyfriend who dumped one for the other, but that doesn't sound right to me. Her mother never believed it. And my father never believed it, neither. He said she wasn't the type. Too much of a fighter. He said they must've got her, too, in the end. Anyway, none of it made any sense to me," she says. "Jumping off a cliff? And one that's not even that high. Seems to me there are better ways. If you really want to die." She stares at me. "Unless she wanted to make a statement."

"But what if that's exactly what she wanted?" I say. "If what you're saying is true. Maybe it was revenge. A big fuck you to whoever hurt her."

"Only she's the one who's dead, isn't she? Some revenge. And Sadie . . ."

"What did her mum say? When you told her the truth?"

"Sadie's? I couldn't get hold of her."

"How hard did you try?"

I see her mood turn. "You think this is easy for me?" she hisses. I can smell garlic on her breath. See the pale, bleached hairs around her mouth, even in the semi-dark. "He was my father. You think I like what he did? You think I'm on his side? You think I don't fucking hate him, even though he's dead?"

"Why are you telling me, then?"

"Who else?" she says sarcastically. "Gavin?"

"Why not?"

Her laugh is like acid. "I don't trust him. All that running-the-film-club stuff? Sounds desperate, if you ask me. Like he wants something. And when he arrived he was asking even more questions than you."

"About Daisy?"

"Zoe, mainly."

"But he's been here a fair while. Hasn't he?"

"Two months. Maybe three."

I go cold. He'd told me a year, at least. "You're sure?"

"Just watch him." She takes a deep breath. "Anyway, I wanted to talk to *you*."

I realize then.

"Was it you who sent the postcard?"

"What postcard? I don't know what you're talking about."

I believe her. I feel sorry for her. She lost her father, and the good memories of him, too. In some ways, she's just another victim.

"I thought you could help."

"Help?"

"You see it, too. Something's still going on."

"What?"

"I don't know. I see the girls every day in the café. There's a lot of drink. Drugs, too. And they act weird, sometimes. Scared. They get calls, then just leave. Like they're terrified of someone." She sighs. "Maybe I'm reading too much into it."

I look over toward the yew. "You're not," I say. "I've seen it, too."

25

I drive Liz back. On the way I resist the temptation to ask more about Gavin, but once I've said goodbye I decide I have to find out what's going on with him myself.

It doesn't take me long. A phone call to Jess and I have his surname—Clayton—then two minutes online and I have his LinkedIn profile. From that it takes no time to find his most recent employer, a financial services technology company based in London for which he worked as coder.

The next step is a little trickier. A rather breathless call to their HR department at first fails to elicit details of his next of kin, even once I've told them it's an urgent but confidential matter and hinted that something awful has happened. The best they can do, they say, is to take my number and ask Tanya to call me back. *Tanya?* I think, as I tell them that'd be great. His mother, perhaps? His sister? Or is he married, after all?

"Hello?"

"Who is this?"

The voice is American. She sounds either anxious or annoyed; it's impossible to tell which.

"It's about Gavin Clayton."

"I know, they said. What's he done?"

What's he done? I think. Not *What's wrong?* Or *Has anything happened?*

"Nothing," I say. "It's just . . . who is this?"

"His wife. Now, can you tell me what's going on?"

It's not a surprise, not really. I keep my voice level.

"I'm in Blackwood Bay," I say.

"He's still there?"

"Yes. He's here."

"And you are?"

"A friend," I say. "I suppose."

She laughs.

"I suppose? Are you fucking him?"

"No," I say. Her voice is clipped, precise. I imagine her in a black jacket, a pencil skirt. A solicitor, maybe.

"I'm making a film. Gavin helped to set things up locally."

"I bet he did. So what is it you want from me?"

"He didn't tell me he was married."

She laughs. "He's not."

"You're divorced?"

"Nearly."

"What happened?"

She snorts. "It's none of your business, but if you want to know, ask him yourself. Ask him what he did."

I hesitate. "Does it have anything to do with Zoe?"

"The missing girls," she says. "Oh yes. With him, everything's about them. Haven't you worked that out yet?"

Gavin waves cheerfully as he pulls into the car park, and I force myself to smile. I've been passing the time, calming myself, filming the view over the village. The long shadows from the low sun look almost abstract in the warm light. He strides confidently over.

"Morning! Everything okay?"

"Kind of."

"What's happened?"

I glance around the car park. There's no one here, but still I don't want to do this in public.

"Not here. Can we go in?"

"Sure." He takes out his key, glancing back as he unlocks the door to the village hall. He's grim-faced; he looks worried now, he knows something's wrong. For a moment I wonder what Tanya didn't tell me, whether I'm as safe as I think I am.

"What is it?"

I close the door behind me, wipe my feet on the mat in the lobby. There are toilets off to the left; on the right a door leads to a small kitchen. The whole place vaguely smells of disinfectant and stale coffee.

"How long have you been here? In Blackwood Bay?"

"I told you," he says quickly as we enter the hall itself. Fluorescents hang from the ceiling and there's a serving hatch through the kitchen. At one end sits a small stage. He turns to face me. "Almost a year. Why?"

"I've been told you've only been here a couple of months."

He closes his eyes, then nods, slowly. It reminds me of Aidan; it's what he used to do when I'd caught him out after he'd told me he wasn't high, he hadn't had a drink, he was fine. I can't decide whether it endears me to him or not. "By whom?"

"Liz," I say. "Why did you lie to me?"

He hesitates. "I . . . well, I wanted to help you. Show you around, you know? Just wanted to be helpful. I'm sorry."

"Gavin. I spoke to Tanya."

He grimaces. It's almost comical.

"What?"

"She told me."

He runs his hand through his hair. "Told you what?"

I've decided to take the risk. "Everything. She told me what you did."

His head falls to his chest. He mumbles something I don't quite catch. It might be *Shit.* Or *Bitch.*

"Gavin?"

He doesn't answer.

"If you want me to trust you, you'd better start telling the truth."

"It wasn't my fault."

What wasn't? I think. *Tell me.*

"That's not what she said," I say instead. "Is it true?"

He pushes a chair over toward me. "Let's sit."

We do so. He faces me. He looks contrite. Disappointed. Angry, too. He begins to pick the skin round his thumbnail, twisting it as he does. It looks painful. Soon he'll draw blood.

"I want to hear your side of the story."

He closes his eyes and draws breath. It's a gathering of energy, and when he looks back up his eyes are moist. Tears glisten in the harsh light.

"I was angry. I mean, my boss, of all people. She couldn't have picked anyone else?"

I look straight at him. An affair? It must be.

"How long?"

"She said it'd been a few weeks. But who knows?"

I imagine bolshie Tanya in her corporate suit and her neat blouse.

She seems the type, I think, but then I realize what a ridiculous thing that is. The type? Aren't we all the type, in the right circumstances?

"So? When you found out . . ."

"I didn't mean it to get . . . physical."

I go into fight or flight. It's not what I expected.

"You hit her?"

"Is that what she told you?"

"What, then?"

"I hit him."

I almost laugh with relief. I try to imagine it, try to see him waiting outside for his rival, or perhaps visiting him at home. I try to imagine how it happened. Perhaps he threw a punch, calculated and cold, shaking as he did so, worried about where it would lead but feeling there was no alternative. Or maybe his anger came out of nowhere, clouding everything out. I wonder if he surprised himself, looked down and saw the other man on the floor and only then realized what he was capable of.

"You hit your boss."

"He said he'd ask for the charges to be dropped if I quit. So I didn't really have a choice."

Levelheaded Gavin won out. "I'm sorry," I say.

He tries to laugh it off. "Looking back, I wanted a change anyway. I just didn't see it at the time."

His cheer is clearly false, for my benefit if not his own. But I say nothing. Part of me is relieved; the truth isn't as bad as I'd feared.

"Anyway," he says wearily, "it's history." He looks up. "I know who you are, by the way."

The air rushes out of the room. My vision splits, the image distorts. It's as though I'm looking at Gavin through a cracked lens.

"What?" I wonder briefly whether I can run.

"You can't keep secrets here. Not for long . . . What's wrong?"

"What did you hear?"

"Oh, just that it was your film. How come you told me you were only helping out?"

Relief surges through me. "Oh," I say. "No reason. It's just . . ."

"Being modest? I read all about you. Didn't realize you were so famous. *Black Winter*, wasn't it?" He's clearly been googling and I'm flattered, despite myself. "I haven't watched it yet."

"You don't have to."

"I want to."

He does, too. I can tell. He's not just trying to butter me up. Or, if he is, he's being very subtle. We sit for a moment, each regarding the other.

"It seems we've both been telling lies."

I scan the roof. There's a bright green balloon way up in the rafters, half deflated. "Looks like it."

"I'm sorry."

"Me, too."

He lowers his voice. "I do want to help, you know. Find out what's been going on here."

I know, I think. He's determined, I'll say that for him.

"I saw Liz," I say. "She climbed into my car. Virtually hijacked me."

His jaw drops. "What?"

"She wanted to show me something. Out on the moor."

I watch for a reaction. There isn't one, just a slight nervous twitch, patience as he waits for me to continue.

"She thinks Daisy is buried there." I pause. "Or Sadie."

"*Sadie?*"

"Yes."

"But Sadie ran away."

I tell him the story and, when I've finished, he whistles.

"It sounds crazy."

"I know. But what if they got to Daisy's body? When it was washed up. Before the police, I mean. Buried it to cover the evidence."

"Who's *they*? What did the police say?"

"She hasn't told them."

"Then we should tell them."

I shake my head. I can't have that. I can't have the police involved. They'd find out who I am.

"No."

"No?" He stands up. "There's an unmarked grave, for heaven's sake!"

I need to backtrack. Quickly.

"It's not a grave, it's just a sick joke. Some flowers under a bloody tree. It seems her father wasn't making much sense, toward the end."

"But—"

"Sadie can't be buried there."

"Why?"

"Just trust me."

He looks at me quizzically.

"So what's your connection? To this place? Blackwood Bay?" he asks.

I look down at my lap. My instinct is to deny it, to say none, nothing, but I know it's too late. He would never believe me, not now. He'd never leave it alone.

I sit as still as I can. I scratch my forearm but feel nothing.

"I know Sadie's alive. I knew her. Down in London. We were on the streets. Homeless. We met in one of the hostels. So one thing I'm sure of is that Sadie can't be buried there."

"Unless she came back."

"She didn't."

"You seem very certain."

"I am."

"Why? What happened to her here?"

She doesn't know, I think. That's the problem. She wishes she did. She thinks it might have something to do with why Daisy died.

But I can't tell him that.

"I don't know."

"You never asked?"

I fix him with a stare. "No. I didn't. People will tell you, if they want to, when they're ready. You don't push."

I'm not sure he understands. This man, with his neatly pressed clothes and his career that I've no doubt he could return to if and when he wants to. He thinks little Sadie got fed up one day, a bit miserable, someone stole her pencil case or called her a nasty name, so she packed a bag and hitched first to Sheffield and then to London. One day, I'd like to tell him how it really is. I almost envy him his solidity, his certitude that there are clear moral lines.

"You don't know where she is now?"

"We lost touch."

"I thought you were friends."

"I didn't say we were friends. And anyway, it was a long time ago."

He sits. Silent. I wish he smoked; I'd ask him for one. Now would be the time to start again. I close my eyes briefly and imagine it, the cigarette between my lips, the spark of the lighter, drawing that first, head-spinning drag, feeling it scour the back of my throat, gently abrasive.

He waits for a moment, then says, "Did Liz mention Zoe?"

I remember Tanya's comment, her parting shot.

I shake my head. Gavin speaks softly. "We really should tell someone, you know?"

"About the so-called grave? I said no. I said—"

"No, I mean tell someone you've met Sadie. Her family—"

No, I think. *No.* I want desperately to find out what happened, why I ran, what I did to Daisy before I went, but I can't go back. I can't see my mother; there's no way she won't recognize me, and what can I possibly say to her when she does?

"Her mother would want to know she's okay."

But she's not, I think. *She's not.*

"I just . . . no."

"Alex," he says, softly. "That's very selfish."

Again, that certainty; he's straight down the line. He's right, I think. And maybe I've run out of options. Maybe she's the one who can tell me why I ran, what happened between me and Daisy. She can finally give me the answers I need.

And if she does, if I can remember who hurt Daisy and why I ran, then maybe I'll know who Liz is scared of, and what's going on with Kat and Ellie.

"How will we find her?"

"There's a way. Someone will know. Or we can look online."

Of course. I'm running out of excuses. And maybe it wouldn't be so terrible.

But then I think about her seeing me. Seeing through to who I really am. The life I've constructed for myself would fall apart.

"Gavin?" I say, and he looks over. For a moment he looks as though he'll do anything for me. It's as if by each sharing a secret we've moved into different territory, come together at the gray line that divides the light on the moon, night from day.

"Yes?" he says.

"Will you be the one who talks to her?"

THEN

26

ALEX'S DIARY, WEDNESDAY, 6 JULY 2011

I've found her! It's not all good news, but at least I'm getting somewhere!

I've been going back to Victoria every day for a week. I haven't been telling Aidan. I know he'll disapprove. I've found a café on the other side of the road, almost opposite. It's really posh, it sells fancy sausages and ham and organic lemonades (whatever that is!) and stuff, but it has seats in the window so I sit there with a coffee and watch the door that leads to the flats. Sometimes I film it on my phone. The woman who runs the café is okay, yesterday she gave me a sandwich and said it was on the house.

Anyway, today I finally saw the girl I recognized. She was coming from the other direction with a guy, wearing the same clothes from that first day, although I think I'd have recognized her anyway. Today I even thought I knew her name—Daisy—though it turns out I was wrong. I wonder if that's the name of someone from before?

When I caught up with her I thought she was going to run again, but I asked her not to. The man she was with said, "Sadie?" and he sounded really surprised to see me.

"Please," I said to them. "I need to talk to you."

At first I didn't think they would, but then the girl said I should wait, they'd be ten minutes. Then they went upstairs.

The girl came down by herself. "C'mon," she said, and we went back toward the coach station to a car park above a row of shops. "In here," she said.

It stank really badly in there, and there was pee everywhere, but we climbed the stairs to the first floor and found a spot near a big silver Volvo.

"You're back," she said, just like that. I felt excited, but scared, too.

"What's your name?"

She didn't answer, just lit a cigarette. I had to ask her again.

"Alice."

Alice. *I wondered if that's the reason I chose Alex as my name, when I needed to tell Dr. Olsen something. She gave me a cigarette and asked where I'd been. I told her as much as I could.*

"That was you?" she said. It turns out I was on the news, in the papers. MYSTERY GIRL FOUND ON DEAL BEACH. I really hope no one back home in London saw it, though I still didn't know why.

Then Alice said something weird. She said I shouldn't be there, that I'd promised not to come back to Victoria, especially not back to the squat. When I asked why, she just said, "You're in danger, girl."

I asked why, but she wouldn't say, so I asked if I'd done drugs at the squat. She just laughed, like it was obvious. She said she didn't, but her friend, Dev, did.

Dev. The name rang a bell. She said it was the guy she'd been with. "He's using again," she said, like I'd be really disappointed.

Anyway, she said we'd met at Waterloo. I'd been living on the streets since I arrived in London, and I'd had my bag stolen so I had no money or anything. I wouldn't tell her what had happened to me, though I said something had, something pretty bad. She said she'd got the sense someone had died. A suicide, but I'd said no, it was worse than that, but that I'd never tell anyone.

She'd managed to persuade me to go and stay in the squat. She said it'd taken ages, and when I asked why she said she didn't know, but it was almost like I was scared of Dev.

But that's all I know. We arranged to meet again, and she says she'll tell me the rest then. I got the sense it was bad. It was the reason I disappeared to Deal. It was the reason she ran when she first saw me. I'm scared, but I'm glad I went, I'm glad I met Alice. The more I see of my old life, the more I seem to remember.

NOW

27

*T*he house is down a dirt track off the main road. I must've been here thousands of times, but I feel only a faint resonance. There's a sign that reads *Concealed Entrance* which I don't remember, the driveway has been newly graveled, and the house itself, standing alone as it does, seems somehow much smaller. I suppose it would've been the farmhouse once, back when there was a working farm here, though that thought never occurred to me when I lived here. We had four bedrooms, and it looks as though my mother has converted one of the outhouses into a fifth. At least that's what I assume she's done with it; I can't think what other use she'd have for it—no need for a granny flat, or a home office—though it seems unlikely that she'd need all those beds, either.

"This is it?"

Gavin seems surprised. I wonder what he'd expected. I lied and told him I'd done some digging, that it wasn't hard to find Sadie's address.

"Uh-huh."

"Looks very grand."

I look out at the pots lining the driveway, ready for plants. All neat and tidy. I know what he means. It doesn't look like the kind of house you'd want to run from. But what does he know? What do any of us?

"I wonder if anyone's in. No cars."

The drive is empty, the house unlit, though it's early, only just starting to get light.

"Let's wait here for a minute," I say, and stop the car opposite the house. I need to get my breathing down. Part of me wants to forget all about it, to stay as I am, lost memories and all. I don't want to face it. But I can't give in to that part. I'm in too deep; this isn't even about the film anymore, it's gone beyond that, it's about me now. Knowing who I was. What happened. How I'm connected to Daisy.

I look up at the house again. I wonder why so many of my memories of my time here are missing. I wonder what happened to me. Dr. Olsen told me I was blocking the things that hurt the most.

It makes sense, I suppose. If you can't remember it, then it didn't happen.

"Gavin? Maybe you could go in now?"

His eyes soften, just a touch. "Okay. I'll go and see how the land lies, then, if she's in, and if she's happy to talk, I'll report back and maybe you could go and talk to her then."

I thank him. He opens the door, then looks back. His eyes are wide, expectant, and for a moment I think he's going to try to kiss me, and know that if he does, I'll let him.

"Wish me luck," he says, then he gets out of the car. He walks up to the gate. That's new, too. It was just a gap in the hedge when I was here last, big enough for the car. He unlatches it and I watch him approach the house. He rings the bell and after a minute a light comes on, a shadow appears, movement behind the frosted glass.

The woman who answers is young. She's holding a baby. I watch—somehow both hugely relieved and bitterly disappointed—as they talk for a moment and then, without a backward glance, Gavin goes inside.

I sit back in the seat. Dr. Olsen told me once it was common, that people often didn't remember the details of what had happened to them that made them run, just the generalities. But it seems I lost even that. I look again at the house. My bedroom was at the back, looking out over the fields, down toward the sea, though I couldn't quite see it. At night, the lights of Blackwood Bay shone in the distance, the lighthouse visible beyond it.

But what happened in there? With my mother's boyfriend? Was there anything? Why have I blocked it, overwritten every memory like a disk too full? And is it related to Zoe, to what's happening now, to Kat and Ellie and the rest?

I slump down in my seat. I'm glad Gavin is here; I don't feel so alone.

After only a minute or two, he reappears at the door, followed by the woman with the baby. He turns and says something to her, and she smiles sadly then waves him off.

"What happened?" I say when he gets into the car. My voice is barely a whisper. "Who was that?"

"They've lived here for seven or eight years."

A weight settles on my chest. I have to force the question out.

"So, what happened to Sadie's mother? Did she leave a forwarding address?"

"No," he says. "We're too late. She died."

"You sure you're all right?"

It's the third or fourth time he's asked. We're halfway back to Black-wood Bay, sitting in a café in a tiny village. He wanted to buy me breakfast and I couldn't think of a decent enough excuse to refuse, but all I could face ordering from the brooding teenager behind the counter was toast. I pick up my knife as Gavin slides my food nearer. The scrape is loud, like a tomb being sealed.

"I'm fine," I say, trying my hardest to sound it, to pull myself together. "Honestly."

"You look a bit pale."

He's frowning; he looks concerned. It's nice that he cares.

I watch as he cracks the shell of his boiled egg and peels it from the top, placing it carefully on his plate. The sound seems too loud: the way the crisp shell breaks reminds me of a skull shattering and as he cuts through the hard, rubbery albumen I think of a scalpel slicing through flesh.

The room begins to shrink and I put down my toast, close my eyes. I can't just sit here. Things are gathering momentum, I can feel it. I'm worried about Ellie. Kat. I can't stay here another minute. "Can we go?"

"What? Now? But—"

"Can we just fucking go?"

He puts down his spoon and stares at me. I wonder what's flashing through his mind, what to say, how to react. I now know he has a
temper. He could tell me to get lost, that there's no need to be angry.
He could demand to know why, tell me there's no way this is about my
film, that much is obvious. I see him weigh it up, then decide.

"Let's eat," he says softly. "I bought you food. Eat it. Then we can
go." He pauses. "I wish you'd tell me why, though. Really, I mean."

"I'm worried," I say. "About the girls."

Still, the irritation in my voice is unmissable. He glances down at
my plate, the food untouched, then up. For a second I see him, furi-
ous, standing over me, his belt in his hand, eyes incandescent, spittle
flying. *Do as you're told*, he's saying, *you little bitch*, and all I can do is
cower, and hope, and tell myself this doesn't mean I'm weak, doesn't
mean he'll own me forever, this is temporary, just until I can get
away, but still he hits me, over and over and over.

But none of that happens and I remember he's one of the good
guys. He's never hurt me.

"Come on, then," he says gently. "I wasn't that hungry anyway."

We drive in silence. I sit forward, gripping the wheel to stop my
hands from shaking. I feel no better than I did in the café. The car's
stifling; my defenses are crumbling away. I wish I had my camera
to hide behind. I spot the turning that leads down to the church
and know I have to stop. Somehow, I know that's where I'll find my
mother.

"I'm turning off," I say.

"What?"

"The cemetery. The light's perfect."

It sounds unconvincing and I know it.

"The cemetery? But—"

"I want to film it."

"Now?"

Shut up, I think. *Shut up.*

"I want to film Sadie's mother's grave."

"I thought you wanted to get back."

"I do . . . I just . . . I can't explain. Gavin? Please?"

Again, he complies. We turn off the main road and into the tree-lined lane. The road is little more than a track, overhung with black, leafless branches, stark against the sky. It dips and curves, the road narrows, and I have to slow almost to a crawl to navigate the bends, but then, finally, it opens out. We're right down at sea level and, ahead of us, silhouetted against the graying sky, is a tiny, dark church. Everything seems off slightly, like the world's tipped, the angles all wrong. A weight presses in on me, as if I'm being buried alive.

She can't be here. She can't. She's alive. I switch off the engine.

"Can you wait here?"

"I'd rather come with you. You seem—"

I get my camera from the back seat and hand it to him.

"Film me, then?"

He agrees, and together we walk down toward the church. The door is closed, the place shuttered. The distant wind is quiet and desperate and Gavin's footsteps echo behind as we circle the perimeter. There's a bench on the far side and the sea is just over a low stone wall. Before it, the headstones lie, shattered like broken teeth.

"Wait here."

"Why—?"

"Please," I hiss. "Just give me a minute?"

He does as I've asked. He wipes the damp bench clear but then declines to sit. He watches me instead—still filming, as far as I can tell—as I enter the overgrown, mossy graveyard. I lean in close to read the inscriptions on the stones and eventually find the one I'm looking for.

Rebecca Davies, it says. 23 November 1968—4 August 2012.

That's it. I don't know what I expected, but that's it. It's small; it seems insignificant. There's no quote, nothing from the Bible—not that she'd have wanted that anyway—not even a Sadly Missed, or Never Forgotten. Just the facts, unvarnished, unadorned. Her name, the year in which she was born, the year she died. Two thousand and twelve. Just over a year and a half after her daughter disappeared. Nineteen months after Daisy died. Dimly, I wonder what happened to the boyfriend, then realize I couldn't care less.

I step closer. There's a sound from underfoot, a soft, sickening crunch like stepping on a snail, and I imagine the sharp shell piercing its pulpy body, the crush of death from something that until that moment had meant protection and refuge. My legs shake as I crouch down. I reach forward; the stone is freezing, a layer of frost clinging to it. I trace the lettering with numbed fingers. Rebecca Davies.

I sit on the hard ground and draw my legs up tight beneath me. Through my jeans I can feel every bump, every rough stone, but I ignore the pain. I deserve it, and plenty more besides. For what I did to her.

I close my eyes. I'm aware that Gavin's over there, not twenty feet away in the shadow of the church, my camera in his hand. But I don't care. I let my head fall; I rock forward.

"What happened?" I whisper, but the only reply is the stone's resonant silence. I begin to cry.

I could've helped. I should've. I could've asked what was wrong, why she'd changed, why she was behaving the way she did, why she let the bastard she'd met drive us apart. But I didn't. I gave up. I turned my back on her. I went out, to clubs and parties. I started drinking, getting wasted, getting laid. Fuck you, I thought. Two can play at that game, two can screw up their lives.

The tears come harder now. It's all coming back. I think back to the day I ran. I walked until my feet bled, then hitched. First one lift, then another, and another. They blend into one. I made it to Sheffield, then London. There's a blank after that, a long, vast emptiness, with only snatched images and jump cuts from one scene to another. Alice, Dev. Gee. Needles, burning smoke. Nodding off in the back of strangers' cars. Giving everything away because I wasn't worth any-thing. Opening myself, first for money, then for drugs, then because it was just what I did. I was barely there; I didn't know who I was most of the time. I thought I was running away from hell but in fact I was running into it, toward holes in my memory and not even being sure I still wanted to live. And then something happened that took me to Deal, and I woke up on the beach, soaked and alone, and my mind gave up, reset itself.

I open my eyes. Although small, the gravestone looms in front of me, and now there's no escaping the truth. She lived only nineteen more months, if that. It wasn't just my life I destroyed when I went. I took with me any hope she might've once had.

"Mum," I whisper. "It's me. Sadie. I'm sorry."

Nothing. Just the wind and my thudding heart. Guilt slams into me, its finger reaching into my mouth, my gut. But there's no way I could've stayed. I have to remember that. I have to cling to that, no matter what else tries to throw me into the raging water.

And what was I expecting? A reply, ghostly and ethereal? For-giveness?

It's too late for all that. I had my chance, and I blew it.

"I'll figure out what's going on," I say. "I'll put it right."

28

We reach the car. Gavin hands me the camera, wordlessly. Its solidity is reassuring and I hold it in my lap for a moment be-fore pressing *Play*. The grainy scene resolves; I hear the crunch of a boot. A figure ahead, a woman staring at the gravestones. She steps forward, then bends down.

I know it's me, but it doesn't feel real. There's a disconnection. My body shudders as I touch the stone, then there's a jerky, vertiginous plummet before the image stabilizes. When it does, we're seeing the same scene but from a lower angle; the camera's resting on the bench. Then Gavin appears, walking toward me. He crouches beside me, but I make no movement; there's no sign I've even noticed. He holds out his hand to help me up, then together we walk back toward the camera, me in front, him following mutely behind.

I press *Stop* and put the device on the dashboard in front of me.

"It's what you wanted," says Gavin. "Isn't it?"

I don't know what to say. I don't know what he saw, how much he heard. I've stopped crying but, even so, my eyes must be ringed with red.

"Are you okay?"

I'm leaving her again. Out here in the cold, in the dark, loamy earth. Just like I left Geraldine. And Alice. And Aidan, though that was more a gradual drift.

And Daisy. I left her, too. I turn to Gavin.

"I'm fine." I start the engine. "Let's go."

I park at the top of the village. The silence fans out like thick, black smoke.

"I'm here for you," he says after a while. "If you want to talk about it."

He means it. He wants to help me. It's not about me being in his debt. It's not about him wanting to rescue me again, like that first night. It's not like it was on the streets, people who wanted to help but only to make themselves feel good. Dare to deny them the opportunity, dare to tell them you're fine, you don't need anything right now, and they're not pleased for you. Suddenly, you can go to hell. They've done their bit and you're an ungrateful bitch throwing it back in their face.

"Where had you been?" I say. "That time you found me on the road. The night we met?"

"What d'you mean?"

"You told me you'd been with Bryan."

He hesitates, just for a second. "I had."

"He says not. Why would he do that?"

"I don't know."

I realize I want to believe him. "I know you want to help," I say softly. "But tell me the truth."

"I hadn't been with him," he says cautiously. "Not exactly. I'd seen him. In the pub. I was on my own." He glances up. "But it amounts to the same thing. I knew he couldn't have been driving the car that didn't stop."

I say nothing.

"You believe me?"

"Yes."

"What can I do? To help?"

"Did she tell you how Sadie's mum died?"

He seems confused for a moment then realizes I mean the woman with the baby.

"No."

He's quiet for a minute, but I can tell he wants to say something else.

"Is Sadie the real reason you came here?"

I consider telling the truth. But how can I?

"Partly, perhaps. I couldn't stop thinking about her. I wish we'd stayed in touch."

"So how old would she be now?"

"Dunno. Twenties?"

"Why did you pretend your film wasn't about what happened to the girls? You could've told me, you know. I only want—"

"To help," I say. "I know. Thing is, it wasn't, originally. But my producer suggested it. He'd read about Daisy. And Zoe."

"And it was too juicy a story not to come up and take a look?"

Juicy. The word stings. I've heard it before, back when I made *Black Winter.* It took a long time to win some of the girls over, to convince them I wasn't just a voyeur trying to use their misery to make something of my own. "We just make a juicy story for you," one of them said. Several, in fact.

I look at Gavin. "You make me sound like I don't care."

"Do you?"

"Yes."

He's quiet for a long time. I remember after the awards, going back to find the women I'd filmed. They weren't pleased to see me, though neither were they particularly upset. To them, I'd moved on, that's all, like everyone does, if they don't die first. As I handed over the envelope of cash—three thousand pounds—I told them it was theirs. It always had been, really.

Gavin clears his throat awkwardly. "Zoe didn't run away."

He sounds so certain it might almost be a confession.

"I just know," he continues. "I can't explain. I think you're right, though. Daisy and Zoe are both dead. Sadie is the only one who got away." The air in the car is still. I can't breathe. My teeth are chattering, but I open the window.

"What is it with you and Zoe?"

He shrugs. "Nothing. I just . . . I suppose I thought I could find her. When I arrived, I mean. I thought . . . I don't know. Maybe I thought the people here might accept me if I showed them that I cared."

"And? How's that going?"

He ignores my question. "We should go to the police—"

"No."

Once again, he ignores me. "I mean, Sadie's the one who'd know what was going on."

But she doesn't, I think. *She doesn't.*

"We should find her. You can tell them you were in touch with her."

"No!"

He looks at me. Into me. Through me.

"No," I say, more gently this time, but more emphatically, too. "Sadie made me promise. And as for the grave, it's nothing. It can't be."

"But—"

"You don't understand, Gavin."

I've hit a nerve. He knows he'll always be on the outside, trying to understand. I'm soaked by another wave of guilt.

"I thought you were worried about the girls. Ellie and Kat?"

"I am," I tell him. I imagine myself buried back there on the moor. I'm alone, naked. It's like I'm there, I can feel it, the soft earth, warm despite the weather, it's surrounding me, engulfing me, swallowing me whole. But then it's as if a cord running through my middle has been pulled tight. Surrounded by so much death, all I want is to live. The atmosphere in the car thickens. I realize, almost from a distance, how easy it would be to reach out, to put my hand on his leg, his thigh, to lean in close to him. He'd open his mouth, surprised. There'd be the smell of licorice, not unpleasant. We'd kiss, and it would go on for a while, becoming more urgent as it does.

Something stops me, but only for a moment. I put my hand on his. Why not? Why shouldn't I take what I want? You only live once, after all. I kiss him. He resists at first; I think he's going to say, *No, stop*, and the shame begins to swell and bubble. But then he gives in. His lips are rougher than I expected; his mouth tastes of coffee. His kiss is hesitant and he keeps his hands to himself, and for that I'm glad.

"Let's go," I say, murmuring into his chest, but he shakes his head. "Do you mind if we don't—?"

"Don't—?"

The familiar sting of rejection. I almost want to laugh.

"I'm sorry. I just . . ."

I wait for him to finish, but he seems unable to. He opens the car door and steps out.

"Gavin?" I say. "Don't tell anyone, will you? About today."

He looks hurt. I realize he thinks I'm referring to our kiss.

"About the graveyard, I mean. About me knowing Sadie."

He smiles, then nods gently.

"I won't."

I thank him, then get out of my car and walk down to Hope Cottage.

29

Once there, I can't settle. I need to do something. I'll shoot some more footage for the film, I decide. The village at night, maybe. From up top, the park, for example. It's nearly dark, so I set off. But as soon as I get to the bandstand and try to film I realize the memory card in my camera is spent and I've forgotten to bring another. I have to go back.

I feel eyes following me as I walk down Slate Road, pricking my skin. I scan left and right, and each time think I see a flash of movement, as if a figure is hiding in the darkness, anticipating my every move but slipping back into the shadows in the instant before I see them. I'm relieved as I duck through the alleyway that brings me to the courtyard, but still I feel under scrutiny. I fancy I see the curtains in Monica's place move slightly, just a shudder, but when I look again everything is still.

I turn my key, but the door is open. I must have forgotten to lock it earlier in my haste, left it on the latch. I need to be more careful.

Rain to *Stormy*. My bag is in the bedroom upstairs, but a second before I switch on the light I realize something's wrong. The door is ajar, the light from the landing shining in, illuminating a patch of the carpet and the edge of the bed, leaving the rest of the room in darkness. I hear the soft sigh of an exhaled breath and see a flicker at the edge of the shadow. The bed creaks as someone stands and steps toward me.

I see his feet first, his ugly black shoes, blue jeans, a black jacket. I freeze. His face is still in the shadows cast by the door, but whoever he is I can tell he's staring at me, his hollow eyes burning.

"Alex."

He says my name as if it's in quotes, and then I know I've been seen. I try to step backward, away from him, but I can't. I'm stiff with fear.

"What the fuck?"

He steps forward. "Don't . . . I'm not going to hurt you."

I half recognize his paper-thin voice but my brain has slowed to a crawl and won't process it, won't make the connection. I'm not even sure I've tipped into fight or flight, since I seem to be able to do nothing but grip the door handle. A second later, I realize.

"David?"

My voice unfreezes me. I find the light switch and flick it on. I'm right, he's coming for me, treading lightly, his hand in his pocket. In a moment he'll withdraw it; the glint of a blade, a length of rope. A gun. I have to act.

"Stay where you are!"

It shocks him. He takes his hand out of his pocket. It's empty.

"Keep away from me!"

"I won't hurt you," he says again. "Just let me go."

I realize he doesn't know what he wants to say; he hadn't been waiting for me, he's been caught. I begin to laugh, even though it's not funny. My fear seems to have turned into something else. I know, since I'm between him and the door that, if I were to run, there's a pretty good chance I'd make it outside.

"What're you doing here?"

"Nothing, I just—"

I scan the room. It's as I left it. The drawers haven't been upended, my stuff doesn't look disturbed. He wasn't expecting me back so soon. I look him in the eye.

"How did you get in?"

"The door," he says. "It was open." He steps closer. "Look, I just want to—"

"Just back the fuck off. Okay?"

He stands stock-still. He's pale in the bright light, even thinner than I remember him. He seems unwell, like he's going through hell and hasn't slept. This close, I can see his smooth, blue-tinged skin, the nicks on his chin where he's cut himself shaving. He almost looks made of wax, but when I look down at my own arm I realize that I do, too.

"I'm on your side," he says quietly. "But you have to leave. You shouldn't be here."

"No."

"It's for your own good."

"Is that a threat?"

His head falls, as if he's disappointed that I'd even think such a thing.

"You shouldn't have come back."

There's a vicious splintering of my perception, as if a train has jumped the switch, there's been a jump-cut in a movie. It's true, then. He knows. He's known all along. Is that why he's here, he wants to find proof? As if I'd be stupid enough to carry anything with me that bore my old name. He knows me, so I must've known him before. Why can't I remember?

"David, I . . ."

The words won't come. He grabs my arm. Static shoots into my shoulder, the feeling intense, like biting on tinfoil.

"Why? Why are you pretending?"

I gasp for air, but it's leaked away. I manage to shake him off, but pain grips my arm.

"Leave me alone!"

He reaches out once more but, this time, his hand hovers.

"You know I'm on your side. I always was." He reaches for my hair. "You've changed."

I shove his hand away.

"You know I've always looked after you."

"Get the fuck off me!"

"Please—"

I battle to keep my voice level. "I don't know you. I've never met you before."

"Don't lie," he says. "There's no need, not with me. What happened to you?"

"What?"

"After you left. What happened?" I shake my head and he reaches out once more. "It's really you."

I react without thinking. It's as if something takes over, an automatic reaction. I slap him. The palm of my hand sings.

He staggers back. "Please. I've heard nothing. Barely a word. I—"

You brought me here, I think. You sent Dan the postcard. It's the only explanation.

"You have to leave. Now."

"What are you doing to the girls? Tell me, you fucker. Tell me!"

He's trembling, shrinking as I watch, retreating within himself. He reminds me of Geraldine, a mind turned rotten. He seems almost elsewhere, as if he's talking to someone only he can see.

"We said we'd never tell. It was our secret."

"Daisy . . ." I say. Certainty hits me, I don't know where from. "You killed her. She was in your house, she was seen."

"No!"

I reach into my pocket for my phone. If only there were a way to record this, I think. Without him knowing.

Fuck it. I point it at him and press *Record.* His hands fly to his face, as if I'm about to spray him with mace.

"Stop! No!"

"Admit it. You killed her."

He freezes, his eyes wide, as if he's about to confess. But then he seems to change his mind.

"You know that's not true!" he says instead. "You know it wasn't me who killed her! Daisy—"

"What are you hiding?"

He backs away.

"Daisy . . . what happened to her? Who pushed her?"

"No one. You know that. Talk to Monica. She was there. She saw it. She saw it all. You know she did."

I want to slap him, force him to tell me why he remembers me when I don't remember him, why I find myself torn between wanting him on my side and wanting to kill him. And I want to beg him not to tell anyone who I am. I open my fist, then close it again.

"Get out," I say. The words reverberate, but I feel curiously, eerily calm, as if something inside me has taken over. Like an automaton, I stand back, watch as he nods slowly then goes past me. He stops at the top of the stairs and turns back to face me.

"Don't stay here," he says. "Please? If you stay, it'll have all been for nothing."

30

I sit in the armchair, my hands balled into fists, knuckles white. The door is locked, but still I watch it.

A shadow, then a face through the window. I recognize Gavin's glasses.

"Alex? It's me."

I stand stiffly and unbolt the door. He's barely through but already he's hugging me, or maybe it's me holding him.

"What did he want?"

To tell me he knew I was Sadie, I think, but I can't say that.

"I think he killed Daisy," I say instead. "And I'm worried about Ellie. She denies it, but he's seeing her, I'm sure of it."

"But—"

"There's something else. He told me Daisy was seen. Jumping. By Monica."

"Monica? But how can that be? If he killed her?"

"I don't know," I say. "Maybe he's lying."

He buries his head in my hair.

"Are you okay?" I look up. I can feel the warmth of his skin. I think of his lips touching mine. "You're shivering. Come on."

• • •

We sit on the sofa. His arm is around me, his warmth spread over me, holding me like a blanket. He's lit a fire in the grate. The silence between us buzzes with things unspoken and desire fills the air, thick as syrup. I look up at him, but his face is unreadable in the shadows. I realize I want him and at the exact moment I lift my chin to kiss him he lowers his. His lips brush mine, inexpertly at first, but then we each find the rhythm of the other. His hand moves to the back of my neck, then down to my breast.

"Is this okay?" he murmurs, and the words won't come so I answer only by removing my sweater, tugging at his belt. "Let's go upstairs," he says, but I shake my head. I can think only of David sitting in that room, watching us.

"No," I say. "Let's stay here." I glance toward the fire. "We might as well enjoy the cliché."

He laughs and lowers me gently to the floor before removing what clothes remain. He's hesitant at first, as if he thinks that at any moment I might ask him to stop, but when I reach for him with every bit as much fervor as he had me he grows more emboldened, less gentle. I guide him into me, closing my eyes as I do, willing myself to stay where I am, focused on what's happening here and now, on my body. "Alex?" he says, and I open my eyes, then kiss him. I realize he's still wearing his glasses and take them off.

"That's better," I say.

It doesn't take long and when we're done he stands up awkwardly. He hands me the blanket from the back of the sofa and I see his body for the first time from a distance. He's skinny but lithe; his sweat-sheened muscles glisten. He seems suddenly embarrassed; he finds his boxers and turns around to put them on. Already I'm replaying what we did, wondering whether we might do it again, more slowly next time and with less silence.

But does he feel the same? Or is that it for him, now he's got what he wanted? I doubt it somehow, but I've been wrong before. More often than not, in fact.

"Was that okay?" he says.

I nod. He deserves more, but the words won't come. "Can you get me some water?" I say instead, more to fill the silence than anything else. When he returns, he seems forlorn. He gathers the rest of his things and begins to dress.

"Stay?" I say.

"No," he begins. "I'm sorry, I shouldn't—"

"Stay," I say, more forcefully this time. "Please? It was great."

He pauses, about to button up his jeans. "You're sure?"

I nod, and he kisses me again.

We stay in bed. He doesn't leave until late morning, and even then he says he'd rather not. I lie still for a while, then shower. I take my time; my arm still feels raw from where David touched it last night. It's as if he's poisonous, something I'm allergic to. Even Gavin's tenderness hasn't overridden it. When I'm done, I dress in my jeans and thickest sweater, then leave, too, locking the door carefully behind me and checking it twice.

Monica's cottage is still. There's no movement, no answer when I ring the bell. The streets are empty, too, the snow all but disappeared. The Rocks brood in the distance and on their edge, silent and empty, sits Bluff House.

I can't bring myself to look at it, so I look forward instead, toward the pub. The walls outside are bare; there are hooks drilled into them at intervals. I tell myself baskets of plants must hang from them in summer—fuchsias, perhaps, violent pinks and vibrant reds—but that seems unreal. Instead, I see meat swinging from them, butchered pigs, slaughtered lambs. Bodies, strung up and bleeding. A girl, crying out in pain. Suddenly, I want to turn and run.

But no. I'm not thinking straight. I force myself to climb the steps that lead up from the street and enter the warmth, ignoring the momentary hush as the lunchtime drinkers regard me to slide purpose-fully over to the bar.

"How's it going, pet?" says the landlady as I approach. She seems subdued.

"Not too bad. Can I get some water?"

"That all?"

I consider for a moment. It's early, but so what? "Actually, I'll have a whiskey."

She pours it for me. It clings to the glass like blood, oily and viscous.

"Has Monica been in?" I say as I hand over my cash.

"Over there, love."

She points to one of the tables tucked into the corner. Monica sits alone and, when she notices me, beckons me over. As I sit down she closes the book in her lap.

"Everything okay?"

Her head tilts, and I wonder if she heard us last night. The walls are thin, after all, thin enough for me to hear her moving around.

"Is it true?" I say.

"What?"

"You saw Daisy jump?"

Her face falls.

"What makes you think that?"

"David told me."

She seems surprised. "He did, did he? And why were you talking to him? And about that?"

I don't want to answer. "So?"

She sighs, then glances around the room. "Not here. We'll go up-stairs."

She stands and we approach the bar. Monica asks Beverly if she minds and when the landlady says no leads me toward a door in the corner. As I approach, a deep fear begins to burn like smoke in my gut, unnamable but alive.

"Come on," says Monica. The doorway yawns, black and cavern-ous, and there's a strange smell from above, salty with a sulfurous edge.

I'm gripped with the desire to run, but I know I'm being ridiculous. I force myself to follow Monica up the steps.

At the top, she flicks a switch and the feeble bulb overhead glows dully. We're on a narrow landing, the yellowing wallpaper peeling, doors off to the left and right. We go through one and into a messy living room. Old coffee cups litter the furniture, there's a huge TV playing in the corner, the sound muted. The whole place smells of stale cigarettes and I begin to feel sick; my heart hammers in my chest like a wild thing desperate for release.

Monica sits on the sofa and indicates the chair opposite.

"Bev lets me come up here," she says, even though I haven't asked. "When I want a cigarette."

"Right."

She smiles and pulls one out. "So. David told you I saw Daisy jump."

"You didn't tell me."

My voice sounds weak, reedy and pathetic. I cough, but it makes no difference.

"No."

"Why?"

"No reason."

"What did you see?"

"What d'you mean? She jumped. That's what I saw."

Sometimes I see it, too, I want to say. I see her standing there in a long, flowing dress; it catches the moonlight, whipped by the wind. She resembles a ghost, ethereal in the bluish light. I see her walk forward, toward the edge of the cliff, almost floating. There's no pause. She takes one step too far, then, soundlessly, disappears.

But I know it wasn't like that. She was wearing jeans. Boots. A jacket. Nothing ethereal about that. Nothing delicate and fragile. Nothing poetic.

"Where were you?"

"Just out for a walk."

She lights a cigarette and the sound is like gunfire. I recoil, and when I glance up there are two of her; my vision is split.

"Alex?"

I blink and the room resolves itself once more. I have to say something. I have to stay present. I dig my nails into my palm but feel nothing.

"What exactly did you see?"

She shakes her head; either she's reluctant to tell me, or it's the pain of remembering. When she speaks, her voice is quiet.

"She were just up there. Standing. I didn't recognize her, not at first. She were too far away. Right on the edge. Just sort of looking out."

"She was definitely by herself?"

"Yes. It were just her."

She's lying. She has to be. David killed her. He was about to confess.

"Did she see you?"

"No. She looked round, just once, but she were in a world of her own. I shouted out to her, I think. Then she jumped."

She states it simply, matter-of-fact. *She jumped.* That's all. As if it were no more nor less than stepping off a curb to cross the road.

"And?"

"And what?"

Did she scream? I think. *Did she cry out? Didn't you do anything to stop her?*

But what could she have done? Dived off the cliff herself? Sprouted wings and caught her on the way down?

"What did you do then?"

"Well, I ran, of course. There were nothing else I could do."

She blows smoke through her nose.

"I looked over the edge. I shouted, I suppose. I can't really remember."

"Did you bang on David's door? The trailer?"

"Yes," she says. "David said he'd been in bed. Reckoned I woke him up."

"Did you believe him?"

She hesitates.

"What? What is it?"

"I'm not sure. You can tell, can't you? I dunno. He was yawning and all that, but it kind of looked . . ."

"What?"

"False, I guess. It's probably nothing."

"I don't know," I say. "He knew Daisy, and Zoe, too."

"How d'you know that?"

"I just know. I think Ellie's seeing him, too."

She shakes her head. "She'd tell me. I'm sure of it."

"So what did you do then? Once David had opened the door."

"We called the police."

I watch her for a moment. Her eyes have misted, as if she's re-living it.

"Is that why people think David had something to do with it? Because he lied about being asleep?"

"I didn't tell anyone that. No point. It were just a hunch. A feeling."

"So? Why, then?"

"A few folk say they saw Daisy there."

"But she lived there. They'd had to move the trailer to his garden—"

"No. In the house. On his roof. There's a terrace, I think. And when she was asked about it she denied it. Like she'd been told to keep it quiet. So people thought he must've had something to do with her deciding to . . . y'know."

"Kill herself."

"Yes." She pauses. "Look. I wish you'd leave it. Honestly. It's not good to get too involved."

But I am. And if you only knew how much.

"It were ten years ago," she says. "It won't bring Daisy back."

I stand my ground.

"But what if whatever it was is the reason Zoe ran, too? That was only a few years ago. Two girls have gone missing from here already."

"Three," she says, her eyes narrow.

"Three, then. And it's still happening. How many more are going to disappear?"

"It's not. Still happening, I mean."

"But—"

"Look," she says. "I need to get on."

We go back, onto the landing. *That door . . .*

"What's in there?" My voice is weak and stretched. Sweat beads on my brow.

"What? Oh, that's just the bedrooms. Kitchen and stuff. Store-room, I think."

I see it, then. An open door; there are crates of bottles in there, coiled plastic tubes, packets of cable ties. A deck chair. A thin mattress on the floor.

I feel something bite into my wrist. A punch in the stomach. I double over.

"Alex?" says Monica. "What's wrong? What is it?"

No, I think. *No.*

Not here, it didn't happen here.

But maybe I'm wrong. Maybe it did.

THEN

She closes her eyes. His hands are on her, but she tries not to feel them.

There's music from downstairs. She feels it pulsing through the floor.

He says she asked for this, which means she must've.

He says her boyfriend said it's fine, which means it must be fine.

He says her boyfriend has said he doesn't mind, which means he doesn't mind.

First it was "Fancy a threesome?"

No.

Then it was "If you loved me, you'd do it."

I do.

"So do it."

Then the threesome became just two. And not with her boyfriend. For the first time, and now it's too late, she realizes that was the plan all along.

She remembers the other girls' advice. Don't cry. Don't fight back. It makes them worse. It's not so bad, if you don't think about it.

So she doesn't. She thinks of her boyfriend. He said he loved her. She knows he's been with lots of girls, but he's told her they meant nothing, she's the one he loves. So that means he must, or else why say it? And if she loves him back, like she says she does, then surely she'll do this, this one thing, this one tiny thing, for him? For them both?

After all, she owes him. She owes her boyfriend, she owes the man on top of her. She owes them both.

She hears the sound of something rip. She feels him breathing in her ear, grunting like a pig. His breath stinks. She lies as still as she can. Maybe, if she tries hard enough, she can imagine it's not happening. It's not her.

He said he loved her, and this is what you do for love. Something is running down her face. Tears, she thinks. Just tears. But at least this is the end, the last time. He's promised. Once and no more.

But this is just the beginning. She knows that already.

NOW

Monica leads the way, back downstairs. The place seems busier—several people have arrived and are sitting at the bar, and a group huddles around the entrance to the lounge—but somehow more subdued. The landlady's face is pinched with worry; everyone's is, in fact, and their voices are low. There's no frivolity in the air.

"Something's happened," says Monica as we push our way through the throng toward the bar. "I'll ask Beverly." Something stirs in my gut, something that's been dormant but is stretching to wake. Monica gets there first and speaks to the landlady in whispers. I don't want to ask the question; it's as if by doing so I'll make it real, but I have no choice.

"What's happened?"

"It's Ellie. She's disappeared."

A strange sense of something like relief washes over me. The thing I've been dreading has finally happened. "When?"

"She was supposed to meet Kat," she says. "She never turned up. And she's not at home."

"They called her?"

"Kat did. Her phone's off."

"And the police . . . ?"

"They said it's too soon."

"Too soon? They told them about Daisy? And Zoe?"

"Aye. They said she'll probably turn up, but they're sending some-one over anyway. Her father is on his way. A few folk're already talking about going out to look for her."

I feel weak; my shoulders sag. I was too late to save her. Beverly slides over the glass of whiskey I ordered earlier.

"Drink this, love."

I take a deep gulp, savoring the burn in my chest. This can't be happening. Not again. Suddenly, I want nothing more than a cigarette. I almost ask Monica for one but manage to resist. There's a commotion in the far corner, raised voices, not quite in anger but on the edge of it. One penetrates the rest.

"I don't give a fuck! I know what I saw. What we waiting for?"

"No!" comes the response, a voice I recognize. Bryan. He sounds imploring, frustrated, trying to keep control. "Guys! C'mon . . ."

Beverly shouts across the crowd. Her voice flies, silencing the rest of the pub.

"Fellas!" she says. "What's going on?"

"Well, go on, then," says someone from the depths of Bryan's huddle. A guy steps forward; it's Pete, from the arcade. The rest of the room is more or less silent.

"I were just saying," says Pete, surveying the room. "We know 'e were filming 'em. So it stands to reason. We should go up there."

I freeze. A few people glance in my direction. I know who he's talking about. I know which film.

"How d'you know it was him?"

Now Pete stares straight at me. For a second I'm not sure why, it's as if I'm missing a few frames of footage, but then he asks me what I mean and I realize it was me who'd spoken. I cough and repeat my question.

"How do you know it was David? Filming the girls?"

Another guy steps forward, from over by the door.

"I saw him."

Everyone turns to look.

"He were down the way," he says, pointing out toward the slipway. "Had some kind of camera. He were acting weird—y'know how he does. Then a bit later I saw the girls. Kat and Ellie, and he started filmin' 'em. Out o' sight, like. Up Smugglers."

He means the alleyway just beyond the pub.

"An' what were you doing there?" comes a voice from the back.

His reply is instant, and sharp. "Minding me own fuckin' business. Like you need to, eh? The point is, it were him filming 'em. Why would he do that, eh? And what with what happened with Daisy an' all, it stands to reason."

"What does?" Again people look at me. "You think he's taken her?"

"What's it to you?"

"C'mon now," says Monica. "She's on'y trying to help."

"Yeah, well no one asked 'er 'ere."

Eyes burn into me. I don't know what to say.

"He knew Zoe, too."

As soon as I've said it I know it's the wrong thing. There'll be questions; I'll have to tell them that I know she was raped by an older man, one she still called a boyfriend. A murmur ripples through the crowd.

"Shouldn't have done that," says Monica in a whisper. Not unkindly, but still it's an admonishment. The place falls silent for a moment, but a decision has been made. There's a shift toward the door.

"Come on, then," says someone near the front, a short guy with cropped ginger hair. "Let's go and sort this out."

"Wait!" says Bryan, but he's near the back and most ignore him. "Let's just think about this—" The crowd splits. About a dozen people troop out, led by the ginger guy. They seem energized by purpose; they think they know where Ellie is, they're going to get her back, and perhaps avenge Daisy and Zoe, too.

I imagine them with pitchforks. The blanket of guilt falls over me, heavy and oppressive and weirdly familiar. I did this, I think. It's my fault. I glance over to Bryan, as if he can stop them, bring them back, calm them down, but he doesn't notice. He comes over, speaks to Monica. "We'd better go," he says. "It's gonna get nasty." He turns to me. "Come on."

We reach The Rocks and begin the climb toward Bluff House. The air is charged, it's raw in my throat, but when I look over at the others they show no sign of it. Bryan forges on up the path until Bluff House is in front of us, somehow still darkly malevolent even in daylight. I take out my camera with another wave of guilt, but I remind myself it's what I do, tell myself I'm not here to make friends, I never was. The crowd has arrived ahead of us, swollen now by a few others they must've picked up on the way. Most are standing back, gossiping in urgent murmurs, but the ginger-haired guy is at David's door. He bangs on it, once, twice, then stands back, calling out as he does. "Get out here, you fucker!" he shouts, his voice raw with anger and burning with hate. I zoom in as he does. There's part of me that can't help being pleased that I'm here to film this, though I'd give even that up to bring Ellie back safe.

Bryan strides forward. "Come on now," he says, and the other guy seems to change his mind. He says something I don't quite hear, to which Bryan responds equally quietly, then steps off the porch to let Bryan knock on David's door. "David?" he says. "It's me, Bryan. Come out, mate."

Mate? I think. It sounds wrong. Still, we wait. Will he answer? A ghostly calm descends; the crowd is silent, holding its collective breath, as if waiting for a show to start. There's a movement from inside, just visible through the stained-glass window, a glimmer of light and shadow. Bryan leans in closer to the door but says nothing. I was mistaken. It was just a reflection. He's not there. A few minutes later Bryan addresses the onlookers.

"He's not answering," he says. "Let me check the back."

"We're wasting time!"

Someone else shouts out. I don't see who.

"Let him check, eh?"

It seems to placate the crowd, just a little. Bryan disappears around the back of the house and a minute passes. When he returns, he announces, "No sign."

"Like fuck," comes a voice. "He's fucking in there! Look!"

As one, we raise our heads. A definite movement this time, in the window above us. The curtains are moving, as if they've been pulled aside and left to fall back. The heat in the crowd rises and someone sends a largish rock sailing toward the house.

It's a good shot. It hits the window in which we saw movement and flies through, shattering it. There's a cheer from below; it's as if the pack has smelled first blood. I look over at Monica. She's on her phone and I'm relieved when I realize she'll be calling the police. Things are on the brink, about to boil over. It's my fault, I think again. It's all my fault. I see them smash their way through the front door and rush in; they drag him out, his nose bloodied, face already beginning to bruise. I see the house on fire, smoke rising, black and caustic.

Or maybe Ellie is in there. Maybe we're wasting time and bursting in to get her back is exactly what we should be doing. Bryan faces the crowd, his hands palm up. "Guys," he says. "Let's calm it, shall we?"

A murmured chorus of disdain.

"Just let me talk to him," says Bryan, turning back toward the house before anyone can answer. He calls out. "David! Come down. We just want to talk!"

We fall silent, but the only answer is the biting wind whistling around the house. Another voice sails over the crowd, high and piercing, as a figure approaches fast over the uneven ground. "Stop it!"

It's Kat. "Stop it!" she says again. "Leave him alone!"

Monica runs to meet her, but Kat pushes past her, determined. "*Stop it!*" She's screaming now. "She's not in there!"

The ginger guy spits. "Where is she then, eh?"

Kat stands her ground. "I don't know," she says through her tears. "But not there. He had nothing to do with it."

"You don't know that."

"I do," she says. "Leave him alone! Whatever's happened to Ellie, it's not his fault!"

The guy shakes his head and gazes down at the ground, as if making a decision. When he looks up, it's clear he wants blood now he's tasted it. He mumbles something to Kat, then turns back toward David's door. "Let's get the fucker."

Kat launches herself at him. She's taller than he is and, though nowhere near as heavy, she has the element of surprise. She knocks him off balance, almost bringing him down, but after a brief moment of confusion he recovers and sends her flying backward, to fall gasping into the mud, the remains of the melting snow. Monica rushes to help her up. "Pig," she says, but the guy ignores her, returning instead to his work on David's door. A siren pierces the silence. Beneath us, on the other side of the outcrop, in the tiny turning circle where the road peters out into nothing, there's the flash of blue and red. A police car pulls up. I glimpse two or three uniformed figures, the flicker of yellow, a fluorescent Day-Glo vest. The officers approach on foot, followed by a few more villagers. As they get closer, I see Gavin among them and wonder whether he called them, how he'd heard, how deep exactly he is in this. When he arrives, he hesitates, as if not sure what to do.

"You okay?"

I tell him I'm fine and we look back at the house. The officers seem to have separated. One is knocking on the door, shouting through the letterbox, while the other is heading round toward the back of the house.

"Can I see you later?" he says, his hand brushing against mine.

"Yes," I say.

"Some of them are talking about going out, searching for Ellie."

"Good," I say, looking up at him. "We should help."

He says nothing. David emerges from Bluff House, flanked by officers. The volume of the crowd swells as he's marched past us. He seems terrified; his eyes are fixed on the ground. Someone shouts at him—*Pedo*, it sounds like—and he flinches. The officer on his right stares them down.

"We'll have less of that," he says, tightening his grip on David's arm. "And you lot had better make yourself scarce."

"What's 'e done, then?" comes a voice. "Where's the girl?"

The officer responds once more, still without breaking stride. "He's done nothing, far as we know."

"Why've you arrested 'im, then?"

There's no answer, and I realize he's not under arrest but being protected. There are more calls, and finally the officer responds.

"Look, we still don't know where Ellie is. So you lot'd be better off trying to find her than standing here causing trouble. Okay?"

There's a mumbling in the crowd. A few look back toward Bluff House, but Bryan's gone inside and the door is closed. I can't see Monica anywhere.

"Is that it?" comes a voice. "That's all you're going to do?"

The officer on David's left responds. "Someone's on their way," she says. "Now, get lost."

I turn to Gavin. "Let's get away from here."

33

We decide to walk. The tide is out. Before we even reach the slipway we hear laughter, shouting voices, and the hard clink of bottles. Music floats over, surfing on the crash of the ocean, *thump-thump-thump*. A little way along the beach, near one of the groynes, five or six boys sit bunched around a fire, smoking and drinking. There's a joint being passed round, from what I can see. A bottle of vodka.

"Come on," I say to Gavin.

We skirt the teenagers, keeping away from the water, walking next to the scrub in the shadow of the cliff.

"What d'you think has happened to Ellie?"

He swallows. "I don't know."

"It's happening again, isn't it?"

He gazes at the distant clouds. "Who knows? Maybe she just lost track of the time. It hasn't been *that* long."

We stop walking.

"You really think that?"

He shakes his head. "No. I suppose not."

I think of what I saw upstairs in the pub. Of what Zoe's parents told me.

"The girls. I think they're being abused."

It's the first time I've used the word since coming back. It sticks to my tongue. Gavin folds his arms and I can't tell whether it's because he doesn't want to believe it or because he doesn't want to admit he's thought the same.

"No—" he begins, but I interrupt.

"You know Zoe was pregnant?"

His body seems to slump. "Who told you that?"

"Her parents. Well, her mother."

He stares out over the water. "You went to see them? When?"

"A few days ago. But—"

"You didn't tell me."

He's staring at me. I regard him for a moment. Is this anger? Annoyance?

"No," I say. "I didn't."

"Why not?"

A weight settles on my chest. I'm in trouble, I'm going to be punished. I've opened my big mouth when I should've kept it shut.

Fuck that. I stare straight at him.

"Since when do I have to tell you everything I do?"

He stares down at the ground. I wonder if I've handled it all wrong, whether he'll turn on his heel now and walk away. But when he raises his head he attempts a smile.

"I'm sorry. I just . . . I could've come with you." He hesitates, and we carry on walking. "What else did they say?"

I don't feel inclined to share everything, not now, so I just say, "Not much."

"Who was the father?"

"They didn't know. But her mother thought she had a boyfriend, an older man, out here in Blackwood Bay. There was an uncle she was close to, but they didn't think he had anything to do with it."

"They're sure?"

"They said not." I pause. "They're not convinced Daisy killed herself, either."

"So maybe it is all linked?"

I nod. "We need to find Ellie."

Gavin glances back toward the group of boys at their campfire.

"Is it worth asking them?"

"Can't hurt."

We go over. My camera is hanging round my neck and I start re-cording as we draw near.

"Excuse me," I say. The boys look up. One tries to hide the joint in his cupped hand, but the smell is pungent and unmistakable.

"What?"

It's the boy from the café, the one who'd been with Ellie and Kat. He somehow manages to look both aggressive and utterly uninter-ested in anything I have to say.

"I was wondering. You know Ellie?"

"What's it to you?"

"You know where she is?"

"No idea, sweetheart."

I want to react, to tell him he has no right to call me that, that unless he watches it I'll teach him a lesson, but I let it go. There are times to fight that battle, and this isn't one of them.

"You know she's disappeared?"

"Yeah."

"But you don't know where she went?"

"No. I dunno where Ellie is. Okay? Nothin' to do wi' me."

There's no response, just the noise of the speaker they have hooked up to one of their phones, the music they haven't bothered to turn down. He stares at me defiantly, so I turn my attention to the others.

"How about you lot? No idea either, I suppose?"

A couple of them shift uneasily. The one with the joint glances over, first at his friends, then at Gavin, then finally at me.

"It'll be him, won't it? That pervy cunt." He waves his cupped hand in the direction of Bluff House, as if anyone were in any doubt to whom he was referring. I glance up, and for a moment I think I see someone there, a lone figure standing right on the edge of the cliff, watching us. Or preparing to jump.

I look away. "He'll have taken her," says the boy. "Like he took the others."

I stare at him. He's a spotty kid. He knows nothing.

"What makes you so sure?"

He laughs. "Everyone knows. Just no one'll say it, like."

I look back at The Rocks, but there's no one there.

"Come on," says Gavin. "We should go."

We step onto the slipway. The clouds are thick; it's getting dark. Ellie's out there, somewhere. Perhaps alone, trying to escape. That is, if she's lucky.

"We need to find her," I say to Gavin, but before he can answer his phone rings.

"It's Bryan," he says when he's finished the call. "They need the keys to the village hall. The police. They've arrived."

When we get there, there's a group waiting outside the front door. Monica's there, and Bryan, too. With him stands a woman I don't recognize, plus two police officers in uniforms. The last thing I wanted, but here they are.

"Sorry," says Bryan as we approach. "I didn't have my keys." The woman with him holds out her hand. She's wearing a long black jacket, trousers, boots. Her face is pinched and severe; I imagine she's not someone who enjoys, or is used to, being kept waiting.

"Detective Superintendent Butler," she says as Gavin shakes her hand. "Heidi. Pleased to meet you." She turns to me. "And you are?"

"Alex Young," I say. "I don't live here. I'm here . . ." I hesitate, and she cocks her head. "Working."

"Working? As?"

"I'm making a film."

She glances briefly from me to Gavin. "Right. Shall we?"

Gavin unlocks the door and we troop in. I look at Butler from behind. She's compact, efficient. She exudes confidence, and it's obvious Bryan at least is already under her spell. He's following her like a hungry puppy. She scans the room, then speaks to one of the officers.

"Where's the girl?"

At first I think she means Ellie, then realize she's referring to Kat.

"On her way. The father, too."

"Right." She shakes her head. "So does anyone know anything?"

The officer fumbles with his notebook, and she sighs then looks round the room.

"Anyone?"

Monica steps forward. "Kat," she begins hesitantly, "that's Ellie's friend, said they'd arranged to meet, but Ellie didn't turn up, and when—"

"When was this?"

Monica glances at the clock at the end of the hall. "Almost three hours ago, now."

"Meet where?"

"The bandstand, I think."

"What for?"

No one answers. No one knows. Hanging around, I suppose. Smoking a joint. Doing nothing and everything at the same time, in that way that teenagers have.

"No sightings?" says Butler.

The officer to her right answers. "No."

"No witnesses to an abduction?" He shakes his head. "She just didn't turn up to meet her friend, and switched her phone off?"

"Yes," he says. "But—"

"She's a teenage girl."

"I know—"

"They do that all the time?"

"—but this place," he continues. "It's not the first time it's happened here. We might need a Child Rescue Alert."

She scans the room. "Tell me."

She must be new to the area. Monica steps forward, and Bryan. They're both clearly nervous.

"Ten years ago," says Monica. "A girl disappeared. Sadie Davies."

I look down at the floor. I can't help it. I'm like a toddler who's been found out.

"Ten years. She didn't turn up?"

The officer shakes his head. "I don't think so."

"You don't *think* so?"

"She sort of did," says Bryan. "Her mother was told she'd been found. In London. But she didn't want to come back."

"Right," says Butler. "So we have one girl who ran away to London. Ten years ago."

Gavin steps forward. "There's someone else. Zoe Pearson. She ran, too. About three and a half years ago. And she was never found."

And Daisy, I think. *And Daisy*, but I say nothing. Officially, she's dead. Officially, it was suicide.

Butler's head cocks.

"OK. Anything else?"

"Zoe . . ." He glances at me. "She was pregnant."

Both Monica and Bryan look over.

"How old was she?"

"Fourteen."

She turns to her officer. "It's a bit early for a full CRA," she says. "At least until we've talked to the friend and the parents. But start the ball rolling, just in case. Let's try and get hold of the girl's computer, and track her phone, if we can. Are people out looking for her?"

Monica answers. "A few."

"Good. Someone should be coordinating that."

It looks as though Gavin is about to volunteer, but then Bryan steps up, barely disguising his eagerness. "I can. We can do it from the pub."

"Or here?" says Gavin.

"The pub is better," says Monica. "More people down there than up here this time of year."

Butler looks at the three of us, waiting for us to decide. After a moment, Gavin backs down.

"Right," she says. "That's settled." She turns to her officers. "Let's set up base here. Now. Where the hell is the father? Are they crawling here?"

34

I get up quietly, before dawn, leaving Gavin snoring gently. We were out until late last night, searching the cliffs, looking for clues. When we returned, empty-handed, to The Ship, we found we weren't alone. Maps had been spread on the table, sectioned off with marker; areas allocated to different groups. No one had found anything; she's vanished without sight. Her parents told Butler that it was out of character, Kat said Ellie had never failed to turn up without letting her know, and finally, late last night, an alert was issued.

In the kitchen I pour myself a glass of water before texting Monica to ask for news. I sit at the table to wait for her reply, watching the sky. I think of Ellie, as if by doing so I can somehow bring her back, but when it comes Monica's reply is brief. *Nothing yet. People are going back out soon. I'll let you know.*

No body, at least. No clothes washed up on a distant beach. Or none that have been found yet. I put down my glass. I need to move.

I take my tripod and walk on to The Rocks, past Bluff House. I angle my camera back toward the cliff and look through the viewfinder. Crag Head is just visible out to the right, at the very edge of the frame. If I pan left, Malby shimmers in the distance. I focus instead on Bluff House itself and the edge of the cliff, just a few yards from the front door. Five steps down to the path, a few more past it and to the edge. Then there's nothing but the sea, black as tar, thrashing with secrets, with bodies, with death.

Is this the view that Monica saw that night? Is Ellie down there, too? I press *Record*, then hesitate for a moment before stepping away from the camera and walking into shot. One step, two, three. I keep my head down, my arms wrapped tight around my body. I walk up to Bluff House. I try to imagine I'm Daisy. I begin to walk toward the cliff—four steps, five—farther and farther, toward the vertiginous drop, toward endless death. But why? Why am I here? What happened to me? Who is making me do this? A boy in a leather jacket who won't tell me he loves me? A friend who let me down? A man who took advantage?

Six, seven. But Monica saw her. And there was a note. Eight. Nine. The note that Daisy's own mother told me means nothing. Ten, eleven, twelve, and I'm over the shingle path, on the other side, the springing grass.

But how can it mean nothing? Is she telling me Daisy never wrote it? But it was she who identified it, she who told the police it was her daughter's handwriting. Thirteen, fourteen, fifteen.

Why would she do that, if it wasn't true?

Sixteen. I'm there now. I can look straight down, over the edge. Another step and I'd be on unstable ground. Tufts of wet grass, loose rocks, hard mud. If it weren't for the thaw, it'd be icy here, another hazard, another thing to send me tumbling. I want to turn and run, but I don't. I peer over, into the waves below. It's like looking backward, through the white crests of the present, and down into the blackness of the past. The truth hangs just out of reach. It hovers in the air; I can almost touch it. If only I could go forward, one more step, or two. Then I'd know, I'd know how she felt, I'd know what happened. I'm almost tempted to, for a moment. Almost.

"Alex!"

The voice is distant, harsh, the name it's calling alien. It takes me a second to understand it's mine and another before I look up to see who's come after me. Farther along the path toward the village a figure has emerged, still too far away to be recognizable but running toward me.

"Alex!" he shouts again. "Stop!"

Stop, I think. *Stop*. I look into the water. I imagine Monica calling out to Daisy. Why didn't she listen?

"Don't!"

I step backward. Arms go around me, I'm gripped, lifted, and for a moment I think whoever it is might be about to push me forward, to throw me in. It's Gavin, I think, come after me. He was lying. He's the one who took Ellie, after all.

Or David, back from the station, knowing I'm the one who pointed the finger and wanting revenge. I prepare myself to fall, but I'm spun round until I'm facing the house. Only then does whoever it is holding me let me go.

It's Bryan. His face is red; his spittle lands on my face and lips. "What on earth are you doing?"

He holds me at arm's length. His nostrils are flared, his voice quivers: he looks terrified.

Or angry. For a second I think he's about to shake me, to draw back his fist and slap me. I resist the urge to fight, to lash out, dig in, go for the eyes; a knee in the balls, if nothing else. It's a primal response, instinctive. I don't know where it comes from.

"Nothing," I gasp, and his hands fall limply to his sides. For a brief, shocking, moment I want them round me again.

"You scared me! I thought . . ."

I look at him. It's just Bryan, anxious and worried. I know what he thought. I know what it looked like. "I was just looking." I point out the camera. "Filming . . . why?"

"I need to speak to you."

"What about? Oh, God. Is it Ellie? Has she—"

"No," he says. "No. She's still missing." He glances up at the windows of Bluff House. "Look. It's . . . can we go somewhere else?"

"How did you find me?"

"I went to Monica's place. I spoke to Gavin. He said you'd be here." He coughs awkwardly and puts his hand out once more. It rests on my arm. Solicitous this time, but still I find myself resisting. I wonder if it's because he wants to get me away from the edge of the cliff, if he wonders what I might do.

"Are you coming? We can talk about it on the way back down."

"No!" I say again. "Tell me what's happened!"

He lowers his voice, even though we're alone. He sounds nervous, and I try to imagine what he's scared of.

"I've had a postcard," he says.

A nervous excitement judders through me.

"A postcard? From who?"

"David."

A weird stillness descends. Even the wind seems to have died away. I was right, then. It was David who sent the card to Dan, luring me up here. But why?

"David? What did it say?"

"Look."

He fumbles in the pocket of his jacket and fishes it out.

"Here. It was put through my front door."

My hands shake as I take it. On one side is a photo of the lighthouse on Crag Head.

"But he's still at the station. Isn't he?"

"They let him go. I don't know where he is. Read the card."

I turn it over. *I've got something that will prove everything*, it says. *She can have it. Tell her to meet me tonight. 8.00. Alone. Don't tell anyone else. Please. I'm sorry.*

"Have you shown the police? That Butler woman?"

"Not yet."

"Why not?"

"I still . . . I don't believe David's involved—"

"But this card! It sounds like he wants to confess."

He glances up toward the clouds. "If he has got Ellie, then she's probably fine. Let's just see what he's got to say."

"But—"

"If he knows we've involved Butler, he'll run. Or worse."

I remember what he told me about David's breakdown. Maybe he's right.

"You're sure it's even from him?"

"It's his writing."

I look again. The letters are small and neatly formed. It doesn't match the card sent to Dan.

"Meet him where?" I look up at Bluff House. "Here?"

"No," says Bryan. "I reckon he's too scared to come back here, after what happened."

"Where, then?" I flip the card over. "The lighthouse?"

"I suppose."

Apprehension envelops me. What does David have for me, and what will it prove?

"Will you come with me?"

"He says to come alone."

No.

I try again—"He sent you the card. He knows you know"—and he nods reluctantly.

I have to go, for Ellie, but David knows the truth about me, something I don't know myself, and I'm not sure I can hear it.

But I've been through this before, I remind myself. I woke up in Deal, not knowing why I ran. I was in the hospital, then they transferred me to the memory clinic, to Dr. Olsen. I became Alex there, found Alice in the squat behind Victoria and, gradually, I pieced it all together. Or some of it, at least.

That's why I went back there, I suppose, why I made *Black Winter.*

And I suppose that's why I'm here, too. To discover the truth. About then, and about now.

THEN

*I*t was at a party in the squat, a few weeks after I moved in. I was exhausted; I felt constantly bloated, yet I couldn't stop eating. That afternoon, one of the others—a girl who called herself Krystal-with-a-K—had asked me whether I was eating for two. I'd shaken my head but couldn't be sure; my periods had become so irregular that being late was something I'd long since stopped worrying about. I'd spent the rest of the afternoon googling signs of pregnancy, and by the time Dev's mates arrived with vodka, beer, and who-knows-what-else I felt anxious and belligerent.

Gee—whose real name was Glenn—cornered me in the bathroom. "Sadie!" he said, almost as if he was surprised to see me. He was wasted, his words slurred, his movements sluggish. He began to sing—"Sadie, Sadie, Give me your answer do . . ."—then leaned in for a kiss. His mouth looked like a wound and I told him I'd rather die. He looked like I'd slapped him.

"You think you're better than me, is that it?" he said. "When you're just a fat slut, giving it away to everyone."

He put his hand on my crotch then, and tried to kiss me. I don't know what happened next. I remember I saw our reflection in the mirror above the sink and recognized neither of us. It felt like I was watching through a camera, a film unspooling on the screen with actors playing out roles. There was an empty wine bottle on the windowsill behind the toilet and, before I knew it, it was in my hand, then a moment later Gee was on the floor, blood running down his face and neck, pooling beneath him. I knelt down, but he wasn't moving.

I ran out. I found Dev and told him. "I've killed Gee."

When we went back to look, Alice was already kneeling next to Gee's prostrate body, a towel pressed to the wound on his head. "It's not as bad as it looks," she said, and Gee's eyes opened, his ugly mouth moving.

"I'll kill that bitch."

Alice turned to Dev. "Get her out of here."

I was stuck, watching the whole thing as if it were on a screen and had nothing to do with me. Dev grabbed me and steered me out through the handful of people crowded in the corridor. At the front door he told me to wait in the park opposite. "I'll come and find you."

I did as he'd asked. An hour or so later, he appeared and handed me a mobile phone.

"Take this."

"What is it?"

"One of my spares," he said. "You have to go."

"But my stuff."

"What stuff?" He sighed. "Look, Gee isn't someone to mess with. You're gonna have to lie low. I've put my number in the phone. Call me. But leave it a few weeks, okay? He'll ask me where you are and it's better I don't know."

I switched the phone on.

"What's the code?"

"Thirteen seventeen," he said, then he kissed me. "I need to go."

I watched him leave, then turned back to face the night.

NOW

I press *Play*.

The film fades in. A cellar; the damp walls ooze and shine. There's a bright light attached to the camera, harsh and unforgiving, and the shadows have hard, precise edges. Without warning, we move back and the angle widens, then there's a violent sweep to the right and a face appears.

It's Daisy. She's snot-nosed and crying, her hair tangled, her eyes bloodshot. *Help me*, she says. *Help me, please.* Over and over she says it, but then the film changes. It cuts suddenly, smashes through black before another image appears. We're outside, the camera is unsteady, the same bright light flashes on the ground, dead leaves and frost, the starry sky, booted feet, trudging at first, but then we pick up the pace until we're running, sprinting toward a distant yew. Underneath it there's a pile of stones. The camera flashes on dead flowers and a woman kneeling over the grave; she's tipping forward, her hands are in the soil, her forehead almost touching the ground. Her body shudders, as if she's crying. We approach and, finally, she hears us. She lifts her head. *Help me*, she says. She sounds relieved. *You're here!* She begins to dig frantically at the earth. *We have to get her out*, she says. *Help me. Help me, please.*

We step forward. She's uncovered a body in the soil, a face buried a few inches deep. It snaps into focus, bright in the circle of light. It's me.

A second after that is when I wake.

Bryan is already waiting when I reach the car park at the top of Slate Road, lounging on the wall by the entrance. He greets me cheerily, but worry is etched on his face. "We'll be early," he says as he gets into the car.

"Good. You'll need to direct me," I say as I buckle up. I'm lying. I know the way, but I don't want him realizing that. I pull out of the car park.

"Left at the top," he says.

"Still no sign of Ellie?"

He shakes his head. We were both out all afternoon, though not to-gether. That's why I fell asleep, I suppose. I filmed some of it, too. Dis-creetly. The guys in the pub, allocating areas to be scoured. Crowds of villagers combing the cliffs, calling her name. I spotted Liz among the searchers, and Monica and Sophie, too.

It doesn't take long to reach the lighthouse and I pull off onto an uneven gravel track. It's desolate, no sign of David's car, and when I switch off the engine the place falls into total blackness, save for the regular flash from the lamp above.

"Have you got a torch?"

"I'll use my phone," I say. Silence wraps itself around us. "You trust him? He won't try to hurt me?" I go on, though it's not the thought of physical distress that swells in the pit of my stomach.

Bryan smiles reassuringly. "You'll be fine."

I find the gravel path that climbs up toward the lighthouse. To the right, there's a low, squat building, and when I draw near I see it was once the visitors' center. It has a wooden terrace on three sides, rotten now, and the windows are all either broken or boarded up. Above the door the remains of a painted sign spell out the word *Head*. I look back. Bryan is sitting in the car, still in darkness.

I climb farther. The lighthouse is painted white, a few abandoned buildings dotted at its base. The tower isn't tall but still inspires awe, standing on the edge of the cliff, solemn and brightly majestic.

I lift my camera and film before letting it fall around my neck, still recording. I reach the top of the path, but there's no one here. I choose a low wall from where I'll get a good view of anyone arriving and sit down.

I switch off my torch and wait for my eyes to adjust. Everything is still, then I hear the machinery behind me, the slow, rhythmic hum of the lenses as they turn. A gull soars overhead, catching the light, its loud shriek mocking.

This is your fault, it seems to say. *All of it.*

My fault. My mind turns instantly to what happened back then, to what I did to Gee, the night of the party. But I wrench my thoughts away and gaze out to sea. The wind bites, my hands turn red and I shove them deep in my pockets. Eight thirty creeps toward eight forty-five and still there's no sign of David. I realize I'd half expected him to turn up with Ellie, to say sorry as he handed her back before skulking back to Bluff House. My feet are numb, and when it's almost nine o'clock I'm about to give up when a figure appears through the dark.

"I was worried."

I shine my torch on Bryan's concerned face and stand, both relieved and disappointed.

"He didn't show."

His face falls. "Let's go back."

"No," I say. "Let's take a look around."

We circle the outhouses, intending to check each one, but when we reach the second and I see its door is ajar I know something is wrong.

Bryan's right behind me. "What is it?" he says, and I tell him I don't know. Inside, I see the room contains nothing but a few shelves and steps that lead down into the darkness.

"Must be some sort of storeroom," says Bryan. He sounds as scared as I feel. "Come on. Let's go."

"No," I say. I'm going in."

He follows. The walls are damp, the brick stairs treacherous. I step cautiously down, filming as I go, my breathing loud in my ears. At the bottom I see nothing but a pool of blackness. "Ellie?" I say quietly, but the only response is the echo of my voice, then Bryan from the steps behind: "Anything?"

I raise the beam of my torch. The dust motes dance like stars. It's a small cellar; there are barrels in the corner, empty paint cans, a pile of wood stacked inelegantly against the wall. I sweep the room, and then something lying on the floor catches my eye. One of David's ugly shoes.

"Bryan?" I say, my voice breaking. "Look."

We find him behind the stack of barrels, slumped in a corner, his head lying awkwardly to one side. At first I think he's dead, but his chest rises and falls gently and when I force myself to touch his hand it's warm.

Bryan kneels next to me. "Any sign of Ellie?"

I shake my head. There's something next to David, though, half covered by his leg. An empty brown bottle.

"We need to call an ambulance," I say. "He's taken an overdose."

37

*B*ryan returns to the car park to wait while I stay with David. I touch his hand but feel nothing. No crackle of electricity, no charge of recognition. Just weary flesh.

"Where is she?" I whisper, but of course there's no reply. I unzip his jacket and feel for his heart. *Don't die*, I think. *Don't die. Tell me what you know.*

It's beating steadily, but the gap between each pulse is a fraction too long. It feels like it's slowing. In the distance, over the roar of the sea, I hear sirens. I withdraw my hand and close his jacket. What was he going to give me? In the pocket I feel the weight of his wallet.

What harm can it do? I take it out and examine it in the dim light from my phone. It's purple nylon, fastened with tattered Velcro. It weighs almost nothing. I tear it open and the rip echoes in the dark chamber. Inside, there are a few notes, tens and fives plus a solitary twenty, and a credit card. There's a supermarket loyalty card, and one from the chemist. In the other compartment, behind clear plastic, there's a key, and also a photograph of a girl.

My heart thuds as I take it out. It's Zoe; I recognize her instantly. She's sitting at a table in a fast-food restaurant, smiling happily. It seems to be a birthday party; there are meals on the table in front of her, eager hands reaching for the food. I bring the picture close to the light. *Where are you?* I think. *Why did you run? Tell me.*

Footsteps on the stairs. I don't think. I pocket the photograph and the key, then replace the wallet. A moment later Bryan arrives, the paramedics behind him with powerful torches. "We'll take over, miss," they say.

"So what do we do now?" I ask Bryan once we're back in the car. He's spoken to the police, he says, and they'll want a statement, but for the moment we can go. "You think David tried to kill himself because he's done something to Ellie?"

He sighs and the air crackles. "I don't want to think that," he says. "But . . . who knows? Maybe he did do something and the guilt was more than he could cope with."

It doesn't sound right to me.

"But why did he send the postcard? What was he going to give me? Was it just so that I'd find him?"

I can't say what's really on my mind. *Did he never intend to tell me about Daisy, about me?*

I pull myself back. "Where will they take him?"

"St. Mary's, I expect."

I start the car. Zoe's picture burns a hole in my pocket. "Maybe he'll be okay. Maybe he'll wake up and tell us what he knows."

Bryan nods. "So what now?"

There's something about the way he says it, as if it's an invitation. But when I look over, he's just sitting, his expression drawn. I must've been imagining it.

I press the accelerator. "Let's carry on looking for Ellie. Back to The Ship?"

• • •

They're playing music now, but at a lower volume than usual. The atmosphere is heavy with hushed conversation and things left unspoken. Several people look up as we enter, nodding at Bryan in greeting or giving a muted wave. I feel self-conscious, arriving with this man. I wonder how it appears, what people will be all too quick to assume. I wonder what Gavin might hear and whether I'm right to even care.

We go through to the bar. A couple of guys are standing over the maps that are fanned across the table. Others must still be out searching.

"I'll get the drinks," I say, and Bryan heads over to talk to a couple of the men. When I return, I hand him his pint and he takes a hefty swig.

I lower my voice. "Have you told them about David?"

He nods. "But something's happened. According to the Butler woman, someone phoned in, said they saw a girl being driven away, said it looked like a taxi." He pauses. "I need a cigarette," he says. "Coming?"

I nod and we go outside. We step down to the alley round the side of the pub. He offers me his pack and, without thought, I take one. He's lit both mine and his own before I fully realize what I'm doing. I take a tentative drag, my first in who knows how long, and notice I'm holding the cigarette between my ring and my middle finger; someone told me the nicotine stains are less visible that way. We smoke in silence for a minute or two, then I see he's looking at my hand. He coughs self-consciously.

"You're not married," he says. It sounds more like a statement than a question.

"No."

"Are you seeing Gavin?"

My head spins from the nicotine but still I take another drag. Why's he asking? Does he think I've led him on?

No, I tell myself. Don't be ridiculous. I face him.

"Why?"

He stares down. "I just . . . wondered, I suppose."

We fall silent. From above us comes the buzz of the pub, still sub-dued. The streetlights cast their faint glow on Slate Road. The moon hangs low over the water. For a moment I feel certain he's about to say something, to make a declaration, and hope desperately that he won't. He grinds out his cigarette beneath his boot, as if in prepara-tion, then sighs. But all he says is, "I'm going back in. Same again?"

I look round, trying not to show the relief I'm feeling. "Yes," I say. "Thanks."

He climbs the steps back into the pub. Nausea stirs in my gut as I put out my cigarette and lean back against the wall. I breathe in deep. Suddenly, I want to see Gavin; I wish he was here. I'm about to go back inside to tell Bryan not to worry about the drink when I hear a voice.

"I want to speak to you."

My heart bangs like a door slamming in the wind. I spin round. Kat is standing right in front of me.

"You went to see him."

She sounds wretched. Angry.

"Who?" I say uselessly.

"David."

"David?" She must've seen me, or overheard Bryan telling the others in the pub. "No, I just—"

"What did you say to him?"

"Nothing, I just—"

"You must've said something. You must've."

She's crying. I move toward her, but slowly, as if she might bolt at any moment. Even in the dim light I can see what her makeup is not quite covering. A bruise pulses on her face, purple and blue and black.

"Did he do that?"

"What?"

"Who hurt you? David? Was it him?"

Her laughter bites. "Don't be stupid. David? He wouldn't. You don't know anything."

"Did he take Ellie?"

"Of course he didn't. He'd never."

"Who did, then?"

She falls silent, and I realize she's terrified. I put my hand out and touch her arm.

"Daisy," I say softly. She yanks her arm free, and a second later I understand what I've done.

"I mean Kat. Sorry, I—"

"What did you call me?" she says, but she doesn't give me a chance to explain. "It's true," she goes on. "It is all about her. You're crazy. It's your fault David did what he did."

She shakes her head, as if she's disappointed in me, then turns to leave.

"Kat!" I say, but she ignores me.

"Talk to me!"

Now, finally, she looks round. "If he dies," she hisses, "it's your fault. You know that? And whatever happens to Ellie. That, too. It'll all be your fault."

38

I'm shaking as I go back inside. Monica has arrived, and she nods in my direction, but I barely respond. My mind is fizzing. When I reach the bar, Bryan and the others are handing out torches, checking they work. Their tone is hushed; there's an atmosphere of subdued camaraderie. A uniformed officer in a hi-vis jacket stands in the corner, chatting to one of the locals. When I go over to Bryan, he hands me my drink and asks what's wrong.

"Nothing," I say. I don't want to tell him about Kat, what she's accused me of.

"You're sure?"

I nod, then sip my wine. It's corked, it tastes of damp cardboard, but I say nothing and put it back on the table. I feel trapped. I'm about to tell him I'd like to join in the search when there's a sudden increase in volume from the rest of the pub, a gasp from over by the door, then a general commotion. I look across to see what's going on, but Bryan is already on his feet.

"Jesus!"

I stand up. There's a figure by the door; she's being embraced, welcomed. I can't see her face, but there's a shock of red hair and instinctively I know who it is.

"Is that her?"

Bryan looks over. "Fuck," he says. "I think it is!"

I follow him over. Ellie is soaked, shivering. She's wearing a pair of jeans and a T-shirt, trainers with a pink flash, but her clothes are encrusted with mud, her shoes wrecked. I switch on my camera. It feels wrong; I hope nobody has noticed, but so what if they have? Things are spiraling for me, I feel I'm losing control, but the documentary is one thing I can hold onto.

"Ellie!" says the woman holding her. "Ellie, love! Where've you been?"

The girl raises her head. It's as if she doesn't understand the question, but then she mumbles something.

"What?" says the woman. "Speak up, love." Then, over her shoulder, "Phone her parents, for God's sake!"

The officer talks urgently into his radio. "No," says Ellie, but her voice is weak even on that single word. Her legs buckle beneath her, as if saying it has taken all her remaining energy. "Where is he?"

"Who? Where's who, love?"

Her eyes dart around the room; mine, too. Kat is nowhere to be seen.

"David," says Ellie.

The volume in the crowd rises a notch.

"Where is he?" she says, frantically. Bryan steps forward, suddenly assertive. "Stop crowding the poor girl," he says, then, "Ellie? You're freezing. We need to get you warm. Then you can tell us what's happened. Okay?"

She looks up at him but just says, "I want to see him."

Bryan glances around, catches Monica's eye. "Has anyone got any clothes she can change into?"

Monica steps up. She slips an arm around the girl.

"I do. I can take her to mine. That okay, Ellie?"

The girl nods, though despite the warm embrace she still seems petrified. The officer looks uncertain but nods his assent.

"C'mon," says Monica softly.

I follow them out and jog a few steps to catch up. "Monica!"

She waits for me.

"Let me help."

She doesn't protest. Together, we take her weight, such as it is. I can feel Ellie's bones through her clothes; her skin is cold and clammy; it's like touching someone already dead.

"There you go," I say, and though it's clear it's effortful she responds with a mumbled "Thanks." I want to ask her where she's been, how far she's had to walk, but realize it would be better to get her into the warmth of the cottage first.

We reach Hope Lane and Monica opens her door. Her living room is a mirror image of the one next door. In the far corner a pile of boxes sits, stacked three or four high, and the coffee table sags under the weight of books and leaflets and old receipts, held in place by a variety of paperweights, a stapler, and what appears to be a rock from the garden. On the floor next to the sofa sits a plate, encrusted with the remains of what I'm guessing was breakfast, next to a mug and an overflowing ashtray.

"Sit yourself down, love," says Monica, and Ellie does as she's told. Monica lights the fire. "You want a drink? Hot chocolate?" Ellie says nothing. "I'll go and find you something warm to wear first." She looks over to me. "Stay with her?"

I nod and sit on the sofa next to the girl as Monica goes upstairs.

She's shivering, and I put my arms round her. She tenses beneath my touch.

"It's okay," I say gently. "I'm not going to hurt you."

She seems to relax at that, though still she stares at the carpet. I wait for a moment, then say, "Where were you?"

She shrugs.

"You can talk to me," I say. "I won't tell. I promise."

"I went to David's."

"Was he the one who took you in the car?"

She shakes her head. Of course not. Why would she go to his house, ask to see him, if he's the one who hurt her?

"Someone else?" I say.

Nothing, though somehow I know her silence means yes.

"Who?"

"No one."

"Where did they take you?"

Again, nothing. But I feel her tense, even through her wet clothes.

"How did you get back?"

"Walked."

"Was it far?"

Her chin dips slightly.

"What direction?"

"The moor," she says, and I think of the yew tree.

"Where on the moor?"

"I don't know."

She's walked all this way. It seems impossible, yet the state of her clothes suggests it's true.

"You want something to eat?"

"Please."

I stand, but then Monica comes down the stairs with a pile of clothes. "Can you get these on her?"

I help Ellie peel off her damp T-shirt. She winces as I do. There's a bruise across her back, another on the inside of her upper arm, and when I help her take down her jeans I see her legs are in the same state.

I know the wrong question now will make her clam up completely so I keep quiet. When she's dressed, and though she hasn't asked, I tell her her parents are on their way. There's no response.

Monica returns from the kitchen with hot chocolate and a plate of jam sandwiches. "There we are," she says. "Tuck in."

Ellie eats slowly and in silence, nibbling at the bread, forcing it down as though swallowing it dry. She blows on her drink and sips at that, too. It's as if she's embarrassed to be seen eating, as if consumption is shameful. When she's done, she says she's tired. Monica takes her upstairs to sleep while we wait for her parents to get here.

"She's in trouble," I say, once she's returned. "She's bruised. She's scared. She's protecting someone."

"David."

"She says it's not him."

I take the glass of wine she's poured without asking. "There is something, though."

"What?"

I take out the photograph. "I found this. In David's wallet."

She examines it for a moment. "It's Zoe."

I nod.

"But why would he have that? Unless he was involved?"

"I don't know. I just . . . Kat says he isn't. And Ellie didn't seem scared of him."

"So? Who took her, then?"

"I don't know. Do you?"

She seems momentarily offended. "What makes you say that?"

"Nothing. It's just . . . you've lived here all your life. You know more of what's going on. Who everyone is." Monica looks skeptical. "More than me, anyway." I hesitate. "Someone drove her out to the moor and left her to find her own way back."

"But why?"

I remember the stories Alice used to tell me. "Punishment? To teach her a lesson. And it worked. She's terrified."

Monica closes her eyes. By the time she opens them a decision has been made.

"I need to show you something."

"What?"

She goes over to the table next to the sofa and grabs a sheet of paper. She hands it to me and I unfold it. It's a handwritten note; the words are tiny, meandering, as if it'd been written in a hurry.

"Read it."

I'm sorry, it begins. *For what I did. I killed her. I killed them both. It's my fault. I never meant to, but I didn't have a choice. I loved them. I know it was wrong, but I couldn't help it. I persuaded Daisy to jump when she threatened to tell on me after what I did to Sadie. I killed her. I buried her on the moor. And then Zoe ran away. I'm sorry. I'm so, so sorry. Please forgive me.*

There's a signature, scrawled at the bottom. *David.*

I hold the note steady in my hand. I read it again, then look up. *It's wrong*, I want to say. *Fake.* He can't have written this. Sadie isn't dead.

But how can I? She'd ask me how I know.

"Why did he give this to you?" I say instead.

She looks me straight in the eye. She can hear the doubt in my voice. It occurs to me that she'll confess, admit he never wrote it, that she did. It's as if she'll tell me why, why she wants him to take the blame for Sadie's death, for something that never happened, and for Daisy's, too, something that did.

I will her to be honest. To tell me who she's covering for, who really wrote the note. To reveal who hurt me, who really killed Daisy.

But she doesn't.

"I don't know. It was put through my letterbox, this afternoon."

I say nothing. Another thought comes. If David's note is fake, then maybe his attempted suicide is, too. Maybe it was attempted murder.

"Will you take it to the police?"

She hesitates. "Should I?"

I'm about to say yes, she should. I'm about to tell her why, that I don't think David wrote it, which means his overdose might not have been self-inflicted. But then I realize they'll question everyone. Including me. I'll have to be honest about who I really am and my secret will be out.

I can't have that, not yet, not until I'm sure I understand what's happening here. I shake my head.

"You're sure?"

I nod. She sinks down into the armchair, seemingly relieved. I wonder what reasons she might have for keeping the note between us.

"We need to help the girls," she says.

"You said they were alright. That you were looking after them."

"I am," she says. She looks exhausted now. "I was. Or I thought I was, anyway." She reaches for her cigarettes. "But after what happened with Ellie? I thought she'd come to me, rather than run away. Maybe she doesn't trust me anymore."

I think of some of the things I've done. Things that made no sense at all, even at the time.

"Don't blame yourself," I say.

"You think?"

I pick up the photo of Zoe from the arm of the chair and look at it again. I notice something. There's someone in the background, smiling and in profile, as if they're talking to someone out of shot. His hair's different, longer, but it's him. He's even wearing the same glasses.

Gavin.

I put it in my pocket, where it sings its accusations.

"Where was Gavin tonight?" I ask.

She shakes her head. "I have no idea."

39

It's getting late, but the lights are on in the village hall and the door is unlocked. Inside, there's a uniformed officer tidying things away and I say hello.

Everything feels muddy; I can't put my thoughts in order. But one feeling comes to the fore. I feel ashamed, though why, I don't know. It's almost like Kat was right, I caused it all, and by sleeping with Gavin I somehow made it worse.

"We'll be done in a few minutes," he says, oblivious. "Thanks for coming to lock up for us."

"Oh," I say, forcing a smile. "That's fine. The investigation's over then?"

"Yeah. The girl reckons she ran away, then changed her mind and came back. Nothing to investigate."

"You believe her?"

"It's not up to me. Anyway, I need to get on."

I go through into the kitchen. Gavin will be here soon, I think, and then I'll have to explain why I lied to the officer about him having asked me to come over to close the place up. But I might as well use this time, see whether I can find anything out. The serving hatch is open and through it I can see the officer, but at the far end of the room a door leads into what I'm guessing is a cupboard or storeroom.

It's not locked. Inside, I find shelves stacked with catering boxes of teabags and huge tins of coffee and hot chocolate. In the corner sits a box of toys, and the projector screen Gavin must use for the film club is propped against the wall. Everything is neat, nothing tossed randomly. There's a filing cabinet in the corner behind the door.

I try the top drawer, but it won't open. On the wall there's a lockbox, but inside there are no keys that might fit. I lean my elbows on the cabinet. Shit. I don't know what I was hoping to find, anything that might be a clue to his connection with Zoe, I suppose. I realize once again I've fucked someone who turns out to be a stranger.

"Alex?"

My head jerks up. Gavin is standing in the doorway, watching me. I don't know how long he's been there. He seems disappointed, I think. Or angry. From the main hall I hear another voice.

"I'll be off, then."

Gavin looks briefly over his shoulder and calls out with false cheer,

"Right, then! Bye!" He looks back to me and lowers his voice. "What're you doing?"

I raise my head defiantly. "I could ask you the same."

He glances at the filing cabinet, as if reassuring himself it's still locked.

"Alex?"

"You knew Zoe."

He shakes his head. "No. I just—"

"Gavin! Just fucking stop, okay?"

His eyes narrow. "You went to see her parents again."

"No," I say. "I found this." I show him the photo. "It's you, isn't it?"

He looks at it closely, then, eyes closed, draws a deep breath.

"Where did you get that?"

I ignore him. I scan the room: he's between me and the door, I might need a weapon, something I can use to defend myself. But there's nothing, just the camera round my neck. Pretty weighty, but not enough.

"What did you do with her?" I say. "Where is she?"

His eyes dart open. "What? You think I . . . ? I'd never—"

I shove the picture toward him.

"Explain this, then!"

He shakes his head. "Did she give it to you?"

She? I think. He can't mean Zoe.

"Who?"

"Jody. Or Sean?"

"What? No. Why? How would—?"

"Come on." He takes my arm. "I need to tell you something."

His grip is firm, but he's not rough. He tries to steer me out, through the kitchen, but I shake him free and walk there myself. In the main hall I turn to face him.

"Tell me. You knew Zoe. How? Where was the photo taken?"

"Her birthday. Her thirteenth. McDonald's."

"And why were you there?"

He stares at the floor. "I'm her uncle."

"What?"

"Jody's my sister."

It's the last thing I expected.

"But—"

"We don't talk. Not anymore."

"She knows you're here?" He shakes his head. "Why *are* you here?"

"To find her. Or find out what happened to her."

"So all this finding a new life . . ."

"Half true, I suppose. I had nothing else to do."

"But why sneak up here? Why not tell her? She's your sister! What happened?"

He sighs. "We argued, after Zoe went. The two of them were frantic. I took some time off work, came and stayed with them. I was trying to be supportive. I thought it was what they wanted."

"It wasn't?"

"I dunno. We got on fine at first. But then . . . Zoe still didn't come home, and everyone started painting this picture of the perfect life she had, of what fantastic parents they'd been."

"They weren't?"

"Well, they were no worse than most. But I'd seen them fighting one Christmas a couple of years before she disappeared. It kicked off at Mum's. Yelling and screaming, they were—"

"In front of Zoe?"

"In front of all of us. They said it was a one-off, that everything was fine. But Zoe came to see me afterward. She said she was sick of it. She didn't know what to do. They were arguing all the time—her mum was convinced her dad was having an affair. The usual stuff."

"Did your sister tell you any of this?"

"No. Not even after Zoe went. It was all everything was perfect and we were all getting on fine and she had no idea why Zoe had started to run wild and . . . well, it seemed like she was more worried about not getting the blame for Zoe being unhappy than actually finding her and bringing her home."

"And you told her that?"

He smiles wryly. "Let's just say it came up in conversation. They weren't too happy. Sean asked me what it'd got to do with me anyway. Pretty much implied I'd been . . . well . . . y'know?"

"What?"

"Too close to Zoe, shall we say. Only they're not the words he used. Pretty much said it was my fault she'd run away."

I hesitate. "I don't think they believe that now."

He grimaces, then gazes up toward the ceiling.

I regard him for a moment. "Maybe you should speak to them. Jody was pretty difficult, but I think she wants to talk. Maybe—"

He turns his gaze back to me. "Not to me, she doesn't. And I don't really want to talk to her, either. I just want to find out what happened to Zoe, and Daisy, and Sadie. And Ellie, now. And make sure it doesn't happen to anyone else."

His eyes glisten. I want to believe him, but can I? I imagine myself walking away, him a few steps behind. A blow to the head and I'm down. No one knows I'm here. No one cares. It'd be that easy.

"Where were you?" I say.

"When?"

"Today. When Ellie came back."

He stares at me. "You think I had something to do with it?"

I don't, I think. *Not really.* But I've been mistaken before and I need to be sure.

"So?"

"Alex, I was out looking for Ellie. Like everyone else."

I retreat.

"But—"

"Ask Bryan," he says. "Liz. Any of them. When they came back, I stayed out, on the moors. Trying to find her."

He steps toward me, his arms out. "Believe me." His face is pleading, imploring. "Look," he says. He holds up his phone. "I filmed it. In case it was, you know. Useful. For your film."

He presses *Play*. A shot of the moor, blanketed in darkness.

"Could've been taken by anyone. Any time."

He shows me the time stamp. An hour ago. "Look." He scrolls through the clip. Right at the end his face flashes into view.

I lift my head, about to speak, though to say what, I'm not sure. Sorry, perhaps, though I don't feel it.

"Don't lie to me again," I say.

He shakes his head. "I won't." He looks up at me, and something hovers in his expression, just beyond reach. It's as if he's considering something, weighing his options, deciding how to reply. But in the end all he says is, "If you promise me the same."

40

Gavin brings me coffee, then leaves. It's early, before light. Loss wraps itself around me, as if I've left something behind but can't remember what. Something important and irreplaceable. I lie in bed, thinking of Daisy's mother withering in her tiny room, her confused brain turning to fantasy, and of my own, lying in the cold ground, rotting to nothing. I think of Zoe, gone, perhaps for good, her room still waiting for her, her parents trying to keep it together, to remain optimistic in the face of the evidence. How do they go on? I think. How do any of us?

Then there's Ellie, returned from who knows where. Am I right about it being a punishment, or was it an attempt at getting away and, if so, from what? On the way downstairs I glance at the barometer. The needle hasn't budged; it sits stubbornly between *Rain* and *Stormy*, as if it's a warning. I know that all it's doing is measuring air pressure, or humidity, or temperature, or perhaps a combination of all three. It's just science, that's all; there's no mystery, nothing supernatural. Perhaps it's broken. I think of David, coming into my bedroom. Perhaps it's me that's broken.

I pick up my computer. As I do, it pings with a new submission. *Play.*

A shot of the sky. There are trees, way over in the distance. It's blue, a clear day. Sunny, but the shadows are long and the trees have shed their leaves. Winter, and something about the film makes me think it's years old. A bright, clear winter's day. As the camera turns a trailer flashes into view. Pegasus.

I shrink away. A girl appears, her head and shoulders filling the frame. She's smiling, grinning. Daisy. The image is clear and sharp, it might almost be recent, but no, it can't be, she's dead.

Still it's as if I'm looking at a ghost, as if I could reach into the screen and grab her, save her. Ask her what happened, who hurt her, why she jumped and why I ran away.

And who sent this? Who is it who was holding the camera?

I need to get away. The night sky is cloudless, the air frozen and still. By the time I'm halfway up Slate Road, I'm out of breath. It's as if the air itself has thickened, closed around me. It's as if I'm back on twenty a day.

My car is where I left it, but now I'm here I don't know where to go, why I'd thought escape was even an option. I know what Dan would say, and I know he's right. Finish your film.

I continue farther, to the park, and push open the stiff sprung gate. My feet crunch on the frozen gravel path. Up ahead, the bandstand looms, but the wind has picked up and I head for its shelter. As I draw close, I see it's not empty; there's a figure hunched in its recess, head down.

I don't turn back. It's as if my subconscious worked out she'd be here and brought me to her. I climb the steps and stand in front of her. She's smoking; she has a jacket wrapped tight around her but still she shivers in the cold. I clear my throat.

"Kat?"

It's only then she notices me and raises her head.

"What're you doing here?"

Her question lacks conviction. She's glad, I can tell. Secretly, perhaps without even knowing it. I'm company, if nothing else.

"Can I join you?"

"It's a free country."

I sit next to her, leaving a gap between us. I look out at Blackwood Bay for a minute or two, at the sea beyond it. I used to come here too, I think. When I was upset. Finally, Kat speaks.

"How did you find me?"

"I didn't. I had no idea you'd be here."

She stubs out her cigarette and folds her arms.

"You're not filming or nothing?"

I shake my head. "D'you want me to?"

Her laughter is a short, low bark of derision. We fall back into an uneasy silence.

"Have you seen Ellie?" she asks me, after a while.

"Briefly," I say. "Last night."

She grunts. It's unreadable, defensive.

"Have you?"

She shakes her head. "They won't let me."

"Who? Her parents?"

"She's told them she ran away. They say I'm a bad influence." She's staring out to sea; her mouth is a thin, hard line.

"And are you?"

She inclines her head toward me. Her lips are twisted into a scowl, but I think I see something else there, too. A grudging respect, maybe. A hint of pride. We're the same, me and her. A friend in nameless trouble and us, rightly or wrongly, taking the blame.

"You drink. I know that. Drugs, too, I imagine."

She says nothing.

"I was the same at your age, you know?"

"That right?"

Her sneer lacks conviction and I laugh quietly. "You'd be surprised. There's not much else to do, is there?"

She gazes back out to sea.

"I remember it, you know. Too young to go clubbing, or even drinking in the pub. It was speed with me, at first anyway."

"Speed?"

"Just a bit. Then . . . well, other stuff."

She stares down at her lap and fiddles with a ring she's wearing on her middle finger, twisting it round. The cheap silver glints.

"How about you?"

"Just weed," she whispers. "And booze."

"You're sure?"

A shrug tells me no, but that's all she's prepared to admit to.

"Ellie, too?"

She shakes her head.

"Where d'you get it? Is it the boys?" I think of the one we saw her with in the café, the charmer I'd encountered on the beach. "Your boyfriend?"

She looks away, breathes deep. Is she crying? I can't tell.

"Tell me what happened to Ellie."

"I don't know, but she didn't run. She wouldn't. And if she did, why did she come back?"

"So . . ." I speak hesitantly, as if the wrong thing might startle her into flight. "She was taken? Dumped out there?"

She doesn't answer, but I take her silence for a yes.

"You were worried about David," I say. "Last night."

She freezes, for a moment. "Is he going to be all right?"

I speak softly. "I don't know."

She looks round now. Her eyes are dry.

"David is your friend?"

"Yes. Ellie's, too." She hesitates. "It's not what you're thinking."

"I'm not thinking anything."

"He helps with homework. He gives us food. A sandwich. When . . . you know."

When your mothers don't bother, I think. Or your fathers.

"So that's all?"

She reaches into her jacket for her pack of cigarettes, and I remember a different time. Daisy is sitting where I am now, and I'm on the bench just next to her. It's dark, winter, the bandstand feels cavernous.

Both of us have a lit cigarette. I take a final drag and flick the butt under the bench opposite, where it lands with a shower of red sparks.

"I mean," says Daisy. "He's all right. He has this telescope. It's really cool. He lets us look through it. You can see the stars, the planets. I've seen a galaxy, even. You should come up some time."

I shiver. A telescope. It's like I knew all along. I suppose I did.

"He has a telescope?" I say to Kat.

She nods.

"Where?"

"On the roof."

I close my eyes and picture it. David's right there, taking the plastic cover off. He's asking the girls what they want to see; it's bright tonight, he's saying, the seeing is good.

The seeing? Somehow I know what that means—there's not too much turbulence in the atmosphere, the image will be sharp and clear—but how? Did Daisy tell me? Or did he?

I shut my eyes and see him. He's looking down at my hands. "You brought your camcorder."

My eyes flick open. I'm back in the bandstand, Kat next to me.

A camcorder. My first.

"There's Betelgeuse," says Kat. She's looking up, and I follow her gaze until I see the reddish blob.

"Want to hear something interesting?" I say. "The thing you're looking at now probably doesn't exist."

"But I can see it."

"Yes. But the thing is, it's so far away that the light it gives off takes over five hundred years to get to us. That means that what you can see through the telescope now is what Betelgeuse looked like in 1500 and something. And Betelgeuse is a supergiant right at the end of its lifespan. Any day now, it'll explode."

We both look at the red star.

"But don't forget you're looking back in time. By the time we *see* it explode from Earth, it will already have happened. Five hundred years ago."

She's silent for a minute, then she says, "It's your favorite, too?"

I search for Andromeda. *No*, I want to say. But I keep quiet. I hug my jacket against the cold.

"Shall I tell you what I think?" I don't wait for her to answer. "I think Ellie was taken out onto the moor to teach her a lesson." I pause. "Or as a warning."

Her silence is enough.

"A warning not to tell anyone what's going on. That's what I'm guessing."

She stares into the distance. Her hair falls over her face.

"I can help you," I say. "If you let me. If you tell me who's hurting you."

She's silent. The cigarette glows in her hand, forgotten.

"It's not your boyfriend, is it? Or not only him. Who else?"

I wait but, still, she doesn't answer. I reach into my pocket and find my phone.

"Can I show you something?"

I find the film I was sent earlier and press *Play*.

"What's this?"

"Watch."

She does, wordlessly. When it's finished she looks back to me. "That's the girl they killed."

She says it without question, without thought. There's no doubt; she knows that's what happened.

"Who sent it? Do you know? Who'd have this?"

She shakes her head. I press *Play* once more. Daisy poses and pouts. She puts on her sunglasses and turns away from the camera.

How's this? she's saying, even though I can't hear her; there's no sound, it's just her voice in my head.

Am I doing it right?

I freeze the screen, zoom in. There's a reflection in the mirror of her sunglasses, a blur really, only vaguely recognizable as a human face, impossible to know whose it is.

Except now I do know. I've known all along, I've just been pushing it away, keeping the certainty at arm's length, avoiding it like it's a dead thing I don't want to look at. An animal, bled out in the snow.

It was me. I was there. Behind the camera, telling her what to do, directing her, lending her my jacket and my glasses and my heels. It was me filming her as she pouted and preened outside her trailer. It was me.

But why? And how did the person who uploaded it get hold of it?

I put my phone away. "I think it's a warning."

"Who from?"

"From the person who killed her. Who else? They want me to stop asking questions."

She doesn't argue. She knows I'm right.

"It might not be a bad idea."

"I'm not scared, Kat. I've been through some shit you wouldn't believe. It'll take more than this to scare me."

She stares straight at me. "You really have no idea," she says. "No idea at all."

"What d'you mean?"

She stands up. "I have to go."

"Kat," I say. "Please talk to me. I can help you."

"You can't," she says. "No one can."

I watch her leave the park. I knew David, too; I know that now. So why do I have no recall of him? I lift my phone once more. Daisy's face fills the screen.

My head falls. I try to think back to the day I filmed it, but I can't. The memory is there, but hidden, or it's like looking through gauze; the film is scratched and burned, too many frames are missing for it to make sense. I get only sensations. Walking up there. Getting ready. Sharing my makeup, even though surely she has some of her own, taking the camcorder out of my bag.

The camcorder. Why don't I remember it? It must've been my

first. It must've been where all this started, this need to record and preserve. But where did I get it?

It means a lot to me. That much I know. But did I steal it, get the bus into town and slip it into my bag, walk out of the shop, praying I hadn't been seen and that there were no security cameras?

No. I don't think so. That was never my style. Lipsticks from the chemist's, perhaps. Cans of cheap cider, maybe. But not a camcorder. Not something worth hundreds.

So where, then? Where did it come from?

Maybe it was a gift? Yes. Not wrapped up with a bow, it was in a plastic carrier bag, but a gift, still. I remember not knowing what it was. I remember it being a surprise. I remember being told I'd earned it.

But from whom? And how? The voice was a man's. It belonged to someone I loved but was also scared of. I knew even as I took it out of its box that the camcorder came with conditions. I've rubbed your back, now it's time for you to rub mine.

I shiver. I feel a hand on me, on my shoulder; it's pushing me, gently. *Go on*, it says. *Go on. Like we agreed, like you promised.* You can't back out now. It pushes harder; I almost stand. I open my eyes, but I'm alone.

Can it have been my mother's boyfriend? When I remember him I see only his face, crumpled with dislike. There's no way he'd have given me a camera.

David, then? Maybe. I can't stop feeling that he'd be all right now if I'd never come, if I'd never started shoving my nose into other people's business. And I can't stop feeling guilty. I can't stop thinking I loved him once.

I need to remember him. He's the key.

41

I ring St. Mary's and tell them I'm a friend of David's. As I wait to be connected I think of the telescope on his roof, the scratched mark on the trailer wall in Daisy's bedroom, the photo in Zoe's. I need him to wake up. I need to see him, to make him tell me how we're all linked, what's happening. Who took Ellie and why, who killed Daisy. I've hit a wall; as much as I try to remember, I can't get through it. But when I call the ward the nurse she tells me there's been no change in his condition. She doesn't sound optimistic.

I put down the phone as a wave of guilt swells through me. I breathe through it and try to focus. I have work to do, a film to make. It's nearly Christmas and they want the taster by the end of the year. And for me, I have to find out what's happening to the girls and try to stop it. Someone is getting them into drugs, abusing them. Someone is taking them out and leaving them on the moors to teach them a lesson. I have to work it out. I mustn't unravel.

I press *Play*. Two kids—twin boys, it looks like—whiz past on a bike. An open pizza box lies on a table with five or six hands grabbing at it. A farm, pigs snuffling at the trough. A bunch of kids flying a kite somewhere farther along the cliff, near the lighthouse. A black screen, a flash of light, a blurred shape as the camera struggles to focus but which resolves itself into a person. Into Ellie.

I lean in. She's laughing, exuberant; her head is thrown back with joy. Next to her there's another girl I don't recognize, and slightly behind her two older boys. As the camera is steadied I realize they're sitting on camping chairs arranged in a loose circle, the ground underfoot is muddy, and behind them a horse peers over a half-door.

The stables. This is good, I think. It'll go with the footage I shot there. Monica's voice cuts in.

"Any more for any more?"

Ellie looks up; the others too. The screen is blocked momentarily by the back of someone's legs as they walk into shot and I realize the person with the camera is sitting on a chair opposite Ellie and trying to film without being noticed.

"Ellie?"

Monica hands her something, though I can't see what.

"Anyone else?"

A couple of the others mumble something.

"Grace?"

The girl next to Ellie holds out her hand and receives her gift, too. Monica walks into shot and turns to face whoever's holding the camera.

"Kat?"

A voice from behind the camera. "I'm okay, thanks."

So it's her filming. The girl called Grace laughs as the screen goes dark and the sound becomes muffled. Kat's covering the lens, I suppose; maybe she's shoved the phone between her knees, or rammed it under her arm. "Oh, come on!"

"I said no."

"Leave her," says Monica, and a second later the camera lens is unblocked. Ellie is in the corner of the screen now, and I see she's holding a cigarette. I zoom in. It's a joint, of course. Monica holds a lighter in front of her face, but as Ellie leans forward to light it she almost topples off the chair. She giggles as she rights herself, stoned already, perhaps drunk, too. At her feet there are empty bottles, wine and vodka, plus a carton of orange juice and a discarded stack of plastic cups. The camera wobbles as Monica turns to sit herself on one of the empty chairs.

"Right," she says cheerily. "So we're all happy?"

There's murmured assent, a giggled profanity. "Happy, Ellie?"

Ellie nods vaguely. She's inhaling deeply on the joint.

"And you're looking forward to the party?"

Grace answers.

"Party? What party?"

"I told you. There's a party tonight, Grace. You said you wanted to go. Remember?"

Grace nods, once. "Kat?" says Monica. "You're going, too? And Ellie?"

The smiles drops from Ellie's face, but she says nothing. I wonder whether it was filmed before she disappeared. Before she was taken.

"Richey will be there to look after you. Don't worry."

Ellie looks over to Kat. Is Richey her boyfriend, the one in the café? The younger girl's eyes flash briefly on the camera that Kat must have cradled in her hand and it's as if she's looking straight at me, but then she raises her gaze. Her eyes are wide and desperate, and she seems both unspeakably young and far, far too wise for her years.

"Now," says Monica. "There's something else. That woman? Alex? She's asking questions." She surveys the girls. "And we must all be very careful about what we tell her. Mustn't we?"

A murmur, but no one replies.

"Or else there'll be no more of this. Understand?"

She looks round, but if there's any more I don't hear it. Kat must've realized she was about to be spotted, that she'd lose her chance to send it to me.

The screen goes black as the film ends and silence rushes in.

I hear voices, interrupted occasionally by music. A radio. With my ear pressed against the wall, I can just about hear her moving around, too, right at the very threshold of perception. She climbs the stairs right next to me and a minute or two later there's the rumble of pipes as the boiler fires.

I return to the window and wait. I walked up to the bandstand last night, as if I expected Kat would still be there, but it was empty. Just a broken bottle under the bench, a littering of spent cigarettes carpeting the floor. A girl, out in the far corner of the park, barely visible in the gloom. But no Kat, and neither have I seen her today.

Not that it matters, I suppose. I didn't know what I was going to say to her. To thank her for the film, I guess. To ask her when it was taken and what happened at the party, and why Ellie didn't want to go with the other girls. As if I couldn't guess.

I know what happens at these parties. Young girls stand around, terrified but trying not to look it, hoping they seem keen enough to not get a beating. Men choosing which they prefer, a nod and a grunt and then it's fifteen minutes upstairs.

But does Monica know that's what's going on? In the film she hadn't seemed cruel. When she'd insisted that Richey was there to protect the girls, she sounded like she believed it was true.

A creak from next door. She's on the stairs again, and at first I'm hopeful she's leaving. But then I hear the TV go on and a little later the noise of cooking.

It's after lunch when I hear her key in the lock. She appears at the window, carrying a jute bag, dressed in a weatherproof jacket despite the weak sun. I sit back out of sight and watch as she locks the door behind her before setting off, glancing at my door as she goes. I wait five minutes, counting each of them off on my phone's digital display, then leave Hope Cottage. It's now or never.

Monica's front door is locked; the handle doesn't give. When I peer through the frosted glass I see a light in her kitchen at the end of the corridor, but there's no noise, no flickering light from the television, no radio. I step back. I have to get inside. I have to find out what's going on.

All that separates her yard from mine is a wooden fence. There are some rickety garden chairs beneath the table in the far corner and I unfold one and stand on it. It's high enough for me to get over the fence, and I drop down on the other side into the mirror image of the yard I've just left. The same ceramic pots are lined up against it, an almost identical table sits in the opposite corner. She's arranged two gnomes with cracked faces on a low stone wall on the other side, while a third has toppled over and lies beneath them, its head smashed.

The patio door is locked but shifts a little when I try it. I find a rock at the back of the yard, where it's weighing down a tarpaulin, then use it to hammer upward on the bottom of the handle. I've no idea why; it's some instinctive knowledge I don't remember learning but must have. After a few seconds the door lifts and I find I can slide it open. I'm inside.

The kitchen is untidy: pots and pans molder in the sink, a day's worth of unwashed plates are stacked next to the kettle, plus three or four mugs, one of which is filled with dirty cutlery. A stale smell pervades, cigarette smoke and fried food, trash that needs emptying. I'm not sure why I'm here, what exactly I'm looking for. It's as if I thought getting inside would tell me instantly what I need to know, but I'm going to have to search. In the living room there's a crumpled blanket on the sofa, the ashtray that still hasn't been emptied since the other day, or else it has and has since been refilled with dead cigarettes. Two wineglasses, both empty other than the dregs of red. I suddenly see Monica as unutterably sad; I picture her lying under the blanket, staring at the television, smoking, drinking wine, pickling herself in her misery. Why are you living like this? I think. What is it that's eating you up? A failed love affair, and now you channel your love into the girls and fester in your disappointment? Is it this place? Then get out. And if it's guilt, then tell someone. Get it off your chest.

Like you did?

The question is abrupt and in a voice that's not my own, almost as if I'm hearing it for real. I look up. She's there, sitting in the chair opposite. She's watching me; it was she who was speaking.

"Daisy?" I say, my mouth dry. The room begins to wobble, as if it's about to spin, as if I'm about to fall. Just in time, my hand finds the back of a chair and I right myself.

"Daisy!" I say again, but still she sits there, silent and impassive. "How—?"

She interrupts me.

You haven't figured it out yet, have you?

"But—"

You haven't got long, you know? I'll get you. I'll make you pay.

I step toward her and then, as instantly as she appeared, she's gone. The chair she was sitting on is empty; there's no one there. Just a cardigan thrown over the back and a cushion, a mark on it, a stain that could be anything, could be coffee, could be wine, could be blood.

Had I imagined her? My legs are unsteady as I run up the stairs and into the bedroom, slamming the door behind me so hard that it bounces open. I half expect to see her sitting on the bed, but no, she's not there, I was imagining it, imagining it all. It's my mind playing tricks. That's all.

I breathe in deep. Monica's room is the same shape as mine, the bed equally unmade and identical, except her duvet cover is floral and bleached by the sun. There's a dresser piled with paperwork, letters, bills, newspapers and magazines, as well as cans of hairspray and deodorant, bottles of cheap perfume.

I don't know what I'm looking for. I open one of the dresser drawers, and it's full: blister packs of pills, a can of insect repellent, and a yellowed paperback. I try the next, and when I find that full of junk, too, go over to the chest of drawers.

I breathe deep. It's an invasion of privacy, worse than just breaking in, and I almost give up and go back to my cottage. But then I remember why I'm here, what I saw in the film Kat sent to me. I have to know.

In the top drawer is her underwear. A selection, mostly cream or white and chosen to be comfortable rather than flattering. I dig deeper and find a pale pink vibrator tucked underneath some balled socks. Deeper still, my fingers brush against something soft and flat, a book, and I pull it out carefully, disturbing as little as I can.

It's a pale blue exercise book, bulging slightly. When I open it I find Polaroid photographs tucked inside. I scan them; they were clearly taken at the stables and each of them is of a girl looking straight at the camera, smiling with varying degrees of gaucheness. There are at least fifteen different girls, all of a similar age. Between thirteen and sixteen, I'd say, though in some cases it's hard to tell.

Most I don't recognize, but third from the top is Kat. Ellie's here, too, and the girl from the film. Grace. I cycle through the rest, already suspecting what I'm going to find.

I'm right. Zoe's picture is here, and farther down I find Daisy's, too, wearing the same clothes she'd had on in the video I'd been sent. Finally, at the very bottom, there's a picture of me.

I force myself to concentrate, to stay in the moment. I put the photos down and go back to the book. On the first page is a list of names, and next to each a sequence of numbers and letters. Over the page there are more lists, dates of birth, phone numbers and addresses, plus more, apparently random, numbers. Nothing seems to correlate with anything else, and though I guess there's a code here it's one I don't have time to figure out. I use my phone to photograph the first page, then I arrange the pictures on the bed and film them, a slow pan from left to right, before returning to the book. After several more pages of information there's a blank, then a few sheets are filled in, this time with men's names—Dale, Shaun, Bill, Mark, Karl, Kevin—plus more phone numbers and more dates. No Bryan, to my relief, and no Gavin either. I examine the dates; they're too recent to be dates of birth and when I flip to the back of the book I see one from only a week or so ago.

I flip to the pages with the information about the girls, forward to the pages dealing with the men. There's nothing concrete here, no hard evidence, but it's not difficult to see what links them. I think of the video I was sent. There's a party tonight; and a single word escapes from my lips.

"Fuck."

Suddenly, I hear a sound. Footsteps outside, then a key in the lock. It's as if I've summoned her. "Shit," I mutter, and I scoop the photos off the bed before stuffing them back inside the book, aware as I do that I have no idea if they're in the right order. I bury the book inside the drawer, in more or less the same place I found it, then scan the room. The place is tiny, there's nowhere to hide, and my mind races—what can I tell her? Why am I here?—comes up with nothing. Already I can hear her downstairs, taking off her jacket. Then I hear her voice. She sounds flustered, unnerved.

"No," she's saying. "No. It can't be. It doesn't make any sense."

She's on the phone. I try to work out what she'll do, where she'll go. I slip through the door and into the bathroom. I hide behind the door, taking in as I do the uncleaned toilet bowl, the sink that's encrusted with toothpaste and remnants of soap. My body is numb, as if it's someone else's, a costume I'm wearing, nothing more. I think of the word Dr. Olsen used. *Dissociation.*

I force myself to concentrate. I grab a pair of nail scissors from the sink and dig the point into my palm until I feel the stab. I focus on what's happening downstairs. I hear Monica close the front door behind her and listen as she hovers at the bottom of the stairs, just a few yards away.

"Slow down," she's saying. Her tone is urgent, confused. What's happened? If only I could hear the other half of the conversation.

She goes into the kitchen and I hear the kettle being filled, though she sounds in need of something stronger.

"But what makes you so sure?"

Silence, then the husk of a laugh. I strain to hear what comes next. "You really think she would? She wouldn't dare!" A pause. "Would she?"

I try to convince myself it's gossip, but it doesn't sound like it. It sounds serious, the discussion of a problem that will need dealing with, one way or another. I will her to say the name of whoever she's talking to, but she doesn't.

A sigh she tries to conceal. "You know me," she says. "I've never let you down."

Her voice is louder now. She's on the stairs. My heart thumps so hard I think she might hear it, then misses the next beat. Did I close the drawer? I can't remember, but still it's better she goes in there than comes in here, where there's no escape. I slide down the wall and into a crouch, the scissors in my hand. There's a tiny hole in my palm, a trickle of blood. It could be someone else's.

She's right outside the door. I can almost make out who's on the other end of the call, though that might be my imagination. She speaks again. "I don't know. We'll have to think of something." I listen to her breathe. I smell her, the same cheap perfume I saw on her dresser; it smells like flowers, like toilet cleaner. Stand, I tell myself, stand. At least face her on your feet, if that's what's going to happen.

She goes into the bedroom. This is it. My chance. I get to my feet as silently as I can and peer at the bedroom door. She's left it open but is nowhere to be seen. I have to move. Now.

I round the bathroom door, not taking my eyes off the bedroom. I can see through, into the mirror on the dresser. Monica is reflected there; she's getting changed, her phone still clamped to her ear, and has already taken off her sweater. She's wearing only a bra, and on her upper arm I make out a faded tattoo. It looks cheap, homemade, and though at first I think it's a heart, after a moment she turns and I see I'm wrong. I head off, across the landing, then to the stairs. They creak, I know that, but what can I do? I tread lightly, miss out every second step, jogging down quietly, holding my breath. The door is at the bottom and, as I reach it, I pray it's unlocked. My hand goes out to the handle, I'm not even thinking anymore, and suddenly there's a noise, loud as a gunshot, and I freeze.

The kettle switching off, that's all. I grab the handle, but as I do I hear Monica upstairs. "Don't worry," she says, her voice brittle. "I'll deal with it. You know I will. It's not like I have a choice. Not if you're sure she's back." She waits. "Carol's?" She laughs, again without humor, and I wonder who Carol is. "'Fraid so. I'll see you then?" A pause. "No, not now. Afterward."

I turn the handle and the door opens. I'm outside. I exhale, deeply, but then think of Monica's tattoo. A perfect circle. An unbroken O. And of her warning to the girls on the film. I've been asking too many questions. And, somehow, they've figured it out.

THEN

SPENCER STREET GROUP PRACTICE

Clinic notes: Zoe Pearson, DOB 7/3/2003

Date: 17 May 2017

Zoe in today with mum. Complains of excessive tiredness,
weight loss and loss of appetite, not wanting to go
to school, nausea accompanied by vomiting. General
lethargy. Mum said she stays out late at night. General
examination no concerns. Advised bed rest and plenty of
fluids. Will call for telephone consultation in three
days.

Suspect Zoe has started smoking, but she denied this
on questioning. She says she is doing well at school and
has no worries either there or at home. She has lots of
friends. Bruise visible on her upper arm, which she told
me she got during PE at school. Also a round mark on her
forearm.

Plan: Review as above. Monitor for general health and
well-being and consider referral to social services if
any other signs appear.

Signed: Dr. Wiseman

Date: 22 May 2017

Called mum. Family friend answered—Monica Browne. Said
Zoe is fully recovered, back at school today. No further
action necessary.

Signed: Dr. Wiseman

NOW

43

She's back. I'll deal with it. I've never let you down.

They're talking about Sadie, about me. They're going to deal with me. I've been foolish, coming here, asking all these questions. I'm in danger. Should I call Gavin, ask him to help? But what could he do? He's only a newcomer, and where's he got with all his questions so far? Bryan? He knows Monica, so maybe that could work to our advantage—to my advantage—and I know he won't turn his back when he knows what's happening to the girls.

I rush down toward the slipway, hoping to find him tending to his boat. He's not there; the whole village seems deserted. I make my way to The Ship and go in. A young woman I don't recognize sits behind the bar, alone.

"Oh, hi," she says when I approach.

"Where is everyone?"

"Carol's," she says, as if I ought to know.

"Where's that?"

"There's a service," she explains. "A carol service. Over at St. Julian's. Everyone'll be there."

Of course. Carols. That must be where Monica's going, and maybe Bryan will be there, too. I ask the woman behind the bar when it starts and she glances at her watch. "Soon. Four, I think. What'll it be?"

I shake my head and tell her I've changed my mind. I climb Slate Road as quickly as I can and get into my car. It would be there, I think. The church where my mother is buried, somewhere I'd be happy never to go again.

It's almost completely dark by the time I turn down the road that leads to St. Julian's. The car park is full so I have to stop the car a little way down the track. I jog the rest of the way, keep my eyes forward; I don't even glance toward my mother's grave. Inside the old church the nave is empty and my boots echo on the cold stone floor. Despite the lit candles that cast their soft orange glow all over the church and the cars parked outside, I wonder for a moment whether I've come to the right place after all, but then I hear a noise from farther in. Raised voices, laughter. Through a door I find a smaller room, this one brightly lit, with a Christmas tree in one corner, and full of people. Children and adults; most, I don't recognize, but Liz and Beverly are here, and Monica, too, just shrugging off her coat. I hesitate in the doorway then spot Gavin in the far corner and enter. Bryan sees me almost as soon as I come in. He waves, and though I return his greeting I push my way over to Gavin.

"Is everything all right?"

I shake my head. Bryan is approaching. "I need to speak to you later."

"What's wrong?" he asks. "What is it?"

"Not now," I say. "Later."

He lowers his voice. "You're scaring me."

I glance at Monica. "I just . . . I can't speak now."

Bryan arrives. "How're you?" he says jovially. He's holding a mince pie in one hand, a plastic cup in the other. "Want some? It's mulled wine. Well, it's supposed to be, only no alcohol, see."

"No, thanks," I say. I turn back to Gavin. "I'll catch you later. Okay?"

Bryan watches as Gavin moves off. Something flickers across his face. Jealousy?

"How're you?"

"Fine," he says. "Have one of these. They're delicious."

He hands me a mince pie on a paper plate. It's homemade; the pastry crumbles as soon as I pick it up. He lowers his voice. "Did Monica tell you about David's note?"

I nod. "There's something else, though. Can we go outside?"

He frowns but steers me toward the door. He stops en route to talk to some guy who laughs and thumps his arm playfully before allowing him to continue. Gavin watches us leave and, though I acknowledge him with a slight nod, he doesn't smile back. I dump my mince pie on the table by the door and together we go into the nave.

"Let's sit," he says, heading toward the front pew. "It'll be starting soon anyway."

"Not there," I say. "It's . . . Can we go farther back?"

We choose the fifth pew from the front. It creaks as we sit and there's that stale, musty smell that's in every church I've ever been. The door to the side room has swung shut and we're now in echoing silence.

I keep my voice low, but still my whisper seems to bellow.

"It's Monica."

"What?"

"Giving the girls drinks. Drugs, too. I'm sure of it. And there's worse. I think she's been . . ."

I falter. He shifts in the pew to face me. The candlelight glints orange on his face.

I search for the word. "Using the girls."

"No," he says emphatically, shaking his head. "None of that. Not Monica."

The door to the side room opens. The vicar enters, a young man dressed in black vestments, his hair thinning. He's laughing as he goes, and pauses to let the woman behind him pass. Behind her follows a man, two children and then, as if on cue, Monica herself.

Bryan leans in close. "That's . . . that's just not possible."

"No?"

Monica scans the room. She notices us, gives a tiny wave. We should've sat nearer the back. I will her not to come over, but she heads toward us.

Bryan sighs as she draws close. Others are coming in now to take their seats. A couple sit on the pew directly in front of us. "Look. I know her as well as anybody. We went out. A long time ago. It's not something she'd do."

I watch Monica approach. They went out? It doesn't feel surprising, and again I wonder whether I'd known them both back then, whether I've somehow forgotten them since.

"She's the one who got me off drugs, you know?"

"People change," I say.

She's level with us now. I force myself to smile in her direction, but at the last moment she seems to change her mind. She waves to us both and mouths, See you later?

Bryan returns her greeting, then, once she's continued toward a rear pew, turns back to me.

"Not her. I just . . . I can't believe it."

A young couple pushes past us, trailing their child.

"I'd be dead without her," he goes on. "She's the one who set me right."

"She loved you."

People are still coming in, though it's slowed to a trickle. It looks like it's about to start.

"It weren't just that. She's a good person."

"So, why did it end? What happened?"

"I stopped needing to be rescued, I suppose. It turned out there wasn't much more to what we had, once you took that away."

At the front the vicar clears his throat. "Welcome!" he says. I fade him out.

"How old were you?"

"Teenagers," he hisses. "Look, why these questions? Monica wouldn't hurt anyone."

"You know she takes the kids to the stables?"

"To give them something to do, yes. They love it."

"That's not all she does it for."

The woman in front of Bryan looks round, her eyes narrowed in admonishment. She smiles when Bryan mouths an apology.

"Let's get out of here," he says. "There's a door at the back."

I duck down and half jog toward the back of the church, Bryan a few paces behind, eyes on me the whole time. For a second it feels naughty,

adventurous, like we're sneaking out of assembly to go and have a cigarette behind the toilet block, but then I lock my gaze with Monica.

"I can prove it," I say, once we're out in the cold air. "Look."

I take out my phone.

"Don't," he says. "Please. Just drop this, okay?"

"No," I say. "You have to watch."

I find the film Kat sent me and press *Play*. At first he refuses to
look at the screen—a sense of loyalty to Monica, I suppose—but then
he watches. Watches as Ellie takes the joint, as Grace and the other
girls are told about the party, as they're warned not to say too much
in front of me.

"Who filmed this?"

"I can't be sure. Kat, I think."

"You've spoken to her?"

"I can't find her."

"And this was before Ellie ran away?"

"I'm guessing so. And I don't think she ran. I think she was taken
out there, as a punishment."

"By Monica? But it doesn't make sense."

"No," I say. I pause, unsure for a moment. "I can't prove it, but I
think there are more people involved."

I tell him about breaking into Monica's cottage, about the book I
found, the photographs, the men's names.

"And there's something else," I say. "She interrupted me, and . . ."

"What?"

I hesitate. I want him to help expose Monica, find out who else is
involved. But do I trust him enough to risk him finding out the truth
about who I am?

I have no choice. I need help.

"She was on the phone," I say. "I heard her say 'She's back.'"

He tilts his head toward me. "She's back?"

"Yes."

"She meant Ellie."

"No," I say. "She didn't sound relieved."

"Who, then?"

My stomach clenches as it comes to me. Maybe Monica doesn't know who I am. How could she? She's back. They were talking about Daisy.

I say it out loud. "Daisy."

"What?"

I nod, but in voicing it, it's all become clear. He shakes his head, incredulously, as it tumbles out.

"She's been seen," I say. "On the Rocks. At Bluff House. And I saw her, too. I was down at the beach, the day Ellie went missing. I saw her—Daisy, I mean—just standing there outside Bluff House, watching me."

He pauses. "My god. You're serious."

I remember last night, when I was up at the bandstand looking for Kat. The figure in the gloaming. Maybe she's following me.

"It was her. I'm sure of it."

"But she was seen jumping."

"By Monica."

He shakes his head.

"And what about David's confession—?"

"You believe him?"

"Do I believe what someone wrote in their suicide note?" he says. "Yes."

I take a deep breath. "It was faked. David's note. I think someone tried to kill him."

"Slow down—"

"I think Daisy tried to kill him."

"Alex, really—"

"She sent me this film of herself," I say, in a hurry to get it all out before I'm dismissed completely. "It was a warning. And I know David's note is a lie, because I knew Sadie."

"What? How—?"

"Back in London. It's why I'm here. She asked me to come up and see what was going on. But the point is, she's alive, so—"

"So he couldn't have killed her. But—"

I grip his arm. The carols have started beyond the door. "Away in a Manger."

"Don't you see?" I go on. "He didn't kill Sadie. He can't have, she's alive. But he said he did. Someone's trying to frame him, but more important—"

"That means the rest of the note might be a lie, too? His confession to killing Daisy?"

"Yes! Exactly! And it all ties in to Monica."

"Fuck." He hesitates, and I know what's coming next. "Have you been to the police?"

"No. I can't. Not yet. I need to be sure. About Monica. That she's behind it all. Back then, too. Then I can tell them."

I can see he's struggling to take it all in.

"Will you help me?"

His confusion seems to clear, just a little. "Of course. But Ellie went to Monica's the night she came back; she's not scared of her. There must be something more going on, someone else. So I think you're right. Let's not be too hasty in going to the police. Not 'til we know more. Who else have you told?"

"Gavin. Some of it, anyway."

Again, a glimmer of something on his lips.

"But can we keep it between us?" I continue. "Just while I figure out what to do."

"Yes." He smiles and puts his hand clumsily on my arm. "Of course."

44

There's nothing we can figure out together, so when we leave St. Julian's Bryan takes his car and I mine. He follows me most of the way back from the church, peeling off to head home only as we come into Blackwood Bay. I park and walk down to Hope Cottage.

The village is still deserted; everyone is at the concert, and I just about manage to resist the urge to run. Before I turn into Hope Lane I see The Ship, its orange lights haloed in the thickening mist. I picture me and Gavin, the two of us sitting with drinks, chatting as if nothing was wrong, nothing was happening. I see us gazing out over the water, staring at the moon, watching the ships shimmer in the distance. A different time. It wouldn't be so bad.

I double-lock the door. I'm safe, I think. Hope Cottage is quiet. Just the steady, relentless ticking of the clock on the mantelpiece, the faint click of the fridge, a steady drip from a tap upstairs. I rest for a moment by the door, check it again before I go through into the kitchen, and pour myself a glass of wine. Maybe it will help. I need to figure out how Daisy can be back. And what to do about Monica.

I examine my reflection in the glass. I look thin; I can almost see through myself to the yard beyond, the dead plants in their terracotta pots, the chair I left out when I scaled the fence to get into Monica's.

I go over to the window. The moon is bright tonight, but not full. It's waning. Waning gibbous.

How do I know that? Who told me?

A voice comes, then. David, of course.

I look back at my reflection in the glass. I'm forgetting. There are two of me now. The me that's here, looking out; the me that's outside, looking in. The me who grew up in Blackwood Bay; the me who did her best to leave it all behind.

But I can't live like that. I say my name, under my breath. *Alex.* My name is Alex. Anything else is an illusion, that's all. Anything else is just light bouncing off the glass. Sadie is dead and, if I have to, I'll bury her once more, bury her so deep this time that she'll never escape.

I force a smile, and my ghost smiles, too. That's more like it. But still I hear David's voice, distant now, like I'm listening through a radio that's stuck between stations, picking up static.

You know, he says, *they used to think the moon hunted people. They thought it traveled through the skies looking for people to kill and eat. And then, later, people thought it was where dead souls go. Some people think*

the moon makes people do crazy things, that even just by looking at it for
too long you can go mad. The word "lunacy" comes from the word "luna."
That's Latin for moon.

I don't answer.

Finished your drink?

Not yet, I say. *Are they out?*

I look back up, at the stars. I look for Orion. For Betelgeuse. I look
for Andromeda.

Yes. The seeing should be good tonight.

Shall we, then?

David. He said he'd always looked after me, and I'm beginning
to believe it must be true. Both Kat and Ellie have vouched for him,
Geraldine, too.

I turn away from the window, take a sip of red wine and, without thinking, light a cigarette from the packet on the worktop—the
packet I guess I must've bought earlier today—then go upstairs.

Shit. I need an ashtray. I'm about to retrace my steps when I see a
saucer by the side of the bed, a single cigarette butt stubbed out and
standing upright in the center. I stare at it for a moment, trying to remember when I brought it up, when I started buying cigarettes, when
I started leaving filthy ashtrays on my bedside table. The memory
flickers into life: it was this afternoon, or yesterday, I think. Except,
when I probe it in more detail, it stalls. Was it even me?

I think about Daisy. Where is she? That saucer, used as an ashtray. Has she been here? Does she hate me for what I've done? What
did I do?

I try to put myself back in the past, to relive it. Daisy and Sadie,
best friends; they did everything together, except Daisy was being
abused and Sadie wasn't.

How did she feel about that? Did she try to tell me? Did I listen?
Why have I forgotten?

We must've argued; an argument I can't even remember but other
people are certain upset her deeply. What happened to her then? Did I
do something? I *have* to remember. It's clear she blames me, she wants

to punish me. And how can I put things right if I don't even know what's wrong?

I lean back against the wall. Other than a single trainer, plus her jacket, washed up on the beach way down the coast, there's only Monica's word that she jumped at all, and I now know that's worth nothing. Can she really be back?

I reach for my phone. It's late, but I don't want to feel so alone, and the memories aren't coming. I can't seem to force them. I wake it from sleep and see there's an alert. A new film has been uploaded.

I start up my laptop and press *Play*.

The screen is black. Flashes of light, a dull, grayish gloom, but nothing's clear, nothing's discernible. Then, a bright flash, something emerges from the shadows, but it's blurry and indistinct. It resolves as the camera's autofocus kicks in but is instantly lost before snapping sharp.

A wall. A stone wall, dark gray, the color of night but with a strange, sickly sheen. The light is bright and full on; it comes from the camera itself, or near it, at least. There's a dripping sound, magnified, echoing. It's a cellar. A damp, fetid cellar. The camera lurches to the right, and there she is. Daisy.

I press *Stop* and the image freezes. I can't watch, I've been here before; I've seen this before, in a dream. I want to wake up.

But I can't. I'm awake already and on the screen Daisy's face is twisted, a grotesque picture of pure terror. Her features have collapsed in on themselves; all hope has gone, there's only pain. And when I look up, away from that terrible vision, I see my room. The TV on the wall, the circular mirror I still can't quite bring myself to look at. Everything is as I know it. This is real. I'm not asleep, and I can't run away. Not this time.

I press *Play* once more.

Help me, she says. *Please.*

Over and over. *Help me. Please. Don't do this.* She appears to be sick, beyond desperate. She's given up. There's no one in the world who can help her.

She stares right into the camera, through the years and down into my gut. She sobs. *You said they wouldn't hurt me.*

No, I want to say. *No.* I want to reach into the machine, go back in time. *I'm here for you,* I want to say. *I was always here for you.* Why didn't you trust me? Why didn't you tell me who was hurting you? I could've made it stop. I know I could. I'd have never left you.

But I didn't, I know that. I've dreamed this film; it can't be new to me. I must've seen it before. Or been there when it was filmed.

But no, I'd remember that, surely? I'd have done something, back then. I'd have told someone, or gone to the police.

Wouldn't I? I remember what Bryan told me. Sadie and Daisy argued. One threatened the other. Some people think Sadie was involved in what happened to Daisy, and that's why she ran away.

And who'd have this film, anyway? The person who filmed it, I suppose, but could that really be me? Or Daisy—would she have a copy?

If there's one thing I do know, it's that I didn't send it to myself. Which means she *is* back. That *is* who they meant, Monica and whoever she was speaking to on the phone. I'm even more sure of it now. Not Sadie. Not me. *Daisy.*

I slam my machine closed and stand, crashing into the bedside table as I go, sending my half-full glass skittering off. Wine flies, pooling on the floor. It sprays the wall and, for a second, it's like it's raining blood.

45

I have to go to Bluff House, find her. I slam the door behind me. Monica's windows are in darkness, the cottage still and empty. She must be "dealing" with Daisy, like she'd promised. I have to get there first.

I don't look back. I begin to run, to sprint as hard as I can. My mind turns in circles. Maybe I left the drawer open in the bedroom and Monica came back after the carols and noticed the rearranged photographs in her little book of shame. Perhaps she even caught sight of me, watching her in the mirror or running down the stairs. Which means I'm in danger, too. But we're linked. I need to reach Daisy, to keep both of us safe, whether she's angry with me or not.

Or maybe I'm being naive, and I should be running away from Daisy, not toward her.

I reach The Rocks, and the shingle path. I fly, wraith-like. I see no one else, and no one sees me. Blackwood Bay is deserted, but it's more than that. I feel invisible.

I close my eyes against the sting of the icy wind. The closer I get, the more powerful I feel; something is driving me, some mysterious energy that is almost supernatural. My legs windmill beneath me and, for an instant, I feel like screaming, but I don't. I see myself in that room with my best friend as she begs for her life. Is it true? Was I there?

I have to remember what I did.

My eyes blink open and I skid to a halt. I look out at the freezing water. I want to shout, *Where are you? Why have you come back?*

I hear a voice and turn around to face Bluff House. There's no one there. I'm alone. It's just the wind, the bark of the black gulls that roost under the eaves, laughing. The groans of the old house, sagging under the load, buckling.

I close my eyes and breathe deep, drawing strength now from the icy air, then step up. As I do, a light flickers in one of the upstairs rooms in Bluff House. It's like a camera flash going off, or moonlight glinting on glass.

I'm falling; it feels like vertigo. My legs collapse beneath me as if I've tripped, or slipped on the soft grass, though the next second I realize I must've been shoved from behind. My hands fly out and partially break my fall, but still I hit the rocky ground with a painful thwack, barely cushioned by the thin topsoil. My teeth crack, my ears ring. I can't breathe; my mouth is stoppered. I see only blackness, and for a second it looks like a tunnel, but not of light. A tunnel that leads down, down into the cold black heart of the earth.

I spit out the soil from my mouth and breathe. If I was pushed, then whoever did it will be standing over me right now. I force open my eyes. I try to twist my head, but it's painful. Something warm is trickling down my cheek.

Déjà fucking vu.

Breathe, I tell myself. I must remember to breathe. I lift my head. The ringing tinnitus intensifies, swells to a crescendo, then disappears.

"Daisy?" I say, or I think I do at least. It comes out as a croak. I try to lift myself up, to work out what's going on, but I hear nothing but the sound of my own breath, heavy now. I'm not even certain she's there, or that she ever was.

But perhaps this is how she wants me. Helpless and begging. She wants to make me pay, for whatever it is I did.

There's a scraping sound, but it doesn't seem real. It's in my head, pure imagination. My mouth is full of blood; I must've bitten my cheek. I spit a bubbly pearl of pink saliva onto the grass and try to force myself onto my side. I want to see you, I plead. If this is what it's come to, then at least let me see your face, one last time before the end.

I don't get the chance. Something flashes in the moonlight—too fast for me even to guess at what it might be—and connects painfully with the side of my head.

I register what's happened for less than a second, then everything goes black.

46

I wake to darkness. My head pounds like a drum stretched too tight, my eyes blur in and out of focus and, when they finally resolve to sharpness, I see only the edge of a discarded mattress upon which I must be lying. It's dark otherwise; the air is sharply sulfuric with the smell of public toilets and the piercing sting of ammonia.

It's the stink I recognize. I'm in Daisy's trailer. The bedroom. I have to get out.

My heart cannons in my chest. When I try to get to my feet the room spins and I fall painfully, cracking my elbow on the bedframe. I put my hand to my head and feel something encrusted there. Blood, I suppose, though at least it's dry. I try once more and this time manage to remain upright. My eyes adjust to the dim moonlight, but still I can only just see what I'm doing. I try the flimsy concertina door. It's locked somehow; either that or something's tying it closed. I pull as hard as I can but, though it buckles, it gives only an inch.

I spin round. There's a window next to me, plastic with a metal frame. I try it, but it's rusted shut. I'm going to die. I see it clearly. She'll come in, with a gun or a knife or a crowbar, and finish it.

I have to get out. I hammer on the window, but nothing gives. I wonder dimly whether it's shatterproof, but my overdriven mind has gone into panic mode. I look around for anything that might help, but there's nothing. My mind slips a little but I fight to stay in control, to stay present. I hammer on the door, eyes darting wildly. The curtains are moldy and torn, but they hang off a metal curtain pole. It might be enough.

I jump up and grab hold of it with both hands, my weight pulling it off the wall. I swing it at the window as hard as I can, but it's no good. It judders, sending shockwaves up my arm and into my shoulder, but the plastic window remains resolutely unbroken. Not even a crack. I try again—three, four, five times—but with the same result. The door is my only chance. I shoehorn the curtain pole through the gap between the door and its frame and pull on it, using all my weight. It levers the door open a little more, and I edge the pole farther in and try again. Eventually, the gap is big enough for me to see through; Daisy has tied something to the handle—a tie, it looks like, dark brown, from David's house, perhaps—and secured it somehow. It won't budge.

I grab hold of the tie, but my hands are numb. I might as well be watching one of the clips for my film. I dig my nails into my palms, as hard as I can, so hard it hurts.

Suddenly, an idea comes. I take out my cigarettes from my jacket pocket and remove the lighter from the packet. I flick the wheel once, twice, until the flame leaps in the darkness. I hold it under the tie, willing it to catch, and when it does the cheap fabric burns quickly and with the peculiar smell of burning rubber. I pull on the door as it chars and blackens, and then, with a final flare, it burns through and the door crashes open. I'm free, I think, then realize I've only broken into the main room of the van and there's still a door between me and outside.

It's locked, of course. I weigh the curtain pole in my hand and scan the room. The front window is cracked, a point of weakness, perhaps. I hammer on it with the pole first, then with my booted foot. It doesn't give, but the crack splinters some more with each impact. I take off my boot and use it to batter the plastic until, finally, with a sound like a ruler shattering, it fractures. I pull at the shards until there's a gap wide enough for me to wriggle through.

I crash to the ground but then drag myself to my feet. David's windows shine silver in the light. Is she in there, watching me? I should have done this weeks ago, I know that now. I should've barged my way in, pushed open the door, snapped the chain and had it out with David. I should have sat him down and made him tell me everything he knew, demanded to know where Daisy was. If I hadn't been so determined to be Alex, maybe I would have. Perhaps that's been the problem all along. Knowing who I am. A febrile excitement dances over my body, light as a moth.

I know it'll be locked, but still I try the front door first. Sure enough, it's solid; it barely rattles in the frame. I could smash the stained-glass window, I suppose, and reach in, but I'm not certain that would do any good either. There must be another way.

I stand back to look at the house. Was that movement, at the window above? A thin blur, a flash of something? I look again. It's definite this time, movement in the room beyond the window. I stare, half expecting her face to appear, but she's retreated. All is still. Yet I feel Daisy up there, looking down at me. Her eyes are on me. What does she think? What an idiot, what a fool I am. She's lured me here.

My heart clenches tight. I wish she would show herself. For a moment I want to shout out to her. *Daisy*, I'd say. *What happened? What did I do to you? Why do you hate me?* But I don't. Her eyes burn into my flesh. I don't want to let her know I'm scared, or how guilty I feel. I don't want to feel the bite of her temper, her sarcasm, so I tip my head down and circle the house. The back door shifts but doesn't give, and I check for other ways in. Behind the trailer there's a sash window with frosted glass—a bathroom, I suppose, or a downstairs toilet—that appears rotten. I get my weight underneath it and try to force it open but, again, it won't budge. The wood is more solid than it seems; it's the paint that's peeling, nothing more. I find a heavyish rock in the garden and tap the upper sash. The glass fissures with a sharp crack but doesn't break. It sits stubborn in the frame, but I try again. This time, it shatters and after that it's simple. I slide my hand gingerly through the gap, find the catch, and release it. The lower sash slides with a little difficulty and I heave myself up onto the ledge. Then, with a bit of inelegant wriggling, I'm inside.

It takes my eyes a moment to adjust to the dark, but already the stink tells me enough. I'm in an airless room; there's the smell of damp, as if old washing has been hung out to dry, plus a faint, steady drip from a cistern somewhere beneath me. A toilet. I lower myself down to the floor and instinctively reach for the light switch in the corner of the room. It doesn't work. There's just an empty click, the room stays dark and, looking up, I can make out the empty, bulbless socket above my head. Shit, I whisper, and as if in response I hear a scurrying patter somewhere in the walls. Mice, I think. Or rats. I let my eyes close and try to grasp at a lungful of air. I try to tell myself I could turn around, go back. No one is making me do this.

But they are, I think, grabbing for the door handle in the dark. I have no choice. I never did. I see it now. Every road led here.

I use the torch on my phone, filming as I go. The lavatory door opens directly onto a hallway and my light hits on a banister, a staircase in heavy, dark wood, a table by the front door on which there's a phone. Against the opposite wall a grandfather clock sits silent and still. Dust is everywhere; motes swim in the beam. To my left a door leads down into a kitchen, and to the right another to a living room in which I see a huge sofa, mismatched chairs, and an old, boxy television. The room is enervating, and I close the door before continuing.

The next door along opens onto a large dining room—a table with five or six chairs and a sideboard against the far wall upon which there's a pile of plates, also abandoned to the dust. The rest of the rooms downstairs are similarly desolate. A pile of fetid clothes in the laundry and unwashed plates in the kitchen betray evidence of life, but little else. A sadness hangs everywhere; it's clear it's a place designed for entertaining but in which only one person now cooks, and only for himself. As I turn back to go upstairs there's a soft creak from directly above me. It's nothing, I tell myself, just the house settling or the wind, but still I'm shaking as I begin to climb. Already I'm digging my nails into my palms, as if in preparation for what I know will come.

The sound comes again, louder now, even more like a movement within rather than the house itself.

"Daisy?" I say, but there's no reply, and the silence that rushes in after my voice is heavier somehow, more constrictive. "Daisy?" I say again when I'm halfway up. "Are you up here?"

There's no answer, but as soon as my eyeline reaches the top step I can see that something's happened here. The doors on this floor are flung open and, inside, the light from my phone illuminates piles of clothes, papers, and books—an utter mess. I jog the rest of the way and go into the ransacked master bedroom. The drawers are upended, their contents tossed on the floor and bed. Clothes, papers, jewelry, which surely can't be David's. The place is chaos; the contrast to the calm decrepitude downstairs is startling.

Someone has been here—Daisy, perhaps—scouring the place, turning it upside down. But looking for what?

Outside, the wind picks up. There's a howl; it sounds like laughter and I drop my camera to my side. There's something here, there must be. What have I missed?

I go over to the window and realize. I've been here before. I know the view: the sea, the moon hanging low over the water, ships in the distance, the rigs beyond them. The picture is the same, the thin line of the horizon cutting across the center like a wire pulled tight. Imagination maps onto fact. There's no join. When I look farther down, I see the spot in which she stood, preparing to jump.

I hear a footstep, a creak on the stairs, followed by another. As if someone is creeping down.

"Daisy!" I say again. "Wait! Come back!"

There's no sign of her out there, but I can see where she's been; the whole house shudders with the disturbance. It's as if she's a ghost, running through the ether, detectable only by the vapor trail she leaves behind. I almost stumble as I race down the stairs, my torch flashes wildly, my leaden heart leaps.

But where is she?

I edge forward. I keep the light low. I'm aware she could be anywhere. She can see me; I'm lit like a beacon.

I say her name once more. At the bottom of the stairs, next to the kitchen, a door hangs ajar. I hadn't noticed it before, a cupboard under the stairs filled with the sharp tang of vinegar.

"Daisy?"

I push in. Coats, shoes, a couple of folding chairs. Boxes stacked in the depths. She can't be in here, and yet . . .

I take a step. The floor gives a little, groaning as it does, and when I look down I see the floorboard is loose. She's clever; she's led me here, too. I kneel and lift it from one end, knowing somehow what I'll find even as I do.

I'm right. There's a metal strongbox, shoved deep under the floorboards. I lift it out in a cloud of dust and musty air. It's locked, but I have the key I found in David's wallet and, when I try it, I find it fits. Inside, there's a satchel, damp and covered with mold, and I open it cautiously. It's old; the clasps are rusted. Inside there's a plastic bag, wrapped round something rectangular, boxy but irregular. Even as I unwrap it I know exactly what it is. Its weight is familiar, its solidity. I've held it before. I've used it, shot with it; it's the thing that started me on the path that led here. My first camcorder.

I open the case. There's a tape in there, but when I try to switch on the machine it's dead. The battery is empty, I suppose, or perhaps age and the damp conditions have wrecked it completely.

There's something else in the satchel, too. Two postcards. I pull them out, my head swimming. The first is a montage of images—a bright red London bus, Tower Bridge, the Houses of Parliament, St. Paul's Cathedral—all arranged around the single word *LONDON*, as if it were necessary. I flip it over, breath held, but there's nothing on the other side but David's address—Bluff House, Blackwood Bay— and a single stamp.

The second postcard is a picture of the Millennium Wheel. On the other side of this, in the same handwriting as the first, there's a message. *I'm coming back*, it says.

I stare at it for a while. The handwriting matches the card sent to Dan. My heart slows. I'm curiously calm. Now that the uncertainty has fallen away, I'm almost relieved. I know what I have to do. I put the camcorder in my bag and stand.

Something is wrong, though. A light on the kitchen ceiling gutters, an orange glow, as if a candle has been lit.

"Daisy?" I say, but the only response is my own echoing, tremulous voice. "Daisy?" I say once more, and go into the kitchen. The trailer is framed in the window, and the source of the light is obvious. It's ablaze, the flames smacking off the melting windows, smoke rolling from the skylight.

Doubt falls away. She thought I was in there. She's trying to kill me.

47

The following day, Gavin says he'll meet me at Liz's café. When I arrive he's outside, shivering in the cold. The place is empty, the lights off, the door shuttered. A sign in the window says she's closed for the holidays.

"Is that usual?" I say as I arrive.

"No idea."

He makes no move to embrace me and none to kiss me, even in greeting.

"What's wrong?"

"Nothing," he says. It's clear he's lying.

"Gavin?"

He gazes down at his feet and shuffles awkwardly. There's less than a yard between us but it feels as wide as a canyon. I don't know what to say, but when he returns my gaze he looks hurt. He pauses, chewing his lip.

"I've been thinking. And . . ."

"What?"

"You promised."

"What?"

"No more lies."

I have to concentrate: I can't afford to give anything away. Not until I know what he means.

"I thought I meant something to you."

"You do," I say, and in this moment, right when it might be too late, I realize I mean it.

"Sadie," he says. "Stop lying to me. I know who you are."

The ground shifts and the world tilts by an inch or two. An abyss opens in front of me, a black hole. *No*, I think. I can't get sucked in, I won't. I draw breath. I can't let him see what's happening, but there's no way I can stop myself.

"Sadie?"

The word echoes. I wish he'd stop saying it. Anyone might hear.

"Are you okay?"

I don't answer at first, but then I hear myself say I'm sorry. The breath catches in my throat but, even as the words emerge, I'm not sure I mean them. It's none of his business, so why am I apologizing? He has no right to be angry.

Nevertheless, I say it again. "I'm sorry."

He holds my face tenderly in his hands. I fight the urge to recoil, to tell him to get the fuck away.

"You couldn't tell me?"

I say nothing. I want to ask him how he knows, but I suppose it's obvious. He saw me at my mother's grave. Heard me insisting that Sadie was alive and that we couldn't go to the police, that she couldn't be buried there on the moors.

"You put two and two together?"

"And this, too." He reaches for my arm and I let him. He pushes back my sleeve. "I noticed it that first night we were together. There are always signs. Of abuse?"

I try to pull away, but he holds me still. He's gentle, but he's tracing my scars. His fingers leave a trail, like tiny insects under my skin, burrowing.

"I wanted to talk to you before, after we went to your mother's grave, but with Ellie going missing . . . And I understand why you tried to hide it, but it's nothing to be ashamed of. They're nothing to be ashamed of."

No, I think. No. *All that happened later, after I ran.*

"Stop it."

"A lot of survivors self-harm. It's quite—"

"It's not self-harm. I had an accident. Boiling soup."

He stares at me. He doesn't believe me.

"You talk in your sleep, too. You know that, don't you?"

I think of my ex. He'd found it funny. You don't stop, he told me once. Muttering under your breath. It's like you're having a right old row.

"You kept saying her name. Daisy."

I nod. Mute. It seems the truth does always come out, in the end. The lost really are always desperate to be found.

"You won't tell anyone, will you?"

He says he won't, but I'm not sure I believe him. Perhaps I'm too late and he already has.

"You could've been honest with me," he says.

I lean in, close. I want to believe him. I want him to reach out, to hold me. I want to believe someone can love me without wanting something from me. But I'm not sure I can.

He stares straight at me, his head tilted. He has a sad half-smile of compassion pasted across the lower half of his face, though it doesn't reach his eyes. "You can trust me."

I don't know what to tell him. I don't know how to give him enough, without giving him everything. That's the problem; I never have. "I like you," he says. "A lot."

He seems suddenly like a schoolboy. I know what I'm supposed to say, here. The words even form, but they choke themselves off in my throat and I say nothing. He shakes his head sadly.

"You don't feel the same."

"It's not that," I say.

"What, then?"

I hesitate. I feel like I'm wading out to sea; the water is black, the ocean floor precarious. At any moment it might disappear and leave me floundering.

"I just feel so . . ."

What? I think. Lost? Empty? Eventually, I find the word. I'd forced it into a box, locked it away, but of course it's still there. It has to be. I wasn't there for her when she needed me. I ran instead, and then she disappeared, too. There's no getting away from that.

"Guilty."

"It's not your fault."

"What?"

"That Daisy took her own life. You did everything you could. Those men . . . they were hurting you; you were right to run away. You had to. No one would blame you."

But they do. Someone blames me. She blames me.

"You don't understand. I didn't run away because of that."

He lowers his voice. "You don't have to lie to me."

"What?"

He looks down. "I know . . . I know it happened to Zoe, too."

I'm silent. He's right, I think.

"I tried to be there for her."

I don't know what to say, and so I just say, "I'm sorry."

"No wonder she ran. If that's even what happened to her." He raises his eyes. They glisten. "What if she really is dead? Like Daisy. What if—?"

"Daisy isn't dead."

"What?"

I stare at him. The moment stretches until it's about to snap and only then do I speak.

"She sent the postcard. She drove up that first night before you came along. In David's car, I think. She's been behind everything."

He's staring at me. He believes I'm fragile, but he's starting to wonder now, wonder how deeply the fracture of abuse has cut.

"You're serious?"

I can see him struggling. Light begins to bleed from the sky.

"She's over there," I say. "At David's house. I'm sure of it."

I tell him about being locked in the trailer and he swallows thickly. "We should go to the police," he says.

I put my hand on his. "I can't," I say. "Not yet." I dig the camcorder out of my bag. "I just need you to help me. I can't explain. But will you? Please?"

He takes it from me and weighs it in his hand.

"Can you get it working? Or transfer stuff from the tape?"

"Then we'll go to the police?"

"Yes," I say, because I know I've run out of options. "I promise."

48

I press *Record*.

I've balanced the camera on the dresser and am sitting on the edge of the bed. The soft glow from the bedside lamp throws my face into partial shadow. My features are indistinct; I could be anyone.

"This is a message for my friend," I begin. I stare down the lens, picturing Daisy there rather than the blank face of the camera. I take a deep breath. "My best friend."

I pause. I haven't planned what I'm going to say. I picture Monica watching it, Beverly in the pub. Gavin and the rest. I wonder what they'll think.

"I know you sent me the card."

Liz, I think. She might watch it, too. Sophie, Kat, Ellie. Anyone. I have to be careful; I can't let them know Daisy is back. I don't want to expose her, to let her down again. I feel like I'm on a ledge, fifteen stories up; one wrong move and I'll go over. I mustn't look down; if I do, I'll stumble and fall, or be compelled to jump.

"I think I know why. I want you to know. I didn't mean to hurt you. I want to help you."

I lean forward, closer to the camera. I imagine her there, staring at me. Defying me. Her eyes would be wide, rebellious. *Go on*, she'd say. *If you're so sure you can help me, if you're so certain you've figured it out, prove it.*

I remember the symbol I saw in her trailer, right by her bed. "I know about Andromeda," I say. "And I remember when you got your tattoo."

My hand goes to my arm, as if I could feel the bite of the imaginary needle myself. We'd gone together. They were going to match, but only she went through with it. I chickened out, almost as if I'd known about the accident that would have rendered the whole thing pointless anyway.

I remember the woman who tattooed her; she had hair dyed the color of blood but with the glossy sheen of ripe tomatoes. I remember a burning heart on her chest, wreathed in barbed wire.

"I wimped out," I say. I know she'll remember, she'll know I'm talking to her, and only to her. "But I won't this time. I promise."

I close my eyes and draw a deep breath. I stare straight into the camera.

"I can help you. If you let me."

I press *Stop*, then upload the clip and make it public. I wonder how long it'll be before she sees it. I know she's watching. After all, she's been watching all along.

*All I can do now is wait. I don't want to sleep, despite my ex-*haustion. I'm too scared of what might be down there, lurking in the deep. Of what might rise to the surface if I look too hard.

Instead, I keep moving. I make strong, bitter coffee, thick as sludge, and pour myself cup after cup. In the living room, I turn off the main light and sit in the pooled luminosity from the screen of my laptop. I can see my reflection in the window, but nothing else. Outside is darkness. A black void; even the moon is invisible, hidden behind clouds. I know she's out there. *You got away*, she's saying, *while I might as well be buried in the black soil. You wanted me to rot, after all.*

I sip my drink. I'm jittery. It's the caffeine, I suppose. The room goes dark as the screen sleeps. My eyes close. My head sinks. A moment of blackness, then her face appears and with a wordless grunt I jolt myself awake.

More coffee. Slug it down. Back to the circle of light.

I watch the clock, floating in and out of consciousness. Even when I'm awake I feel numb, half dreaming. It's like my body is a puppet, a mannequin. My strings are cut. The clock ticks, endlessly. *Rain* to *Stormy.*

It must be nearly midnight when the knife-tap ping of a new submission jerks me into life. A calm folds itself over me, I know exactly what it is and who it's from. I breathe in deep, filling my lungs, then wake my machine. This is it. My chance to save Daisy. My chance to say sorry, for whatever it is I've done. My chance to win her back.

The screen is black. *Play.* A flash of low cloud, the distant moon, flipping in and out of focus, then the image settles. Bluff House snaps into focus.

The image shakes then, and a second later, low and rough, disguised but chillingly familiar, there's a female voice.

"I'm here now," it says. "Come alone."

49

When I turn my back on Hope Cottage, it's with the feeling I won't see it again. There's a light on next door, a shadow moving in the upstairs window, and from inside floats the sound of voices. Without pausing to think, I knock and wait.

Monica opens the door.

"Alex!"

She seems surprised. I look terrible, I know that. No makeup, my hair's a mess, I haven't slept. Now I'm here, I don't know what to say. I thought I'd hate her as soon as I saw her, but I find I can't. She seems too pathetic. Too weak.

"Can I come in?"

She regards me levelly.

"It's not a good time."

I keep my voice calm. I can deal with what she's done later, once I've met with Daisy, once I know what I did. After all, Monica doesn't know how much I know. She has no idea what I've seen.

I remember her words on the phone.

"She's back," I say. "You know it, and I know it."

She tilts her head with incredulity. It's almost comical, a parody of confusion.

"Come on," I say. "Let's stop fucking about and be honest with each other, shall we?"

For a second I think she's going to slam the door in my face, but then she seems to relent.

"You'd best come in."

I scan the room. The sofa is empty; there's a single wineglass on the coffee table. The voices were coming from a television upstairs. A soap opera.

"You know she's at David's, right?"

"Who?"

"Daisy."

I see her pupils flare but then she turns away to reach for her cigarettes. She sits on the edge of the chair opposite and folds her legs precisely beneath her, composing herself, before sliding them toward me. I ignore them.

"You're wrong. She's dead." Her tone is flat; it lacks conviction. "She jumped. I saw—"

"Tell the truth. Daisy didn't jump."

"I *saw* her."

"She's alive. She contacted me."

She fumbles for her lighter. "How? Through your little film? We've all watched it, you know." The flame stutters as she lights up. "You're just an outsider, come up here to stir stuff up—"

"No—" I say, but she ignores me.

"—stuff you know nothing about."

I take a step forward, try to stay calm. Her anger is a defense. She's scared, I think. I wonder how much she knows.

"That's not true."

She exhales a cloud of blue smoke, cool now. "Just so you can make one of your films. About us."

I shake my head, defiant. "She's not dead."

"We're good people. Understand? She jumped. It's sad, but that's what happened. She jumped off The Rocks and she's dead. We don't need you up here, throwing about all kinds of accusations."

"No," I say. "She was abused. I have a film. You didn't know that, did you?"

"Of?"

"It's Daisy. Pleading for her life. She sent it to me."

Her cigarette halts midway between her mouth and the ashtray.

"What's going on here?" I say.

"Nothing." She stares down at it. "Nothing, I swear."

"You're lying. I know you're involved."

Her head jerks up, her eyes narrowed and venomous. "What?"

I say it again, but she's in control of her reactions now. She's unmoving, impervious. Rigid. How can I break through to her?

"Monica? She's begging in that film. Pleading for her fucking life. Tell me what's going on. What are you doing to the girls?"

She lifts her cigarette once more. Her hand shakes, but she says nothing.

"You might as well tell me the truth." I hold her gaze. "I know anyway. I have evidence."

"You know nothing."

"I know what happens. Out at the stables."

She stiffens.

"I know about the drugs. The booze." I hesitate. "The parties."

"You know nothing. I'm not hurting the girls. I'm helping them."

My skin flushes. I laugh. I can't help it.

"Helping them? How, exactly? You know what goes on at these parties, right?"

"No, it's not like that. The boys . . . they drive them there. They bring them back. They look after them."

"You don't really believe that."

She meets my gaze but her eyes flitter and she looks like an animal caught in headlights, like the sheep on the road in the instant before it was hit.

"It's true. They enjoy the parties. They want to go."

"That's what they tell you? Are you sure they even have a choice?"

She's silent.

"They're raped there, Monica. You know that, don't you?"

"They get paid."

"Paid? What for?"

"They lead the men on. Get a photo. They don't go through with it. Unless . . ."

"Unless?"

"Some of them might choose to have sex. That's up to them! Nothing to do with me . . ."

My body tenses, a tsunami of rage.

"What the fuck? They're, what? Thirteen years old? Fourteen?"

"But—"

"They're kids! It's rape, Monica. However you cut it. Zoe was pregnant!"

Her head falls and I see my chance.

"Why did Sadie run? Tell me. What did she do?"

"No." Her voice cracks, just a little.

"Tell me, or I swear I'll go to the police, show them every film I've been sent, and let—"

"Stop!"

Her interruption is fierce. Her eyes flare; she's twitchy, desperate.

"She died!"

"What?"

"Sadie died! She died. Okay?"

"No. She didn't."

She pays no heed. The energy has flooded out of her and she sighs, a juddering, monumental sigh that seems to leave her whole body diminished.

"It's true. All of it. She's dead and buried. She died, and then Daisy killed herself."

Her voice is tiny. I can barely hear her, but still I say, "No."

I shake my head, but I'm sinking, too, slipping beneath the waves. I need to keep my secret, I think. I can't be exposed. But now another voice comes in, loud and urgent. What's the point? it says. Gavin knows anyway.

"You don't understand."

"Understand what?"

I can't hold it in anymore.

"Sadie isn't dead."

"What?"

I can't stop. I know I should, but I can't. It's out before I can calm down.

"She can't be. She's me."

I've got her. She's shaken. The incredulity on her face is genuine this time.

"It's true," I whisper. "I'm Sadie. I changed my name."

"No," she says. She stands up abruptly. The ashtray slides off her lap and hits the floor in a shower of sparks. She leans forward, looks at me strangely.

"It's true," I repeat. "It's why I'm back."

"No."

"Daisy was my friend," I say. "I just want to understand what happened."

"Sadie?"

"Yes."

"Sadie Davies?"

"Yes. I ran away. I lost weight, had surgery. I wanted a new start."

Her hand goes to my cheek. Her touch is tender but still it burns.

"But . . ."

"What happened to me here?"

"You don't know?"

My hearts thuds. *No,* I think. *No!* Everything hangs on this, and

I can't remember. The airless room begins to spin and I feel myself pale.

"Are you okay?" she says, lifting her other hand to my cheek so that she's cradling me. The kindness in her eyes is more than I can bear and I begin to cry.

"I keep . . . I keep remembering things . . . I'm not sure . . . it's like something happened to me here, something bad, but I don't know what. I've blocked it."

She says nothing. I have to ask her.

"Why did Daisy disappear? Really?"

Again, nothing.

"Was it over me? Because of something I did? I mean, if it was something big, I'd remember, wouldn't I? Please help me find her."

She exhales, lifts burning eyes to meet mine. I feel like she's looking inside me, reaching into my guts.

"I can't."

"Why?"

"I can't explain. I just . . . I can't."

"Then at least don't tell anyone else, will you?" I say. "About who I am? No one else can know."

She regards me for a moment, then her face seems to melt.

"I won't tell. I promise."

I thank her and get to my feet. I'd thought she could help me, but now I know she can't. No one can. I wipe away my tears. I'm on my own.

50

*B*luff House is in darkness, just as I left it a few hours ago. The fire is out; the fire engine I summoned anonymously must've departed. Beneath me the streets are empty and The Ship quiet and still. The streetlamps sputter in the gloom.

I have to do this. I can't walk up Slate Road, head down, and get in my car, turn left instead of right, foot down all the way home. I'd be back in my little flat by morning, my housemate still asleep, washing-up not done, bowls sitting in the sink, crusted with breakfast cereal and pasta. I can't go back with no film, though even that doesn't matter now. I have to find out the truth. Break the cycle.

It's begun to snow once more. The flakes meander as they fall and melt as they land in my hair and on my face. When I look up at the clouds it's like they're rushing toward me, or I'm zooming through them, firing into space. I can feel her watching me. She knows I'm here.

I knock gently on the door. My apology is ripe on my tongue. I'll plead with her to tell me the truth about what happened, to let me make it right. I'm ready, I think, for whatever she wants to do.

When there's no answer I try again, and again, until I'm certain she's not going to come to the door. I retreat and tread carefully toward the edge, lost and uncertain. There's a boulder here and I sit on it, gazing out to sea, as if the waves may tell me what to do.

My phone vibrates in my pocket. It's Gavin.

"Where are you?"

"The Rocks."

"Why?"

I hesitate, then tell him. "I know you don't believe me, but Daisy got in touch. I was supposed to meet her at Bluff House."

"And?"

"She's not here."

"I can't say I'm surprised," he says. "I got that camcorder working. There was a clip on the tape. I'm sending it through."

"What is it?"

"Watch it. Watch it now."

I end the call, and a moment later my phone vibrates with a message. As I press *Play* my stomach contracts, balling itself into a fist. The screen resolves into a view of The Rocks, the very spot I'm sitting. It's night, but bright, the moon is full; it gleams on the shimmering water, glittering the depths. The viewpoint is high, almost like a crane shot. But it's not, of course. It was shot from inside David's house, an upper room. His bedroom, most likely. A song begins, hummed quietly by the person with the camera. David, I suppose. It has to be.

Dai-sy, Dai-sy, give me your answer, do.

We pan down; at the very bottom of the frame a girl appears, walking away from the house. She's wearing a short black jacket, blue jeans, and a pair of white trainers. Her hair is wild, whipped by the wind as if it's trying to escape, or strangle her. She has her head down. She crosses the path onto the grass, then steps down nearer the edge. She doesn't stop. She doesn't look round.

Dai-sy, Dai-sy, give me your answer, do.
I'm half crazy, all for the love of you.

She pauses. I lean in, so close to the screen that my breath mists its surface. *No*, I think. You don't jump. You take off your trainer and toss it into the waves. Your jacket, too. You turn around, go back to the house, to the note you've written. You've already persuaded Monica to tell people she saw you jump—how, I don't know. It's all set. I've seen through your game. If you jump, how can you still be here?

As I watch, she crouches, almost as if she's praying, or looking out over the edge, seeing how far down it is, how far she has to fall. Or maybe she's taking off her trainer.

She stands. The light of the moon catches her. She glows in the dark; she looks like a ghost. Her head falls. She doesn't glance back. She takes one step forward, then another, until she's right at the edge.

And then she jumps.

I watch it again. Over and over, and each time I press Play I think maybe she'll turn back this time and it will be different. But she doesn't. She walks. She pauses, crouches, stands. Then she disappears.

Was I wrong? I thought her suicide wasn't real, she was still here. But this? This is the proof of what Monica saw. Her, alone, jumping off the edge of the world.

I think of David. Why did you film this? Why didn't you help her? There's no panic after she jumps, either. No dropping of the camera, no exclamation of shock or horror. The shot doesn't even wobble. He was expecting it, watching it. The image is static for a few seconds, then it ends, the screen sliding effortlessly to black just as her body must have hit the water.

No, I think. No. It can't be right. And yet, what other explanation can there be? She jumped. It's as simple as that. She wasn't pushed; it was no accident. She didn't invent the whole thing. She walked to the edge of the world and let herself fall into nothingness.

So what's going on? Who attacked me? Who's been sending me the messages, if not her? How can she have sent me footage of her own abuse, her own fear? How did she send me the postcard that lured me up here in the first place?

Could she have survived the jump? I imagine her body, hidden in the darkness along with the fish, clinging to the rocks with the limpets and crabs, swimming under the surface.

But to where? Even if she survived the fall, the currents are strong; it's a long way to swim alone and at night. Unless . . .

I stand and walk to the edge of the cliff. I take a step nearer and look down. Is it possible?

The water is black, flecked with white foam shining in the moonlight. It roils. And yet, it's not that far away, not really. Liz is right: it's not that high. A little way out of the village the coast curves sharply, and beyond that the edge begins to rise, gently at first, but with an increasing slope. She wouldn't have had to go far to find a cliff much higher, a drop much more precipitous, and onto rocks. Why choose here, right outside David's place?

What was it Liz said? *Seems there are better ways, if she really wanted to die. Unless she wanted to make a statement.*

Daisy. You're a clever girl.

I fall to my knees and shuffle closer still. I dig my hands into the soil and peer over, shifting my weight as far forward as I dare. The winds shrieks in my ears, the water rages below, and I wonder what would happen if I leapt, too. But it's no good, it's too dark. I can see nothing.

I need to get closer.

51

I wait for daylight. It promises a beautiful winter's day, exactly ten years since Daisy disappeared. It doesn't feel like a coincidence.

I worked it out last night. David helped her, like he helped Kat and Ellie. And Zoe. He filmed Kat and Ellie eating chips and smoking a joint to try to let me know something was going on, and he filmed Daisy's plummet from the cliff in case anyone ever doubted she jumped. And that's why he wanted to see me, the night I found him by the lighthouse. He wanted to give me the film from his camcorder. The proof.

So Daisy isn't dead. The only missing piece is how. How she survived. That, and why she's back, why she's skulking in the shadows and why, if she wants to kill me, she doesn't just get it over with.

I turn over and look at my phone. It's eight thirty and I've arranged to meet Gavin at ten. I've told him we'll go to the police and tell them what we've found, that he's right, it's the only way.

But there's something else I need to do first.

I meet Bryan by the slipway. The tide is in, the boat already on the water. It looks smaller than I'd remembered it, more fragile.

"You okay?" he says as I approach.

"Fine," I say, even though I'm not. My hands are shaking, my voice cracked. I'm hoping he'll think it's the cold.

"Figured anything out about Daisy yet?"

I fake a smile. "Still working on it," I say.

"You wrapped up? It'll be freezing on the water. You can swim, right?"

I look up at the feathery clouds that hang over Bluff House. There's no point in telling the truth.

"I can swim, yes. I just don't like the water. If I fall in, you'll just have to jump in and rescue me."

He examines me warily; he's not sure whether I'm joking. But there's something in his gaze. He'd do it. If it came down to it. He'd haul me to safety; I know he would.

But how can I be so certain? I stare into his eyes. I recognize their metallic glint. I remember them from way back, from the time before. But if that's true, then why is every other memory of him lost?

"Shall we?"

He grabs a rope and heaves the boat closer to the slipway. The sea is flat, almost still. The birds have gone.

"Hop in."

I do so, and he follows me. I sit at the back of the boat as he unhooks us and starts the engine. We head out into the open water, and every now and again he glances at me to see how I'm doing. I smile weakly. I've begun to shiver, half with the cold, but mostly through fear. I can't help it. A nameless dread has infused every part of me. All I can see is the water, its hugeness, salty and cold. All I can think of are the endless depths beneath me, waiting to suck me down. The creatures that hide in the dark.

He accelerates a little and we begin to bounce over the water, faster than I'd thought possible, faster than I'd like. Is he showing off? After a minute I can't bear it any longer. Nausea stirs in my gut.

"Can we slow down?"

"Sorry?"

I shout louder, over the noise of the engine. I pat my camera, now in its waterproof case.

"I want to film!"

He cuts the engine to a dull thrum and I focus the viewfinder. I record The Ship, the slipway, the groynes that cut into the beach. Material that may well prove useful, but that's a secondary consideration. I'm going through the motions. I look up at Bluff House. It seems farther away from down here, the cliffs higher.

"Can we go over that way?"

"Aye," he says. He steers us toward the cliff, increasing speed once more. My heart beats as loud as the engine's roar; I can't look down at the water as it parts beneath us and neither can I look out at the cliff from which my best friend threw herself. I look up instead, at the blue sky, the thin cloud beneath. Way in the distance a single bird appears, too far away to be identifiable, circling like carrion.

I think of Daisy, here in the water, looking up at the night sky. What did she glimpse? The moon, perhaps, or the stars of Orion, of Pegasus and Andromeda. Deep red Betelgeuse, so distant and already dead. The endless black, above and below.

But then what did she do? Did she swim, after all? Did she find safety?

Bryan glances back.

"Here okay?"

"Can we get a bit nearer?"

We leave the shelter of the bay. The water is choppier here; a fine, freezing spray soaks my face. My stomach turns with the cloying stink of petrol. We're approaching the house now. The cliff is jagged, striated, layered with time. There's an overhang; I see her fall, straight down into the water.

"Any good?"

My camera is limp around my neck and I lift it. I film the house, the rocks. I film Malby in the distance, its blinking lights. Why didn't we go there? Daisy and I? Why didn't we take off together? What did I do to you that meant you had to jump? Again, I try to work out whether it might've been possible to survive the fall, then swim round the bay, to the slipway, perhaps, or in the other direction, to the nearest beach. It looks too far, even for a strong swimmer like Daisy.

"Bit closer?"

We continue, and then I see a shape, under the surface of the water. Nothing more than a dark shadow carved into the cliff; a jagged, shimmering hole. A cave, just a yard or so across at its widest point, but still it's a cave. A place to hide. I imagine Daisy there, trapped below the waterline, squirming like a worm caught on the hook. Waiting to be rescued, but by whom?

Bryan cuts the engine.

"You know," he says, "it's been ten years?"

I look blankly at him, but he's not stupid, he can see what it is I'm filming, that I'm focused on Bluff House and the cave beneath it. He knows this isn't about background footage for a film examining the everyday life of Blackwood Bay, a film I no longer think I can finish. He knows exactly what this is.

"Today, I mean. Ten years since she jumped."

I look back to where he sits. We're bobbing in the water in the shadow of the cliff. He's staring at me. His face is calm, his voice quiet, but there's something deliberate about it, as if he's more upset than he's letting on, having to make an effort to appear this together.

Suddenly, it makes sense.

"You knew her," I say. "Better than you told me."

"You don't understand," he says. "Do you?"

I don't answer, and he makes no move. His eyes are hard, black as pebbles. I feel afraid, though I can't say why. All I can think of is the water beneath me, still beneath the squall. Déjà vu.

He shifts his weight and, crouching, moves up the boat.

"You shouldn't have come back here."

Back here. He knows.

"Monica's told you?"

My voice is blank, but he ignores me anyway.

"What are you trying to do?" he says. "Make your documentary?" His tone mocks me.

"No." I look him in the eye. "Find out the truth."

"About what?"

"You know what."

He laughs, quietly, but his voice is black with sarcasm, bitter. I recognize it. I can hear him back then, the same laugh.

You know what you are, he's saying. *You know what you've always been.*

My mind begins to slip, to fall away. I grip the side of the boat.

"Why are you lying?" he says.

I knew him, I think. *Back then*. I knew him.

"You trying to finish what you started?"

"What *I* started?"

He laughs.

"I don't know what you're talking about," I say. My mind races. "I want to know what happened to my friend."

"Your friend? The friend you killed?"

"*No!*" I say.

My mind cowers, tries to flee into a dark corner, but now I can't hide from the memories. I see Daisy then, back as she was in the film. She's pleading. *Help me! Please! You said they wouldn't hurt me.*

And I'm there. Holding the camera. I'm there now.

I won't, I'm saying, but I don't know if that's true, because there's someone standing behind me, watching me and Daisy, and he wants me to hurt her, he wants me to kill her. I'm desperate to turn around, to tell him I've changed my mind and that this is sick, he's crazy, we have to let her go, but I can't. This is the only way I'm going to get what I need, it's the only way to make the sickness go away.

I hear myself sob. I'm not sure if it's the me—Alex—who's here on the boat, or Sadie way back then.

Do it, comes a voice. I'm back there again. I put the camera down, making sure to keep my friend in shot. I take a step toward her. I hear someone laugh, and I jolt: I'm still on the boat and it's Bryan, here and now, in front of me.

I'm reeling with the pull of the waves, the violent ebb and flow of the past and the present. I stand, and the boat rocks, spray hits, needles of ice. I almost slip but catch myself in time. It shocks me back into my body.

"You'd better watch yourself, baby."

Baby? Despite his venom, the word lands on my skin as soft as falling snow, as if it's a word I could once sink into. I remember him calling me that before. I remember him giving me the camcorder. A present, he said, for my special girl. If only I'd known how he'd one day want me to use it.

Images flicker. I see Daisy; she's on her knees. The camera is running. But what happened next? The memory won't come, it's lost, the data overwritten in the decade since.

He stands up now, moves toward me. The boat rocks once more and he laughs as I stumble.

Bryan. It's Bryan, laughing now, just as it was Bryan who was laughing back then. Bryan who told me my best friend had to die.

"*You!* You killed her!"

He shakes his head, but he's still smiling.

"I remember it now, I know I do. You killed her. And you made me film it."

His smile is black. "No, baby. You did."

I'm falling, I can feel it. Bitten by the salt spray, my mind is corroding, my body eaten away. What balance I had is skewed. My whole being revolts. *No! I didn't kill anyone!* it screams. But even as it does, I realize that it's true.

I've got what I wanted, I think, wryly. I wanted the truth, and here it is.

I clutch the side of the boat and look beyond him. The sun is up, but it's clouding over.

"Take me back."

"And let you tell people what happened?"

I scuttle away from him, but there's only so far I can go. My foot connects with something—coiled rope, perhaps—and I stumble once more.

"Careful, now," he says, but it's without concern. He steps closer and pushes me, not hard, but enough that I'm forced to sit heavily on the edge of the boat. The water soaks through my trousers, numbingly cold.

"We don't want you falling in, now, do we? Such a tragic accident . . ."

I remember my friend.

"What did you do to her?"

"We buried her. You know that."

I have to ask, even though I already know.

"Where?"

"You know that, too."

I try to figure it out. Did she jump, but survive, only to have Bryan kill her anyway? *Bastard*, I think. *Bastard*. But somehow I know instinctively not to say it out loud. I see him, standing over me; he has his belt in his hand. He's wrapped it round my neck. He's going to teach me a lesson, he says. It'll be fun. I need to learn how to behave. I need to learn who it is, out of all of them, who loves me the most.

No, insulting him won't help. I remember now. The only thing that ever worked with him was me on my knees, pleading, begging. And even that failed toward the end.

"Let me go."

"*Alex*," he says, spitting my name with a spiteful smirk. "You know I can't do that."

"Please."

He shakes his head. "I really thought you were gone for good, you know. We all did. Yet here you are. And we can't make the same mistake again."

"No! I'll keep quiet, I promise I will."

"I wish I could believe you."

He's standing over me. He has the boat hook in his hand. I know what he means to do. Kill me, like he killed Daisy.

"Bryan, please."

"She fell," he says, his voice suddenly low, grief-stricken, mocking. He's talking about me, imagining the questions he'll be asked when he reports my death and how he'll answer them. "I tried to save her. But she must've hit her head."

"Bryan, no. Please—"

"I think it was suicide—"

"No."

"She wanted to go. Guilt, perhaps? No, I had no idea who she really was. None of us did. She'd changed so very much."

"Bryan, please," I whisper, as if it'll do any good. The hand in which he holds the boat hook twitches.

"It's for the best," he says, lifting the weapon above his head as if it's a baseball bat. I look into his eyes, and I realize, with utter certainty now, that he means to kill me.

I have no choice. Better to drown, to die by my own hand, than let him win. I take a deep breath.

I jump into the cold, black water.

52

I go under. My ears fill with a cacophonous roar; it's so cold my heart stops and I think it'll never start again. Salt stings my throat and I force myself not to breathe. I must fight, but I don't know how, I don't know which way is up, in which direction I might find life. I kick against nothing, thinking of Daisy as I do, wondering if this is what happened to her, how she went from begging for her life in that cellar to stepping off the edge of the cliff. The questions keep circling in my head. Is she alive, or not? How can she be, if it's true that I killed her?

I can't focus for long. I'm too heavy. My jeans and jacket weigh me down, but I'm not sure whether taking them off will help or instead be a waste of energy; crucial time spent sinking rather than trying to rise. I can't think, I don't know. I feel both weightless and as heavy as a rock.

Then something—I don't know what, survival instinct, perhaps—

takes hold and my legs whip kick. I reach out with my hands and scoop the icy water before pulling them back, as if lifting myself onto a ledge. I feel a tiny thrust upward and begin to move through the darkness. I break the surface of the water and come up, gasping, into the light.

It takes me a moment to orient myself. The boat is behind me; ahead of me, the cliffs. I need to swim, but I don't know how, and a second later something thuds in the water next to me. Bryan is leaning over the edge of the vessel, wild-eyed, the boat hook in his hands. He raises it, and I try to move as it crashes down once more, this time glancing off the side of my head. I go under.

I begin to pull myself through the water, heading vaguely toward the cliffs. Slowly, I make progress. Behind me, the engine starts, sputters, then fails. Some luck at last, but for how long? I pull harder, again and again, and it starts to feel more natural, I get into the rhythm of the swim, feeling the kick and glide. It feels almost like I've always known how to do it, I'd just forgotten.

After six or seven strokes I come up for air. The boat is behind me now, a fair distance, but I don't know how much longer he'll struggle to get the engine going. And when he does I'm done for, he'll come for me, finish what he started. The same thought occurs that I noticed in the car that first night—this is not how it ends, this is not how I die—except this time the conviction feels void and another voice comes in. Daisy's voice. *What if you're wrong*, it says, *and this is it? What if this is what you deserve, after what you did to me?*

I pull harder. I stand no chance of making it back to the beach so I aim for the cliff. I feel anesthetized by the cold, spent. The current is helping a little now but, even if I make it, there's nothing there. It's not like I can climb up and reach David's house.

I see it then. The cave, a tiny half-submerged scar gouged out of the rock. It feels like my only chance. I kick toward it as behind me the boat's engine roars into life. One more gulp of air, and I go under. Kick, pull. Kick, pull. The thrum of the boat grows, ferocious, and I think I'm not going to make it, but then it seems to fade, as if he's given up, decided to set out for the bay instead. Perhaps he thinks I've gone under, one last time. Either way, it makes no difference now.

Kick. Pull. Over and over, and then I'm there. The entrance to the crevice is only a little bigger than I am; I have to dive under the water to make it through. I squeeze into the dark. The blackness is complete, but when I put my feet down they find rock. The cave has a floor. The silence closes over me like the earth in a grave.

I breathe. In. Out. I'm alive. Cold, but alive. Exhaustion gathers in the distance; sleep prepares to roll over me like a wave. I can't let that happen.

My body is underwater from the chest down. My limbs begin to sing with pain. I reach out, upward first, and map the contours of the chamber. The roof of the cave is just a few inches above my head, hard and covered with slime. The walls to the left and right are a bit farther, but not much. It feels like a coffin, stood on end. I have visions of the air running out, the cave filling with water as the tide comes in. I see myself drowning. My body trapped here, for who knows how long. And I know what Bryan will say, if they even ask him.

I've no idea where she went. I haven't seen her.

Daisy, I think. Is that what happened to you?

A woman's voice echoes in the dark.

"Are you going to stand there forever?"

It hits me hard as a punch. I recognize it. I'd recognize it anywhere. It's her.

"Daisy?"

Relief thunders through me as the truth snaps into focus. I was right all along. I didn't kill her. Bryan was lying. She must've jumped from the cliff and into the water, then swum to the cave. She escaped. I didn't kill her. She's here, not buried on the moor.

But has she been here all along? In this cavern under the rocks, waiting for me?

"You came," she says. "I knew you would. Only you're not there yet."

I draw breath. My teeth clash painfully together, stammering with the cold.

"Help me."

"Turn around."

I do as she's suggested. I swivel toward her voice.

"Put your hand out. To the left. Feel the gap?"

I stumble blindly but find the narrow opening in the rock.

"Go through."

The entrance to a tunnel, perhaps? The gap is little more than a slit.

"Daisy?" I say hesitantly. "I can't."

"You can," she says. "You have to. I did."

I turn side-on. The air is stale; there's the sharp taste of salt. If it weren't for her voice, I'd be certain it was a dead end.

"Daisy?"

"You're fine," she says. "Just try harder."

I stretch out my hand. She's near, but how did she get here? There must be a tunnel, a way in from above. It's the only explanation.

I think back to the legends, the smugglers who could land their contraband and get it up to the clifftop without it ever seeing the light of day. This must be one of their routes.

Suddenly, I feel it. It's like I knew about this place, have known it all along.

"Daisy, please?"

She says nothing, and I realize she'd no way of knowing I'd find my way to the cave this morning. Unless . . .

I see what I've missed. Bryan must've told her he'd deliver me here; they must be working together. Even though just a few minutes ago he'd been trying his hardest to kill me, it must've been just to get me to jump into the water, to swim to the cave, to end up stuck here in this gap.

"Come on," she says. "You can get through. You did it before, after all."

"Before?"

Even as I argue, I know she's right. I have been here before, trapped in this narrow gap. Wondering whether I'll make it through. I breathe in; I wriggle. The jagged rock scrapes against my face and the back of my legs, I taste blood, but then it gives and I almost fall through into a larger chamber beyond.

"There we are," says Daisy, louder now I'm in the same part of the cave. It's as if she can see me in the blackness. "A bit farther."

I step up toward her voice. My hands find a ledge and I lift myself up and out of the water.

"I'm right here."

She's near now. I can hear her breathing, mingled with my own. After all this time, she's close enough to touch, yet I keep my hands still.

"What do you want with me?"

"I've been here all along. Watching you."

"The postcard. You sent it."

"Yes."

"The videos. They were from you."

"Some of them, yes."

I listen to the hypnotic *drip, drip, drip* of water from the roof of the cave. I was right.

"*Why?* Why did you do it?"

"You don't get it, do you? You still don't know."

"To get revenge?" I say. "But you're alive. I didn't do anything."

She sighs. "I thought we were friends."

"We were. We are. You're here, aren't you?"

"And you filmed it. You filmed it."

"I had no choice."

Her voice is mocking. "No choice? *They made me do it?* You and your boyfriend? Bryan." She laughs. "You thought he loved you. All those presents; you thought you'd got it made. Until he gave you that first little white line. Until he started selling you to his friends."

"No. That came later. That was after I'd gone to London."

She laughs once more. A brutal snort of derision. I'm so cold. I feel my body closing down. I want to close my eyes, to sleep.

"Really? You can't still believe that, surely? Not even you can be that stupid."

"It's true," I say, but even as I do I see it, shockingly real. Me and Bryan, we're in bed; he's told me he loves me so I'm happy, but at the same time my stomach is cramping. Tiny insects crawl through my veins; I want to be sick, but then he offers me something. "It'll make you feel better, baby," he says. "It'll be like the first time."

Daisy's voice cuts into my memory. "You remember now?"

Opposing forces rupture through me, nausea spilling up from my guts, vertigo spinning me down. *It can't be true. It can't.*

But she's right. He began sharing me. It started with his dealer, or the guy he said was his dealer, anyway. He said he couldn't pay, he didn't have enough money.

"But there's another way," he said. "You owe me, after all." And even though I said no, my resistance didn't last long. By then I was desperate. By then I was squirming on the hook and would've done anything.

"Anything?" says Daisy, and it's as if she can hear my thoughts. "Even get your best friend involved? Deliver her to them? Get her hooked, too? First on love, then on drugs."

"No," I say. "No." But even as I do, I can see it: it's true.

"Then, when she threatened to talk, they had you kill her."

"But I didn't," I sob. "You're not dead. Daisy, you're not dead."

"No," she says. "That's right. I'm not. But she is."

"Who? Who's dead?"

"You know who." She pauses, and part of me knows what's coming.

The truth cleaves me in two. *No,* I say. *No.* It's not possible, I can't work it out. I see us both, in the cellar. I have the camera; my friend is tied up, she's on her knees. I brought her here, told her there was someone who wanted to meet her. I promised her fun, said we could try something, told her my boyfriend had sorted us out and it'd be the best yet, even better than last time, all we had to do was let it take us away.

"I didn't know what they had planned. I swear it."

"But you still went through with it."

I remember putting the camera down. She looked up at me; there was snot running from her nose. *Don't,* she said. *Don't hurt me.*

She was kneeling on the floor, begging for help. Help I couldn't give her, because I was part of this now.

I have to, I replied, sobbing.

Bryan's voice cut in, then. *Do it,* he said. *If you don't do it, we will, and blame you anyway. So you might as well.*

And so I did. I stepped toward her, the belt limp in my hand. I wondered what he wanted the film for, whether it was just to keep me in line, or if he'd found someone willing to pay for it. I didn't know. But still I did it. I wrapped the belt around my best friend's neck. And then—

No!

"You get it now?" says Daisy, but as she does some kind of door opens farther up the tunnel and the cave is lit with a flash. I react without thinking, shutting my dark-adapted eyes against the searing light, but it's no good. I force them open and look around for my friend, but there's no one there. There never was. It's as if someone has pulled the plug and whatever remained of me has run through the sluice.

I see everything in minute detail, high resolution. I stare at the walls of the cave—the damp, dripping walls that curve upward toward the source of the dazzling light, the chisel marks where it's been widened to make the tunnel more passable.

I feel weightless, more alive than I've felt in years. But the momentary, blissful vacuum implodes. It was me speaking; her voice was in my head. Daisy *is* alive, here with me now, like she was at Hope Cottage, like she was down in London, like she was when I ran away. Like she has been all along.

Because Daisy isn't dead. She's me.

THEN

53

*T*he bed is cold, the sheets heavy. David has central heating, but he doesn't turn it on. He's left a fan-heater in the corner of the room, but it blows feebly and smells of burning hair.

So I lie here and shiver. I'm worthless, anyway.

He knocks on the door. "Daisy?"

Don't call me that, I think. Anything else. But not that.

"Can I come in?"

Tonight is the night. It's nearly time. The tide is right. It was my plan all along, but now we're here I'm not so sure.

"Daisy? Are you okay? I've made you some soup."

I sit up. It's true that I'm hungry. And I'll need all the strength I can get.

*I know I have to escape; I can't stay here. My plan started form-*ing as soon as they returned from burying Sadie on the moors. Bryan has told me that he owns me now, that unless I do as I'm told he'll send the film of me killing Sadie to the police. And I know he would, too. Then it'll all be over. The fact that I hate myself already will make no difference, and neither will the fact that they made me do it, that I had no choice. Not *felt* I had no choice, *actually* had no choice. Sadie had started fighting back, had threatened to tell, so Bryan de-cided. He had to teach her a lesson, and if I refused to help, then he'd have to teach me one, too.

Maybe it would've been better that way, I think now. Then at least I wouldn't have to live with myself, with what I've done.

The plan is my idea, then, but now it comes to it, I'm terrified. It's not just the jump I'm dreading, the plunge into icy water, the swim back to the cave and into the tunnel. Even if it works, even if I get away and no one comes after me because everyone in this place thinks I'm dead, I still won't have escaped. I'll have the drugs to kick. I'll need help, and I don't know how to get it. Things will get worse before they get better; the only question is by how much.

Maybe I should stay here and die. Maybe it's what I deserve.

David puts the soup gently down on the bedside table. "Eat up."

"I'm scared."

My voice is weak. I sound like the little girl I am deep down, and I hate myself for it.

"I know," he says. "But you'll be fine. There's help out there. You're a strong person."

He's always believed in me. It's his voice I heard when I felt like jumping for real. His voice telling me I'm a good person, underneath it all. That he's always known it.

"You think I'll make it?"

He puts his hand on my arm. "I know you will." He's gentle, kind. The kindest any man has ever been to me. Kinder than I merit. "You've written your note?"

"Yes."

"I'll make sure it's found."

"You'll show Mum?"

"We have to. She'll have to tell them it's definitely your writing."

"But you'll tell her? Later? You'll tell her I'm all right."

He nods, softly. "I'll try. But it might be too dangerous."

I thank him. I wish I could tell him why I really need to get away, why convincing them I'm dead is the only way to stop them coming after me. I wish I could tell him how Bryan lied at first, told me I'd just have to pretend, it wasn't going to be real. "We just need to scare her," he'd said, and by the time I realized he was lying, it was too late. He made me pull the belt tighter, even once she'd stopped crying and her whole body went limp. He made me.

Yet it was me who did it. Me who wasn't strong enough to refuse, to fight back, to tell him how evil he was. I wish more than anything I could go back and change everything. I wish I could undo the moment I introduced her to Bryan, the moment I met him myself. Then Sadie and I would still be friends, rather than one of us buried in the cold ground and the other about to either fake her suicide or die in the process.

"So, when you jump . . ." says David, "you know what you have to do."

"Yes," I say. I know the tunnel leads back into the rock, and up into David's cellar. "And you'll film it? Just in case."

He says he will. We've discussed this. My body won't be found; I'm going to take off my trainers and my jacket in the water, but it may not be enough to convince them. If it ever comes to it, he needs to be able to prove I really went over the edge.

"And we'll wait? We'll wait until there's someone to see?"

"Yes," he says. "I'll look through the telescope until I spot some-one coming. You'll have plenty of time. Then we can be sure there'll be a witness. All you have to do is jump and then swim back into the cave."

I tell him I'm ready. The plan is I'll wait in the tunnels. We've put towels and a change of clothes down there, a torch, blankets and some food. It's too risky for me to go up to David's straight away, in case they search the area, but when the time is right he'll come for me. He'll get me out.

"Where will you go?" he says.

I answer straight away. I've been thinking about it for days.

"London."

"You can't use your real name."

"I know."

"You've decided what name you will use?"

Sadie, I think. For a long time I used to wish I was her, imagine it was me who lived over in that big house with her mum, rather than in that shitty trailer with mine. I used to pretend I was clever like she was, and good at school, and had prospects. It became a habit, so that, even when her life started to fall apart, I couldn't stop. Every time one of those men forced themselves on me, every time I had to lie there at one of their parties while one after another after another came through to have their turn, I would detach. I would convince myself I was her. At home, watching TV or with a boyfriend who really loved her rather than just saying he did until she was sufficiently in his debt. Even just doing her homework or helping her mother bake. Living a normal life. It's become a habit, this pretending to be Sadie whenever things get bad, so that the real me, Daisy, doesn't have to feel anything.

I was jealous, I realize now. Otherwise, why, when Bryan said it was my turn to bring in someone new, did I choose her? Now I know I can't bring her back, but I can try to live the life she'd have lived. To honor her, if nothing else.

I open my mouth to tell David what name I'll use, but he interrupts me.

"No," he says. "It's better I don't know."

"But—"

He shakes his head sadly. "We can't stay in touch, Daisy."

I stare at my hands.

"Okay," I say.

He passes me the spoon. "Eat."

I try a mouthful, but it scalds my tongue.

"Will you find Sadie?" he says, and I realize people are believing the story that Bryan has put out, that she ran away, that she was seen hitching a lift, heading down south.

I can't do it after all, I can't lie to him. I lower the spoon.

"She's dead."

He falls quiet. I expect him to be angry, shocked at least, but he doesn't say anything. Perhaps he suspected it all along. For a second I think he'll tell me I can't go through with it, I need to go to the police.

"But she sent a note to her mum."

"They made me write it."

"And the people who saw her hitching a lift?"

"Making it up," I say. "Or maybe they were bribed to say it. Either way, it wasn't her."

I wish it was, more than anything. But no. They took her body and buried her on the moor.

I feel my heart collapse.

"I can't tell you anything else."

He touches my arm. "You don't have to."

I'd do anything to bring her back, I think. Anything to change what happened, anything at all. I think I hear her voice then, way out in the distance. *Do what?* she says. *Scrub your arm with bleach? Burn the tattoo away, the one that marks you as Daisy, the murderer? Cut it out?*

Maybe. Even scars are preferable to that mark on my forearm, that perfect circle, that unbroken O. I was such a fool, having it tattooed there, where I could see it, where it was a constant reminder. He gave me the choice, after all. *Anywhere you like*, he said. But I thought I was doing it for love, I wanted people to see it, so I picked there.

I look at the bowl of soup. Steam rises from it like smoke. Burn it away? If that's what it takes, then yes.

NOW

54

And now I'm back here. Lured by a postcard I must've kept for ten years before I sent it to Dan and then forgot doing it. I'm here, shivering in the damp tunnel that leads to David's cellar. He must've recognized me that first time I saw him. And recognized me for real, as Daisy, not as Sadie, as I'd thought, as I'd feared. He must've been certain enough to have broken into my room, to go looking through my stuff for proof. No wonder he asked me why I came back. No wonder he tried to get me to leave, before it was too late. No wonder he tried to show me the tape of myself jumping.

Except Bryan got to him first. Silenced him before he could tell me what he knew. Before he could give me the film of my own suicide. But he made a mistake. He'd left it there for me to find.

I hear a voice, echoing off the walls of the cave.

"Alex?"

It snaps me back to the present, but it sounds alien. *Alex?* Who is she?

It takes me a moment to remember. The voice comes again. "Are you there?"

No, I think. *No. You're not real.* But it's not Daisy's voice, and neither is it mine. It belongs to someone else, someone I know.

"Alex! Answer me!"

My eyes blink in the light. I struggle to focus and, as I do, I feel the last remnants of Sadie disappear. I force myself to speak.

"Hello?"

My voice ricochets from the walls of the cave. A little way above me I see a figure, a torch swinging wildly.

"Monica?"

A pummeling dread hits me. She's mixed up in all this, though I wonder if she really believes the girls are just going to these parties to lure the men, to blackmail them, that they're not being forced into sex. Has she come for me? I might still have to fight, though I think the odds are better with her. I remember then: it was she who'd been Bryan's number-one girl before me, she who brought me on board with promises of booze and cigarettes and a place to hang out when things were shitty at home. She must've stuck with him, all these years, helping him.

And she's helping him now, too. I wonder what happened to Zoe; I expect they snared her, Kat and Ellie, and the rest, the same way they had me.

"Alex?" she says. "Are you there?"

I keep quiet. I'm trapped; there's no escape. I knew her, I think. Just like I knew Bryan. She was a few years older than me, she introduced me to one of her friends, an older man whose name I've erased, the boyfriend in the leather jacket, who gave me drink and bought me presents and told me I was beautiful. We had sex, and it was good, except after a while he told me I needed to earn my treats and started sharing me with other men, men who'd pay. He took me and waited outside, squats in Malby, empty homes in the middle of being renovated, the arcade in Blackwood Bay and upstairs at the pub. I tried to escape but, every time, Monica told me I must have led the guys on, that I was under age and in too deep, and if I spoke out I'd go to prison. I believed her. And then, right when I had no self-esteem left, she introduced me to her boyfriend. Bryan. It was a while before I realized he was controlling it all, but by the time I did it was too late. I was in love.

I hold my breath. I can't let her see me. But then another voice joins hers.

"Sadie?"

Gavin?

The torch flashes off the walls of the cave. Eventually, it finds me.

"Shit. There she is! Sadie!" His voice is flooded with relief. "You're here!" he says, then, turning to Monica. "She's here!"

Can he be in on it, too? I have to get away. I wade back into the water, slipping as I do. I go under; freezing water rushes into me and I can't move. I need to escape, but where to?

There's only one place. Back into the dark, into the cave and out to sea.

The hesitation costs me, though. Gavin reaches me and grabs my upper arm.

"Stop!" he says. "What're you doing?"

I try to pull free, but his grip is firm. Just a little way behind, Monica is clambering over the rocks, wielding her torch.

"Let me go!"

I lash out and, though I manage to free myself, my foot goes over on the slime and I go down, face first into the water. The black depths rush in; I can't breathe. Gavin grabs hold once more and tries to lift me out.

"Daisy!" says Monica. "Wait!"

The name clamps round me like a vise. The urge to escape vanishes; I stop fighting. I'm limp, with shock, perhaps. Gavin holds me and I hear his voice, incredulous.

"*Daisy?*"

Time stops. I don't know how long for, but it's Monica who breaks the silence.

"It's true," she says. "Now come on." Gavin hesitates, his mouth clearly full of questions, but she grabs my other arm. "Help her."

They heave me up onto the narrow ledge and out of the freezing water, then crouch over me. I cough, and warm seawater floods from my nose, mixed with mucus. Gavin is holding my head; Monica, too. She has me by the throat and it feels like she wants to squeeze and squeeze and never let go.

"Daisy," she says, leaning close. "You need to come with us, now."

I shake my head. I feel my body shutting down. I can't go back there, back to Blackwood Bay. Not now. Not after what I did to Sadie.

"Daisy. Come on! It's not safe here. Trust me."

She's talking about Bryan, I suppose. He'll be landing his boat back at the slipway and heading this way. But why is she helping me?

I can't summon the will to ask. Nothing matters anymore, not now I know what I did. I don't care what happens to me.

After a second she turns to Gavin. "Help me get her upstairs," she says. "Then go and get someone from the village."

He stands just beyond her, watching us both. He seems undecided, he can't work out what's going on, whether he should leave me here with Monica.

"I'm trying to help her!" says Monica, and finally, he moves. Together they lift me, and the three of us climb the passageway back to David's cellar. The exit is hidden in the darkest corner, a rotting door behind boxes of papers. A single lightbulb hangs overhead, garlanded with cobwebs.

She turns to Gavin. "For God's sake, go and get help."

I stammer through chattering teeth, but Monica silences me. "You have to trust me. I'm trying to put this right." She looks back at Gavin. *"Go! Now!"*

He makes his decision. He leaves, taking the steps two at a time, and Monica and I slump against the dusty wall, too exhausted to speak. I shiver; my soaking clothes cling to my skin, my limbs are raw. I could die here, go to sleep and never wake up. It's what I deserve. But somewhere else, underneath all that, I know I mustn't. I have work to do; I can't let Bryan get away with it.

"Monica?"

At first she shows no sign of having heard me, but then she breaks her silence.

"You were right about it all. I'm an idiot, I couldn't let myself see what was happening. He told me nothing was going on. The girls went to the parties because they enjoyed it. They seduced the men, took photos. Then he blackmailed them. They were in on it. That's what he said." Her face falls and her hands come up to cover her shame, but she can't hold back her tears. "I loved him," she says, between sobs. "Always have. I believed what he said. But he was just using me."

She goes on, in a whisper now. "He worked out you were back. Said there was a weird way you held your cigarette, just like Daisy. Said we'd have to deal with the situation. He forced me to make that film of Bluff House and tell you to come alone. But then . . . then he said the only way we could keep you quiet was to kill you. That's when I knew. That's when I knew Sadie's death hadn't been an accident. That he'd killed her, too."

I look at her and the shame I share with her skewers me. "No. I did that." It comes out as a sob. I want to sink farther to the floor, let it swallow me completely.

"Daisy, love. He made you. You had no choice."

I try to believe her. I fail, but there's something about hearing my real name again. It shocks me out of my torpor. I'm beginning to feel again. Sorrow, for Sadie, for all the girls. For Monica.

"You're still in love with him."

She shakes her head, but I can see it in her eyes. "How stupid am I? I thought he was the one who'd rescued me."

"Rescued you?"

"My father."

It's little more than a croak, but I know what she means. Abuse goes in cycles, Dr. Olsen taught me that. But maybe this is her chance to break the chain.

And isn't that what I have to do, too? Slowly, I feel myself cranking up, stuttering into start-up like my ancient laptop.

"How did you know where to find me?" I ask.

"We worked it out, me and Gavin. If you jumped but were alive, there must've been a way back in. He's been reading about the smugglers and he worked it out."

And then she asks, "When you came to see me yesterday . . . you really believed you were Sadie?"

"Yes," I say. It was my truth, at least, if no one else's. "But you knew she was dead."

I think about my episode, the fugue state. I must have made up most of the memories that came back afterward, my own fictions, my own beliefs about Sadie's life. And the most important fact—that she was dead and I was the one who killed her—I erased completely.

"My mind . . . it just . . . broke. I've believed I was her . . . for years."

Broke in two, I think. *Half Sadie, half me.*

It hits me then. I have no idea who I am.

Except that's not true. I'm Alex. I make films. I'm a success, or have been.

"Will you go to the police?" I ask.

She stares at the floor. She doesn't want to, of course.

"I suppose," she says. "I'll tell them what happened here. I have to."

"And what I did."

She shakes her head. "It wasn't your fault. You were young."

"Old enough, though."

"Don't blame yourself, Daisy. There was no way you could've saved her."

"But I'm still the one who killed her."

She's about to say something when another voice interrupts.

"Yes, Daisy. You are."

The voice has come from overhead, the entrance to the cellar. Together, we try to stand, but I'm slow, and before either of us can fully get to our feet he's down the stairs. He's holding something in his hand, something metallic, and he lashes out, catching Monica on the side of the head. She goes down, gasping, clawing at me and almost pulling me over, too. She lands with a sickening crunch. I launch myself at him, but he's too strong and has the advantage of surprise; he pushes me backward and I go over. My head connects painfully with the wall, but it seems to open something in me, a pathway to defiance. How dare he? How dare he think he can destroy me? He's pathetic. I was a child then, but now I'm not; I'll die before I let him hurt me again. My eyes burn as I look up and see what he has in his hand. A gun, but it's short and squat, like a toy. A flare gun.

"Bryan," I begin, but there's blood in my mouth. "Don't."

He laughs, steps toward me. I look over at Monica, but she's down. Moving, but her eyes are closed.

"Monica," I plead. "Get up."

"She's not going to help you," he says. "Not now." He glances upstairs. "Neither's Gavin. It's just you and me."

Blood runs down my chin.

"Daisy—" he begins, but I interrupt.

"Don't call me that."

"Why not? It's your name. It's who you are."

"No. I changed."

"Changed your name. Doesn't change who you are, or what you did."

His eyes are as cold as the ocean.

"You made me do it."

"Oh, right. *I made you.* And how did I do that?"

I say nothing.

"How's it going to look, Daisy? I've still got all those notes you wrote. About how much you loved me. I've still got all those photos of the two of us." He pauses. "Doing . . . well . . . you know what we were doing." He shakes his head, sadly. "You with all those other fellas, too. Won't be hard to convince people you were a slut, jealous when I started to prefer Sadie. That's why you killed her, isn't it? You couldn't stand to see me with someone else."

He's wrong. We were supposed to escape together. She was supposed to save me.

I launch myself at him. He's unprepared, but big; he doesn't go over. Instead we grapple, equally balanced, he the stronger, me the more enraged. He tries to throw me into the wall, but I'm clutching his jacket and instead we both swing until his face is an inch from mine.

"You're nothing," he spits. "You never were."

It's like a shot of adrenaline pumped into my veins. I'm not the Daisy he remembers, I've been in too many fights, too many risky situations. My right leg is between his and I lift my knee as sharply as

I can, at the same time yanking down on his jacket. He cries in pain and I push him backward, screaming wordlessly as I do. He crashes to the floor in a shower of dust and, once he's down, I kick him again before grabbing the flare gun. My hands shake as I point it at his chest.

"You destroyed me."

He laughs, a hollow, sick sound, and spits blood onto the floor. "You destroyed yourself. I've still got the film, you know? The one of you killing Sadie. And that kinda proves everything, doesn't it, Daisy?"

I can't breathe. The air is flooded with dust. I see the film, me standing over my friend, the belt around her neck.

It hits me again. He's right. I killed her. I killed Sadie. I should've said no, I should've fought, even if it did mean it'd be me who ended up dead.

I can't forgive myself. Never. The gun shakes in my hand. I can see him, eyeing it, waiting for his chance. For a second I think I can hear sirens, but even if so, they're way in the distance, and getting quieter. It's just my imagination, a last, horrible trick of the mind.

"I was fifteen."

"So?"

I hear Sadie's voice. *Come back*, she's saying. *We can escape. We can beat him, and we can go home and make our film and none of this will have happened.*

No.

Leave her here. Leave Daisy here, lying at the bottom of the sea like you thought she was. Come with me, back home.

"I can't."

"Can't what, Daisy?"

I've said it out loud. Bryan doesn't know there are two people inside me, two frightened teenagers battling it out.

"I'm sorry," I say.

It's Daisy's voice that answers. *No*, she says. *You didn't come here to say sorry. You came to accept your punishment at last. So accept it.*

I look down at the gun in my hand. She's right. I killed Sadie and never paid the price. I'm not here to win. I'm not even here to apologize. I'm here to accept responsibility.

I'm almost tempted to toss him the gun, to let him finish it. But I don't. After what he did? My eyes fall closed. He reduced me to nothing, then made me kill my friend. It's not my fault. Letting him win will solve nothing. And there's Ellie to think about, and Kat, and who knows how many others.

I raise the gun, but it's too late. He's on his feet, he's grabbed the barrel. I grip as hard as I can, but he's too strong; one hard shove and I stagger back. The weapon is his.

He grins. The same twisted grin I remember from all that time ago. I sink to my knees and bow my head, glad that, if this is the end, then at least I know who I am.

"Finish it," I say, and for once—and when I least want to be—I'm totally in my body. I can feel the rough ground under my feet and knees. I can taste the dust in the air, smell the mold oozing from the walls. I can hear Monica's ragged breathing, like something that's dying.

I close my eyes, waiting for my judgment, waiting for death.

"No," he says softly. "Get up. This time you're going to jump. This time you're going to do it for real."

The sky has clouded, the waves pummel the cliff beneath me. I look back toward Blackwood Bay, to The Ship, the slipway, the gentle arc of the coast as it curves toward Crag Head, but there's no one around. No one who can help me. Everything is as it was ten years ago. Everything is as I remember it.

I step toward the edge. It should be night, by rights, the dead sky scarred with stars. Fifteen steps, maybe twenty. I go forward, Bryan behind me. In one hand he's carrying a metal poker he found in David's living room after binding Monica's hands and feet and securing her to the cellar steps, and in the other the flare gun. But they're for protection only. I know what he means to do. A walk to the edge and then I jump, or, if I refuse, he pushes me. Either way, I go down. It will look like an accident, another suicide. He tells the world he saw me fall; he was powerless to stop me.

I understand, finally, now it's too late. I jumped ten years ago because I was trying to escape from Blackwood Bay, and I called myself Sadie because I was trying to escape from myself. I wanted to pretend she wasn't dead, because that meant I didn't kill her and I'm not a murderer. I'm not a monster.

But then the fugue happened. The phone call to Dev, who called me by the only name he'd ever heard me use. And from that moment on I believed it was true. Except Daisy never really went away. Not when I got my qualifications, not when I was back on the streets making *Black Winter*. She was just hiding, feeding her guilt, waiting. And then, after ten years, I made a mistake. I came back, and brought her with me.

I should've stayed away forever. But how was I to know?

I look down. At least I saw my mother. At least I saw Geraldine one last time, and I realize now that she recognized me, too. Dimly, and despite how much I've changed, she knew who I was. Everything she said makes sense.

And David. My friend. He could see who I was, too. He was trying to warn me.

I'm at the edge. I had my eyes open, last time I jumped. I remember now. I look up. I wish I could see Betelgeuse one last time. The dead star. But it's enough to know it's there.

"Stop," says Bryan. He points down to my feet. "See those stones? Fill your pockets."

There are rocks here. They're heavy; they'll weigh me down. This time, he wants to be sure I die. Be certain it looks like suicide.

I bend down and lift the first rock. It's slick with rainwater and nearly slips through my fingers.

"In your pocket."

I do as he says. The scar on my arm itches. Removing it didn't help. How could it? I'm Daisy, whether I like it or not; I did what I did, and I'll have to pay.

But now? Like this?

"How about Monica?" I say. "Gavin? Even if I die, you'll never cover it up. Unless you kill them."

He smiles, a cruel, warped smile. "Oh, don't you worry about them. Monica will realize how much trouble she'd be in and come back to me. And as for Gavin . . ."

He leaves the sentence hanging. I wonder what he'll do. Burn down Bluff House with him inside? It wouldn't surprise me. After all, he had poor Ellie driven to the middle of the moors and left to find her own way back, just to scare her into silence. He forced David to take an overdose to keep him quiet. I know what he's capable of.

"Who's been helping you?" I say. "Is everyone involved?"

"Not everyone," he says with a callous shrug. "But enough. It's amazing what people will do once you've got a film of them with a pretty little thing like Zoe."

"Zoe," I say. "Is she . . . ?"

"What? Dead? No. She got away. No one's seen hide nor hair of that one, for good, or bad. I don't think she'll be coming back, though. She was clever."

I ignore his gibe. I think of the girls on the film from the stable. I think of the girls listed in Monica's book, and Kat with the tattoo she clearly didn't want and which is shared by me, and Monica, and who knows who else? He must've branded us all.

"How many have there been? How many girls?"

"A few."

He gestures with the poker. "Another rock."

I lift one more. Maybe he's right and this is what I deserve. But is it really better if I die? Sadie's gone already; it won't bring her back. It'll just mean he's won.

And if I go, if I jump, then he's free to carry on. Who knows how many more girls will be destroyed before he stops, or is caught, or dies. I unzip my other pocket to slip the stone inside. There's something already there, though. My phone. I fumble, but muscle memory kicks in and I find the button. I press *Record*. It's a waterproof model, but still I'm worried it might not work. Even if it does it'll be sound only, muffled by my jacket, but that's all I need.

"Why?" I say.

"Why what?"

"Why did you do it? Why *do* you do it?"

He says nothing.

"Is it the sex?"

Now, he laughs. "No. It's not that."

"Money, then?" I say. "The men paid you?"

"Of course they did. But no."

"So why?"

He gestures toward the village. "Look around. I own this place. Half of Malby, too. I have something on virtually every man here, you know that? Either them or their father, or their brother, or their friend. They've all got secrets. They've all got things they don't want to come out. And like I say, it's amazing what people will do for you when they're scared."

"You said you loved me."

He laughs. A sneering, evil laugh. "I did? You were fifteen. A girl. You were nothing to me. None of you were."

Despite everything, it stings.

"You said it."

"I said lots of things."

"But . . . why?"

"It was the easiest way to get you to do what I wanted."

"All those men—"

"Don't give me that," he says. "You're a slut. You loved it."

I stare at him. In that moment, my hate is as pure and white as burning magnesium, and I want to rush at him, to tear out his eyes, to rip out his tongue, but I do nothing. I hide it, like I always have, like I've learned to hide everything.

"You got me hooked on drugs."

"You loved that, too."

"No," I say. "You made me. And you forced me to earn them."

"Nothing's for free. And you had what they wanted. Supply and demand, that's all it is."

"But Sadie? Why kill her?"

Say it, I think. *Say it*. He's quiet.

"Was it for fun?"

He sneers. "For fun? She wasn't safe. She'd started to talk. She'd said something to David, I'm sure of it. Her mother, too. She had to be got rid of, don't you see? And by getting you to do it I killed two birds with one stone. Shut both of you up."

"David. You pretended to be his friend."

"You know what they say about keeping your enemies close."

"He didn't know?"

"No. He had no idea. He thought it was someone else, way out in Malby. Even little Sadie wouldn't tell him it was me. She knew what I'd do to her best friend if she did."

"Meaning me?"

"Yes."

"What happened to him? His overdose?"

"You know the answer to that. Stop wasting time."

"You thought by faking his confession to both murders you could make sure they were never pinned on you."

"Maybe."

"You're a monster," I say. "You're sick."

"The world is sick, baby."

My mind is clear now. I can see it all. How the clip I've just recorded will fit into the film I still plan to make. His voice, over the footage of me, back when I was fifteen, walking toward the edge of the world. Not what the channel might've expected, but who cares? It's the film I need to make, the one I needed to make all along.

"Turn around, Daisy."

"No," I say, taking out my phone. "I think we're done. I'm pretty sure I've got everything."

His eyes flare when he sees what I'm brandishing; he tries to snatch it, but I whip it out of reach. Suddenly, everything is still, just the sound of the sea beneath us; even the wind seems gentle, now.

"Give me that."

"No," I say again.

"You can't run," he says. "There's nowhere to go."

"I'm going nowhere, Bryan. I don't need to. I recorded it all." I press the button on the homepage. "And now it's uploaded to the server. Whatever happens here, it's not me who's finished."

I smile. His eyes are darting left and right. He knows it's over. His crimes are public. I draw breath just as he lifts the poker and, as he brings it down, I step to the side, out of range. I'm near the edge, but this time I keep my balance. I don't fall, I don't go over.

"Even if I die now," I say, "they'll find the film. Your confession. Out there for everyone to hear."

His eyes burn but, as I watch, something inside them dies. He knows there's no escape. He knows there's only one way this can end now. He drops the poker and it clatters off the rocks. His head falls for a second, but then he looks up. His eyes lock with mine, and with a sudden surge he reaches out. I think he's going to grab me, to try to push me over, and maybe he is.

"Daisy?" he says. "*Baby . . .*"

I think of what he did to me, to Daisy, to Zoe, and who knows how many more. I summon all the strength I have and push. He stumbles, then falls with a curdled scream that might almost be laughter. I watch as he goes. His body plummets without grace, cartwheeling as it falls, and smashes into the deep, gray water. He goes under. Once, twice, three times. I breathe deep, gasping at the cold, clean air, and wait, my eyes fixed on the sea below.

The waves swallow him one final time then close over his body. This time, he doesn't come up.

TOMORROW

I park the car and get out. It's early morning, not long after dawn. The late-summer light is thin, but already I can tell it's going to be a beautiful day. I check the address. Stone steps lead up to an imposing front door and I find the buzzer and press.

Dr. Olsen has retired, but she's agreed to see me. I've told her the truth, that I've pieced it together; finally, I know what happened. After a few moments she buzzes me up.

"Alex, darling," she says when she opens the door. She looks exactly the same as I remember her. She holds out her hands and takes both of mine. "It's so lovely to see you!"

She pulls me in and we embrace. "It's Daisy, now," I say, and she apologizes. I tell her it doesn't matter. I've only recently got used to it myself.

"Well, you must call me Laure," she says. "Come on in! There's no way I'd have recognized you!"

I smile. Her flat is smaller than I'd expected, but comfortable. She makes me a cup of tea, then sits on the sofa while I set up my camera. I'm making a new film now. It's about what happened in Blackwood Bay. It's about trauma, and abuse, and the effects they can have. It's about shattered lives. It's about me.

I've told her there are still things from back then that I can't remember, and there are still days when I find myself doing something with no recollection of how I came to be doing it.

"You have a tendency to dissociate," she says. "You may have always had that, but it's likely it was exacerbated by the terrible abuse you suffered. It's not uncommon."

"You mean people pretend to be someone else?"

"Not exactly. Dissociation can take several forms, and of course things rarely fall into a neat diagnostic pattern. For many people, it's like no longer feeling they're in their own body. Or they feel they're underwater and their limbs aren't behaving. For you? Back then, I suspect that when you were being abused you would dissociate to avoid the pain. You'd imagine yourself having Sadie's life, rather than your own, and it's possible that when you dissociated during the traumatic abuse you would almost become her."

"Is that why I killed her? Because I was jealous?"

Her voice is soft.

"Daisy, dear. You were being abused, terribly. You were drinking and taking drugs, often against your will. You were told that if you didn't comply, you'd be killed. And let's not forget that you've told me Bryan said the plan was only to scare Sadie, so that she wouldn't tell your friend—"

"David?"

"Yes, David. So she wouldn't tell David any more than she already had. It's likely that after Sadie's death you experienced overwhelming guilt, probably self-hatred. It's my feeling that it took every ounce of strength you had left to go to David and tell him you needed to get away. After that, your mind fractured. Subconsciously, you tried to kill Daisy—the person who had murdered Sadie—while at the same time resurrecting Sadie and giving her back the life you knew had been taken. You ran to London having done this consciously, having decided to call yourself Sadie, but when the abuse continued in London you carried on dissociating and believing you were her, eventually finding it harder and harder to determine which of your memories were real, Daisy experiences, and which were fantasy, Sadie memories."

"And then I attacked that guy. Gee."

"Yes. And you had to run again. Why you chose Deal, I don't think we'll ever know. It's possible you were just going to the coast, and possible, too, that you intended suicide. Anyway, you experienced something called a dissociative fugue, in which people usually lose their memory of who they are, and dissociative amnesia, which meant that your memories of life before your fugue didn't return. And then, when you phoned Dev and he called you Sadie—"

"I thought I *was* her."

"Yes. Your Sadie memories became real. Your Daisy ones were erased completely."

"And then I changed my name anyway. To Alex."

"Yes. Burying the truth even further."

I sigh and gaze out the window over her shoulder. The guilt hasn't gone away, the feeling that I could've done more to escape, that I should've fought harder, tried to save Sadie's life, even if it cost me my own. Even though I know, really, that it was futile. Bryan would've killed us both.

"Is this common?"

"Yours is a particularly extreme example. But dissociation in order to avoid abuse is far from unheard of."

I nod. I've asked the question for the benefit of the camera more than anything. Dr. Olsen has already given me the statistics for my film, and she's approached a few of her former patients to ask whether they'd consider appearing. Already two have said yes, and a third looks likely.

I'm pleased about this. I don't know how much of my own story I'll be able to use, in the end. Monica and I told Heidi Butler everything, or almost everything. She's awaiting trial, but the Crown Prosecution Service said just last week that, after a thorough investigation and review, they've decided not to press charges in the case of Sadie's murder. The tape of Bryan's confession was a big factor there, they explained, along with the fact that I was underage when it happened and subject to coercion and intimidation. Bryan has disappeared.

I realize now that Kat must've known Sadie was dead; perhaps David told her. That's what she was telling me, when I showed her the clip of Sadie outside the trailer, the film I thought was of Daisy. *That's the girl they killed.*

Yet I believed I was Sadie and the film was of Daisy. I must've made the same mistake every time I saw a photo of my friend, so stupidly convinced I knew who I was.

Dr. Olsen and I talk some more, then I switch off the camera and thank her.

"You'll stay?" she says. "I'm making dinner. It's not much, but you'd be very welcome."

I shake my head. I'm meeting Gavin later; he's found a new restaurant he's excited about showing me. It's early days, but I think we're falling in love.

"That'd be great," I say. "But I can't. I'm sorry."

"Never mind," she says. I pack up my equipment and she walks me to the door.

"What happened to David?" she says.

"He recovered."

"Good. You still see him?"

"No," I say.

I've only been back to Blackwood Bay once, when Gavin and I went to pick up my mother and bring her down south. I saw David briefly; I thanked him and told him I'd never forget what he'd done for me. For us.

"You mustn't feel guilty," she says, taking my hands once more. "You know that? Without you, it'd still be going on."

I tell her I understand.

There was one more place I went, on that trip to Blackwood Bay. Sadie's grave, the place she'd lain for ten years, wrapped in a plastic sheet. They'd never even looked for her body, because some corrupt policeman—someone else Bryan had dirt on—said she'd been seen hitchhiking and then made the report that she'd been found down in London and didn't want to be contacted.

She's in St. Julian's, now. At peace, I'd like to think.

"I'm sorry," I said that morning. "For everything."

I realized in that moment that I was glad I'd gone back to make my film in Blackwood Bay. If I hadn't, she'd still be out on the moor. I'd still be Alex. Bryan would have succeeded by now in breaking Ellie and moved on to whoever's next. Monica would still be in love with him, choosing to believe the girls were complicit.

I sat for a while. The sun rose; the sea flashed in the distance. I wish I could bring her back, but I can't. I was stupid to think I could.

I had a bunch of flowers—pink peonies—and I left them there for her.

"Goodbye, Sadie," I said, and then, I came back home.

Acknowledgments

Thank you to Clare Conville and all at C+W; Frankie Gray, Larry Finlay, Alison Barrow, Sarah Day, and all Transworld; Jennifer Barth, Mary Gaule, and all at HCUS; Iris Tupholme and all at HC Canada; and Michael Heyward, David Winter, and all at Text. Thank you to all my international publishers and translators.

Thank you to Maria A. and Bill M,. Alice Keens-Soper, Rebecca Kinnarney, and Sue C-J.

Thank you to Richard, Amy, and Antonia, to Gabriel Cole, Sam Lear, and Reuben Cole, and to Helene. Thank you to Charles, and in particular to Andrew Dell.

Finally, thank you to all my family and friends who've kept me (mostly) sane during the last few years.

Author's Note

"Blackwood Bay" is a fictional location. It shares some of its geography and topography with Robin Hood's Bay in North Yorkshire, but any resemblance ends there, and the events contained herein are entirely fictional.

About the Author

SJ WATSON'S first novel, *Before I Go to Sleep*, became a phenomenal international success and has now sold over six million copies worldwide. It won the Crime Writers' Association Award for Best Debut Novel and the Galaxy National Book Award for Crime Thriller of the Year. The film of the book, starring Nicole Kidman, Colin Firth, and Mark Strong and directed by Rowan Joffe, was released in September 2014. Watson's second novel, *Second Life*, a psychological thriller, was published to acclaim in 2015. He lives in London.

DON'T MISS THESE OTHER
HEART-RACING THRILLERS FROM
S.J. WATSON

"An exceptional thriller. It left my nerves jangling for hours after I finished the last page."
—Dennis Lehane

"Pure page-turner."
—*New York Times*

"Quite simply the best debut novel I have ever read."
—Tess Gerritsen

"An erotic, psychological, and nuanced thriller whose end, I guarantee, you'll never see coming."
—Maureen Corrigan,
NPR's *Fresh Air*

"Kept me on the edge of my seat."
—Reese Witherspoon